Please feel free to send me an e:
filters these emails. Good news

Melissa Bender - melissa_bend

Sign up for my blog for updates and freebies!
http://melissa-bender.awesomeauthors.org

Copyright © 2017 by Melissa Bender

All Rights reserved under International and Pan-American Copyright Conventions. By payment of required fees you have been granted the non-exclusive, non-transferable right to access and read the text of this book. No part of this text may be reproduced, transmitted, downloaded, decompiled, reverse-engineered or stored in or introduced into any information storage and retrieval system, in any form or by any means, whether electronic or mechanical, now known, hereinafter invented, without express written permission of BLVNP Inc. For more information contact BLVNP Inc. The publisher does not have any control over and does not assume any responsibility for author or third-party websites or their content. This book is a work of fiction. The characters, incidents and dialogue are drawn from the author's imagination and are not to be construed as real. While reference might be made to actual historical events or existing locations, the names, characters, places and incidents are either products of the author's imagination or are used fictitiously, and any resemblance to actual persons living or dead, business establishments, events or locales is entirely coincidental.

About the Publisher

BLVNP Incorporated, A Nevada Corporation, 340 S. Lemon #6200, Walnut CA 91789, info@blvnp.com / legal@blvnp.com

DISCLAIMER

This book is a work of FICTION. It is fiction and not to be confused with reality. Neither the author nor the publisher or its associates assume any responsibility for any loss, injury, death or legal consequences resulting from acting on the contents in this book. The author's opinions are not to be construed as the opinions of the publisher. The material in this book is for entertainment purposes ONLY. Enjoy.

Praise for Breaking Old Habits

I actually really enjoyed this. I first heard about it on Facebook, with someone providing some details about the story and asking if anyone knew the title because they were looking for it. I was definitely intrigued and simply **HAD** to read it. This was my first Wattpad book, so I wasn't sure what I was getting into. Yes, there were some editing issues that would need to be cleaned up for publication, but it didn't detract from the story.
The story had twists and turns and it kept me hooked. I hated to put it down to go to work. This is one I'll definitely read again, and I'll also be checking out the author's other works!
Lindsay, Goodreads

I stumbled upon this by accident. Someone had posted about a book they started reading and couldn't remember the title on one of the book groups I'm in and someone said it sounded like this. I signed up on Wattpad and started reading. I finished it in one sitting. It was all angsty goodness. The beginning, I wanted to scream a time or two but then it got really good and I wound up loving it.
Tonya Coleman, Goodreads

Thanks to a post on Facebook, I found this awesome book. I had to download the app to read it but it was so worth it.
This book had everything. Romance, drama and you just wanted to smack the hell out of some people. A definite must read book.
Brenda, Goodreads

Heard about this book on Facebook. A reader was looking for a book by just a description of it. Just by the description I and many others were dying to find ur the name of this book!! I absolutely loved reading it. It had a few writing errors. Nothing huge. A very enjoyable storyline & very believable for many readers I believe. Can't wait to try reading something else of Melissa.
Monica Holloway, Goodreads

Freaking awesome book I couldn't put it down! I loved griffin and Ayla they're perfect for each other. The only problem is he's still deals with his ex because of their kids and Ayla is getting fed up. Can he save their relationship and start putting the right person first. Read it and find out! I wish there was more of these two I'd love that!!
Courtney Wade, Goodreads

Breaking Old Habits

By: Melissa Bender

BLVNP

ISBN: 978-1-68030-869-3
©MelissaBender2017

Table of Contents

PROLOGUE 1

CHAPTER ONE 4

CHAPTER TWO 19

CHAPTER THREE 35

CHAPTER FOUR 48

CHAPTER FIVE 61

CHAPTER SIX..76

CHAPTER SEVEN 91

CHAPTER EIGHT...103

CHAPTER NINE 117

CHAPTER TEN 132

CHAPTER ELEVEN 146

CHAPTER TWELVE 159

CHAPTER THIRTEEN 170

CHAPTER FOURTEEN...182

CHAPTER FIFTEEN 195

CHAPTER SIXTEEN 209

CHAPTER SEVENTEEN...221

CHAPTER EIGHTEEN 235

CHAPTER NINETEEN 249

CHAPTER TWENTY..262

CHAPTER TWENTY-ONE 275

CHAPTER TWENTY-TWO 287

CHAPTER TWENTY-THREE 301

CHAPTER TWENTY-FOUR 313

CHAPTER TWENTY-FIVE 325

CHAPTER TWENTY-SIX 337

EPILOGUE 350

*Bailey, Mason & Everly
Unconditionally, wholeheartedly, you are so loved.* xx

FREE DOWNLOAD

Get these freebies and MORE when you sign up for the author's mailing list!

http://melissa-bender.awesomeauthors.org

PROLOGUE

"I've got a big dick, and you know what they say about big dicks?"

I shook my head. I really did not have a clue, nor did I even want to know. "They're more enjoyable?"

"They need frequent milking. Care to help a man out and milk me?"

I pictured myself sitting on an upside down tin bucket, wearing pink rubber gloves, and squeezing the udders of a milking cow. Major turn off. "Sorry, I'm actually here with someone."

"Oh?" he questioned, his dark brows dipped closer together as his brown eyes stared at me in question. "I don't see anyone."

Make a run for it.

I should have done just that. Unable to find Harvey who had obviously been picked up, leaving me high and dry, I instead, without thinking, reached out and grabbed hold of the arm of the guy passing by me. Too bad if he were in his fifties or more. It was too late to overthink as my palm rubbed the front of his chest. I smiled, leaning in. "Him... He was just grabbing us a drink." Finally, I looked up with relief to see that he was younger and extremely handsome.

The man I was currently clinging to shot me an annoyed glare as if I had ruined his night. I could not tell if he was smiling, though, as his mouth was covered by a dark beard. "Pardon?"

"Weren't you, babe? You grabbed us drinks, right?" I said, pleading silently with him to just go along. I noticed his hands were empty. My plan was failing. "Where are they?"

He was quiet for a moment, eyes directed on mine. I could tell that he was well into his thirties, possibly older. There was a hipster charm about him with that well-kept beard and pulled back hair. His blue eyes were burning holes through my head as he smiled back warmly. Thankfully, his body relaxed as his arm slid around my waist, resting his hand against the curve of my hip. "Yes. I was at the bar waiting." His hand slid further down, taking the whole fake thing we were doing to another level as his hand cupped my ass and squeezed. "I, however, decided I'd rather go home and fuck."

Now it was my turn to be caught off guard. "I'm sorry? What?"

"I said—" he made a point to speak louder over the music, as he leant in "—are you ready to go home, and fuck?"

I almost choked on my breath. He was pushing it. Managing a smile, I glared at him, forgetting all about the horny milk bottle in front of us as I turned to face him. I raised a brow as my fingertips grazed over his crisp, white shirt, fondling with the button below his open collar. "But we just got here. I want to dance." I did a little pout for extra annoyance. "Come and dance with me."

He leant in, his warm breath blowing against my ear. I fought the urge to let out a throaty groan. "Dance on my cock."

If my panties weren't soaking wet already, they were now. "It's my birthday. Buy me a drink then?"

He grinned, tilting his head towards the bar. "One drink for the birthday girl, coming right up. Was there anything else, pretty?"

"Oh, yeah. You owe me a new pair of panties."

CHAPTER ONE

"Oh, my god!" I groaned against the crook of Griffin's neck. My lips pressed against his skin as I opened my mouth and bit down lightly—and not in a good way.

Here I sat, straddling my man's lap, practically grinding myself to an orgasm when his next-door neighbour walked in with the announcement that she needed more milk. His cock was rock solid, straining against my crotch. His long fingers dug against the curve of my ass, holding me in place and keeping me still, unable to move away.

How was I supposed to ignore this? She was in our kitchen at the opposite side of the living room where we were, oblivious to our usual midday fuck while the two boys were in school. This was supposed to be our time.

My bra was on the floor, tossed wherever the black lace material had landed, and my breasts, hidden by a thin, white tank top, was pressed against his chest. I could feel his heart beating steadily, showing me that he was not at all annoyed by our current situation. I wondered how often this had happened when we were not home, and yet he never seemed to mind.

God forbid that she ever walks in while I am on my knees, blowing him to heaven and back. I wondered if his heart would be so steady then. Would he look up, offer her a smile, and continue ramming his cock down my throat? I highly doubted it.

Nothing ever bothered him.

I, however, was very bothered.

A year ago, I thought I had hit the jackpot when Griffin and I met in the club, saving me from the creep bragging about his gigantic penis. He had brought me a drink, and we walked around the city. He spoke about architecture, showing me the buildings as we walked to my mother's café on the corner of Bathurst Street, Sydney, where I then made us breakfast.

Breakfast led to maple syrup being licked off my stomach as the undeniable pull between us became too much to handle. The next thing we knew, we were hot and heavy, ripping each other's clothing off.

Fast forward to the day we moved in together, I found out that my new next-door neighbour was, in fact, his ex-fiancée and the mother of their fifteen-year-old twin sons, Toby and Mack. They were not my problem; the kids were great. It was her.

Slamming the stainless fridge door shut, she walked back towards the door with our milk and called out, "Thanks, Griffin. I'll replace it soon for you." There was no anger or jealousy in her tone. It was said as if they are best friends.

I eyed him, watching closely as he said back, "Thank you, Karen."

As soon as I heard the door close, I mentally screamed *fuck off* to her. She was not going to replace it. She never did.

"Now, where were we?" Griffin groaned, flexing upwards as his fingers dug dipper into my ass.

With a slight twitch of my neck, I squirmed from his hold and pried his hands from my ass, moving to a standing position. This so was not going to happen. "Kind of not in the mood anymore," I said with a dissatisfied mumble as I bent and picked up my bra from the light grey rug in a hasty snatch.

"What?" he asked with exasperation, reaching into his unzipped slacks and pulling out his stiff cock. "I'm rock hard."

There was no denying he was hard. It was hard as steel, pointing upwards with a drizzle of clear pre-cum running down the side.

I just shrugged. "I'm not even wet. It's like a desert."

His lips twitched up into a smirk as he adjusted himself back in his pants. "That's quite an image. I bet I could have you gushing like Niagara Falls in no time."

I shook my head. This man was not getting the hint. "Take a cold shower. It's not going to happen right now. You have to get back to work, anyway."

"I'm the boss. Work can wait."

Fair point.

He raised a brow. "Could you?" He nodded towards the bulge straining against his navy slacks. You could see the outline as it lay over his hip. Oh, how I wanted to run my hand up and down that thing, squeezing it tightly

There was too much annoyance in my system to be in the mood for getting down and dirty, though. That was the last thing I wanted after his ex appeared. I was not about to get on my knees and suck him hard and empty when the idea of my teeth lashing down and biting him was too much temptation.

I picked up a red plush cushion and tossed it at him.

He let out a grunt and caught the next one I threw.

"Suck yourself off. I'm not putting out."

"Pretty, don't be like that." He groaned, stretching himself out on the dark brown leather couch.

Eyeing him, I raised my brow and crossed my arms. I leant against the wall, shaking my head. "Griffin, would you like it if my ex was walking in uninvited and unannounced like that whenever he felt like it?"

His blue eyes darkened even more as he narrowed them. He raised a curious brow back. "You told me you didn't have any ex-boyfriends." His tone was flat.

"Not my point." I wanted to keep my serious face, but I ended up fighting a smile as I sighed in frustration. I pushed off the white wall that connected the living room to the kitchen. "I don't like her coming over here. We could have been naked and fucking."

"We *should* be naked and fucking. Now get back over here."

Blunt, as usual.

There was no sugar coating anything with us. We were always open and honest. Well, most of the time. I stared at him, trying to sound serious. "I'll put a sex ban on you."

He mumbled with a scoff, "You wouldn't last."

"Do you really want to find out?" I was determined not to give in.

With a roll of his eyes, he stood and sighed loudly. "Ayla, she's the mother of my children." His hand came up and brushed through his hair. "Would you rather it be bad between us?"

"She lives next door." This was a dead-end fight, the fight that never went anywhere—the same fight where he would always defend her and tell me I was being jealous and overreacting.

I was not. I just wanted him to see things from my point of view. He was being a coward and letting her walk all over him. How could he not see things from my point of view, that it made me very uncomfortable having her so close to us?

I turned my back on him, giving up, and made my way down to the bedroom.

His footsteps were close behind me. "It's easier for the boys. They get to have both parents close by." I went to close the door behind me with a grin as I glanced over my shoulder. He was only smiling back, a boyish grin on his face as he followed and blocked the door. "Is it that time of the month?"

"Why is that what all men assume?" I groaned. I could not be mad without him asking if I was on the red river week. Flopping down on our king-sized bed, I watched him walk in and groaned. "Tell her to go and buy her own fucking milk! She has enough money to do so since you pay for her living."

"Anything else?" he asked, starting to undo his slacks again.

I raised my hips, tugging down my shorts and panties in one go. I kicked them to the floor as he stood at my feet, unbuttoning his white shirt one button at a time. "Tell her to stop coming over."

Kneeling above and between my open thighs, he lifted my white tank, peeling it above my head and tossing it back behind him. He sighed. "You know she won't listen to a word I say, right?"

"She still loves you; of course, she'll listen," I said through clenched teeth as I spread my legs further apart, watching his hand move down there.

"I don't love her." He assured me, pushing his index finger deep inside me. "Dry my ass. You're soaked."

"Of course, I am. Your dick is in my face." Not quite, but almost. My head fell back on the pillow as another fingered entered.

He curled them both. *Fuck me.* My eyes rolled as I relished in the pleasure.

He let out a groan of his own as I reached for his hot length, giving it a firm stroke. Flexing more into my palm as he hissed, he closed his eyes and tilted back his head. "Ayla. Christ!"

Coyly smiling, I eyed his naked and glorious as fuck body. He stood at six foot four, covered in tattoos and muscle, and had trimmed dark hair. I loved it. He was manly yet so beautiful to stare at. For thirty-seven, he took my breath away with his extremely handsome features—strong jaw line and piercing blue eyes. They were kind eyes, but when he was mad, you knew just by the way he stared. His eyes held an unseen emotion to most. I, however, got to experience it often. Just a look of dominance from them was enough to make me sink to my knees and take him in my mouth without him ever needing to say a single word. Still, he held a boyish grin that made him appear a lot younger than he actually looked.

His dark brown hair reached to his shoulder and was worn up most times. It suited him.

Think Jason Momoa, and you will get the gist of what I mean. Never did I think that I would be in love with a man who had long hair and a full grown beard. He even has spacers in his ear. He had one, and it suited him. I hated them usually, but on him? Damn, I just loved this hipster, bad boy look he pulled off.

I was madly in love.

My mother called him the son of Brad Pitt and Jesus. He was completely beautiful.

"When did you last shave?" I asked, reaching out to cup his jaw. I parted my thighs, and he lowered himself on top of me more.

"Last night." His words came out strangled as he pushed inside me.

My muscles tightened around him automatically as I savoured the moment. That first thrust. It was my favourite.

"You did it before in the shower."

I could not help but giggle. "Not your balls. I meant this." I tugged at his beard. "I haven't seen you with a smooth face before."

He just smirked, laying his full weight on top of my naked body and rubbing his chin against my forehead. "You don't complain when I'm going down on you."

No, I never complained about that.

Moaning as his thrusts went from nothing to hard, I clung to his shoulders. One of my legs went up over his hip as he pushed it back, and the other tightly curled around his thigh, keeping him close. My breasts bounced with each powerful jerk of his hips. When our eyes locked in on each other, his mouth came and crashed down against mine. Our tongues wound together, fighting for dominance as we each battled for control. I did it to wind him up… teasing him. It was not that I liked being in charge. I preferred him to take that control. It did it knowing he enjoyed the thrill of the chase.

Pulling my hips back, I gasped as he went deeper. "Griff…" My words were drowned out when my voice rasped with another throaty moan as his groin angled and hit me right where I needed it. My orgasm was coming on fast, and his was coming close.

"With me, pretty. I'm right there with you," he said, grunting and spilling himself inside me as I tightened once more, erupting in shaking pleasure with him.

We had been together for seventeen months. You would assume we met normally, and I never told my parents about how we truly met that night—that we met in the club, I cooked breakfast, and then had sex on table three in the café, proceeding to spend the next two days hauled up together in a motel room. Instead, I said he came into the café and that things went from there… which was kind of true. He did stalk me for a couple of weeks until I finally agreed to go on an actual date with him. He had taken me to Quay Restaurant, with a view of Sydney Harbour. He may have that hipster charm about him, but nothing about him was low-key hipster.

Tracing my fingers over his chest, I stared at his artwork of black ink as I lay in the crook of his arm. I brushed my finger over my name that was written across his chest where his heart was beating steady. I had his name on the inside of my ring finger. Forever, we would be connected. His lips pressed to the top of my dark hair, and he exhaled. "What time is it?"

Reaching over his naked-as-the-day-he-was-born body, I found my phone on the bedside table and swiped the unlock screen. I groaned sleepily. "We got ten minutes. It's well past lunch time."

It was ten minutes until the boys finished school and twenty minutes until they would be here. Toby was a charming boy, and when I say charming, I really mean going through that teenage rebelling stage. He was older by three minutes and always in a bad mood. On the other hand, Mack was much shyer and blushed whenever spoken to. He was the quietest out of them all.

They both had their dad's charming good looks.

It did not worry me too much that he had teenage children or that I was only seven years older than them, but it did bother his ex, Karen. She called me the "young floozy he was fucking through his midlife crisis." Meanwhile, my personal favourite to call her was his teenage dream.

She never saw their split coming. He told me they were not sleeping together. Had not done it since she fell pregnant. They had separate rooms for six years before he just got up and finally walked out when they were ten. There was no love there, and he thinks there never had been. It was a mere teenage infatuation filled with lust. She, however, was in love with him still. I think he filled her with false hopes when he designed and built the apartments for them to live in.

When she first walked in, I was surprised. She was not what I had been expecting. I was expecting a warm, friendly woman. She was very small, not at all intimidating with her size, until she spoke. And there it was—that resting bitch face look. Griffin had mentioned the skinniness was due to drugs. I knew the moment we met, she would make this tough between us. I could not think otherwise when her marble-like eyes always looked mad, and she kept a cigarette tucked behind her ear, near her mousy brown short hair.

The first time I caught her waltzing in and making herself at home, I thought that they were getting back together and had been screwing behind my back. I instantly turned around and walked back out of the apartment.

For three days, I had ignored his calls and texts and pretended I had not listened to his desperate voice mail messages. I held my ground until he drove for two hours over to my parent's in Mosman and begged me to talk to him. I did, and somehow, that talk convinced me to move in with him. He explained she did that sometimes, but there was nothing even remotely sexual between them.

They were friends for the sake of their children. It was normal, right? *It would stop once we began living together*, I thought.

Wrong.

So, I had gone back to the house and hoped for the best. As I was carrying a box of belongings up the stairs, his ex-fiancée came over and made her thoughts known—clearly letting her bitch side come out without any remorse or regret. She had told me that I was never going to be their boys' mother, and if I ever tried to be, she'd put me six feet under. Griffin, hearing all of that, came over and told her to calm down and back off.

This woman was marking her claim and letting me know. She was the only woman in their life. Sometimes, I think she thought Griffin was still hers, too.

"Do you have work this weekend?" he asked, sitting up and finding his boxer shorts that were at the foot of our mattress.

Staying in bed, I watched him with devouring eyes. "I have it off. Why's that? Do you want to do something?"

"Does it count if I say *you*?" He grinned slipping a leg into the bottoms. Looking more serious, he kept his voice low and words short. "There's a game on." It was not a request. He was simply telling me that he was going.

"Hot men, lots of cash… who wouldn't miss that for the world?" I teased, and a laugh escaped as he raised a brow at me. Correcting myself, I said, "I'm sorry. I meant one extremely hot man."

"Better." Having finished dressing up, he rubbed his chin and bent down to pick up something. Turned out it was my black thong, and he handed it to me. "If she switches weekends, do you mind watching them while I'm out?"

I knew that was coming. Still, he always asked if I was okay to watch them. Raising my hips back up, I pulled the tiny fabric up my tanned thighs and covered the bare part he was staring at. "Of course. I love those boys. You know that I don't mind looking after them. They're safe with me."

Leaning over the bed, he placed a chaste kiss against the bare skin of my stomach. "I know they are." Once he had helped me up, he gave my behind a playful slap. "Behave at work."

"Always do. Don't forget to heat up your dinner in the oven, not microwave like last time." I winked and stood on my tippy toes. Wrapping my arms around his neck as he slid his around my lower waist and squeezed my bare ass. "Tell me you love me before I leave," I asked with a whisper.

"I love you," he said, staring into my eyes and rocking me to my core. "You love me?"

Almost pressing my lips against his, I whispered, "I love you. You know I do."

"I do. I'll wait up for you. Call me when you're finished." He always said that, but I wouldn't call knowing it would only wake him up.

Trying to decide what to wear to work tonight while Griffin took the boys to his studio was routine to me. I ended up slipping into a pair of skinny black jeans that clung to my ass and a long, white tee that fitted loosely but hugged my curves enough. I left my arms exposed to show off the black ink my boyfriend liked to draw all over me. He was making me way more addicted to tats than I needed to be. When you date an architect, who was also a qualified tattooist, you just let him draw. I loved it, though. He would draw something up and show it to me. I never hesitated to let him put it on my skin.

I tied my long black hair up into a messy knotted bun. Working in a café was fun although the hours sucked during the week. I was glad to have most weekends off on a rotating roster. My mum rarely showed up anymore. I would be lucky to see her maybe three times a month. Other than that, I was the girl in charge of opening and closing.

Bending down, I dug through the bottom of the wardrobe until I found what I was looking for: flats.

This room was far too small for my things, but I did not tell him that. This house was designed to fit a man and two children. It was gorgeous and very modern but also boyish. I tried to make it slightly prettier, but I was met with mock horror and a candle that was only allowed to come out of the draw when Griffin was feeling romantic and wanted to drip hot wax over my naked body as he fucked me until I was flushed pink with handprints and marks all over.

Our sex life was extremely fun… spontaneous with a hint of kink to it. Who was I kidding? There was a lot of kink between us.

After doing a thick eyeliner, I glossed up my lips and made my way outside. At almost three pm, I headed to the car.

Trying not to notice the woman sitting on the wooden porch chair out the front of her house. She did not even try to hide that she was staring at me.

I should give her the finger, but I chose my best friend's advice and ignored her.

Harvey was wiping down the wooden counter when I walked through the sliding door. He looked up and smiled. "Afternoon," he called out loudly. I was used to it as his earphones were blasting music, something he always had on while cleaning. "How's the day been treating you?"

I gave him a half a shrug, rolling my eyes. "It was great until Karen appeared."

"You're kidding. She came over again?" He knew without having to ask.

"Too early for a drink?" I asked with a wink.

"Won't say no." He smirked, making his way over to the coffee machine. Harvey made the best coffee ever. My favourite was his dirty hippie. "You look good tonight."

I just smiled. His compliments were a usual thing, but I took no notice. He was just being friendly.

Harvey was what women would call fucking gorgeous. It seemed all the men in my life were. His short dark brown hair was tousled up and shaved on one side, and he had a brow ring and sleeve of tats on both arms. Add to that the nose piercing and his bright blue eyes that looked like pools of crystal clear water. Harvey was a one-night stand kind of guy and never banged the same girl twice. There was no sexual relationship between him and me. We became friends when we first met at work, and it stayed that way. That was probably why Griffin loathed him so much. Harvey did not like Griffin either. If I had a dollar for every time he told me that he was too old or that I could do better, I would be the millionaire.

I'm not kidding. Those two would grin and bear it, but only for my sake.

Passing over a coffee cup, I found my black apron and tied it around my waist. "To work tonight!" I grinned.

Holding it up as if to toast with me, he grinned back. "To one hell of a night."

***

It was more than one hell of a night. It was a nightmare! There wasn't enough coffee to keep me awake at the end of the night once I had finished mopping the floors and locking up.

There were two fights, and one of them ended with a table being smashed and the police arriving to haul their drunken asses out of the café—just one of the downsides of working in a café that stayed open to the late-night diners. At first, it seemed like a good idea, and most of the time, it was. But then random drunks appear, and soon, I was being hit on by the usual wasted men and some women. Apparently, having tats and black hair made me look like a hard-core lesbian. No, I was straight. Even though Griffin would probably love to watch me with another woman, it was not going to happen.

I liked cock, more specifically, his cock.

Also, I did not share what was mine.

Exhausted and eager to welcome our bed, I walked up the stairs to our front door at almost midnight. I was freaking tired. All the lights were out, except for the soft glow of the hallway lamp.

The house was silent. It was small, but it suited the four of us well. Everything was almost always tidy. I loved summer here. The sun shone perfectly into our bedroom as we would often lie in bed, talking and just enjoying each other's company.

I checked on the boys, both passed out in their own rooms. They are twins but very different.

Toby's TV was still on and the movie back at the main menu. I walked over and turned it off. Mack had a book still in his hand. He must have fallen asleep reading as he did so often. They both got a kiss from me. I loved them. They may not be my own children, but I adored these two boys so much.

Kicking off my shoes as I pushed open our bedroom door, I found Griffin passed out with the TV on and the sheets around his naked waist, covering his hidden possession.

He always slept naked… not that I ever complained.

He woke up with a yawn as I stripped off my clothing and quickly slid in beneath the covers. His arms wrapped around me, and he placed a kiss on my bare shoulder. "You didn't call." His sleepy voice was so sexy as his groin flexed into the curve of my behind, making me curl my legs up.

"And you didn't wait up," I whispered, my eyes already closing as my hands slipped over his, interlocking our fingers. I snuggled down, my back against his front as his lips glided against the nape of my neck.

The woman across the road may cause me some grief, but at least I got to come home to this every morning after work. That was not going to change for anything or anyone.

CHAPTER TWO

Loosening my thighs from around his waist as he slowly draws his flaccid cock out, I could not help but grin lazily up at him as he helped me to stand on my feet. I wobbled for a split second but never fell as his hands were still firmly placed on my hips, holding me as I regained my balance on the shower tiles. The warm leak of semen running down my inner thigh was being washed away as Griffin slipped his hand between my thighs with the washcloth and also started washing himself clean from our usual shower antics.

"What time is the game tonight?" I asked, rinsing the conditioner from my hair as I watched him.

The water spilling down his face made him look like a Greek god—so sexy and completely mine. Stepping out from underneath the water, he brushed his long locks from his face. "Around eleven."

I nodded, spitting out the water from my mouth. I rested my bare back against the white tiles and found relief in their coolness. "Can you write down the nights the boys are staying here this week so I can try to get them off work?" I asked. I wanted to spend my nights at home with the three of them.

"You know you don't have to work. I make enough with both jobs to take care of you." He pointed out.

He had offered me this on more than once occasion, and it used to bother me. Now, it just went in one ear and out the other. Sure, it would be great not having to work all night, but on the other hand, I liked it. I could spend my mornings at home, and Griffin and I could spend time together if he were not at work or in the tattoo joint. It was a perfect schedule.

I would not admit to him that I was not planning to be like her. Karen refused to work, and Griffin was paying her half of his income each week. It really bothered me that he was paying her much more than necessary. They had joint custody, so why couldn't she go out and get a job or refuse to take most of the money? No way in hell was she going to get anything from me.

The shower was large enough for the both of us, and then some. There were two sides, but we usually showered together. As he walked from the open shower, reaching for a towel to dry off, I took advantage of the hot water. It was all to myself now. "I like working. I'm young, and since you refuse to let me pay rent, I refuse to stop working." My eyes flickered to his, gauging his reaction.

"They're back at hers tonight for three and then two with us."

"It's very confusing. Why can't you do a more permanent arrangement?" They loved staying here with us... sometimes maybe more than with her.

He stopped drying himself and looked down to me. "It's easy."

I bit my tongue, wanting to mention just how strange it was. "If you say so."

Taking a step forwards, he snaked an arm around my waist, getting wet once more as I pressed my body to his. "Don't worry. You'll still have me."

A smile spread across my lips. "Good. Maybe we can go have dinner with my parents one night then. I know they're missing me and dying to see you again."

"Dying?" He raised a brow. "I think they merely tolerate me to keep their only child happy."

"Nope. Sorry, they love you."

"Good. We'll go there on the weekend. I have it off, and so do you," he said with a wiggle of his brow. I knew what he meant. We would spend those days fucking like crazy.

Pretending to kiss him, I reached for the white fluffy towel instead. "Look forward to it."

He placed his splayed out hand over my shoulder, slowly running it down to my elbow. "You know, getting a full sleeve means having your elbow area done too. Not just upper and lower arm."

Here we go again. He was itching to get me back in that chair, in both ways. "Yeah, but I like how it looks this way. It's different. Kind of cool, don't you think?"

"I know. Have you thought about getting something on your hip done?" he asked, his finger now tracing dangerously low. "It would look incredibly sexy."

I have thought about it, and I had decided against it only for one fact. "No. I don't want it to stretch and look distorted when I'm pregnant."

Something flashed in his eyes, his face changing for a moment, but it was gone before I could notice what it had been.

Maybe it was fear or possibly excitement. I was a long way off babies, but I did want them, and he knew that. It had been a major factor in me moving in. Children were eagerly anticipated.

"Pregnancy… of course," he said with a nod, dropping the towel from around his waist. As he walked past me, I could not help but reach out and slap his cheeky bum before walking into our bedroom to get dressed.

I stood facing the foggy mirror as I rubbed the green hand towel over the glass, staring at myself as my dark blue eyes stared back from the reflection. I could see my black feather tattoo curling beneath my left breast, peeking from the underside. Each of my tattoos told a story. My very first one was the blackbird on the inside of my index finger. It was for when I lost my virginity. My eyes trailed down to my flat stomach, and I sighed. I should not have brought up pregnancy, not after what Karen had put him through with promising she was on the pill and then lying about the condom breaking. Unbeknown to him, she was not on anything and fell pregnant immediately. My bet was that she poked holes through the latex, so it broke, just to knock herself up. I did not like to think about the two of them together, in bed.

Lying, conniving bitch. There, I said it—although I did not really say it. She was the devil in disguise.

That was a big part of the reason he was so adamant about us using condoms even though I was taking the pill. He did not think I noticed, but I knew he was in the bathroom with me every morning to make sure I was taking the pill. I always took it in front of him, not letting him know that I knew what he was doing.

Drying my hair, I dressed in the walk-in robe and made my way to the bedroom where he was sitting on the king bed, tying his laces up. "I'm sorry," I said quietly. "I didn't think that through."

"Don't be sorry. I won't deny you of children. You know that." He spoke so formally, it almost felt forced.

"I'm not asking for them right now. You know that I'm happy with you and the boys. That's plenty for me." For now. We would revisit the baby talk in a year or more… or I would ask him once his cock was inside me, and he wasn't so wound up about the subject. "I just look forward to babies with you. Is that a bad thing?"

Smiling as he stood, he tied his hair back and walked towards me. "I know what you meant. Don't panic."

"So, I'll get the boys fed and ready and wait for you to come back home." Karen had swapped weekends with us yet again, and next weekend, we would likely have them too. She liked to change everything around, and because there was no real set plan, Griffin went along with whatever the boys wanted to do.

"Taking them to the café? They'd like that."

I smiled, running my flat palms up and down the front of his casual red t-shirt, then taking a step back to admire the sight before me. "Okay. I shall do that for dinner."

His eyes on mine, he stared down at me. The strong gaze gave me a shiver down my spine as he said, "Good girl."

I melted. I adored being called that. "Thank you."

"And I will also try not to get a wide on at the thought of you surrounded by men in suits and cash. Are you wearing the suit I came—"

It was his lucky suit, as he claimed.

His hand flew over my mouth, and a grin spread over his mouth. "Yes, dirty woman. I remember that night very well. If you're a good girl, I'll give you something when I get back home."

"You know I love presents." I winked, my voice coming out muffled underneath his palm. With a lick against his salty skin, he moved it away, and I laughed. "What are you giving me?"

"You'll have to wait and see."

"Wait." I frowned slightly. "An actual gift or your dick?"

He walked out and did not answer, but I could hear the laughter, so it was probably sex.

Mack was sitting on the marble kitchen bench doing homework as I went into the kitchen. It was not a large area but enough for a counter and dining table. We rarely ate out here, anyway. It was just for formality. Everything was open planned—bare white walls and furniture Griffin had purchased before we met. I would love to put a picture up, but he was anti-nails in his nice, clean walls.

He looked up when I ran my fingers through his light brown hair and smiled as I slid into the seat opposite him. "We're going out for dinner tonight, excited?"

Sometimes, I felt like their bigger protective sister, and it probably was a good thing. They already had parents; I was not going to step in and take that role away.

Mack, with a shrug, just nodded. "Guess so."

"Or would you rather have a happy meal at McDonald's?" I suggested, teasing him. "Maybe an ice-cream sundae? *Mm*, hot fudge sounds amazing, doesn't it?"

Looking up, he opened his mouth and then closed it again as Toby walked in, wearing a hoodie and baggy jeans. He kicked my chair as he walked past. "I'm hungry." He grumbled, definitely in a hormonal mood. "Like starving."

"Just wait twenty minutes. We're going out." I was bot feeding them before we sat and ate. I was not stupid. I knew he would never eat his actual dinner if he pigged on something beforehand. Checking my watch, I stood up. "Ten minutes, and you can eat all you want."

"Dad…" Toby called out. "I'm hungry!"

Typical Toby. He did not like what I had to say, so he goes to his father. "What?" Griffin called out, doing his black silk tie as he walked into the room, joining us.

I forced my eyes off his irresistible body and went back to helping Mack. He did not need it, but I still did it, anyway.

"I'm hungry… like really hungry." Toby groaned. "I don't want to wait ten minutes."

"Eight actually." I winked, giving him a playful beam which earned me a scowl.

"You're not eating anything now. Ayla is taking you both out." I loved that Griffin did not go behind my back and did the opposite of what I had said. He told me from the day I moved in here that his children were to treat me with respect and that I had the authority to scold them if necessary. He did not want them having one over my head.

Not that I scolded them a lot, but I did not let anyone walk all over me.

Toby, in a grumpy mood, was testing his father's patience. "I'll go over to mum's then. She'll let me eat what I want. She always does."

Griffin raised a brow down at him. "Don't be rude. I said no, and I meant it. You're not going over there, and since you're being a pain in my ass, you can take the garbage out."

As Toby stomped off, Griffin glanced over and winked. I laughed, walking towards him and sliding my arms around his waist. "Are you eating first?"

"No. I'm not hungry." He raised his brow and nodded over at Mack's homework. "Why are you doing your brother's work?" he asked, not sounding angry. He was more amused than anything.

Mack shrugged and put the pen down. "Toby's dumb. I'm helping him, and he's going to pay me for it."

"Is he?" Griffin smirked, grabbing me by the hips as I went to brush past them. He pulled me against him, holding me close. The warmth of his affection made me smile. "Where's he getting the money from?"

"You," Toby answered for him with a wide grin. "When are we leaving? I'm halfway through an Xbox game—*Call of Duty*."

Boys and their toys.

"Toby, what's going to happen when you're tested on the homework Mack's doing for you?" I asked. "You know… they make you sit in a room and watch you answer all those questions."

His eyes widened for a moment, and then they dipped into a frown. "I'll know it by then. He wants to do the work, so he can do it."

I sighed. This boy had no clue.

"Ayla's right. If you get caught cheating, they'll make you repeat your year." Pointing towards Mack, he spoke to him. "Don't do anyone else's homework, except your own. If they offer to pay you, tell them to shove it up their arse."

Mack stifled a laugh. "Got it, Dad."

Griffin's eyes went to Toby's. He was going into stern dad mode. "Your own homework, alright?"

With a groan, he also agreed. "Alright, Dad."

I kissed him goodbye, and Griffin was out the door and on his way to the game. We were soon set for the road to go and eat. Grabbing my bag and keys, I locked the door, and we headed down to the car.

"Where are you going with them?" her nosy voice called out from above us. "It's too late to be up on a school night."

"Dad said it's okay," Toby spoke back, hesitating before he opened the car door and jumped inside.

I internally groaned as she put down the can of Red Bear on the cement and made her way down the steps. For the love of god! Couldn't she keep to her own side of the place? I get that she was their mother, but this was ridiculous. Watching her stalk over in a pair of black leggings and a green off the shoulder top, I contemplated on getting in my car and just driving off. They were in our care. I loved how she was home, though, just drinking.

Sighing, I knew I she was going to want an explanation. "Karen, we're going for a drive."

"You mean he's gone gambling, and you're bringing my children along to watch."

Damn it. He did not want her to know that he had gone there.

I could not lie, and I refused to get in between their chaotic drama. "I'm taking the boys to get dinner. Then we're coming back home."

"You tell him if he wins, then he better not skimp out on me." She narrowed her eyes, placing a hand on her hip to make her small build seem more intimidating. It worked, only because

I knew she could knock me out in an instant. I have heard and seen her scrap, like a bulldog with a bone. "You take your eyes off my children for one second, and I'll have your scrawny ass buried—"

I cut her off with an impulsive eye roll. "Six feet under? Yeah, I get it. You can trust me with them. Griffin sure does."

"The father of my children is blinded by your perky tits and pussy. Once he's over the beauty of you and done with his thrill of fucking another woman, he'll finally see that there's really nothing special about you. He's a man, and well, you just graduated pre-school." I hated it when she brought up the twelve-year age gap between us. Being twenty-two does not make me young and stupid.

I got in the car and ignored her burning blaze of a glare as I drove out down the driveway and in the opposite direction of her.

"Mum doesn't like you," Toby stated with far too much enthusiasm as he scrolled through my iPod shuffle to change the music selection and finally settles on Linkin Park, but I skipped it with the button on the wheel before the swearing starts up.

Mack, in the back seat, raised his head up and joined in on our conversation. "Why doesn't she like her?"

"Mum said Dad's thinking with his dick," Toby replied.

Oh, god.

"Please don't talk that way. Your dad happens to love me. Do you think he would have asked me to move in if he didn't?" Glancing over, I raised a brow and turned my eyes back on the road. "Your mum shouldn't say things like that to you."

"Doesn't matter. We like you, and she's just mad since Dad is happy." As much as Toby could be a pain in my ass with his teenager mood swings, he really could be a sweet kid. It was rare when it happens, but it made being here worth it.

"What is this?" Mack asked, peering out the tinted window. "We're having dinner here?"

I twisted the keys and pulled them out, turning slightly to look over to where he sat in the back seat. "We sure are."

"Why is dad gambling?"

"I don't know." I really didn't.

"Maybe he's secretly planning something like when he changed your car." Toby pointed out, laughing loudly.

"That was the best." Mack joined him in laughing, and I just rolled my eyes, rather wanting to forget how my boyfriend decided to change my little white lancer that I paid five grand for myself for a black pimped out Audi.

After the initial shock of bursting into tears, I realised that yes, it did look sexier. I especially loved that the inside now had pink lighting instead of the usual red or white. But I told him that he owned that car and I would just drive it.

As I held the café door open for them both, I said with a slight grin, "Ever seen *Fast and the Furious*?"

"Yeah," they both said in unison.

"Well, maybe we can do a few hot laps around the city before we head home."

Both boys rolled their eyes, groaning. It did not take much to embarrass them. I loved it.

We took a table by the corner where we were able to see the busy streets at knock off rush hour, and I could not help but worry about Griffin. I knew it was safe, but it was also very dangerous. When I had first found out about his underground poker games, I did not believe him. Then he took me to watch one night, and I still could not believe it. He bought five grands worth of chips and won a total of forty that night. It was easy money—fun money—but it was also very, very illegal money.

They played hard, but they won harder. The drawback was that there was a risk of getting caught. Then comes the fallout if things get way worse. I have only ever asked him to stop playing once, in case he got caught, and he did for a while. But I had since then realised that it had nothing to do with the money. He just loved the adrenaline rush.

There were cops there who were in on the betting. They had their radios with them so everyone would know if any suspicion was being raised and could quickly tell players to take off the moment someone rings the bell, giving everyone enough time to flee the scene before any arrests were made. Usually, they would get a call through the week. The venue often changed, too.

Still, as much as he tried to say it was just a game, it worried me. I could not relax until he was back home with us. After the boys had finished their shakes and fries, I drove home without embarrassing the boys and spotted Griffin's red Mustang in the driveway.

He was back early.

"I tried calling. I thought something happened," he said, walking over as I stepped outside. I had not noticed the missed calls.

"You're home early." I pointed out. He normally did not come back until well into the early hours. "Why? Did something happen?"

"I missed you, that's all. Is that such a bad thing?"

Slowly, a smile crept over my lips as my eyes closed momentarily.

He kissed me, keeping me close once more and inhaling the scent of my hair. He had one of his arms wrapped around my side as he kept a close eye on his sons who were gawking at the beauty before them—their father's sleek red car that had been christened with a glorious fuck on the hood and a blowjob on the drive home.

"We were distracted by cake after dinner. Even brought you a slice home."

"Just a slice?" He cocked a brow.

"Mum said you have to give her half of what you win," Toby said, getting on the driver's side and sitting on the comfortable black leather seat as Mack got on the other side.

Griffin just chewed on his lower lip and shook his head. "Nothing gets past her," he muttered with a grim expression.

"She told the boys you're thinking with your cock. That's disgusting to say, especially to children." He knew I was referring to him and I being together. "It's hurtful."

Sliding his hand over my ass in the jeans I wore, he cupped my cheek and squeezed it. "Ignore her." There he went again, ignoring my feelings over the matter and letting her win. He was never one for conflict. He preferred to ignore and get along than deal with the fighting.

Of course, she was soon coming down, knowing we were here and that Griffin had a fresh lot of money waiting for her to collect. He told the boys he won ten grand and put five in an envelope for their mother.

The boys trotted off inside, and I began to follow when he grabbed my elbow and pulled me to a stop. "Wait here."

I watched him as he reached in and pulled out the envelope from his back pocket. Griffin walked over to where Karen stood and climbed the two steps to her porch, holding out the thick white envelope. He handed it to her and said something which caused her to glance at me and smirk.

I looked away and was about to walk inside when he turned and came back. He took me by the hand and led me up inside our house as the boys were eager to go and do their own thing.

"You didn't answer earlier. How come you're back so soon?"

"I told you, I missed you."

"Griffin..." I raised a brow, crossing both arms over my chest. "Tell me."

He started to loosen his tie and unbutton his shirt. "It was a quick game."

"So..." I started, my smile beginning to grow. "My present?"

His fingers stopped on the last button before undoing it and pulling his shirt off over his shoulders. "You're about to get it."

Throwing me down on the bed after I was stripped naked, he pushed me face first into the white pillow and reached underneath my belly, lifting me so that my ass was in the air. He teased me by dragging his swollen cock between my inner lips, and I sighed in anticipation, pushing out into him with need. Finally, he plunged in and grasped my hips with rough fingers that would surely leave bruises—his marks.

He balled his fists on a tight grip on my hair, and he pulled my head back as his other hand reached in front. The first slap stung, catching me off guard as my clit pulsed from sensitivity. His cock sliding in and out soon set the pace for another slap, and my body reacted. The orgasm was coming on. Then he stopped.

My legs shook, my body aching with the need to get off. He moved from the bed, walking towards his bedside drawer, opening it. "I brought you something."

"Oh?" I said, expecting nipple clamps.

Instead, he pulled out a black velvet pouch, and my pussy clenched in what was to come. A stainless butt plug with a purple jewelled top was revealed before my very eyes. It was very pretty. "For my good girl. I want to stare at this as I fuck your cunt." He then pushed it into my pussy, just enough to lube it up. Easing it out, he dragged it back towards my ass as I stayed on all fours. I bent lower, allowing him full access.

"That feels amazing." I shook in pleasure. My eyes were rolling, and my moans were not at all quiet as the princess plug was pushed into my ass slowly. His voice was husky with desire as his cock pushed back into my pussy, the fullness sending me over. I have never come so hard and fast before. This was indeed the perfect gift.

His dirty talk was pure filth as he pushed my body forwards, pinning my face into the pillow and fucking me relentlessly over and over again.

Panting loudly as I came down from the emotional high, I watched as he fell beside me with his own deep breathing. He leant in and kissed my mouth, a soft tenderness as he sat up. I tilted my head to the side, my cheek against the pillow. "Wow." I was one very happy girl.

He had fucked me like his dirty little whore, and then took me slower, making love to me. There were two sides to him that only I got to experience, the dominant and the romantic.

"Wow, indeed. I love you." He kissed my forehead then proceeded to reach into the bedside drawer and pull out another envelope. It was different to the one he handed Karen. This was thicker, yellow, and bigger.

I read his expression so easily. He was such a liar. "How much did you really win?"

"A lot more, baby, a lot more."

CHAPTER THREE

"Babe!" I called out, peering into the pantry once more and reshuffling bags of chips to try to find what I knew should be in here. "Did you move my coffee?"

"Huh?" he asked, walking up behind me and sliding his hands easily along the curve of my hips, pulling me back against his morning glory. "What did you say?"

"Did you drink my coffee?" I asked, giving up on searching as there was no sign whatsoever of the golden box containing my butterscotch latte.

I yawned. I was tired and could not start my day until I at least had one of my Nescafè coffee sachets. Some people have a coffee and a smoke first thing in the morning, like Griffin, and some go jogging. Me? I had a flavoured latte and never let myself run out. It was probably borderline obsession, but I had multiple coffee flavours and no one could touch them. It was the only thing in this house that everyone stayed away from.

Unless… someone had been sneaking around and taking them without telling me. No guesses who that could be.

Griffin could never understand why I liked them so much when we had an espresso maker or that I was a qualified barista. It was just something I liked. Coffee making all day was my job, but when I came home, I prefer not to make coffee.

Turning, I looked up at Griffin who was also half-asleep and leaning against his arm that rested on the pantry door frame over my shorter body. His chest was bare and warm as I pressed my cheek against his skin.

His hands stroked down my skin softly, brushing through my long hair. "I know better than to touch your coffee. Could you have…" He let his question linger in the air.

My head snapped backwards, and my eyes narrowed. "I never run out."

"Would you like me to go buy you another box?" He raised a brow. "The boys wouldn't have touched it. They're too young for coffee. Hell, they think you'd skin leather off them if they touched it."

"Did anyone else come into the pantry while I was at work yesterday afternoon?" I asked, not wanting to say her name. She already took the milk; just what else has she been helping herself to? I noticed I was running low on my coconut face scrub too, but I did not peg her for the type to use those.

"No." There was no hesitation in his firm answer.

He knew I would be pissed as hell if she was coming over here while I was away and vice versa. We had a major deal breaker in our relationship, and I was not kidding around when I let him know what that was. Unless it was for an absolute emergency, like a house on fire or one of the kids being unconscious, there was no need for it.

"Well, I must have run out then," I said under my breath. I knew I had not.

Spinning on my heels, I was ready to go back to bed. That was until Griffin wrapped his right hand around my left elbow, spinning me around and hauling me up and over his shoulder. I let out a laugh and squealed at the same time.

"We're going to the shop!" he announced, carrying me towards the front door. "My girl wants coffee, and she gets whatever she needs." He made me sound like a spoilt brat. He did spoil me well, though.

"No! I haven't even showered yet. We're not even dressed." I looked a damn awful mess with my hair sticking out all over the place.

Halting in his footsteps, he took a detour and picked up a white shirt from the pile of laundry I needed to wash, and we were back on our way to the front door. Outside, the rain pelted down hard. It was freezing cold, but I knew better than to think he would turn and go back inside. Dashing to the car, he opened my door and practically dropped my body onto the front seat with a thud.

After pulling the shirt on over his head as he sat in the driver's seat, he looked over and winked. "Sorry for getting you wet. Well... your hair and clothes."

"You think you made me wet elsewhere?" I asked, leaning over the centre console towards him. "Because I am extremely soaked from the rain, and that's it." I broke out into laughter as I pulled away and sat with my back to the leather seat.

"Not funny," he murmured with a grin. His hair was flat, and droplets of water covered their ends, dripping onto his shirt. "Let's go get this damn coffee, so you're awake enough to fuck without yawning the entire time."

I could not believe he brought that up. I threw my arms out in front of me to make a point as I snapped back at him. "It happened once, and I had barely slept two hours. Maybe you should have done a better job at keeping me focused."

Faking hurt, he shook his head with a grin. "Ouch, baby. You hurt me hard."

The trip to the store went longer than intended. A stop in at a McDonald's drive-thru, and we were on the way to the store. Griffin came out holding a large white Coles bag. I expected one box, but he had grabbed four and a couple of others.

"On sale?"

"No. I just didn't want to listen to you complain anymore." He winked, and I slapped his thigh. "They were on special."

Good boy. I was training him well. "Thanks, baby."

The rain had not eased up when we returned home. Griffin had one meeting with building contractors that was keeping him busy of late. He had designed the most beautiful home out of the city that would sit on a couple of acres. Griffin had left before the kids finished school, and then we were set to leave to my parents for the night. It was a two-hour drive including traffic, and we wanted to get there earlier, rather than drive in the rain through the night. With a kiss goodbye, my man left for work, I gave the house a quick clean up and then packed us an overnight bag.

It had been a huge deal for me to move out of their home. Being an only child, I was extremely close to my mum. For them to accept my relationship with Griffin without judgement was the type of people they were. They were both extremely supportive.

In the middle of vacuuming, my phone buzzed, and I did not think much of it. Ten minutes later, when I finally got around to reading the message, I freaked out.

I'm going to be later than thought. Can you get the boys from school?

"Shit!" Holding my arm out, I glanced down at my wrist and looked at my black watch. I needed to leave now.

Racing outside, I had the car in reverse before I clipped my belt and headed off to the school. Hopefully, the boys were not waiting too long.

I gathered my hair in my hands as I tried to shield the rain from soaking my straightened locks. Whoever does their hair when there's a storm outside was a total moron. Yep, I was one of those girls who liked my hair straight then cried about it when it got wet. My own stupid fault.

They were both standing at the gate under the bus shelter when I came to a halt in front of them. Mack was sitting on the bench seat with a book in hand, and Toby was leaning against the post, watching the cars pass by.

"I am so sorry!" I was not too late but late enough to know I should have been here sooner.

Toby bent down and grabbed his black Rip Curl bag, slinging a strap over his shoulder. "Where's Dad?"

"He got stuck in work. Did you have a good day at school?" I asked, trying to exchange some pleasantries with them. "I really am sorry that I'm late."

Mack stood and shoved his book into his bag. "You're not really. We only got let out."

Still, I felt terrible. I had never actually picked them up from school before, and it was not because Griffin did not trust me. It had everything to do with their mother thinking that I could not be trusted enough to collect them from school.

"Well, let's head home. Do you boys need anything to take to your mum's?" I asked.

"Nope," both replied.

Seeing as though I had this time alone with them, my curiosity piped up, and I could not help myself from asking them. "Hey, you know my coffee's... Did you drink any today? Or last night?" I asked. "Did Dad have one?"

Mack frowned, confused. "I'm not allowed coffee. Dad said it'll make me hypo."

"Toby?" I asked, in the sweetest voice possible while still grinning. "I won't get mad. I'm just asking."

"And I'm just saying that no, I didn't either. Dad said you'd kick our ass if we touched them."

"He didn't say that!" I gasped. "When did he say that?"

"Before you moved in. I don't like coffee, anyway." Toby just shrugged and dug into is school bag looking around for something.

There was not much talk after we arrived back home. They sat up at the kitchen table and did their homework. Toby was doing his own. Shocker! By the time Griffin was on his way home, the boys were on the couch and watching a movie as I sent Mum a text, letting her know that we would be leaving soon.

She was so excited to have us back there. Apparently, Dad had been marinating the steaks all day and brought the marshmallows and chocolate for me. He knew me well.

When Griffin came home, he walked silently over to the fridge, reaching for a beer but then put it back and chose coke instead. Taking his usual seat beside me on the couch, he stretched out and closed his eyes.

"Can we come over later and play the Xbox?" Toby asked, looking hopeful.

Sighing, Griffin shook his head and opened both his eyes. "Sorry, you're at your mum's so you know you're not allowed." When they were there, they were not allowed here. "Anyway, we won't be here. You know I'm going to Ayla's parents for the night, so if you need me, just call."

Mack looked up, his eyes wide. "When can we go visit her mum and dad?"

I smiled at him. "Maybe over the school holidays, if that's alright with your dad." *And if your mother allowed it,* I added in my head.

Toby turned to face us. "Will they let us swim in their pool?"

"Course they will. No one else uses it." I assured him. They both were treated like my parent's grandchildren, spoilt and loved.

"Sweet. Dad, can we go there?" Toby asked him.

Laughing, Griffin nodded. "Yeah, we might go away for the holidays on a camping trip or to the snow. I'm sure we can stay there on our way through." His hand squeezed mine. "You boys need to go get your bags. Your mother's probably waiting."

Their smiles slightly faded, and Mack murmured, "Do we have to go?"

"I'm sorry, you know that you do." It must be so hard to have to live between two homes. To see them upset now and then was difficult to digest.

They both dragged their feet, walking down to their bedrooms.

Turning to Griffin, I gave him a smile and straddled his lap eagerly. "Do you know what we get to do tonight?"

"Fuck in a hot tub?" His voice was low and seductive as his hands slid over my thigh, trying to pry my thighs with his rubbing fingers.

"You've got a way with words, but no." He was right; we probably would fuck in there, but that was not it. "We can roast marshmallows over the fire pit."

A laugh escaped, and he shook his head. "Sometimes, I forget how old I really am with you. That, or how young you are."

"Not old, baby, just wise."

Before his hand could slide any closer, the boys walked out with their backpacks and a sullen look on their face. I offered them each a smile as we stood up to say goodbye. We would see them again come Sunday night, anyway.

Griffin gave Toby's brown hair a ruffle and then gave him a kiss on the forehead. "Be good."

"Can't we come with you?" Mack asked quietly as I hugged him. "Please."

He was breaking my heart right now. "Oh, buddy. I promise next time you can come, yeah?"

"Promise?"

I was not sure if I had the right to promise him something, part of me wanted to say "hell yeah, bud." But the other part was always reserved as I was not his mother. My eyes flickered to Griffin. I caught him staring, and he gave me a nod.

Giving him a kiss on the cheek, I pulled away, bending slightly to take hold of his blue backpack and hand it up to him. "Promise."

Both their faces brightened. Hugging their dad, they walked to the front door, and Griffin followed to wave them off. Even if they were just going across the road, it was still hard to see them leave, especially for two nights. They would be back Sunday, and I was going to tackle a roast… not like my last one, where it turned into roast chicken and toasted cheese sandwiches. Kind of forgot to put the vegetables on, and no one really wanted a baked dinner at eight PM. The chicken tasted great, though.

Scratching my leg as I let out a yawn, I flopped back down on the couch. "I'm stuffed." I could see the smirk he was trying to fight off, and I raised a brow. "Just say it," I said with a groan.

Shaking his head, Griffin laughed. "Wasn't going to say anything, dear."

"Liar." I rolled my eyes. "You were going to say, not yet, but you will be soon."

"My girlfriend, such dirty words coming out of that sweet little mouth." Standing, he outstretched his arms for me to take his hand. He helped me stand and pulled me flush against his chest. "Your mouth needs a good stuffing."

Laughing, I nodded as I pressed my mouth against his, pulling away just enough to speak. "Yeah, it does." Wiggling my brows, I bumped my hips against his and flexed into him. "Quickie?"

He groaned, and before I knew it, he was already lifting me up and carrying me to the kitchen counter.

***

The car was loaded. I slid in the front seat, waiting for Griffin to lock up the door and drive us to my parents. I was excited to have the days off and was sure as hell looking forward to a night away with the two of us. No one to barge in, take our things, and then complain about nothing.

Or so I thought.

She was charging down the stairs, wiping her nose with a tissue and then shoving it into her bra strap. She walked over the driveway and stood right in front of the car window. Her hands were on her hips, and her eyes gave me that glowering look of hell.

I motioned with my hands, and I mouthed *what* to her. If she were nice, then maybe I would be nice back, but no. I did not think she even knew what nice was. Not to me, anyway, and I had not even done anything wrong to her. She motioned back, wanting me to get out of the car. I did. She then came at me like a hound dog ready for its feast.

"Griffin is inside. He'll be—" I did not know why I bothered speaking when she always cut me off.

"What the hell do you think you're doing?" She menacingly growled, so low that I could hear the venom behind each word. "You're not their mother. You're nothing to them, so back the hell off."

Ouch. That fucking hurt. "I'm nothing?" I was more than nothing. I was the woman her kids wanted to stay with this week. "Watch your mouth around me."

"Or what? Going to hit me?" She scoffed and followed it up with a loud sniff. She obviously had a cold, which grossed me out. "You're obviously not getting the memo. Fuck off!"

"Hey, enough!" Griffin came and took a step between us. "I asked Ayla to pick them up. If you're going to get pissed at someone, then it should be me."

Her eyes widened as he cut her off sharp. "Pissed?" She laughed, mocking him. "Why didn't you get them from school?"

"I was unable to get away from work on time, and I trust her enough with our sons," he firmly said. I hated that they were theirs. They had the family, and I just tried to fit in. "She lives here; it makes sense that she collects them from school if needed."

Her eyes returned to normal. "I could have gotten them from school. I've been home all day!"

"Well, I didn't know that, did I?" He raised his voice back. "Can't do a fucking thing right, never could!"

"I told you I didn't want her picking them up from school."

"Too late for that," I muttered underneath my breath, not meaning for her to hear.

"Shut up!" Karen spat. Pointing a finger, she pushed hard into Griffin's chest. "I told you that I didn't want your play thing anywhere near my sons. It's bad enough she moved in with you. I refuse to have her collecting them from school."

"I'm right here you know," I grumbled, getting annoyed that we were already running behind time.

Griffin nodded towards the car, giving me a pointed look. "Wait for me in the car."

"I'm not—"

"Ayla," he warned, his tone final.

Oh, like hell he was going to speak to me like this. I was not a child. If my looks could kill, he would have had a serious concussion right now. I closed the car door with a harsh thud, more loudly than I should. It was hard to sit and not watch them. They were fighting yet again. I could hear everything she said. She was yelling and pointing towards me, and he was standing there not saying much. This would have been the perfect time for him to fight back.

When he did come back to the car, I was on my phone texting Mum, saying that we were on our way.

Ten minutes into our drive, he spoke again, "How long are you going to ignore me for?"

I had been giving the silent treatment to him. Petty, I know. But, I was a girl, and sometimes we held grudges. Instead of speaking, I swivelled my body and looked out the window as the sunlight began to dim and turn into a glorious sunset.

It did not stop him from speaking to me.

"So you're angry?"

Of course, I was angry.

"Come on. I didn't mean to raise my voice at you." This time, he reached over and rubbed my leg. He was not going to give up.

Trying to push his hand away, I finally answered. "You scolded me like I was a child playing up and needing a time out."

A sigh escaped his lips, and he gave my thigh a squeeze. "I didn't mean to."

"You never defend me."

"I do."

A shook my head. "No, you don't." He knew he didn't. "She was so rude to me, and I didn't do anything to deserve that! I may not be their mother, but I shouldn't be treated like a girl you sometimes fuck."

"Don't say that, Ayla!" he warned with a growl. "You're not just a casual hook up. You know that."

I was quiet for a moment, then placed my hand over his for him to link our fingers together. "She hurt my feelings, Griffin," I said, my voice so soft. "My feelings were hurt, and I didn't do anything wrong. I didn't know she would react like that about the boys, but I drive them to town, and I don't see why I can't take them to and from school."

Heaving another sigh, he shook his head and lifted my hand up towards his lips. "I don't know either. You know how she gets. She threatened to keep the boys away longer."

She could not do that. "You can do something about that."

Placing another kiss to my knuckles, he dropped our hands so they were in his lap. "Let's talk about something else. I don't want to fight with you. Not when we're going to your parents."

He knew I was right, but he had never taken her to court. I think he was afraid that they would take one look at him being tatted up with piercings and judge him by that. He was a good father, and I just wished he would see that.

I also wished that his ex-fiancée would not hassle us this trip. Ha, one can only hope, right?

CHAPTER FOUR

"Why don't you ever go see your parents?" I mustered up the courage and finally asked him.

He kept his eyes ahead, focusing on the road in the darkness as we reached Mosman. We had passed the welcome sign and would soon be at my parent's house. Griffin answered me, "They're pissed at me."

"For walking out?" I could not help myself. That was what I had come to believe. His side of the story was that he up and left when the twins were ten. "Sorry."

He peered towards me for a split second and then looked back at the road. "Don't be sorry. It's true. I left my family, and they're pretty pissed about it still."

"Would they prefer you to be in an unhappy relationship?" I asked. Surely, his parents would not want their son to live a miserable life with a woman he did not love. I know that was the last thing my parents would ever wish for me.

He laughed softly, shaking his head. "Ayla, there's plenty reasons why I haven't introduced you to my parents.

They're not like yours." Yes, because they still had no clue about me. "Your parents didn't really care that I'm older or have teenage boys. My parents... they'd make it a point to drive you away."

"No one can drive me away from you," I said confidently.

"You sure about that?"

Karen could try, but I was not giving in and letting her win. I was sticking around. Reaching over, I ran my hand over his thigh and gave it a gentle squeeze. "Positive."

"Good. I'm just glad I never married her. Divorce would be a fucking nightmare," he murmured.

I agreed to that.

"I'm glad you didn't marry her too." I smiled. Hell, I was over the moon that he did not go through with that. "You did propose, so maybe you wanted to marry her in some way, though?"

"My parents pushed me to propose when she was pregnant. I didn't even ask. Just got her a cheap ass ring and left it on the dresser," he admitted for the first time to me.

Wow. "Uh, well, if you're going to ask me, then I expect to be romanced big time, baby!"

He let out a loud laugh, shaking his head but still grinning. "Yeah? Would you like me to get down on one bended knee and ask you? Should I wear a suit? You better tell me your favourite flowers. I'll need to organise them."

I smiled. He had no idea, but I loved him all the more for being so clueless with this. "I'm not really a flowers kind of girl, so any will do. But not yet, it's too early." It was way too early to be thinking about marriage. "Just make sure it's a white gold ring or even platinum with a lot of sparkles."

"I'll keep that in mind."

We pulled into the driveway of my parent's home. It was a two-story waterfront place, and I was looking forward to seeing them after so long. Griffin pulled the keys from the ignition and grabbed his phone and wallet. I shot him a questioning look, and he shrugged, not seeing that it was not the boys who were going to call but her.

With my bag half slung over my shoulder, I felt a hard stinging slap to my ass as Griffin passed by me towards the front door and opened it like it was his own home. That was how comfortable my parents made him feel.

My mother was first to rush and embrace him with a hug. "We were starting to worry. The storm's getting bad, and it's late."

"We stopped for food. Ayla was hungry."

Liar, I internally commented, faking an eye roll. "Yeah, and that burger that you ordered ate itself." I gave him a slight shove as I passed him into the house. I could hear him chuckling as I waltzed straight to my father and pecked him on the cheek. "Missed you, Daddy."

"Missed you too, sweetheart, Now go unpack so we can finally eat or are you not hungry now?" He winked with a glint of humour in his eye.

"We're hungry. We didn't eat much. Just a snack." Heck, I could eat a horse right now. I was that hungry.

***

I dropped down to my old double bed. The room was still the same with light pink walls and a white dresser near the door. Even the TV mounted on the wall for when I would have all night Netflix sessions was still there. I watched Griffin pull off his jumper and make his way towards me, slowly creeping up over my body. "I don't understand why you used to live here and work so far away."

"Because…" I giggled as his lips hit the bare skin just below my belly button. "It didn't bother me driving each day. I drove up, worked, then came home." I tried to pry his hands away as he went to pull the fabric of my bottoms down. "No, we can't," I hissed, swatting his hands away with a sharp slap.

"Ayla, you're killing me."

Good. Suffer my lover.

I rolled to my stomach as he lay beside me. He let out a yawn, and I narrowed my eyes. Reaching over, I ran my fingers through his hair. "You look exhausted. Maybe old age is catching up with you."

He shook his head with a scoff. "No. I'm just exhausted after work today and that drive."

"Griffin…" I moaned with a yawn. "We need to get off this bed before I fall asleep."

His hand went to the back of my head, trying to move me. "Your mouth around my cock would wake me up."

I squirmed away. I was not going to do that. "No, it wouldn't. You'd blow then fall asleep."

Rubbing his eyes with clenched fists, he laughed. "You're absolutely right. I probably would after the way I'm feeling right now."

"Work was really that exhausting?" I thought designing buildings would be easy and fun. "I mean, why are you so tired?"

"My girlfriend exhausts me."

I sat up, raising a brow. "It can be arranged for your girlfriend to never exhaust you again."

As I went to get off the bed, he caught me and pulled me back down, rolling so he was between my thighs as he held my hands above my head into the mattress. "I love being exhausted by you. I just had a busy day, that's all."

"Okay. Well, you can ride shotgun tomorrow, and I'll drive us home." I suggested. "Now kiss me like you mean it."

His smile broke out into a huge grin. "Oh, I love it when you're bossy, mistress."

***

My parents were sitting outside when we walked out. The rain was pounding against the roofing, but still, we were sheltered and free from it all. The fire pit was burning with a blazing orange flame in the middle of the room as Dad had the food cooking on the barbecue. The smell of kebabs and onions made my mouth water almost instantly. Not as instant as the packet of marshmallows on the table did, though.

It was just the four of us and the stunning view of the harbour.

"So, how are the boys?" Mum asked once we had taken a seat and grabbed a drink. I was having a glass of red wine even though I did not really want one. I did not say no.

Smiling, I answered before Griffin could. "They're great. Mack got an A in class the other day, and Toby got his first B." I sounded like a proud parent. When I realised everyone was staring, I blushed and sat back in my seat. She had been asking Griffin, not me. "Sorry."

Griffin, with his hand on my thigh, looked at me with an expression I was yet to learn. I'm going to say it was with pride, though. He then went to speak, "Yes, they're both great. It's sad that they couldn't make it, but they're looking forward to visiting in the summer holidays."

"Wonderful. I have something for them each for you to take back." Mum smiled. She and I looked way too alike when we smiled. "I hope you do bring them soon."

It was easy to tell just how much she adored those boys, and it made me a little sad because Griffin could not even tell his parents about me living with him. Why the hell did it bother me so much? Oh, yeah, because we had been dating for almost eighteen months, and I had never met them—my potential in-laws, who should already love me. I mean, I love their grandchildren, and let's face it, I have way more class than that woman living beside us.

He must have noticed my disappearing smile and leant in, whispering, "What's wrong?"

Now was not the time to bring this up. "Nothing, we'll talk about it later."

Later. Everything was getting pushed back on the back burner for later. Sooner or later, it was going to blow up in a fireball of flames and burn us all... or it might just burn me, mostly. I needed to decide if I could wait it out or just lay everything that I feel on the table and get the answers I was too scared to hear out loud.

The food was amazing, as always. Mum was telling us about her new café she was opening up closer to home and possibly not coming back to the city café. She was giving me more control and management of the other one. It was great in a way but still terrifying.

Griffin and Dad were talking about cars when I left them to be and went inside to help Mum with the empty plates and silverware. Scraping leftover salad in the bin, I caught her smiling at me, but this was not her usual smile. It was a sad one that warned me of an imminent little chat—one of those mother-daughter talks I usually dreaded. She would talk, and I would listen.

"Yes?" I asked, trying to pry my way out of it.

"Ayla, you know I love you, and you know that I adore Griffin. Your father and I both think the world of him." She glanced out at the men on the deck, watching for a brief moment, and then turned back.

"But?" *There was always a but.*

"But, are you happy? I mean really happy?"

Whoa. Where did that come from? I could not help but giggle nervously. "Mum, of course, I'm happy. Why wouldn't I be?"

"No. I don't mean like that. I just..." She paused and took in a long sip of her tall glass of red. She set the glass back down, curling her fingers around the crystal stem, and looked back at me. "He's older and with children. I worry that you may be too young... that you're headed for heartbreak."

As much as I loved her, I refused to listen to this. "Mum, I love him. Stop it. He's great. I'm great. We're great."

Raising a perfectly shaped brow, she said, "You just said great three times."

Did she really need to point that out? I dragged my fingers through my hair, rolling my eyes on purpose. "Don't."

"Is his ex-wife giving you trouble still?" She knew all about her. I did not really keep much from my mother, except for how we really met. She did not need to know about that one.

Ex-wife my ass. "Ex-fiancé. They never married, and yeah, she still hates me."

"You shouldn't have to put up with this. I just hope she isn't going to come between you both. It would break my heart to see your heart broken."

This was getting too real, and I did not want to think about that. I know things may be complicated, but I knew Griffin, and I knew that he would defend me if things become too difficult between her and me.

Ending the conversation by reaching for the pink bag of Pascall Marshmallows and heading back outside, I tore open the packaging and grinned shamelessly as I found the skewer I used to toast them in. "I'm going to eat this entire bag."

"I have no doubt you will." My Dad knew me so well. Tilting his empty beer bottle from side to side to see if he had any left, he sighed and stood. "I'll be back with a couple more."

Off he went, and I heard the chair grate along the tiles. Griffin came up behind me, placing one hand on my lower back as he took the pink marshmallow from my hand, piercing it through the fire poker and giving me a wink. "You and sharp objects don't mix so well. Would you like me to toast them for you?"

"I dropped the damn steak knife once," I reminded him. It may have landed on his foot. Anyone would think it sliced off a toe. "I can manage."

"Are you sure? I could do this and save any pain you may cause."

"Would you like me to call you daddy?" I cocked a brow, smiling when he snorted in disgust. *Yeah, I didn't think so.*

He handed the poker back to me with a grin. "Point taken. I will let you handle it yourself, big girl."

"Thanks, baby. Or should I say daddy?"

"Ayla..." He didn't like that one bit.

My tummy hurt from laughing hard. "Kidding."

It was all right to joke about it and tease him, but in no way was I going to be screaming out daddy during sex anytime soon... or ever. Not when he had kids. It was just plain gross. The only time I ever used that word was when I would ask my father for money and bat my pretty little lashes to him. Any other time? No way.

"Good. Are you going to tell me what you were thinking earlier?"

On second thought, I would rather call him daddy than talk about this. I set myself up in front of the fire pit and shrugged. "Not really. It's nothing."

"It's never nothing. What's on your mind, pretty?" I loved when he called me that.

"Nothing, it's just..." How could I bring this up without causing a fight? "I'm still upset."

Silence followed until he took a few more soft steps and sat beside me. His hand landed on my thigh, giving it gentle but firm squeeze. He knew it obviously. "I know you are, and I will try to make it better."

Not try, you fool. Just make it better.

"There's another thing..." I paused. I did not want to be this girl—the girl who complained and became needy with emotions—but I was turning into her because he was not giving me anything back. "I want to meet your parents."

"Hmm." He was mulling it over, his hand loosening and dropping. Leaning forwards, he ran a hand through his hair and rubbed his chin, deep in thought. "You do know what could happen?"

Of course. How bad could it be? "I live with you, and I want to meet them. Unless you're embarrassed by me?" *Could that be it?* "Are you embarrassed, or is my age a real issue for you?"

"I'm not embarrassed by you."

I met his eye, and he just stared back. "Then show me off to your parents. I want them to like me."

"I don't need their approval."

Right. "Fuck's sake! I can't even." I was annoyed. That just answered that. "You know what, Griffin? Don't bother. I'm going to bed."

Just my luck! Dad walked in as I started to stand up. I dropped the bag of uneaten marshmallows on the table and placed the stick down.

"Don't tell me you've finished already?"

"No, I'm just tired. I'm going to get a good night's sleep." I shot a glance at Griffin. He avoided eye contacts, his jaw clenching. He was obviously annoyed, but I did not care. "You can stay up. Talk about whatever you want." *Your fear of me meeting your parents... Your crazy ex who you refuse to deal with...* Oh, I knew what they could talk about. "Talk about the ghost who keeps stealing all my coffee."

Walking inside, the last words I heard were my father puzzled voice. "You have a ghost?" That made me chuckle all the way to my bedroom.

The shower did not help ease my thoughts. I was agitated and annoyed big time. Couldn't he just tell his parents about us and let them see how happy he was? Of course not because that is just too hard to do. I laid in bed, closed my eyes, and fell asleep listening to my dad's sixties rock music vaguely playing from outside.

***

It was pitch black when my eyes fluttered open. My body was tingling all over, aroused and turned on to the peak of explosion. Bucking my hips, I let out a low moan and ran my hand down my naked chest, towards my lower abdomen and to where his mouth was hungrily licking me.

"About time you woke." He groaned, making my clit pulsing from his words.

Then he did it—the one thing I absolutely loved. His fingers began to pound faster into me, hitting my G-spot while his face shook. His beard was prickling against my body and setting every nerve on fire. I was going to lose it any second now.

Nothing. No sound came from my throat except the low, throaty moan of a delicious and delirious orgasm that shook my body wide awake.

His tongue, licking up every drip of the wetness that left my body, began to kiss up my lower belly and towards my breasts, nipping at me with his teeth until finally, his lips came crashing down on mine. My hands were pulling his boxers, and I kicked them further down with my foot as I spread my legs wide open for him.

A single thrust came. That first thrust always had me clenching around him tightly. "Yes." I breathed out.

As our hips were slapping together, my fingers dug into the curve of his ass, pushing him deeper inside until his own orgasm blew out his dick in four long, deep thrusts. The rope of his semen was deep inside me.

"That was too quick." He groaned, pulling out but not moving off my body.

Sleep was coming back, and I was utterly spent. "It was perfect."

***

I was awake and annoyed as I sat up with my arms folded over my bare chest and my eyes glued to his sleeping body. *Hurry up and wake up,* I screamed in my head. I wished men could sense when their girlfriends needed to talk. With a slight nudge of my foot, I kicked him, and he moaned in his sleep. He was starting to move, and bingo! He was awake.

"Morning." He yawned, covering his eyes from the sunlight peeking through the blinds.

"You took advantage of me last night."

"What?" He was still half-asleep. "When?"

Shrugging, I lay back down in bed and faced him. "When I was asleep. You ate me out and then screwed me."

"I prefer the term making love with my mouth... then dick. So you're still mad?"

Was I mad? Yeah, a little. "Just a bit. How would you have felt if I didn't tell my parents about you or said not to mention you have two children?" I asked, trying to get him to see my side.

"You're right." I knew that already. "I'll give them a call and tell them about you."

That brought a smile to my face. Curiosity filled me. "Really?"

"Really. Now come here and turn around so I can spoon fuck you."

Yeah, such a romantic.

Saying goodbye to my parents was not too hard. Ok, I lied. I may have shed a tear or fifty on the drive home. I missed them and wished we could have stayed longer, but we had to get back home, and I had to make sure nothing was taken from our house. I did not like that I worried about someone snooping through my things, but how could I not be suspicious? I was not crazy paranoid, right?

Griffin opened the car window and lit up a smoke. *Yuck.* "How about we go and catch a movie tonight? I'll take you on a date."

"Sure. What one?" I asked as his phone rang again for the tenth time. Ok, this was the second time in an hour, but it was annoying me. "Are you going to answer that?"

Reaching in and grabbing the phone out of his pocket, he sighed. "It's Karen." Of course, it was. "I don't have to take it."

I gave in, and dread filled the pit of my stomach. "It might be one of the boys. Answer it."

What was worse than driving home in the morning and missing the Macca's breakfast menu? Believe me, when you're in a drive-thru, and the boards switch around mid-order, and they say, "Sorry, breakfast is over," that can really get under your skin. So at ten thirty-six am, I was eating a Big Mac as I drove us home.

That was nothing, though.

My problem was beside me. Listening to your loved one talking to their ex was way worse. I am not talking about a quick one-minute chitchat. I am talking about a forty-five-minute-long conversation where they are both laughing and talking like long lost friends all because she needed his help and could not call anyone else.

What could I do, though? I just gritted my teeth and sucked it up.

CHAPTER FIVE

We pulled into the driveway, and who else would be waiting for us at our steps? Well, for *him* actually. Yes, it was the one and only Karen. I was starting to lose my patience after having to endure him talking on the phone for almost an hour.

We lost forty minutes—valuable time that he and I could have shared!

What did they have to chat about? Random, stupid stuff that did not need to be spoken about. She asked him how to set up her DVD player like she did not already know that, and then she had the nerve to ask him about his night away. He even started to tell her until he noticed my death glare aimed directly through his skull. That was when he told her he had to go and tried sucking up by rubbing my thigh.

When she began to walk over, I really lost it. "If you talk to her, I'm going to stay with Harvey."

"Excuse me?" He looked taken aback.

With a low, harsh whisper, I seethed back. "I'm angry, so fucking angry that I'm about to burst into tears."

I was not one to boss him around or ever lose my temper like this, but I was beyond fuming.

"What?"

"You speak to her, and I will leave," I said clearly. My fingers dug into the palms of my skin as I squeezed my hands hard. Taking a deep, steady breath, I continued. "I mean it."

"Ayla..." He was clearly shocked, reaching out to cup my cheek.

I pulled back, my eyes burning from the sting of tears. "No." I did not want to hear it. "Just don't talk to me. Don't even touch me." I opened the car door, pushing it shut behind me.

Griffin stepped out and began walking towards me. His expression was solemn as I refused to make eye contact. "I'll get those," he murmured, taking the bags before I could reach them.

Rolling my eyes, I let the bag go and heard her coming closer.

"Griffy, can you come check out the player? I want to see if it's set up right."

Griffy? I just scoffed.

He noticed and ran a hand through his hair as he hauled the case from the boot. "Uh... I don't think that's a good idea." Yes, because he knew exactly what would happen if he did go over there.

"Wow, she's really got you by the balls—"

"Just go away," I muttered, loud enough for him and her to hear me. I was not in the mood for this right now.

Karen was raising her brows and twitched her lips up in a disgusting snarl. "Got something to say?" I kept quiet, not wanting to lower to her standards and petty behavior, although I think I just might have snapped and did it. She smiled back towards Griffin. "Your parents look well. We all went out for dinner last night. The boys enjoyed it."

I stopped in my tracks. "What?" I could not stop the question from coming.

Seeming to relish in my cluelessness, she smirked. "I thought it was odd that you went away. She said she called you last week about coming down."

My heart hammered against my chest, pounding harder as I snapped my head back towards Griffin, scoffing under my breath. "Unbelievable."

He would not look at me, focusing instead on Karen. Rolling my eyes, I kept walking to our front door. This was beyond a joke. He was not far behind me as I walked inside and glanced around. Everything seemed normal. Nothing seemed missing. I would have a thorough check later just to be sure.

"Ayla, what the hell was that?" His voice raised once he closed the front door, following me as I walked towards the bathroom and picked up my iPod.

There was nothing more I wanted to say to him. I was hurt, embarrassed, and felt like a fool. He knew his parents were here. He had been so eager to pack up and go visit my parents. Was that just to avoid me meeting them? I felt less than good enough… like I was some hidden girlfriend.

Instead of talking, I turned the music on my iPod right up, and I slammed the door in his face. Flicking the lock, I turned on the heat and fan. I was going to shower and cry my fucking eyes out, and he could not hear a thing.

I heard him knocking on the door. I ignored it. There was nothing he could say right now that would make me think differently. I was hurt because Karen had taken what could have been a nice night away for us. He had hounded him with calls and texts. When he had taken a shower this morning, I saw her name flash up with a text. Curiosity had gotten the better of me, and I found several more that he had replied with. It hurt to know that while I had been in bed sleeping, they were texting. Then he just came in and tongue fucked me as if nothing was wrong? That hurt.

She may be in his life, but there must be boundaries. Right now, there was none. She was having free rein over our life, and he was letting her.

I understood why he wanted to keep the peace and remain friends, but she was abusing his kindness.

I hated it. I really hated it.

Griffin had given up on knocking and let me be. When I emerged from the shower, I dried off and walked naked into our bedroom, finding it empty. It was a large room with a view of the street and just our bed, walk-in robe, and side tables. Griffin was a very clean man, but it would be nice to have a few shelves with photos of us up.

I could hear the TV on in the living room, and I was relieved he was now out there giving me space. That or he was possibly working. He usually sketched when he was not in the best of moods.

I had no intention of doing anything except being lazy. I wanted to go and see Harvey, but I knew I would probably end up a blubbering mess, so I opted to stay in and got dressed in a pair of sweats and tied my hair up into a knotted bun. I stayed in the bedroom, lying on my back and just staring up at the ceiling.

We rarely fought. This was probably our second fight since finding out his ex lived next door. Usually, we got along like best friends, joking around and very loved up.

When the bedroom door opened, I rolled to my side, facing away.

"Are you okay?"

"Fine." Girl code for I was not fine.

"Ayla…"

"Just leave me alone, please," I whispered back, my eyes swelling with tears as they ran down the side of my cheek.

He sighed heavily, which only infuriated me.

"Why?"

I sniffed back the tears and sat up, resting my back against the headboard. "I read your text messages."

"You searched through my phone?" When I glanced up, he looked amused rather than pissed off.

"No. I opened up her message and found a heap more."

He was silent for a moment and then leant against the door frame, resting his back on the wood as he crossed his arms over his chest. "Fair enough. Yes, she texted, and I replied. I have nothing to hide from you."

"I wish you wouldn't speak to her again."

"She's…"

Oh, for the love of god. I know what she is.

"The mother of your children, I know. But I'm your girlfriend, and you hurt me. You are hurting me, and I don't deserve to feel second place all the time." I feel like I was at the very bottom compared to her.

"Ayla, what the fuck do you want me to do?" he shouted, causing me to jump. "What the fuck do you want me to do!"

My heart was racing in my chest as I shot back. "How about you defend me when she comes and attacks me?"

"You told her to go away." *Like I needed reminding.* "What if the boys were there? They could have heard." He was lecturing me like I was a child. I was not.

This was not going how I imagined it. My anger was getting the better of me. "How about I tell you to go away?"

"I'm going to leave you alone. You're pissed, and I won't argue with you."

He thought that would solve things, but it was only going to annoy me more.

I did not want him to walk away. I wanted him to tell me he was sorry and would not let her treat me like this again. I wanted him to grab me, hold me, and then tell me everything was going to be ok.

"Walk away, Griffin, ignore my feelings, which you're so great at doing!" I shouted back, angrily punching down my fist on the bed when he had disappeared. It did not help.

I was a ball of hormonal mess, and I hated it.

He came back to the room and flung open the door with a hard push, banging it against the wall. His voice was raised, hard and husky. "I'm walking away before this blows up more than it should. You're making a big—"

"A what? A big deal? Fuck you, Griffin!" I yelled, kneeling up on the bed with hot tears coming alive once again. "You never see my point of things, and I'm sick of it!"

"That's bullshit!"

"Your parents were here! You knew they were, and you didn't even tell me." I pointed out, a sob escaping. "I could have met them last night. You basically lied to my face!" He did not say anything because I was right.

"I was talking about Karen," he finally said. "You are jealous over nothing."

My rage boiled over, and I was off the bed in an instant. "She comes into our home!" I screamed. I was literally screaming that at him until my throat hurt. "She uses our things... my things."

I pushed past him, only to be pulled and spun around as his hand wrapped around my wrist. "Where are you going?" he asked. He seemed calmer, but I could see the silent rage in his eyes.

"Harvey's."

His jaw clenched, and his hand let me go as if my skin burned him. "And if I say no? That I didn't want you to go there?"

"Then I wouldn't go, but we both know you're not going to say that." Then he would be forced to change things with Karen, and that was not going to happen. I knew that. He knew that, and she even knew that.

She was the one who would always have her scrawny fingers wrapped around his balls and holding them like a set of marbles in her hand.

"Ayla..." He sighed. "I don't want to fight with you."

"I'm not fighting, Griffin. I'm upset, and you don't care about my feelings. You've made it clear."

"Let me at least explain. I owe you that much."

Owe me? I deserve a medal for everything I have had to put up with from his ex. "I only want to know one thing. Tell me why you never mentioned your parents coming to town?"

I waited, giving him ample opportunity to confess and reveal the truth, but deep down, I already knew the answer. When he was unable to form words, I just shook my head. "Exactly. How do you expect me to feel when you're keeping me hidden?" I walked out the door after that.

So much for our time off this weekend together.

***

Driving around the block a good three times before I parked, I checked my reflection in the rear-view mirror and made sure no one could tell I had been crying. I did not want to talk about it. I just wanted to veg out and do nothing. Yes, I could have done that back home, but I could not be in the same room with him right now. He would only use sex to win my forgiveness. I was a sucker for sex, and it was a huge weakness of mine. I mean, if you see him naked and hard, you would give in too.

There was no doubt Karen heard us fighting. She was probably grinning from ear to ear like a Cheshire cat.

Harvey was spread out, lying on his couch when I walked into his two-bedroom flat. "Hey, you." I smiled slumping down on the other side of the couch, putting my feet up on his wooden coffee table scattered with junk. It was filled with empty beer bottles and food that looked as if it were about to grow teeth and eyes.

Smirking back at me, he said, "Make yourself at home."

With a laugh, I replied, "Don't worry. I always do. How's your weekend been?"

He gestured his hand to the table cluttered with crap. "As you can tell, pretty fucking great."

"That's the way." I let out a sigh, and he raised a brow. "Don't ask."

He sat up and frowned. "Have you been crying?"

Shit. "No."

"Liar. What the fuck did he do to you?" His fists were balled up tightly, and fresh tears sprung to my eyes. "Fuck me, Ayla. You need to end this if this is how he treats you."

"Please, don't." I did not want to talk about this.

With a shrug, he sat back down on the sofa, reaching over and rubbing my shoulder like a brother would. "I just hate to see you hurt."

And that was why I loved him like a brother. "I'm okay." No, I really wasn't. "Can we just talk about something else?" I just did not want to think and talk about anything that involved Griffin or his ex from hell.

Instead of talking, he put on *Interstellar*, and we began to watch that. Within ten minutes, I was already closing my eyes as sleep welcomed me. The tears and the long drive back home had exhausted me. My heart ached painfully.

***

When I woke, it was due to my mobile vibrating underneath my cheek and the light flashing in the darkness. Clearly, I had slept well into the evening.

I glanced at the bright screen to see Griffin's name with three missed calls and one text. I silenced the call and looked around for Harvey, who was walking back into the room with a woollen blanket in his hands.

His message read, *Please come home.*

I yawned, sitting up as stretched out. "I'm sorry. I fell asleep."

"You're not the only one. I just woke a few minutes ago myself. Are you going back home?"

"Yeah, I should. Griffin called, and I better get back."

"I bet anything he's pissed at you for being with another guy at his place."

"But—" I went to interject because Griffin knew there was nothing between Harvey and me. It was just friendship. However, he kept talking before I could get another word in.

"Don't worry. If you were my girl, I'd be too—although I'd never give you a reason to be with another guy."

This conversation was not going in the right direction. "I really should go."

"You can stay, you know." He stared at me, and I felt the meaning of his words hit me slowly. He liked me more than just a friend.

That was not a good thing.

***

The light was on next door, and I could hear faint yelling as I walked towards our doorway. Karen was screaming at one of the boys, telling them to pick their shit up. I just wanted to run over there and bring them back here. It was a frequent occurrence, probably why they loathed staying with her so much. She always yelled at them.

A pair of arms engulfed me as soon as I turned the key and locked the door behind me. Griffin's front pressed against my back, his warm lips kissing down the base of my neck and towards the curve of my shoulder. He was holding me a little too tightly and stunk of booze. That did not surprise. He had been drinking all day.

"I didn't think you'd come home."

Me either, until I realised Harvey did in fact like me. "I fell asleep."

Turning me to face him, he held my cheeks in a firm grasp. His blue eyes focused on mine. "Where did you sleep? You were gone all day. I was worried you weren't coming home."

Jealous much? Glad to know I could make him green with envy at times. It was just a small bit of what I felt on a usual basis. "On the couch. He wanted me to stay there instead of driving back."

"I'm sorry about earlier. I'm sorry about the car and texts. You were right. I should have your back more." *Finally.* He finally admitted it. "The boys… I want them here with me all the time, but you know how she is and what she could do to keep that from happening."

She would make it her sole mission to ruin his life if he even tried to apply for more than fifty percent of custody rights. "Can't you move away?"

"And go where?" He took my hand, leading me to the couch. I noticed an empty pizza box on the floor along with tipped over empty beer cans. Paperwork was strewn around the coffee table with his iPad. He had been working.

Shaking my head to the side, I pulled away from him. "I don't like her, Griffin. It's uncomfortable being around here. I get it; she's your ex, but it's not fair for me. I don't know if I can keep—"

He cut me off. "I can't lose you," he murmured. "I'm so sorry, baby. I can't lose you, Ayla."

"You won't." I did not know what the future held, but I loved him, and at this moment, I was not leaving. Leaving was not an option.

He did not believe me. He pulled me down to sit on his lap, and I tilted my head to the side, sadly. "Yes, you will."

This was a rare side to him. Right now, he was an emotional drunk who was spilling his feelings as well as his tears. Time for a change in subject. I untied my hair, letting my black locks fall past my shoulders. "She's yelling at the boys."

He nodded and sighed, rubbing both hands through his hair then over his face. "I can't do anything about it."

"I don't like them being yelled at," I informed him. He already knew it though. "I would never yell at our children like that." When he was drunk, it was the only time I could talk about her and not have him argue back. He would listen and almost agree to anything.

It was kind of bad, but I used it to my full advantage tonight. Well, I was.

"Ayla..." he began. "I don't want any more kids."

Wow. Full blow to the chest right there. The words have not completely sunk in yet, and I just stared at him in confusion. I swallowed hard, stroking my fingers through his hair and trying to keep calm when I wanted to rip the long hair from his skull. My brows dipped together as I asked softly, "You don't want to have a baby with me?"

"That's not it. Of course, I would love to have children with you."

"Well, then what is it?" I frowned, clearly confused.

With our fingers laced together, he squeezed them tightly and rested his forehead on mine. "I've been there before and did the whole diapers and sleepless nights. I just can't see myself doing it again."

Tears began to run down my cheeks, and I bit my lower lip, shaking my head. I was unable to believe all this. "But you said—" I choked out a sob. "If I were older, would you?" Was I too young for him?

"Your age has nothing to do with this, pretty." He took my face in his hands firmly, holding it tight. I felt his warm tears hit my skin as he blinked them back. "You want a baby. You deserve to have one, and I can't give you those things."

Have you ever seen a man crying? It was absolutely heartbreaking.

"Griffin, you could change your mind."

He had to be talking rubbish, right? It was just the fear talking. There was a niggling voice in the back of my mind saying, "Drunk words are sober thoughts."

The hold he had on me loosened, and he began gently caressing my cheek. "I love you, Ayla, and I can see myself spending the rest of my life with you, but marriage and babies? I just don't want that."

He had filled me with false hopes. I should scream and call him a liar. I should be packing a bag and leaving him for leading me on with a hope that we would have a future together. But I was not moving. I was stuck there, stroking his long locks as his eyes began to close, and more tears spilled out. I sat there and promised him that it did not matter.

"I won't leave you. Toby and Mack... they're enough for me." Were they? Did I really need a ring to commit to him fully? It was just a name, right? It was only a piece of paper, and not having that would not change the fact that we were madly in love.

"Promise me that you won't leave."

Walk away, Ayla. Don't give it all up for him. "I promise." *Stupid girl.* I was just a stupid girl in love.

His salty tears mixed with mine as he leant in and kissed me passionately. His hand then slid from my cheek to around the back of my head, drawing me in closer. We kissed until it felt like a dream, our bodies pressed together. Griffin stood, lifting me with ease, and carried me down to our bedroom. Laying me on the bed, he touched me all over like we had not been together in years, a sweet reunion to make up for.

He stripped his clothes and mine too, as we lay naked, kissing and holding one another with primal need. Our bodies were joined, sweaty and desperate for more. Nothing was enough right now.

"I love you, Ayla." His sweet murmurs were caressing my skin, and his fingers were starting to dig into the curve of my ass, pulling me into him as he began thrusting quicker, needier. "I love you so much."

Clinging to his shoulders, I raised my hips as my orgasm hit, and I came undone around him. "I love you too." I cried in sweet ecstasy until he came and collapsed against my body. Not pulling out just yet, he held me tightly and kissed me down my body, making his way between my thighs.

His tongue circled my tender bud, licking back and forth as two fingers slid deep into me. Another went into my ass. His teeth were gently nipping and biting against my clit—sucking, licking until that blankness began washing back over me, sending me clutching the bed sheet as another blinding orgasm ripped through me.

His tongue was replaced once again with the thick head of his erection, slowly pushing back in and starting all over again. This time with more dominance. We spent a good part of the night this way, fucking and making love, changing from hard to soft and fast to slow. Our bodies slapped loudly, and our lips rarely left each other. Griffin's final orgasm came out with hot spurts as he groaned deeply and gave me a final thrust.

Lying naked in his arms, I could see he was heavily asleep, and I should have been too. I just could not sleep, though. Too many thoughts were running through my mind. There was too much to think about. It was slowly sinking in… his words and what I had promised him.

As I lay there, I could not help but feel the full impact of the promise I agreed to. I was giving up becoming a mother of my own children, of being a wife.

Tears began to spill anew as I regretted it, and I would, for as long as he and I were together.

CHAPTER SIX

"I'll have a large chai latte, one blueberry muffin, and two croissants. Thanks."

I took the cash and slipped it in the front of my black apron as the woman juggling two little kids at her feet placed her order. I felt a tug in my heart as I smiled down at them before hastily starting on her coffee.

With a killer migraine coming on, I really could not wait to knock off and head home. We were going out to friends for barbecue and drinks.

"You're leaving already?" Harvey came over as I was in the back room grabbing my coat. "I thought you worked until five?"

"I changed it so I could head home early." I slipped my arm into the long, thick, grey sleeve and started doing up the buttons. "We're still on for next week, right?" He and I were swapping shifts. I had something planned for Griffin's birthday and wanted to surprise him. Really surprise him.

Harvey smiled, leaning against the wall. "Yes. You know…" That cheeky grin of his spread across his face, and I, too, smiled back. "You could give me something for helping you out."

Rolling my eyes, I crossed my arms over my chest. "I'm not sucking your cock."

"Jesus!" He snorted, clearly not expecting that as he brushed a hand through his dark hair, laughing. "You think that's all I'd want off you?"

"Well, who knows with you?" I winked.

He just laughed and shook his head. Taking a step towards me, he placed a soft kiss on my cheek, very close to my lips, and whispered, "Don't stay up too late."

I was unprepared for that

My heart was racing as he shuffled backwards, a smile tugging at the corner of his lips. I was stunned, unsure whether it was just a normal friendly kiss or intended to mean more. I quickly reached for my bag, grabbing it and slinging the strap over my shoulder. I spoke to no one in particular. "I'll see you later."

I never uttered a word of what happened to Griffin. How could I? He would assume the worst and make me feel as if I had done the wrong thing. It was not intentional. I had come to the decision that it was not anything more than just a friendly kiss.

Kicking off my boots as I walked into the house, I noticed it was dead quiet. It was unusual.

Well, not quite since the boys were over at their mother's and Griffin would normally just lie in bed waiting for me. He would usually send me a couple cock pics now and then to let me know he was hard and ready for me. When was he not?

"Baby?" I called out.

I internally wanted to smack myself in the face at that word—a word I would love to transform into an actual baby. That promise I made him was still heavy in my stomach, swirling around with regret. Stupid was I to promise that. I was weak and gave in.

I should not have said that.

I could not help but think that perhaps he would change his mind and that later down the track, we would have that together.

He lied to me. He knew I wanted a family of my own, and I deserved that. But I loved him, and love made people blind. We have the boys: Toby and Mack. I loved them, but I have never had the chance to experience being pregnant or holding my own child in my arms.

Why was I craving babies all of a sudden? Last week, I was happy to wait a few years for them, but ever since Griffin had taken that future away from us, it had been on my mind quite a bit.

No babies, and no ring on my finger.

My mother will just love this. I could not tell her. I was too embarrassed to tell anyone that my boyfriend did not want these things with me. Maybe it was an age issue, and he just did not want to admit it.

"You know I hate it when you call me that." I heard him grumble from outside.

I followed his voice to where he was leaning against the open door and watched him bend down to pick up one of my pink bras, pegging it on the line. "I don't care." All other thoughts left my mind as I walked over, snaking my arms around him from behind to engulf him in a tight hug. "You're all mine, and I find you sexy."

He smelt like home as I inhaled his scent, still holding him close. Turning, he brushed his forefinger and thumb through my hair and smiled. "I missed you today."

I honestly was not sure if he was mine or not. "I missed you. What time are we leaving?"

"Once I finish these," he answered. "Ayla," he said immediately after. My arms were raised above my head when I caught his worrying stare. "Are we ok?" he asked as I pulled away, picking up a black pair of socks to peg out.

Clipping down the peg, I forced a smile. "Course, we are. I need to shower, though. I smell like coffee." I moved away quickly.

"I'll just finish up out here. She wants their uniforms washed, dried, and folded for tomorrow."

I paused, turning with a frown and glancing over her way. At least he was smart enough to build a privacy wall between the two houses for when we were outside. "Tomorrow is Saturday. Why does she need them then?"

"I don't know. You know how she gets." He sighed heavily.

***

We did not miss the movement from her bedroom window. Karen was peeking through the curtains as Griffin reversed out the driveway, gawking at us both with curious and prying eyes. It would kill her not knowing where we were off to. She always needed to know if it was a date night or just for a drive.

I could see the bonfire up ahead when we pulled into the front driveway of Charlie's house. I was excited for a fun night, needing to enjoy a night out and forget the weeks' stress that was weighing down on my shoulders.

Charlie and Griffin had been friends since high school. Their group of friends had grown up together and remained close. It was a little weird at first meeting them since I was the odd one out and Karen was no longer hanging around. From what I could tell, they did not go too much on her, but the girls were still friendly with her.

Maggy waved over at us with a pair of tongs in the air as she held a plate full of steaks and burgers. I waved back. I was slowly easing into new friendships with the people Griffin had grown up with. They were nice enough to me. They were polite because they had to be.

Griffin was already in for a big night as he cracked open a Jack Daniel's can, swigging a large mouthful. His other hand was firm on my ass as I carried our cooler bag of drinks, and by drinks, I meant my coke and his alcohol. I would have to drive us back home afterwards.

"I see you've finally learned how to use a grill," Griffin called out, giving my ass a squeeze as we walked over to Charlie.

"Yeah, sure is. Don't worry. I'm keeping an eye, so we all don't get food poisoning." Maggy turned to me, wearing a smile, but it wasn't genuine. "Hi, Ayla, how are you?"

"I'm alright. Thanks." I found myself shy around his friends, knowing that all of them were judging me. How could they not? I was years younger, and their other friend loathed me.

The guys? Not so much. Bryan was the only single one, and he was coming back to ours tonight to crash with us. The poor fella was in for a loud awakening if he does not sleep deep enough. Then again, maybe Griffin would be too drunk to perform. It has happened before. He literally passed out and left me naked and spread with his head resting against the inner of my thigh.

"Aw, you didn't bring the boys?" Maggy asked, brushing her blonde hair to one side and pulling open her own drink of a vodka mixed with raspberry drink as Charlie joined us. "Stefan and Ethan were looking forward to playing on the trampoline with them."

"It's not our weekend," Griffin mumbled. He could have brought them. Karen was just being a dog about it, saying she already had plans with them.

"Where are they?" I asked, looking around until I spotted them jumping and playing wrestling. They were also twins, nine years old, and god could they be rough with each other! They were always wrestling and pushing just to agitate the other.

Griffin gave them a wave, calling out loudly, "Hey, boys! Ayla wants to get on with you and fight too!"

I laughed, nudging him in the side. "Liar." I did love trampolines and bouncing. Well, on something else that was more pleasurable.

"Please, Ayla! Come and jump with us!" Stefan called out, waving with both arms in the air. He was trying to look over the black netting around the trampoline, but he was too little to see above it.

"Soon," I called back out with a promise.

"Charlie wouldn't let me invite Karen..." *Oh, boy.* Maggy sighed. "I didn't see the problem since you live so close and get along well."

I clenched my teeth. *Breathe. Just breathe.*

Griffin shrugged and pulled out a lighter for his cigarette.

"I don't think it's any of your business, Maggy." Charlie frowned at her, shaking his head. "It would have made things awkward for Ayla."

"She's my best friend," she countered.

"And he's been my friend longer. Now, stop this crap and quit bringing up unwanted shit none of us want to talk about…"

I just got up and left them to their lover's quarrel. Griffin followed closely behind, letting out a whistle every time I wiggled my backside at him.

This was what it was often like between us—playful and fun. I missed it terribly.

Laughter bubbled inside of me as I giggled hysterically, bouncing up and down, trying to catch and jump up with them. Ethan was the smallest and would just fly into the air whenever I got close enough near him. I jumped until my legs began to hurt, and that did not take too long. I was puffing hard when I collapsed on my back with both boys jumping around me. I let out a yelp as one stomped on my hair and pulled on it.

It turned into a game of try-and-jump-on-Ayla's-hair, which then turned into catch-the-boys-and-put-them-to-bed.

"See ya, Ayla! Goodnight!" Stefan grinned, coming over and hugging me after I sat back down on one of the cloth-covered hay bales.

"Night, boys." I hugged them both back and leant in to snuggle against Griffin, trying to keep warm. "That wore me out big time."

"You two need to get your arses into gear and have a baby. I bet the boys would love a little sister running about." Maggy's other friend, Helena pointed out as she walked by us, nudging Griffin in the side. She and I actually did get along.

Crickets. The crackle of the fire burning was the only thing everyone could hear. It was one of those awkward moments where you just laugh and roll your eyes because deep down, you're actually dying of heartache about the topic.

I could not look at Griffin. If I did, he would know that I lied to him about it. Picking up my can of soft drink, I shook my head with a smile. "I don't think so."

"You're great with kids."

"And other people…" I corrected her, looking for a distraction while Griffin sat stone cold beside me. "Oh, yum. Food!" I jumped up and went to help Maggy bring over the cooked meat, trying not to trip on anything in the darkness.

"Charlie, you sure this is cooked? You've never used a grill before, have you?" Bryan looked at the tray of meat and tried to light it up with the flashlight of his phone.

I was already taking a bite of my chicken kebab and pulled it out, trying to inspect it closer. "It looks okay to me."

Clapping his tongs together, Charlie defended himself. "I cooked them all long enough, and you'd be able to tell if the chicken was raw."

I ate too much and was going to dig into the dessert when Griffin grabbed me by the wrist and pulled me to a stop. "Come for a walk with me. I need to take a piss."

Ah, charming as ever.

"And I have to come because? Do you need me to hold it for you?" I smirked, teasing him as I poked his hard stomach with my finger.

He smiled a little, raising his brow. "You can hold it if that turns you on."

Flirting back, I whispered, "In your dreams. I'm not holding it unless you're hard and going in deep."

We walked for a few minutes, and I heard Griffin starting to unzip with his smoke still hanging out his mouth. I just stood there, not watching as I leant against a tree and waiting for him to finish. I pulled out my phone. It was nearly two am, and the cool air was picking up.

"Are you ready to leave?" he asked, zipping back up and stumbling a little. The booze was kicking in.

"When you're ready, we'll go."

"I fucking love you." He grinned, coming towards me like a predator and trapping me with his larger frame. "God, you're so sexy."

Mm, keep going. "You're not too bad yourself."

Quickly, he had my jeans unzipped and pulled down. With my one leg out, he lifted me by the ass, and I wrapped my thighs tightly around him. His cock thrusting in dry had us both hissing with uncomfortable pain. That bloody hurt.

"Sorry. I should have licked you out first." *Yeah, ya think!*

After our quickie in the paddock, we made our way back and tried to act like we had not just done what we had done. Spontaneity was one of his best qualities. That, and his random love notes that were placed in the fridge if he left for work early.

"What did you two get up too?" Charlie grinned, breaking out in roaring laughter. "Ayla, your cheeks are a bit flushed. Bit out of breath, are we?"

"I told you they'd be able to tell!" I slapped Griffin's stomach, and when the guys laughed even more, I knew I had just given myself up. "It's dark, and you can't see my cheeks. Ha ha." Yep, I had given us away.

Charlie smirked. "How many times a day do you two fuck?"

And so began the uncomfortable questioning about our sex life as Griffin happily bragged about our twice a day sessions at the very minimum while looking down at his phone. I could not help but think it was her, and jealousy roared its ugly head inside me at once, making me feel ill. I hated that I just assumed he was texting her when it could easily be someone he played poker with, someone wanting a tattoo, or some client he was designing a house for.

"Try having kids, then the sex goes." Maggy pointed out. "That's what happened once the twins came along, and you decided to leave Karen over it."

The liquid in my mouth was almost spat out as I sat back on the hay bale. "Can we not talk about that, please?"

She rolled her eyes, shaking her head. "It's just the truth, Ayla. You need to accept Karen."

"Karen and I haven't fucked since the night she fell pregnant," Griffin muttered, shoving his phone back into his coat and pulling me closer to his side. "A night I'd much rather forget if you don't mind."

"Yeah, but that was one night, compared to how many times?"

His voice was cold, and I could tell he was growing annoyed by her questioning. "I screwed her once and barely remember it since I was stoned out of my mind."

"Who's better?" Charlie asked, drunk and with no filter whatsoever.

Griffin smirked. "Well, Ayla doesn't lay there like a dead fish."

"Can you just stop talking about this, please?" I asked quietly. "I don't want to know about you and her."

Looking down at me, he closed his eyes and sighed, his breath smelling strong of bourbon. He then smiled. "It's just you and me baby. No one else since her. Just you. I mean it."

"Good, because I like to think that I taught you all those hot moves."

His smile grew, and he began to laugh loudly. "Oh, baby, you did. Trust me. I've never had sex like the way we do. It's fucking incredible to share that kind of passion with someone else who feels the exact same way."

"You're making me wet."

He took my hand and placed it over his jean clad groin. I could feel the outline of his arousal as his dick was thick, hard, and ready. Leaning in for a deep kiss, I pulled back instead and nuzzled my nose against his. I could not wait to get home.

And so, the next topic was about cars, and it stayed that way until Charlie and Maggy began to make out in front of us all. I knew it was time for us to leave then. Helena and her husband, Travis, were also getting frisky. The baffling part was when Helena had her hand slyly moving up and down Charlie's lap while being obviously fingered by her own husband.

"I need a fucking girlfriend." Bryan yawned, falling into the backseat of the car. "Were they having a group thing back there?"

"They share and care." Griffin grinned, opening another can and doing his belt up, while I started the car.

"They, swap partners?" I asked. "Did you ever...?" If his friends were into that, then did he and her had a go at it too?

"No. Not on my part, anyway." His answer was firm, referring to when Karen would fuck other men once he left for work. "And I'd knock another man out if he even hinted at taking you."

I had to smile. I loved his possessiveness.

Not on his part? Did that mean Karen had done stuff with the four of them behind his back? I really did not want to know.

"So guess the three way's out of the question then," a slurring voice spoke from behind us.

His hand dropped to my thigh possessively. "You can use your hand. Ayla's not for sharing."

Walking behind the two drunken men who were stumbling and singing loudly as they made their way up the steps to our front door, I pulled my phone out of my bag and saw I had a message four hours ago from Harvey.

My heart raced as I quickly walked down to our bedroom, opening it.

I hope he realises just how good he's got it. You deserve better.

How could I respond to that? Hearing Griffin come into the bedroom, I turned my phone off and placed it on the bed. He cocked his head to the side, raking his eyes up and down my body to the point that I began to shiver with anticipation. Walking closer, he easily skimmed both his hands over my hips. "I want you."

"Bryan will hear." I giggled, trying to pry his drunken lips from mine. Once his hands slid between my thighs and rubbed that spot I loved, I was his. Clasping his shirt and clamping my thighs around to grind more pressure against me, I moaned. "God, just fuck me... and don't stop."

"Planning on it, baby. Get on your knees."

And down I went.

***

I woke with what anyone would assume was the worst hangover from hell and a pounding in my head that would not go away. As my eyes fluttered open, I realised that it was not just my head pounding but the front door. My phone was somewhere tossed around the room, so I peered at the wall clock. It was not even nine am. I wanted to sleep in and sleep most the day away.

Yawning as I sat up, I winced. I grabbed my stomach and slightly nudged Griffin with my foot. "I'm going to throw up." I barely got the words out before I was indeed throwing up in the middle of our bed.

Yes, that was right. I did not so graciously make it to the bathroom. Nope. I, Ayla, spewed right in the middle of our freaking bed. Once I had realised what I had done in front of Griffin, I automatically burst into tears. I had peed in front of him before, and he farts like a maniac in front of me, but spewing? That was not for his eyes to see.

"Hey." He soothed me by rubbing my back in slow circles. "Are you okay?"

Shaking my head, I buried my face in my hands. "How could I be okay after that? I'm so embarrassed."

"It's ok, Ayla. I've got morning wood, so you feel like..." Yawning loudly, he rubbed his neck. "Jesus Christ, my head is throbbing."

"It's the door, and I'm definitely not in the mood." *Shit.* I almost forgot about that. "Someone's at the door."

Confusion swept over his face as he looked around the room, tossing the covers off and grabbing the doona in a big ball. He then dropped it while putting on some boxers. "You grab the door. I'll get this washed up."

Major crushing on him right now. "You don't have to do—"

He cut me off with a kiss to the mouth and shut me right up.

The banging kept going, and he groaned, yelling towards the open bedroom door. "We're fucking coming!" he bellowed out. We were both assuming it was she who lived next to us. "I'll clean this up for you." Making his way to the door in a pair of boxers and the doona cover, he popped his head back in with a slight frown. "You weren't drinking. How come you're throwing up?"

Stepping into a pair of boy short panties and grabbing a bra, I looked at him. "No, but I did eat the chicken."

"I told him to cook those kebabs for longer. Fucken oaf," he muttered and walked off again.

Tying my hair up, I glanced at my reflection in the mirror as I walked to the front door. Ugh, he had left a huge love bite on my neck. I almost pulled my hair down but stopped. Screw Karen. I just had on my underwear and an oversized jumper of Griffin. She can look at me and see that we had spent a better part of the night fucking each other's brains out.

I got to the door looking like a hot mess and turned the handle. I almost rolled my eyes at the two elders standing in front of me. A woman, dressed immaculately in all grey and a mauve dress scarf, and a man, also in a neat shirt with pressed slacks, stood at our door.

Great, people trying to sell us something or preach about religion.

"Uh, no thanks," I mumbled, beginning to close the door, until Griffin ran up behind me and flung it back open, looking slightly embarrassed.

"Mum, Dad! Wasn't expecting you."

Oh, dear. Not good. Really not good.

"Well, we tried calling." Her eyes looked at me up and down, showing instant disapproval. "But I see you've been busy."

"Umm." I tugged the bottom of the jumper, trying to cover more of my thighs as I felt like a low-class hooker getting sprung for giving a freebie. "I'm Ayla." *You know, the girl crazy about your son and living with him and your grandchildren.* She should know this by now, but now was as good as ever.

"I don't care who you are, dear. Get some clothes on and leave my son's house," she scolded curtly, making me feel like an ant about to get squished by someone's finger.

Griffin's groan was auditable as he rubbed a palm over his face. "Mum... She's, uh..." I waited and waited for the *girlfriend* part, but what came was something even more disappointing. "She's Bryan's girlfriend."

I was like a punch to the gut, and I was ready to throw up again. I could not look at him. I just stood there, trying to make sure I heard it right. "Yeah. Bryan's girlfriend," I mumbled and turned away as tears sprung to my eyes.

CHAPTER SEVEN

"Ayla, wait..." he called out. It was his quiet but panicked beg as he came following me into the bedroom, moments after I had walked off—no, I had stalked off and left a trail of smoke behind myself after purposely shoving my elbow into the side of his abdomen.

I was already reaching for my bag and some clothes to pack. I could not stay here.

"What are you doing?" he asked.

What does it look like, you big friggin baboon! I rolled my eyes instead of speaking.

"Why are you packing? Stop it." His breathing was starting to pick up. "Ayla, talk to me. Damn it!"

The moment I felt that touch I craved, I lost my shit with him. Spinning around with tears racing down my cheeks, I shook my fist in the air, threatening to hit him. "Get the hell away from me before I... I am so close to punching the lights out your head, Griffin." I was seething with rage. "How could you? I am your fucking girlfriend. No, I thought I was! But obviously, I'm not."

"You are." He stepped closer, taking my wrist in his hand. He was trying to calm me, but it was not working. I was too hurt, too mad at him for this. "I didn't know what to say to them. You see what my parents look like. They're snobs, and you'd be eaten alive by my mother."

"Well, I guess we will never know, will we?" I shot back sarcastically, shaking my hand to free it from his hold. "You're embarrassed of me."

His eyes narrowed, and he attempted to cup my cheeks, but I stepped back away from him. "I'm not."

"Don't put words in my mouth."

Oh, he won't get to twist this around and make it sound like it's my fault. "You are, otherwise you'd have said I was your girlfriend a year ago. I don't need to put anything in your mouth when your actions are speaking louder than your words. You're embarrassed by me."

"Ayla, please…" He walked to my bag and began to unpack it.

Turning back around, I wiped the hot tears away with my sleeves. "You're thirty-seven years old. Grow up and act like it!" I tried to push him away from my belongings. "Don't touch my stuff!"

"You're fucking not leaving, Ayla. I mean it," he said through gritted teeth, his tone firm and raised. "I won't let you walk out of this house with your bags packed."

I raised a brow. *Like, really? You're going to threaten me?* "I don't need my bags to walk out on you."

"I won't let you leave this house, Ayla."

"I'll go into Bryan's room them. I'm sure he'd love his girlfriend to wake him up with a good morning blowjob."

That hit a nerve, and he shot me a glare to kill. His jaw tightened, and his arms folded over his chest. "Finished yet?" He spat.

"No. Maybe..." A big, wide smile grew on my face as an idea popped into my head. "Maybe Bryan could finish me off. Maybe—"

"I'll do anything to make this right," he pleaded.

Damn right you will.

"You get out there and tell them the truth, or I'm gone, Griffin. I mean it. I don't deserve to be hidden if you really love me."

He looked like he was ready to tear his hair out, roughly dragging his fingers through his locks once more. "I'm not fucking hiding you."

A wave of sickness came over again. I took in a steady breath, wobbling on my feet as I clutched my stomach and took in a deep breath. I really wanted to curl up and sleep this food poisoning away. "You don't want me to leave? Then you tell your parents about me and that this is my home, too." I swallowed hard, letting out a slow breath. "I'm going to be sick. You need to move."

Pushing him out of my way, I ran into the bathroom. Griffin followed behind me and closed the door behind him as I was on my knees, throwing up once again.

I heard the shower turning on and was slowly helped into an upright position. "Don't touch me." I looked away, more of my tears coming alive.

A pained expression was across his face as he dropped both his hands. "I want to take care of you."

"You should have thought about that before hiding me and making me feel embarrassed about myself."

"I'll tell them."

"Don't bother."

"I'll tell them," he repeated more firmly. "You're right. I panicked and hurt you. I'll tell them now. Once you're out of the shower and dressed, I'll introduce you to my parents."

My gaze dropped to the floor. "Your mum thinks I'm a whore. I see the way they both looked at me... like I'm just a young, naïve girl who likes you for your cock and money."

He snorted. "I doubt that's what went through her mind."

"I can't believe you would lie about me to your family," I said, dead serious.

"Ayla, I love you. I love you so much, and you're right. You deserve to be shown off to the fucking world."

Finally! Let's throw a party to celebrate this sudden and long overdue realisation.

Looking back up at him, I smiled sadly. "You really hurt me, and if you hurt me like that again, I will leave, Griffin. I'd do anything for you, and sometimes, I need to feel like you'd do anything for me."

"Anything. I'll do anything for you."

Except propose and have a baby with me.

"Ayla..." He crouched down to the floor beside me, taking my cheek in his palm as he reached for the washcloth to wipe my mouth clean. "Let me fix this. Let me fix us."

"We aren't broken... yet."

"There never will be a yet," he promised, and I believed him. I fucking *believed* him again.

After my shower and telling Griffin once more that I would not leave him, I dressed in a pair of black leggings, a long white shirt, and a zip up jacket. I honestly could not care about my appearance right now. I felt like shit.

His parents were sitting at the dining table when we walked out, and I have no doubt that they heard our spat. If they did, they were not showing it. I soon realised they were not listening. They were too busy looking at the family album of the boys that I had been making. Well, they were more of a scrapbook.

"Mum, Dad…" Griffin said, rubbing his hand against my lower back where his mother's eyes darted straight to. "This is Ayla."

"Yes, you introduced us already… She's Bryan or Braun's girlfriend." She sounded exhausted even talking to him about it, and with a flick of her hand, she dismissed him.

"It's Bryan and no, she's not seeing him. I should have just told you the truth."

"Oh…" His father suddenly straightened up and reached into his back pocket. "How much do you owe her?"

Holy fuck! Was I just referred to as a hooker? I would prefer the term escort. I have more class than banging just anyone for a quick buck. I'm definitely worth more.

"Twenty." I shrugged. May as well give it back to them.

He began pulling out a twenty dollar note, and I shook my head. "Thousand."

"Oh, just pay the girl for heaven's sake, Paul." His mother snapped, flicking another page in the book and not once lifting her eyes.

"Christ." His father's cheeks reddened as he went for the check book. He could not be serious, right?

"Dad, please stop," Griffin chuckled. He got my twisted sense of humour, but his parents sure did not. "This is Ayla, my girlfriend. She lives here."

It was quiet for a moment. Their confusion was clear.

"The prostitute?" his mother spoke, her jaw dropped.

"Mum! No. Now stop it. Ayla, meet my mother, Theresa, and my dad, Paul." Griffin's hand gave me a gentle squeeze as I stayed glued to the spot. It was not how I wanted to meet his parents, but it was better than nothing, I guess.

"Nice to meet you," I said quietly, feeling shyer than usual.

"I'm confused." Paul stood up and walked around the table where we were standing. "You're not a..." A grin swept over his face. "Ahh, smart girl! I would have handed it over without a thought." He laughed, and I was wondering just how much money they have. "Ayla, pleasure to meet you. Sorry for the confusion. You just never know these days. How long have you been shacking up with my son?"

"Umm..." *Should I tell them the whole time? Or just...*

"She moved in after a year of dating. Been here roughly around—"

"I've been here almost six months. We're together for—"

"Six months off two years. I'll have to get you—"

"Flowers for our anniversary."

We were finishing each other's sentences, and I could see it was not sitting well with his mother. She looked repulsed.

"How old are you?" she asked

Ugh. That was not what I wanted to talk about.

"Twenty-two."

"Thirty-Two?"

Shaking my head, I said it clearer. "I'm twenty-two."

"That's quite the age gap. Fifteen years is a big difference. What do your parents think about this?" she asked, now giving me her full attention. "You're just so young."

I took a seat only because I did not want to throw up again. "They don't have a problem with it. They love him and the kids, so it's no big deal."

She clicked into gear at the mention of the kids. "You... You're around the boys?"

Duh. "Yes. Would you like coffee?"

"Griffin? Why are we just finding out about this now?"

I'll take that as a no. "I thought you and Karen we're working on things."

That was news to me.

"No, Mum. I'm with Ayla. I'm happy with her, and the boys love her."

"But she's—"

"Age means nothing. It's just a number. Now, coffee?" he spoke with evident anger, but he did not lose his temper.

If he hated conflict so much, then why did he have no problem hurting me and not the others in his life who were hurting him purposely? I really needed to sit and think about things seriously. Was all this worth it?

I left them in the kitchen to catch up while I went back to the bedroom, bumping into Bryan on my way out who was wearing nothing but a pair of boxers and his morning glory. He just smirked, winking as I looked away, rolling my eyes. There was no shame in that man. He was good looking as hell but had absolutely no shame when it comes to flirting.

There was no point in me trying to get any rest. That went out the window with the loud Jane Fonda cackle from Monster-in-Law that his mother kept making every few minutes over something Griffin was saying.

Tears sprung to my eyes as I thought about the earlier fight and how much that really hurt. Was Harvey right about him? Yes, I deserve better than to be treated this way, but I love Griffin, and I could not picture a life without him. My heart literally ached thinking about him and me no longer together.

Sleep soon overtook me as I curled on my side and closed my eyes. I was never eating Charlie's cooking again.

***

I felt a bounce on the bed and groaned, keeping my eyes closed. "You just love waking me up, don't you?"

"Dad said to see if you're okay. He's saying goodbye to Grandma and Grandpa. Grandma doesn't like you, said you're closer to my age than dads."

I giggled, opening my eyes at Toby. I sighed. "You're seven years younger than me. I never really thought about that before."

"You could be Dad's daughter, she said." Toby scrunched his face and shook his head. "Yuck."

That took the daddy I playfully called him to a whole new level. "Yeah, like if he was like fifteen when he had me, but yuck is the right word." I sat up, taking the hood off my head, and waited for the wave of nausea to hit, but it did not. I felt normal. Well, better than I had been when I woke up this morning. "How about we get some food? I'm starving."

"Dad said you'd say that." Toby laughed, getting off the bed. "Oh, and Mum said to say hello."

Yeah, like she really meant that. *Bitch*.

"So let's go and get some food, big guy." I yawned, putting my feet on the floor and fixing the bed back up.

Griffin was just closing the front door when I walked out with Toby, flashing me a somewhat relieved smile as he walked over and kissed the top of my head. "Feeling better, pretty?"

"A little." I was fine, but I was going to milk this a little longer. I wanted him sucking up big time to make up for the hurt he put me through this morning. "I'm a bit hungry."

His hands began to massage my shoulders, and I felt my eyes start to roll just from how good it felt. "That feels amazing."

"Oh, he's got amazing hands." A voice broke all my thoughts, and I looked up to see Karen sitting in our living room with Mack. "He used to rub my shoulders all the time. When I was pregnant with the boys, he gave the most incredible massages."

What the ever-loving fuck is she doing in here? How did I even miss her sitting there in front of me? *Fuck me.* He could not be serious right now. How was this making up for anything? I was just going to be in a worse mood if he kept this up.

"Karen, you're in our house?" I almost threw up at the sight of her.

My stomach was swirling, and my heart was beginning to beat faster. Jealousy was swarming through my veins as I thought about him touching her. Griffin's touch suddenly irritated me, and I moved away from him to grab a drink from the kitchen.

I looked up just as she made her entrance into the kitchen.

She grabbed a bottle of coke and took three large mouthfuls before speaking. "Oh, yes. Mack and I are doing some reading for his school work. Seeing as though the kids are back with you two tonight, I thought I might as well come over and help with homework." She then, and ever so ladylike, belched in two parts, giggling afterwards.

She was a pig. There were no other words for her. She was a lazy, mooch of a pig.

My eyes were piercing through Griffin's skull as he made eye contact with me for a moment. "Well, we haven't discussed that yet. I don't see why you have to do that when I'm here to help. We both have been doing so without your help, Karen."

"I'll be helping, Griffin. I'm their mother."

"Okay." I could not make a scene in front of the kids. I knew that was what she wanted. She wanted me to go all crazy in front of the kids so she would have more of a reason to gain full custody.

Right now, I wanted to drink. Going into the pantry, I grabbed out a sachet of caramel latte and made myself a hot drink. Watching the kettle boil was the only thing that calmed me down right now.

Griffin was hanging around like a fly, and I sighed, finally talking to him. "What do you want?" I felt like I was going to be in a permanent pissed-off mood.

"Uh…" He hesitated. "Look, I tried to get out of it… just so you know."

"Spit it out," I demanded, stirring my drink roughly. The delicious coffee spilling over the edges only irked me more. "Her in here. Not on."

"Mum invited her over. She got here literally two minutes before you woke up. I swear, I've barely even spoken to her, Ayla." He really felt the need to tell me this. He was feeling the heat of my silence. He was panicking because I was on the verge of walking out on him.

"Fuck me." I turned and looked at him. "Take me to bed. I want you to make love to me right now."

"The boys…" He hesitated, his eyes flickering over to them. "Later…"

"Bullshit," I muttered. They never bothered him before. All those times we snuck off for a two-minute quickie, he never once turned me down unless the kids were not busy doing something, then we waited. "Forget it."

"Ayla…" He sighed, finally taking hold of me and pulling me against his chest. My tears spilled out, and I lost it. I silently cried in his arms. The water must have gone through his shirt because he moved aside and tilted my chin up, meeting my sight, and a pained expression crossed his face. "Fuck, it rips my heart out seeing you like this."

I knew he meant that, and it just made me cry harder.

The pad of his thumb brushed just underneath my eyes as he wiped my tears away. "Tell her to leave, Griffin. Please." My voice was giving my hurt away as I buried my head back against his chest and silently sobbed.

I needed her gone today. I just needed her to leave me and this shitty day alone.

"My parents will be back in half an hour. They're taking us out for lunch."

I did not know if that was meant to make me feel better, but it did not. I said nothing, and he kept talking.

"I told them no, but the boys said yes, and she had already spoken with Karen. Seems like they speak regularly."

"Wait… what?" Was he saying lunch with his parents and us or the all of us as in that thing in the living room also? "I'm not going."

"I need you there with me."

"Doubt it," I muttered just as Mack walked into the kitchen wearing a huge smile.

"We're all going out for family lunch! Mum said she's coming too!" He was excited, and this is where I felt like a bitch. I had to put my issues aside and do this for the kids. "You're coming too. Right, Ayla?" he asked, hopefully.

It was not about me and my problems anymore. It was about the kids wanting to have dinner with their Mum and Dad and grandparents—a family. But how did I fit into it all? I was not anything except the girlfriend. I needed to be more supportive. I needed to suck it up and do this for Griffin and his sons.

With a smile, I nodded and wrapped my arm around Griffin's waist. "Of course, I am. Your dad's going to buy me dessert! Couldn't pass that up."

Griffin looked down at me and whispered in a voice low enough for me to hear. "Thank you."

"That's called putting you first," I whispered back, moving away to go and finish my drink in peace before spending an irritating few hours with his ex and parents.

You can do this. It's just a family lunch. "You're a big happy family," I told myself as I rummaged our wardrobe for an outfit worthy of his mother's approval.

A big happy fucking family we were not.

CHAPTER EIGHT

My pussy was purring... and no, I did not own a kitten.

"Oh, my... That... keep doing that!" I cried out, and it came out muffled in his hand. My legs were shaking, my hips were tingling, and my toes began to curl at the start of my orgasm as it climbed that mountain of bliss. "Fuck... fuck... fuck... I'm cumming."

"Yeah..." He grunted, his hips taking long and hard strides between my thighs. I kept my legs wrapped around him tightly as my fingers dug into the skin of his bare ass, wanting him in deeper and deeper. "I'm going to cum... Shit, Ayla! Fuck..." he moaned as I raised my hips and squeezed him empty just as my own orgasm rippled through my body.

My pussy was clenching uncontrollably around his swollen cock as he slid in and out. Our bodies were slapping together, and my hips raised to create a faster friction with each one. Juices spilled, tongues tangled, hands grasped—we could not get enough of each other. Neither of us wanted it to end.

Lying there half-dressed and sprawled out on the bedroom floor, I panted heavily. Griffin collapsed on top of me. "Happy now?" He smirked, giving me a kiss before pulling out and tucking himself back into his boxers.

I just lay there, watching him. "Mmm." A sleepy, exhausted, and sated smile escaped my lips. "For now."

"For now?" he asked, raising a brow and grabbing a shirt he had only just changed out of to wipe me clean. "You're insatiable, Ayla."

"Only for you," I replied, finally sitting upright and reaching for my top. "How is it that all you do is just lower your jeans and I have to get completely naked for a quickie?"

"Your skin... your body... It's very addicting," he said with a growl that went with his aroused state.

I smiled, blushing as I stepped into a pair of boyfriend jeans and did the button up. "You came in here like a predator on a mission. I was dressed and ready to go."

"I was hard at the thought of you in here naked and dressing." He came over and pulled me to him. "I love you, pretty."

"I love you too." I wrapped my arms around his neck and began to kiss him once more. I felt the bulge growing once again in his jeans. "I can't wait until we get back from lunch. I can't believe you fucked me with her out there."

"Maybe hearing us will keep her away." *Hmm, if only.* His mouth lowered once again. "God, you're sexy! I can't get enough of you."

"Me either." I could not. "I love you like crazy."

His long, lean fingers ran through my hair, and he kissed me with a deep, knee crumbling passion "I'll love you until my heart stops beating, Ayla, and even then, I'm pretty sure I'll still keep on loving you."

"You're so romantic." I smiled against his soft lips as our tongues wound together once again.

The bedroom door began to open, and Griffin instinctively wrapped his arms around my body to cover my exposed front. The boys now and then did walk in unannounced but always covered their eyes. Bless their little hearts.

This time, however, it was not Toby or Mack. It was their mother.

"What do you think you're doing?" I exclaimed, seriously annoyed. This was our room—our private room for him and me. She now tainted it. "Get out!" I could not help it. She had no right to be in here. Of all the rooms, this was ours and off limits.

Scowling, she scoffed. "Fucking hurry up. We'd like to leave sometime soon."

"Get out, Karen." Griffin's order was clear. "You have no need to be in here. Ayla is right. You need to leave."

Oh my, did he just take my side?

She stuttered, refusing eye contact. "I was just... I was uh... Never mind."

Could she be? Oh please, tell me she was. She was actually jealous. She heard us. And *baboom!* I hoped it hit her in the heart. I hoped it made it clear to her that she and Griffin are really never getting back together again.

He sighed once she had left, checking the door one last time to make sure. "I'm sorry, baby. I'm at a loss. She's doing my head in."

"It doesn't seem like she's doing your head in."

"I might not show it, Ayla, but I'm not liking her in our house as much as you are. I don't want to fight because that'll make the boys take sides, and she'll go to the cops about the betting. We almost got caught the other week."

"Why don't you stop betting then?" I suggested, sitting on the bed to slide my shirt over my head. "You have the tat shop. Can't you just stick with that?"

He took the spot beside me, putting his hands over his face and yawning. "I like playing poker."

"Well, then keep playing." I grinned as I hooked my leg over his thighs and straddled his lap, running my fingers through his hair to massage his scalp. "Harvey loves my massages; just so you know."

"I'd rather not know that," he grimly muttered. "And I never massaged anyone until you came along. She barely even got a hello some days."

She said it to get a reaction out of me. Damn her. "Well, Harvey has never experienced my massages, and by the way, I think she's jealous of what she walked in on," I said, remembering the look on her face as those marble eyes darted from him to me. "She's never heard you tell me that you love me before, and she probably heard it all."

"She heard me fucking you?" He raised a brow, cupping my ass and flexing up his body in a slow, tantalising grind. "She heard me eating your pussy? What about when I came inside you? She heard that too?"

I giggled. "How should I know? It's not like we were listening to others."

"You sure you're not feeling sick? We could, you know, cancel and stay in."

What has happened to the man who hurt me earlier? He has done a full change and swapped directions, wanting to stay in and then kicking Karen out. Maybe he finally saw that his actions were a complete fuck up and was trying to change. I liked it.

Patting his chest, I slowly climbed off him. "I feel much better. Now tell me how good I look, and we can leave."

"You look incredible. *Edible.* As always, beautiful."

Suck up, baby. I don't mind a bit.

His parents were at the wharf already when we arrived, and we were seated outside on the deck. The place was fancy, stunning, and expensive. I did not know what to eat. I would have been happy with a pizza.

It dawned on me that this is how Griffin had grown up. I had wondered about the tuxes in his closet and why he had not worn them. He just said they were from years ago. It never clicked that his parents were loaded and that he was, too. Maybe he had a trust fund. Oh, now that made sense. Looking at him, he really did not look like the guy who came from one though.

Gazing over the menu again, I settled on something I could not pronounce and pointed it out to Griffin so he could order for me. With a soft chuckle, he nodded. His hand on my thigh inched higher, and I tried to pry it away, but lost since, well, he was stronger than me. Besides, I kinda liked being felt up on the sly by him in public.

Karen, who has been quiet since we arrived, picked up her glass of water and adjusted her bra strap. She was in a dress—a fucking dress while I wore jeans and a v-neck t-shirt. Even his mother was wearing a dress. The two of them were talking about everything from TV to the boys and how well they had been doing in class.

"Toby is even getting Bs all on his own." She smiled over at him.

"Yeah, Ayla has been helping me. She does pretend tests so I can prepare for real ones," Toby replied back in a way that had my heart melting like an adoring parent.

"That's lovely." Teresa gave him a tight-lipped smile. "What about you, Mack? Still top of your class?"

"Yep," he replied in a mumble as his head was buried in the book he had been currently reading.

I said current because his mother snatched it out of his hands and tossed it beside her on the floor. "Put that garbage away while we're about to eat."

"But Mum... Dad said I could read it."

Karen shot him a pointed look. "I said, no." Even I felt the sting of the scolding. "Listen to me and do as you're told for once."

I offered him a smile. He looked sad, and it hurt that she had embarrassed him in front of everyone like that. Griffin said nothing, but his jaw tensed, and his hand tightened on my jeans.

Paul, clearing his throat, ordered drinks for the table and then proceeded to start on his order. Turned out that mine was not that complex after all. I was loving the toasted sourdough bread with garlic butter and could have eaten an entire loaf on my own.

"This is really good." I smiled, about to take another bite, when Griffin reached forwards, taking the piece from my hand and bringing it to his lips with a crunchy bite.

My open mouth had him laughing softly. "You're right. It is good." He then continued to eat my second piece.

The conversation was light, and not much was said as main was delivered. Paul and Griffin both got the rib eye, rare and bloody. My mouth began to water, but not in a good way. I felt sick and queasy. I forced myself to look away and start on my bowl of potato gnocchi, but it was not helping much.

"I need to use the bathroom," I whispered, turning inwards towards him to keep my voice low. "Your lunch is making me want to throw up."

Looking down at his plate, he clicked his tongue. "Uh, yeah. I was wishing they had pizza or burgers for adults on the menu. I'm hungover as all fuck."

"We'll pick up pizza and burgers afterwards." I smiled, kissing him on the cheek, before I stood and excused myself.

I was not sick, but I felt like it. I just pulled out my phone as I sat on the toilet and read Harvey's text over again. I had not responded to him. It was not a simple thing to answer. I felt like I deserved better, and if I wanted it, then I would have to make that change, but moments like this, with how he was being all sweet and romantic, made me want him more. I loved him and could not see a life without Griffin and his sons in it.

Shoving my phone back in my bag, I stood up to leave when I heard the bathroom door open and talking voices. Like any normal girl, I peered through the door crack to spy on them.

"Karen, she actually seems lovely. I think she might just be shy," Theresa said, opening her purse and pulling out her lipstick. "The boys seem to be quite taken with her."

Karen sighed and shook her head. "She's after his money. She works in a café, and can't give those boys a stable home. She's trying to take them from me. Do you really want Griffin to marry a girl half his age? She walks around in her underwear, for crying out loud. You said you'd come down to help me get rid of her."

"Calm down, sweetie. I called her a prostitute. I don't think I could have offended her anymore although Griffin did introduce her as Brian's girlfriend, to begin with."

Her giggle was annoying. "So fucking hilarious. Wish I could have heard. She can't stay there anymore. I want her gone."

Theresa smiled as she checked her teeth for stains. "You want my son back? I think you need to take things further if you're afraid of that happening. Make a move to get back with him. You have children together. You'll always be family. She can't take that bond away."

My heart was hurting. How could his mother suggest that?

Karen, with a smile, brushed her hair to the side. "Don't worry. I have something that'll make him see we're meant to be."

"Well, then..." Theresa said, placing her lippy away back in her purse. I watched as she turned to face Karen and placed both her hands on either side of her shoulders. Her voice was determined as she spoke. "Get my son back and away from that young trashy thing. I don't want her anywhere near my grandsons any longer."

"Don't worry. I told you before, she's just a young pretty thing for him to get a thrill out of."

I exited the bathroom a few moments after they had left and lingered by the fish tank for a moment before I made my way to the table again. I did not utter a word about what I had heard to anyone and played it cool, telling Griffin I was watching the fishes when he asked what took me so long. He leaned in, kissing me on my cheek and telling me he had chosen a raspberry crepe with whipped cream for dessert. I only smiled in return.

My mind was elsewhere.

All through lunch, it was all I could think about... this plan of hers to break us apart. What would she do? Would Griffin believe her and fall for it? No, I doubted it. There was really nothing she could do. She had done all the crazy things she could possibly do to hurt me.

I had thought her mother was defending me at first, but I should have known better. She wanted him and Karen back together. The entire conversation after I came out was just about them and reminiscing about the earlier years with the kids.

At the end of lunch, his parents were saying goodbye to us. After she had hugged Karen, she came towards me with a fake smile and put her arms out. As her lips went to touch my cheek in a goodbye kiss, I murmured in a voice low enough so only she would hear me, "I love your son and you, and Karen can do whatever you want to try and push me away... but I'm not going anywhere."

"I don't—"

"You really should make sure nobody is in the ladies room when you decide to talk about others."

Her eyes grew wide, and I smiled with my own sweet fake smile.

"Everything alright?" Paul asked, coming over. "It was lovely to meet you, Ayla. Hope to see you again soon. I told Griffin to bring you down home for a visit. I'm sure you'd like to come out on the boat."

I hugged him back and did not miss the thunder glare from Karen, either. "Sounds great. We'll have to do that." Pulling away, I watched as the boys said goodbye.

After that, we all went our own ways, and the boys came home with us. Karen made a throat slitting signal behind them as she got out of the car, and I just gave her the finger on the sly. As if he would go back to her. She was crazy.

Burgers and pizza were devoured by us all, and our lazy Saturday was underway in the usual way—my favourite kind of way: movies, snacks, and pyjamas.

"You okay? You were pretty quiet through the rest of lunch."

"I'm okay. Just want to watch a movie and snuggle on the couch." I yawned as I curled into his side, placing my leg over his with the blanket pulled up close.

Toby and Mack were playing Xbox in their room while we were in the living room about to watch something on Netflix. I was not even paying attention.

Shifting slightly, so he was half leaning above me, he stroked his fingers through my hair soothingly. "Thank you for today. I know it wasn't easy for you."

"Are you happy with me? Like, really happy?" I asked. I did not mean for those words to slip out, but they did. "I mean, is there any part of you that wants to have your family back together for the sake of the boys?"

Without hesitation, he answered me. "Not at all. I love my sons, but Karen? I don't love her, I feel nothing but anger and repulse for her. She lied to me too many times and destroyed any trust I had in her."

"Because of the pregnancy?" I asked quietly.

"Yes. I was going to leave, but she announced she was pregnant, so I stayed for the sake of them."

"Did you love her then?" I hated bringing up the past, but like I said, jealousy got the better of me. "I mean, I hear that men fall more in love when they watch their partner give birth."

My head rose and lowered with his deep breath as his heart rate beat on a steady pace underneath my ear. "I should have," he whispered, "but my only thought was how much I despised her."

"You'll tell me if you ever begin to despise me, right?" I looked up, needing a guarantee that he would never stay with me for the sake of it.

Placing a kiss on my forehead, he spoke against my skin as if in a promise, "You're nothing like her."

No. I definitely wasn't.

Mack and Toby walked into the living room, scrunching their noses in disgust as they looked at us loved up and cuddling on the couch.

"Yes?" I said, and Griffin looked up. "Can we help you both?"

"We want to play *Just Dance*. Will you play with us?" Mack's eyes lit up. "I'm on Ayla's team."

I giggled against the crook of his neck and smiled, looking up as Griffin groaned loudly. "Oh, I definitely want to watch you and your dorky dad dancing."

"My dorky dad dancing was the reason you're here with me now." He smiled, tightly wrapping his arms around my body. "Alright, set it up, and we'll play."

***

The next few days passed, and nothing exciting really happened. Griffin and I had a free night, so we planned a date night at the café. Harvey was working, which did not seem to faze him as far as I could tell. I was excited to have a night out with my main man, have dinner, and then a movie afterwards.

I sat and sipped on my hot coffee, trying to keep myself awake as I held my phone out and snapped a picture of Griffin who was reading over the menu.

"Babe, you know what's on the menu already." I pointed out, yawning.

"I know." He flashed a smile. "I'll take a steak pie with sauce."

How original. I rolled my eyes. "I think you need to take me out to a fancy restaurant for dinner. I'm over eating between here and home."

"Am I not keeping you happy, dear?" He just grinned as he reached over, taking my hand. "I'll surprise you next week with reservations somewhere expensive."

I heard a slight scoff beside me as Harvey muttered not so quietly, "Money doesn't keep people happy for long."

Griffin did not respond as I shot Harvey a glare.

"I need to make a call outside. I won't be long."

As I watched him leave, I walked around the counter to where Harvey was. "What the hell is your problem?"

He shrugged. "Nothing. Just keeping him on his toes. Does he have any clue about next week?" he asked.

I grinned, forgetting all about my annoyance. My plan was underway. "Nope. Not a clue. It's going to be great. The boys are at hers for that weekend."

"Have you told her that you're going away and not to call him?"

I scoffed. "No. Why would I tell her that? She would figure out some excuse to give the boys to him."

"I can't believe he dated her, let alone fucked her. I wouldn't even touch it with someone else's cock."

"Umm…" I busted out laughing, bracing myself and sitting up on the counter top. "That's disgusting."

He was laughing hysterically, fixing his eyes on mine, and I thought for a moment that my heart would explode. The smile he wore was squeezing around my heart. There was pure joy between us. It was easy, and it was never complicated. My laughter died down as his hand began to reach up and tuck a lock of hair behind my ear. Our eyes were still connected, and a part of me worried that he was about to kiss me.

"Should do that more often."

My brows furrowed together, confused. "Do what?"

"Smile. You're so beautiful when you smile."

Everything came to a sudden halt when the door closed, and we broke apart. Griffin was standing there, glaring with his jaw tightly clenched. His fists scrunched as he looked from me to Harvey and back again. "Get in my car. Now."

"What?" I choked out.

"Dinner is over. Ayla, get in my fucking car now!" he growled as he turned and walked back outside. He was pissed.

"Umm… I'll see you later. Sorry." I did not know what I was apologising for. I just felt the need to.

"You don't have to go with him. I can take you home," Harvey whispered as I began to move off the counter. "He's not your keeper."

I looked at Griffin who was already in the car waiting for me. I smiled back to Harvey, giving him a slight shrug. "I have to go."

"Hope he realises how fucking good he's got it. Maybe if I treated you like shit, you'd come to me." He grumbled, shaking his head as the horn out front honked loudly. "See you around, Ayla. Text me when you're home, so I know you're safe."

Griffin floored the car before I even had my belt on. "What the fuck was that?" he asked, his words seeping with anger.

"What was what?" I asked back. I knew that he had seen Harvey and me. "There's nothing going on between us."

"Are you sure about that, Ayla?" he said through clenched teeth, taking a sharp corner and then slamming into a lower gear.

There was nothing between him and me; I was sure about that. "Yes. Now slow down and tell me about this expensive restaurant that you're taking me to next week." My hand slid over his groin, and he began to calm down as I unzipped his jeans and began stroking his already hard cock.

He was jealous, and I fucking loved it.

CHAPTER NINE

"What's for dinner?" Karen asked, coming into the kitchen and setting her glass of water down on the counter where I was chopping up vegetables to go with the marinated roast beef I had been cooking all day. "Oh, veggies? Yuck."

I smirked, watching her retreat from the kitchen. "Figured you'd say that."

"Excuse me?" She stopped, turning around. "What's that meant to mean?"

"Nothing." I kept chopping the carrots, placed them in the steamer, and looked up. "Karen, I think it's time you leave. Dinner is almost done, and homework has been finished for almost an hour."

I was not being rude about it, but this was dinnertime, and I had to leave for work and wanted to spend some time with the kids and Griffin alone before I left.

"Griffin, tell your hussy to fuck off," she called out, keeping her eyes on mine as she purses her lips into a puckered pout.

"Don't speak to me like that. You're in my home, and you're going to show some respect." *For once in your damn fucking life!* "Oh, and how about putting your rubbish in the bin instead of leaving it laying on the floor for someone else to pick up, you lazy—"

"Ayla!" Griffin raised his brow as he entered the room. "Problem?"

Yeah, a shit load of them, I wanted to say. "Nope. All good, babe. Can you please tell the boys that dinner will be ready in half hour?" I smiled at him. "I cooked your favourite."

"Pizza?" Karen asked, butting into our conversation.

He ignored her, walking over and lifting the lid on the slow cooker. "I've been smelling this all day, and it's not my favourite thing to eat. Second maybe, but something else is first." My core warmed up as his eyes travelled over my body. I heard a cough behind him, and he pulled away, standing up straighter. "Uh, yeah… I'll tell them. Karen, you should be getting over to your place. We're having a family dinner soon."

I did a victory grin as I watched him walk away, and Karen was left grinding her teeth from the dismissal she got. Family dinner with me, him, and the boys? Yep, sounds perfect to me.

"You'll never replace me."

"I'm not trying to replace you, but I'm not going away. So, you should really figure out a way to get used to me being around because I'm here to stay."

She walked closer and shoved a pink-painted nail into my chest, poking it. "You'll never be anything to them. You're a little slut who is nothing to my sons. You'll never be their mother, and you sure as hell won't be his wife!"

I stood there, tears forming in my eyes as her words hit me right in the heart. She was right, but I did not want her to know that. I would not be his wife or a mother—something I desperately craved to be. I wanted to have his children growing inside my belly and to share a surname with him and his sons. I wanted a real family.

I was kidding myself and losing who I had become. I felt as if I were nothing.

"Hey, Ayla?" Mack called out. "Can I have a friend stay over my birthday tomorrow night?"

Cutting me off before I could get a word in, she barged past me and blocked my view of him. "That's right. It's your birthday, big boy. You're going to love what mummy has brought you."

Yeah, with money that she hasn't earned herself.

"Ayla?" he asked again, stepping around her with big, hopeful eyes. "Please? Dad said to ask if you're ok with it." *Well, that was a change.*

"Umm... sure." I smiled, composing myself and wiping away the tears before anyone noticed. I kept my back to them as he said goodbye to his mother and walked her out. I hated her more than anything for doing this to me. If she just kept away, I would be more than ok.

***

Work kept me busy, but Harvey and I barely spoke. We were not purposely ignoring each other; the nights were just busy, and I did not want to stop. I would end up thinking about the situation at home and get all depressed. I did not want that. I needed to keep busy and focus on the good things in my life, the positive ones.

Holly came over, holding a bottle of champagne and a tray of glasses, after we had closed the doors. "Who's up for a drink?" She grinned, popping the lid off and squealing when the cork flew into the wall and literally went through it.

"Ahh, not me." I laughed. "You're not meant to pop the cork that way," I said as the bubbles foamed like crazy from the bottle. "Oh, and I just finished mopping. You can fix that up."

Pouting, she groaned. "But I wanted to get drunk."

"You get drunk every night." Harvey pointed out, joining in our conversation as he picked up his bag. "Why did you pop a bottle of that?"

"I wanted to try it." She took a mouthful, and she spat it out. "Eww. Gag. No, thanks. Anyway, I'm off. Gotta meet my lover for some fun."

She was a crack up—funny, and gorgeous. Oh, and also a lesbian who liked to wear the strap on.

Harvey shuffled nervously on his feet. "Yeah, me too. Uh, see ya."

"Yep! I'll clean this mess up. Thanks!" I called out, going to the storage room and finding the mop again. It was just something else to clean up that was not mine.

It was two am, and I lay in Griffin's arms after we had made love, tangled together in naked bliss. Stroking my fingers over his chest, I ran them up and back down. "I want to move." It had been on my mind most of the night. "I want us to move."

"What?" he asked, his voice vibrating against my cheek.

"I want to move and have a house of our own." I wanted something more from him. This? It was not enough for me anymore. I needed a big commitment. This was his house, and I wanted one that was ours.

"Ayla…" He sighed. "What's wrong with this place? You don't like it?"

"I don't like her coming over here. You get the kids, and she's over here constantly helping with homework that they can do on their own. She-"

"Stop it," he said in his normal tone. "Moving wouldn't solve anything. The boys like having their mother close, and it's easier on them."

"It's not easy to me, Griffin." None of this was.

Sitting up, he reached for a pair of boxers and began to put them on. "Look, I told you about all of this before you moved in."

"No, you never did." I reminded. "You never told me she was across from you or that she would be coming over daily. I don't like it."

"So what now? You want to break up? Is that it? You want to go fuck Harvey?"

Woah. That was uncalled for.

"Jesus Christ. You're back to this?" We already had this fight two days ago. "I told you nothing is going on between us. You keep throwing it in my face. That's not fair!" Sitting up myself, I found my panties at the end of the bed where he had slid them down my thighs and tossed them away.

"Ayla, I watched him fucking caress your face like a lover. He's into you."

"Big deal!" I almost shouted. "Karen's into you."

"So he does want you?" Shaking his head, he pulled his long dark locks into a bun. "I fucking knew it. I fucking knew it, and you did too! You should have told me!" He pointed an accusing finger at me. "You should have told me."

I should have, but I would be damned if I admitted that right now. "Sleep on the couch. Get out."

"You're kicking me out of my own bed? Really?" He laughed. "For doing what? Being pissed that another man was hitting on my girl all this time and she knew about it?"

Jumping out of bed, I grabbed a pair of actual pyjamas and began dressing into them. "Fuck you. I'll sleep out there."

"Ayla, don't be ridiculous. You're overreacting."

"No. Don't you dare tell me I'm overreacting. You're an ass, Griffin, and... and..." All words were failing me. "Just go call Karen. I'm sure she's waiting for an all-night text session that you normally have when you think I'm asleep!"

I was a hormonal mess. Not waiting for his comeback, I slammed the bedroom door and stalked to the linen closet, grabbing a couple of blankets and pillow to set myself up on the couch for the night.

Fuck him and fuck her. I was so mad.

I could not stop crying. I hated it. I rarely cried, but this past week, all I had done was cry and be over emotional. Wiping my eyes, I took in a shaky breath, and another round of salty tears stung my eyes until I fell asleep wishing everything was different.

When my eyes finally fluttered open, it was still dark, but I could hear the cars pulling out of the drives as people got ready for work. It took a moment before it all came crashing down and hit me. I remembered the fight we had last night and the constant bickering. Just four more sleeps, and we could go away—just the two of us and be stress slash *Karen*-free. I could not wait.

As I sat up on the couch, the passage light came on, and Griffin walked down in just a pair of his boxers, looking like he had slept about as well as I had. "We've never spent the night apart because of a fight before."

He was right. "I know."

"I hate it."

"Me too."

Coming around to the couch, he pulled the covers back and laid down beside me. His arm was around my body, drawing me in. "What's going on with us? We never fight like this."

"I'm just…" I began to speak, but my voice gave away again as tears pooled in my eyes once more. "This is hard on me—her being here all the time. I feel like she's everywhere lately." She was also coming into the café, which I had not mentioned to him. I probably should, but I just could not deal with that right now. "It's just really suffocating."

"I'm sorry," he said after a few minutes, rubbing circles against my skin with his fingertips. "None of this is fair to you."

"I just… I don't like her coming over here, Griffin. It's every day now. She's making a mess and talking to me rudely. Between working and coming home to her, I feel like I'm never getting any time with just you and the boys." I hope he could hear my desperation. To hear him telling her enough was enough. No more. I needed him to put a stop on her constant meddling.

Looking up at him, I wiped my eyes on the blanket. The words were on the tip of my tongue. *I want to have a baby.* I wanted to have one with him. My body craved a child with him, but I swallowed the words like a coward and looked away, letting the sobs escape once again.

"Don't cry. Fuck anything else but crying… It kills me." His hands tightened, and he held me tightly.

Pulling me down with him, I cried, and he just held me, rocking me back and forth until the darkness washed over once again.

***

We were both asleep on the couch when we were awakened by a loud voice calling out. "It's my birthday! Dad! Ayla! It's my birthday!"

Griffin yawned, chuckling. "Happy birthday! Now pipe down. You'll wake the damn neighbourhood."

"Happy birthday," I called out. "What do you boys want? Presents or breakfast first?" I knew exactly what they wanted.

"Presents!"

"Shut up!" Toby yelled. "I'm sleeping! But I'll take presents, too."

"Ahh, wonderful mornings with the kids as usual." Griffin sat up but pulled be back as I went to leave his side. "Are you… I mean, are we okay?" he asked, looking almost too afraid to hear my answer.

Were we okay? I guess every couple has its up and downs. "We will be. We just need to get on a page that works for us both."

"What page is that?" he asked, letting me go finally.

I gave him a shrug, brushing my hair away from around my face. "I don't know. I think we need to have a conversation about that. But things… they need to change, Griffin. This doesn't feel like my house anymore. I don't feel like it's just us in this relationship."

"It's your home, Ayla." He stood up, cupping my cheeks as his body pressed to mine. "It's our home. Just you and me, pretty. It's just us here."

"Then please respect me. Show me it's just us and keep her out of it."

We pulled apart as one of the birthday boys came running in with his school clothes already on and his hair done. It was a first. "I'm ready. Please tell me I can open my presents before school?" Mack beamed, very excited.

Griffin hugged him, kissing the top of his head with a grin. "Course, you can. Sit, and I'll go grab them."

"Top shelf, my side," I called out. I had been excited to experience birthdays with the boys and could not wait to see if they liked what we had brought.

Griffin came back in carrying a large box and a couple other smaller parcels wrapped up in blue paper, and Toby followed sleepily behind him. I had the camera out, taking photos of the birthday boys and watching as they took their first gift.

They smiled, but I was not expecting him to jump for joy over clothes and new shoes. It was just the general basics they were given before the main gift.

"Thanks." Mack put them aside, and Griffin handed over a large box to each of them. Mack went first, slowly opening the card to read.

"I don't know what this is, do I?" he asked coming to sit on the floor beside me.

"Nope. I picked it out, so hopefully, he likes it." I hoped so. It took me hours to find and only just arrived in the mail last week.

Slowly, his eyes went from excited to confused to wide and surprised as he tossed the paper aside and spun the large box around, scanning his eyes over the front. "No way!"

"What is it?" Griffin asked.

"Dad! It's like the best present ever!" He beamed, holding up the Hogwarts trunk with all the Harry Potter collector's books inside. "I can't believe you got me this!"

Griffin took the trunk from him and opened it up. "Ayla got you this. I had no clue until now."

Mack was suffocating me with a hug as he kissed my cheeks. "Thanks, Mum. I love it!"

My heart. I felt like I could not breathe. Did he just... no... But the way Griffin was staring at me was telling me yes. Mack had just called me mum for the first time! He had just called me mum, and I really liked it. Tears were threatening to fall down my cheeks. It was a one of a kind experience that I really relished and savoured.

"You're welcome. I know how much you love to read, and you lost that other book." No, she threw it out and made him believe it was lost. "So, pancakes or waffles for breakfast?"

"Both!" Toby answered. "And bacon, please." He began to unwrap his gift, and just as eager as Mack, he let out a scream as he held the Nintendo Switch and three games. "Fuck, yes!"

"Language." I reminded as he too came and hugged me. I think their birthday morning was a win.

***

A pair of strong arms slipped around me from behind as I flipped the bacon over, and lips nuzzled against my neck, showering it with a flutter of kisses. "Smells good."

"It's bacon; of course it smells good." *Really mouth-watering good.*

"Those books... they're not a cheap set, Ayla." His scolding was light and playful. "Nor was the Nintendo."

"It was worth seeing the expression when they opened them up," I responded, bumping my ass against his groin as I reached to grab a plate.

"He called you mum." I knew where he was going with this. If she had heard, fuck us all. We would never hear the end of it.

I smiled. "He did, but I think it was a slip-up. It's ok. Don't worry about her finding out and raining hell on your life."

"That's not what I meant by it. I was just saying." He did not seem mad or upset. He seemed... happy.

"Come on. Let's have breakfast and once the kids are at school, we could—"

"Do anal?" I knew that was coming. It had been awhile.

I laughed. "Fine, but in the shower and after you've eaten me out."

"When do I fuck you without making you cum that way first?" True. "Now come on. I'm starving."

Eyeing my plate, he smirked. "Eating for two?" Then his expression immediately changed, and his cheeks slightly reddened. "Uh, fuck. I didn't... Toby," he called out and left the room to find his son.

In other words, he left out of awkwardness.

Shit. Eating for two? Like seriously, he actually said that. No, unfortunately, I was not eating for two, much to my dismay.

Dropping my sight to the plate, I looked at the food and put half of it back. I suddenly was not that hungry anymore.

I took my pill and jumped into the shower after clearing the table while Griffin took the boys to school. Leaning my head against the tiled wall, I soaked up the hot water raining down over my naked skin. I was rubbing my shoulders when I heard him walking in the room.

No words were spoken as I felt his hands on my skin, sliding down between my welcoming thighs. I rolled my head back, lifting my leg and placing my foot on his shoulder as he began to circle my hardening bud slowly.

My breathing picked up, and my fingers found his hair, pulling and flexing my hips forward. "Griffin…" I moaned. "Faster…" I wanted to just get off.

With his tongue lapping me up, he curled his fingers inside me, hitting my G-spot, and then slid another into my puckered ass as I started to see nothing but a flash of white. *Fuck.* I was lost. I held my breath has I threw my head back and came loudly, holding his hair in a fist and pushing his face against my pussy more as I rode out my orgasm.

His hand stroked his cock up and down, squeezing the tip, as his free hand spun me around and pushed me to the wall. His hands took their place on my hips, and his mouth kissed up the nape of my neck as his thick length tapped my clit, sliding down to my folds and teasing my pussy with a slow dip. His cock was almost in when he pulled out and slammed into my ass.

I groaned with pleasure as he began taking a slow, steady pace of fucking me. Reaching around, he rubbed my clit with one hand as the other played with my breast, rolling a nipple between his fingers as he started moving faster.

Turning my head to face him, he met my need and kissed me hard. His tongue was taking command. He did not last long, coming in hot spurts over my ass as I held his cock from behind and jerked him off until he was limp and heavily breathing.

No words were exchanged, but none were needed right now. He held me in the shower until the water began to turn cold, and we made our way to the bedroom where we would spend the rest of the morning until the kids were due home. Karen was picking them up and bringing them over like they were too stupid to walk five feet on their own.

"Don't forget, Samuel is staying over, so we have to cool it on the sex tonight."

Griffin lay on the bed, resting on his elbows. "But I want you. I'll have you silently."

"You can have me tomorrow."

He just shook his head and stretched out—gloriously lying naked on the bed, might I add. "What I said earlier… about the eating for two—"

Shit. "Oh, I have to check on the sausage rolls. It's not a birthday party without them."

"Ayla…" he called out as I had taken off to avoid that conversation. "Get your sexy ass back in here."

"No. I know what you're going to say," I called out, laughing. "I don't want to talk about it."

***

Griffin was opening the door for the kids when they came running over, and I saw the annoyance in his face as Mack showed him his new mobile phone. He had never had one before and was not allowed one until he finished school. That was the rule. Four more months would not have hurt him. Just like Toby had to wait. Griffin was adamant about it.

"Look, Dad. How cool is this?"

"Great." He smiled and headed out the door, straight over to where she was standing.

I glanced out the window, noticing he was pointing back to the house and she was yelling. They were fighting. Ooh, I should have grabbed the popcorn and pulled up a seat for some rare action. I wanted to, but I had a party to set up and food to finish cooking, and I would rather hear what was being said instead of trying to lip read.

Griffin came back in all flustered and grabbed his car keys. "I'll be back."

"Are you okay?" I asked, and he just nodded. "Okay. Well, don't be too long. We've got cake, remember?"

He smiled for a moment and walked over, kissing me quickly. "Love you. I won't be long."

"I love you, too."

The table was set, and the food was as ready to be eaten as ever. There was still no sign of Griffin, and the boys were all off doing their own thing. Toby was playing his new Nintendo, and the other two... Well, I had no idea.

"Boys," I called out, but there was no answer.

Walking down the hallway, I stopped, pushing open Toby's door. "Where's your brother?"

"In his room, showing Samuel his Potter stuff," he said, his eyes never leaving the screen.

"Okay. Well, it's food time as soon as Dad gets back," I said as I made my way to the next bedroom door and pushed it open. "Mack, it's time for—Oh, my god!"

My eyes were not prepared to see what was in front of me. The two boys looked completely stunned and mortified as their mouths ripped apart. They were both standing far away from each other, on opposite ends of the room like there was an explosion, looking on the verge of tears.

The front door closed with a thud, and Griffin's voice echoed in the room. "Pretty, I'm home!"

"Don't tell Dad... Please..." came Mack's quiet plea. "Please."

I just closed the door and covered my mouth. *Oh, fuck.* I did not know what to do.

CHAPTER TEN

Today was the day. It was Griffin's birthday. Well, tomorrow, it would be. Tonight, I was taking him away for two nights—two nights with just him and me.

We were going to do something that I knew he would love, and no, it was not fucking me even though I planned to do that a lot with him. I was taking him camping, and I really could not wait. I had even brought him a new fishing rod along with all the tools to go with it. It took me so long to choose rods. I called Dad who gave me some advice, but I was still confused. In the end, I put Dad on the phone to talk to the guy, and he told him what to sell me. It was all packed. I had everything loaded up in the boot of my car… marshmallows and all.

I spent the morning being all giddy and excited. I suck at keeping secrets, and since I had a major secret I was yet to tell Griffin, I was desperately trying to keep myself busy. Riding his cock kept me distracted well enough to focus on something else. I did not even think.

Mack is gay.

That was a lie. Truthfully, I had thought about it a lot.

He and Samuel are apparently not just friends. Yes, and I was yet to get used to that.

Dinner was awkward. The poor boys were afraid, assuming I was going to out them both to Griffin's father. I did not know how he would handle that, and I did not feel it was my place to tell Griffin. Mack needed to do that himself and have that talk. I just hoped it would be soon.

The boys were sleeping in the living room watching movies, and I made sure that Toby stayed out with them for the night too—in between them because, well, same rules apply as if it were a girl staying over with Toby. None of that hanky panky was happening in this house anytime soon.

I would only have a quick conversation with Mack about what I had walked in on, and although it was just kissing, I wanted to have more of a talk. It was something he promised we would do when we came back home. Hopefully, he would also decide to tell his father about this. The secret was eating me up, and I could not keep it for long… not something this big. Griffin would be so hurt if he knew that I had known and not confided in him. My point was that Mack trusted me with this, and I somewhat felt it bonded us closer together.

He chose *me*, not his mother.

"Your bags are packed. Please be good, and don't get in any trouble." I knew Karen had a love of yelling at them while they stayed there.

Toby nodded, picking up his duffle bag and sighing. "I don't want to go over there."

"Me either. Can't we stay here with you?" Mack asked. "We will be good."

"Boys, I'd love that, but your mum wants you both over there."

"What's wrong?" Griffin came inside. "Your mother is out there waiting, and you know how she gets."

Yeah, we all knew her ways. "They don't want to go," I told him.

His eyes softened, and he walked over, pulling them both to him and hugging each of them with one hand. "When you're back here, I promise we'll all go do something… just the four of us. How's that sound?"

"Like what?" Toby asked, cocking his head to the side. He was a perfect likeness to his father as he did that.

"Something fun. This weekend. Just us."

Just us. I liked that.

Kissing them both goodbye, I watched as they walked down and over to their mother's house, slowly and unhappily. It broke my heart, but I guess we were not that far away from them. Only, I felt like shit for planning to go away for Griffin's birthday without them. I did ask her if we could have them here, and she said no. She had plans, she said.

Turning to me, he slowly swept his tongue across his lower lip. "Kids are gone. Bed and undress?"

"Why go to bed when you can have me right here?"

I squealed and giggled as Griffin charged at me, lifting me up by my thighs as he held the curve of my ass and pushed me over his shoulder. "I'll have you all over the house."

"I have work, remember?" I said between laughter as he gave my ass a swift spank. "Oooh! Daddy… please hurt me since I've been such a naughty girl."

"Ayla." He chuckled, giving me another smack. "Kinky girl."

I had tricked him into taking a shower with me before I left for work even though I was not really going anywhere. I wanted us to be clean before we took off to the camp site with no shower or power. We would really be roughing it, something Griffin once told me he loved to do when he was younger—camping without the worries of technology getting in the way. We would fish, talk, hang out, and drink. I could manage that.

"Can't you stay here?" he asked, watching as I straightened my hair. Like I said, I was preparing for the days to come.

Glancing through the mirror at his reflection as he stood behind me, I nodded. "I'm sorry. I can't chuck a sickie now. It's too late. Hey, let me straighten your hair?"

He made a scoffing sound when I snapped the tongs in the air. "Dream on, baby."

"Please, just a little part. It's long; what do you expect me to want to do with it?"

"Pull it when I'm fucking you."

Rolling my eyes, I parted my hair to the side and began to iron it out. "I do that already."

"Well, then nothing else needs to be done."

"What if you cut it?" I suggested. "I haven't seen you with short hair before or a smooth face. I want to see it."

Shaking his head, he ran his fingers through his long hair and then rubbed his beard, laughing. "It's taken me a long time to grow this out. Ten years, nearly."

"Fine." I rolled my eyes at him, snapping my tongs together once again. "I have to go. You going to wait up for me?"

"I'll be in bed waiting, my love."

Oh, I could not wait for this surprise. I was so excited. Turning to face him, I slipped my arms around his neck and jumped up, wrapping my thighs around his waist. "I love you. Don't fall asleep on me, and maybe I'll just come home in a willing and very giving mood."

"Mmm." He raised his brows. "I'll have to stay up and keep ready for you."

"You better." I inhaled his scent and slowly began to kiss him. "I miss you already."

"I miss you more, baby." His mouth covered mine as I slid down his body and landed on my feet. "Would you like a lift?"

"It's okay. I'm getting a ride tonight. I'll meet her at the end of the street." I smiled and kissed him once again. "I love you."

It was freezing outside as I walked down to the end of the road. It was only a ten-minute walk but long enough for my legs in this weather. Pulling my phone out, I sent him a text to let him know that I was with my so-called friend who I worked with.

On the way to work now. God, I miss you.

His reply came in fast, almost instantly. *Miss you more, sexy girl. Hurry home. I'm waiting.*

I waited twenty more minutes before I began to make the walk back to the house. My hands were shoved into my pockets, and my stomach was swirling with butterflies at my first big surprise for him. It was dark, so hiding was not too hard. The lights were on at Karen's, and her music was thudding, but it was something I did not care about tonight.

She could party it up all she liked, but I was not going to be around to listen to it.

Walking inside the house, I crept down to the bedroom, finding it empty. All lights were off as I walked around. I even checked outside for him. Nothing. He was not there.

Oh, god. He knew. I suck at keeping secrets, alright. "Griffin, very funny. You can come out now." I called out with a slight laugh. My laughter stopped when I realised he was not here. There was no sign of him. He was not in the kitchen, living room, office, or bedrooms. Both bathrooms were empty, and it was silent outside.

His car was in the driveway, but where was he? My eyes went straight to the window where the loud music was coming from, and my heart began to beat faster. *No way.* He would not.

Bile rose in my throat as a wave of sickness washed over me. Nerves of doubt filled me as I flicked the living room light off and made my way to the front door, peeking out over to her side of her house as people came in and out of her front door.

There was no way Griffin would do that to me. He knew how I felt, and he promised me. I did not want to believe it. So I picked up my phone, and I dialled his number. He would answer me if I called, and if he were there, I would hear the music.

On the sixth ring, I hung up. He did not answer.

I kept scanning across the road, looking around, and could not see him... until I spotted him walking up the driveway. Relief filled me for a slight second as I quickly hid behind the door, peeking out the curtains and watching as he took the stairs. My smile dropped. They were not ours but hers. He had a beer in his hand, laughing and lighting up a cigarette with Charlie.

I wanted to march over there and scream my lungs out at him. I wanted to hit him and make a scene, but I could not move. I was frozen to the spot, unable to move. Just staring at the man who lied to me made every possible emotion course through my body. Still, I watched him laughing away and talking with his friends. Karen was also there. She came out and joined them for a smoke, and he did nothing.

She looked happy—like she had won the fucking lottery.

I stayed in my spot until all of them disappeared inside. I found my feet and spun on my heels, down to the bedroom where I grabbed a suitcase and packed my things for real. He thought I was at work and would not be back for a few hours. I wondered how long he would stay over there with her for. All night? Would he come home? Would he get drunk and sleep with her? Oh, god! The thought just made my stomach churn.

Running to the bathroom, I fell to my knees and threw up until it hurt.

The sight of them all stuck in my mind killed me. It drove me insane.

Rinsing my mouth and going back to the bedroom, I pulled out my phone and dialled the person I knew I could count on to come and get me. I did not even hesitate.

After two hours of sitting here and spying through the blinds, which turned out was like front row seats at a movie theatre, I have had enough. Karen had her blinds wide open, and I could see them all inside, partying with drunk girls dancing around.

He was having the time of his life, so I sent him another text. *I'm on the way home. Not feeling too good.*

I wanted to see his reaction. I wanted to be here when he walks in and sees me.

He exited her door, downing another beer and laughing as he waved bye to his friends. I was so angry, I was pretty sure that I was going to lose my shit with him once he walks in. My bags were at the door, packed and ready to leave.

There was no denying it. I was losing myself here. I had given up things, and he gave nothing in return.

My heart thudded loudly as the door clicked open, and he stepped inside. He turned on the light, and then finally, he looked up at me sitting on the couch with tears streaming down my cheeks. I had been crying most the time I packed and watched him enjoy himself over there.

"Ayla..."

"Hey..." I did not look at him. "Been out?"

"I can explain."

"Go ahead. I'd love to know all about Karen's house. Is her bed comfy?" Sarcasm mixed with anger was laced in every word I spat out.

"It wasn't like that."

Standing up, I shook my head. I did not give a shit anymore. "I had one deal breaker between us—two, actually: you sticking your dick in another girl, and you going inside her house."

"I..." He stammered, at a loss for words. Then the lights clicked in his head. "No."

"I'm done." It was final. He broke my one fucking condition with him.

"No, Ayla."

"Fuck you. I'm so fucking done with you and this bullshit."

We were using sex to push aside all our other problems, and it could not keep happening. We desperately needed to talk, but there was no longer anything to talk about. I had been spineless, and now, my backbone was back. I was not going to let him walk all over me again with his fake promises.

He was in front of me, holding me by the shoulders, as he tried keeping me close to him. "I didn't plan it. I swear."

"Really? How long were you over there for?"

"Not long…"

Fucking liar.

"I never went to work tonight. I was planning on surprising you for your birthday tomorrow. My car is in the shed full of camping gear. I came back after half an hour. So how about you answer me with the fucking truth this time because you have been over there all night?" I yelled, every word growing louder. "How many times have you been over there?"

"Just this once."

"I don't believe you." I pushed him away. His touch was like a burn to my skin. "Don't touch me."

"I'm sorry, Ayla." He was running his hands through his hair, obviously stressing out. "I didn't plan to go there. Baby, I swear. Charlie and Brian… They pretty much showed up just after you texted me you were on your way to work, and then they wanted me to go over there. I said no, but fuck… you know how they get. They wanted to have a few drinks for my birthday tomorrow. Karen was throwing a party, and yes, I fucked up by going over."

I listened, and he sounded as if he were telling the truth, but I did not care anymore. "It's too late. You were in her house. You were smoking and drinking with her. I saw it with my own eyes, Griffin. Did you fuck her too?"

Hell, I was losing my mind. Sitting here and stewing over everything for the past hours really did my head in.

"What? No!" He shot back, offended. "I would never cheat on you." I stayed silent, no longer sure if I believed him.

"It's not too late... Baby, please, let me fix this. I'll go get the guys. They'll tell you I barely spoke to her the whole time."

"I don't give a shit anymore. I'm done."

"Don't say that. I fucked up badly. I know."

"No, you don't know! Christ! You're fucking up every fucking day by having that bitch coming into our home. You fucked up by letting her speak to me the way she does. After all the shit I've given up... You have no clue how hurt I am about anything, do you?" I screamed, wiping my eyes to see clearer.

He took a step away from me, and his eyes went to the large case by the door with a smaller bag. "What's that?" His eyes widened. "Ayla, please don't do this."

"I told you!" I screamed until my throat hurt. Thanks for the music next door, they could not hear the fight we were having. "I told you, you step one foot inside her house, and it's over. For all I know, you've been doing this every time I go to work. I don't believe a word that comes out of your mouth anymore. I don't trust you anymore."

Swallowing hard, his own eyes began to grow teary. "Sweetheart, don't end this. It was just one time, I swear on my life. I swear on everything, it was just tonight."

"I gave up everything for you." I sobbed. I could hardly believe it hurt this much. "I always chose you. I put you and your sons first all the time. I love them like my own, and you don't give a shit about that. You're just a selfish asshole who doesn't care about me."

"I care. I care about you."

"I wanted a ring..." I looked up, my voice a mere whisper. "I want a baby, and I want a wedding. I want to be a mother and a wife, and you don't want that with me."

His mouth formed a perfect O as he looked at me, speechless. No words he could say would change anything. Swallowing, he spoke back calmly. "You told me you didn't want that anymore."

"I thought I could give it up, but I wanted a baby with you and have the chance to be a mother. You took it away, and I stupidly agreed because I was afraid of losing you. I wanted to marry you, but why stay with someone when we both want different things?"

"I wish you would have just told me this. You didn't need to agree to what I wanted."

Shaking my head, I could not help but be sarcastic. "And I wish you'd have grown a pair and told your ex to fuck off away from us, but that never happened either."

His anger rose as he narrowed his eyes in on me. "What about Harvey? He's been trying to get in your panties for how fucking long? And you haven't told him to piss off."

"He's never been a lover, and he's my friend. Yes, he may have feelings for me, but I make it quite clear that I am with you. Hell, I talk about you constantly. All I do is talk about you to him." Could he not see that I absolutely adored him?

Ignoring my declaration, he calmed down slightly. "I need you."

"I needed you until I realised she needs you, and you always make sure she's happy."

"I don't love her." He ground out, blinking away tears as he came closer to me once again. "I love you. I don't feel anything for her."

It could have fooled me, but it did not this time. "I want a baby. Don't you want to have a baby with me? Does the idea of me pregnant really repulse you that much?"

"It's not that." he sighed, letting out a frustrated groan. "The boys are teenagers, and they're able to do things for themselves. I don't want to go through that fucking stage again of having to watch a newborn constantly, dealing with nappies and screaming."

My lips parted. "Okay." Well, I wanted that.

"I didn't know you were planning a surprise," he said, giving me a sad smile.

I shrugged back. "No big deal. I had brought you a new fishing rod and tackle box gear. Surprise! Happy birthday, Griffin." Pulling away, I ran a hand through my hair. "Ah, I hate this house."

"What?"

"I hate that you let her come in here. I hate that she's always around, taking our milk. She stole my coffee. How do I know that? She makes herself one every day since she's been here! But, yet again, you never believed me. She steals my face masks. I know that because she sits outside having a cigarette wearing the black mask." I reached up, wiping my eyes on my cotton sleeve.

He swallowed loud enough for me to hear. "I didn't know that it was her for sure."

"From the second I moved in here, you should have told her not to come over." I sniffed. "I can't even hang anything on the walls or buy things to make it feel like mine. This house is a man cave."

"Buy anything you want. Change everything, Ayla. Just don't leave. Don't do this to us."

I just rolled my eyes, walking towards him and bringing my hands to his chest to touch him one last time. His hands were tangled in my hair, curling into a tight fist as our lips drew together and crashed like ocean waves. Heat and electricity lighted up my insides as our tongues tasted one another. He tasted of liquor and cigarettes, but I was still addicted to him.

Pulling back, I shook my head. He looked pained, and it killed me to hurt him.

No. I could not do this. I needed to leave before I changed my mind. "I have to go."

He pleaded. "We can work this out."

"No, we can't. You refuse to change, and she's always going to have some sickening hold on you. You won't do anything about it. I understand you needing to do this and keep the peace for the boys, but you need to draw the line somewhere. She's in our home every day. Imagine if you were in my shoes and my ex was coming over, hanging out daily. You'd have beaten the shit out of him." Heck, he wanted to beat the shit out of Harvey, and we weren't even a couple.

He was about to speak when a horn honked outside, and his brows dipped. "You called Harvey to come get you?" he grimly said. "Unbelievable! I should have known."

I shook my head as I walked towards the door, passing him and picking up my case by the handle. "No, Griffin. I called my mum because I'm going back home."

"You're honestly leaving me?" Turning, I watched as he kept walking towards the couch. He blinked away more tears until he stopped trying and let them fall to his cheeks. "I've lost you, haven't I?"

I nodded as the reality set in. He had lost me, and I found myself.

"What am I going to tell the boys? You're not just leaving me, Ayla; you're leaving them too."

My hand stopped on the doorknob as my voice shook from the pain of leaving them all. "How about you tell them that you fucked up for once? You screwed up and lost the girl who worshipped you all."

"Ayla…" He sat, his head in his hands. His shoulders fell with each silent sob. "Don't do this."

"I'm only doing this because you couldn't respect me and my feelings enough. I love you, Griffin, and I probably always will. But, I deserve a man who'll put me first for once. I need a man who wants the same things as I do, and you've made it clear that marriage and babies are out of the question for you. I need more, more than what you could offer me. As long as Karen's in the picture, we don't have a chance."

He nodded, finally looking up with bloodshot eyes. He opened his mouth to speak, and I wished he did. If he had promised me the world, I would have stayed.

Instead, he said nothing. He said nothing, and I walked away.

CHAPTER ELEVEN

There was a loud knock on the bedroom door, and I paused David Guetta's "I'll Keep Loving You" on the iPod as my dad entered.

"Sweetheart, I love you, but that song... It's been on repeat for the past two days."

"Deal with it," I muttered with a blank expression as I kept on staring at the ceiling. "I like it."

"Maybe there's something a little more..." He lingered, leaving the unspoken word hanging in the air.

Blinking, I turned my head to see him in the doorway. "You mean, something happier?"

"Could it help?"

Maybe I did not want it to help.

I instantly went into depression mode after crying my eyes out on the drive home. Since I came back here, moping around in my old bed, I had only gotten up to shower and use the bathroom. I did nothing else. I ate all my meals, though. Surprisingly, I was hungry, which I did not think I would be.

Perhaps I was turning into a fat, depressed slob who ate her feelings away. Yeah, that was it.

"Dear... I don't mean to be—"

"I told you to leave her alone." My mother shooed him away and popped her head in, giving me a sad smile as she left the room and closed the door.

They let me be after that, leaving me to press play once again and listen to the same song over and over. It was the only way I knew to describe my feelings. I would love him. I did love him. I would *always* love him, and at this moment, I could not see a life without him in it.

I had done the hard part and walked away. However, deep down, I was still wishing that he chased after me—that he would come begging for me to stay and make all those promises I wanted to hear from him. Even if I very well knew that they were not true, I knew I would have stayed—and that was the worst part.

I lost myself to him. I gave him my all, and for what? I got nothing in return. Well, maybe a good fuck, but that was about it.

He had called me—not right away, though—the next day. The realisation that I actually was not coming back and that I was really gone and done with the drama that came with him must have finally hit his thick skull. *Karen.* Gahh! Just thinking about her had me glaring at the ceiling as I sat up and reached over to my bedside table, grabbing hold of my phone.

Griffin. My eyes began to fill up, blurring his name into a puddle of tears.

His name flashed over the screen again. I had not called anyone, but he drained my battery from the number of times he kept calling. They started at eleven am yesterday, and he was still calling every half an hour today. He never left a voice message. He just kept calling, and I ignored them all every single time.

It was killing me not to pick up and say hello. It was not like he could persuade me into coming back to him. I did not have a car. I had left the keys with him at the house. It was his, in the first place. I was only driving it. Being here, it gave me the time to think about everything we had been through. That was all I had been doing, and it was only making me angrier and more pissed off with him.

How I missed the boys, though. I regretted that I did not say goodbye to them, but I could not. It would have made things too hard. They were great kids, and I loved them like my own. Mack and I shared a bond. Toby was always the smart ass, but not once did he miss giving me a kiss and cuddle me good night.

Then again, there was her, and I could not compete with that.

Karen was always his number one. They have some sick emotional affair. Even if Griffin did not realise it, that was what it was. *Whatever.* They were always texting and talking. Her constant visits did my head in, and I knew if I stayed, I was going to be the girl who whined and sulked. That was not me.

I was already turning into her, though. I was emotional, clingy, and going crazy with jealousy.

I could have easily told him about the plan I had overheard from his mother and Karen, but like I said, I was not that girl. I did not do drama. Probably why I did not really have a female best friend. It was mostly Harvey and the girls at the café. I needed a life again. Playing house made me happy—until it didn't.

Becoming fed up, I answered the phone in a huff through the silent tears that were still coming from my eyes. I thought I would have cried them all away by now. "What!"

"You answered." He breathed out. "Don't hang up."

"You've got to stop calling me. I mean it. Just leave me alone."

"Is that what you want? You want me to stop calling?" He sounded as if he had not slept a wink since I left.

I was silent. Was it what I wanted? Truthfully, *no*, but it was what I needed.

"Griffin," I whispered, tears rolling down my cheeks. "Please. I need space."

"I need you."

His words brought a sob to my mouth that I was sure he heard as I ended the call and silenced the phone. Throwing it across the room, I fell face first into my pillow, sobbing loud howls of heartache that felt like they would never end.

The next time I woke from that blackness of doom, I closed my eyes again and rolled over. I did not want to be awake. Couldn't I just sleep until the pain ripping my heart out ends? Not that easy, apparently.

Noticing a woollen blanket over my body, I kicked it off with my feet. My bladder felt ready to explode, so I walked to the bathroom, yawning. Going downstairs, I heard voices in the kitchen, and for the tiniest moment, I assumed that he was here. I hoped.

"Hey, sleepy head. You're finally up."

I eyed him, confused. Was I dreaming? "Harvey?" I asked. "What are you doing here?"

"Well, your..."

"I called him, hoping he'd be able to get you out of that bed you've been in for days," Dad spoke up, looking quite pleased with himself. "Plus, he kept asking how you were. Nice boy he is."

Mum sighed, rolling her eyes as she stood from the table. "I had no idea about this, but you can imagine my reaction. Something to eat?"

"Umm, yeah… I guess, and you called him?" *Oh no.* He told him. "Dad, I told you I'm fine."

"Horse shit, young lady." He scoffed. "You're not fine, and be damned if I'll let my little princess sit in her room, crying for days."

"It's been two," I reminded.

"Long enough. Now, sit and eat."

He could lecture me and think he was helping, but he was not. Harvey was not someone I wanted to see just yet. I had planned on locking myself away from everyone to deal with all of this… grieve or whatever for the loss of my fucked-up relationship with a man who did not deserve me. Yes, he never deserved me.

Maybe at the start, but not now.

Sitting down, I rubbed a hand over my stomach. It was cramping up a bit. Must be hunger pains. "So you just drove down here?" I asked, finally looking up at Harvey.

"Yeah, is that not okay?" he asked, somewhat cautious.

I shrugged. My hair was a mess, and my eyes were puffy. I was in my pyjamas and did not really care. I had no intention of impressing anyone. I was not sure if I had even brushed my teeth since coming here.

"It's fine," I said back as Mum placed a full plate of veggies and roast meat in front of me.

"You're looking a little thin. Just want to make sure you're eating well." A for effort, Mum.

"Thanks."

Normally, I had a thing where I could not eat in front of others if they were not eating, but that went out the window tonight as I dug in hungrily. It was so good that I finished with a piece of bread to soak up the leftover gravy on my plate.

Like I said, I was not trying to impress anyone.

"Why don't we go for a walk?" Harvey suggested after dinner.

I shook my head. "Not really in the mood to walk around."

"What about roasting marshmallows?"

That got my attention. Not wanting to admit it, I looked up and pursed my lips. "Just to the fire pit. I'm not going anywhere else."

I wondered for a moment if Griffin had found all the camping gear I hid in the car. I hoped the milk in the esky spilled somehow and left a curdled, smelly mess all over the car that he could not get out.

"What happened?" he asked.

I sighed, knowing it was coming. Of course, he was not going to drive two hours from his place and not ask me about the breakup. Digging my hand into the hoodie pocket, I sighed again. Could I talk about it without becoming a blubbering mess in front of him?

There was only one way to find out.

"We broke up."

"No shit. I meant, how did it happen? I thought you were going away."

There was no sugar coating with him. Good, I did not want that. "He was in her house."

"Oh, and that's a bad thing?" he asked, looking back to the fire as he rolled the stick between his fingertips. "I mean, she's always over yours, so why is he being there any different?"

My mood was turning sour. "Because it's disrespectful to me."

"You come over to my place."

"We've never fucked." I snapped, annoyed at him. "He went into her house and lied to my face about it. Him going over there is the same as cheating in my eyes, only he didn't put his dick in her. He still went there knowing very well that I would be devastated and hurt."

"Oh."

"I hadn't even gone ten minutes, and he was in her house. She was throwing him a birthday party with their kids and friends. You should have seen them."

"You were there watching?" He began to smirk. "Spying?"

I'm his—*was* his girlfriend. "Not spying, gathering intel. Ok, maybe I was spying, but how could I not?"

"Did you hide in the bushes?" He chuckled, finding this whole thing amusing. Why wouldn't he? He hated Griffin.

"No, only through the living room window at home—his place. I couldn't hear them talk. The music was so loud. But I sat there and watched him having the time of his life with her. They looked like the perfect family," I said the last part in a bare whisper. It hurt, but they did. "He still loves her."

A scoff came beside me, followed by a roar of laughter. "Fuck off. We both know he hates her, and if he loved her, then he would be with her, not threatening to smash my face in if I touched you."

"He said that to you? When?" I did not believe it.

"Yesterday, when he turned up at my apartment. Almost kicked the door in too," he added.

"He came to your house?" I asked. Why was I so surprised by all of this? I was meant to hate him, not thinking of a guy coming for his girl.

Harvey pulled back his hand and blew against the burnt marshmallow, handing it over to me. "He said you left him, and if I even thought of going after you, then he'd know and make me regret it. He fucked up and lost you, huh?" He smirked. "So, your dad called, and I couldn't pass up the chance to really fuck him off."

I just forced a smile back. "Yeah... He lost me." He did.

All I had was this vision I had forced myself to see for the past few months. We were not meant to be, but I was not ready to let go completely then. I needed to see the real him, and I finally did. My heart could mourn the loss of him, but my brain knew it was the smart and right thing to do.

"I think we should go back inside." I had not checked my phone, and I wanted to check it. Pathetic, I know.

"In a minute." He placed another marshmallow on the stick as I kept eating mine, and he began to toast that too. "Did you decide to take some time off work? I can cover for you."

"Oh, no. It's ok. I'm going to call and see if I can work weekends again like before. Maybe Mum could transfer me to her new café here. I need the money." *To buy a new car and look for a rental closer to home.* Then I could find a new job.

He nodded, once again bringing the toasted marshmallow closer to him, sliding it up the stick with his fingers and bringing it closer towards my lips. I frowned but parted my lips to take the gooey deliciousness and eat it—only he kissed me instead. He *kissed* me.

I froze. His cold lips were against mine for a few seconds before he pulled away with a smile, popping the marshmallow into my mouth. "I love you."

Oh. "Harvey, I…" How could I respond to that? I was not ready.

"Don't say anything. Just know that when you're ready, I'm here for you. I won't hurt you. You know I wouldn't." I knew he would not hurt me, but I was far from ready to get myself back into another relationship.

He kissed me, and you know what I felt? *Guilt.* I felt guilty.

I did not want him to kiss me. He should not have done that. I was here crying over my breakup, and he thought he can just drive up and kiss me? Oh, no. Not happening.

"I think I'm going to go to bed." I pretended to yawn, stretching, but immediately pulled my arms back down as my stomach cramped again.

"You okay?" he asked, standing with me. "I'll walk you to your room."

"Umm, it's okay. You don't have to do that." I assured him, but his blue eyes were insisting, and he was already following behind me.

At my door, he smiled handsomely and went to hug me goodnight. His arms didn't offer any comfort, though, just an awkwardness that I clung onto tightly. Was it bad that I closed my eyes and thought of Griffin holding me? It did not do any justice. His touch was too soft… his body too thin. I craved the manly hug—the feeling of belonging and possession when Griffin held me.

Pulling away, I said, "Goodnight."

"See you in the morning. Remember what I said, Ayla. I'll wait for you. You deserve that."

I could not respond to that. The man was standing in front of me, pouring his feelings out and promising to treat me great, yet it did not give me any solace at all. I foolishly wanted the man who kept hurting me.

My phone was under the bed, and there was a total of seven missed calls in the past two hours. More guilt racked me as I touched my lips and wiped them with my sleeve, wanting the touch of Harvey off me. It should not have surprised me that he would kiss me. It did, though. I had never given him mixed signals. I was his friend, but he knew how much I adore and love Griffin.

I climbed back into bed, my home of heartache. I snuggled down feeling alone and cold. Grabbing a cushion, I hugged it tightly, closing my eyes and waiting for the tears, but they never came. They would, later on.

I fell asleep to the vibration of my phone buzzing underneath my pillow, and I felt that tomorrow, I would wake up feeling better than I had been today. *A day at a time*, so Mum told me as she had held me in her arms and promised everything would work out and that I'd get through this.

They did not know the full story, like how we met. I had only given them a short half-truth version of it all being too much for me, and I needed to move on.

***

The next day, after tossing and turning most of the night, I was eating with everyone else but did not eat much. I felt off this morning. The juice burned my throat, and toast was the only thing I could stomach.

"Do you feel like doing anything today?" Harvey asked, cutting into his bacon and eggs that made me want to throw up.

Did I? "No." I wanted to go back to bed and put on my music. I wanted to listen to nothing but the song that spoke so many words to me. "I think I might take a shower."

Carrying my empty plate to the sink, I heard my dad coughing awkwardly, and I looked up, frowning slightly as Harvey was straightening up in his chair, his cheeks slightly rosy. "Time of the month?"

I looked at him like he was crazy. "You didn't just ask me that. I'm not moody because of my period."

"Ayla... Uh, you're bleeding." Harvey pointed out with his knife poking towards my legs.

Looking down, I felt my cheeks flush. "I'm not."

Mum turned around from the kitchen sink and looked over with a worried expression. "Dear, let's get you to the hospital."

I shook my head. There was no need. I would just put a pad in after I showered. "Mum, I'm—Ahh," I cried out. "Ahh..." I screamed louder this time as I clutched my stomach. I lost my footing and fell forwards, but my father jumped up from his seat just in time.

A set of strong arms caught me, and all I could remember was curling up in pain as I screamed in agony. My stomach tightened with the worst period pain I had ever felt before I passed out.

***

There was an annoying beep filling my ears as I fluttered my eyes open. My lips were dry, and my throat was sore. Looking around as my vision focused, I spotted Harvey asleep on the chair across the room. Then my eyes drifted down to where there was an IV hooked into my left hand.

"Hey." I croaked, trying to move forwards, but my stomach ached and hurt. Swallowing, I tried again. "Harvey."

"Hmm?" he murmured sleepily. Then his eyes opened and widened. "You're awake?" He stood and walked over.

"Can you bring me water?" I nodded towards the tray at the end of the bed. "Thirsty."

Reaching for the plastic cup with a straw inside it, he brought it towards my dry lips, and I took a refreshing mouthful, drinking the entire thing.

"I'll get your parents," he said as he set the cup back down. "Won't be long."

"What happened?" I felt stupid for being so clueless.

"Ayla…" He began. "I'm sorry. I really am."

"What did you do?" I asked. You would never know with him. "Oh, the kiss."

A sad, solemn expression crossed his face as he sat on the edge of the bed beside me. "No, I didn't do anything. I don't regret kissing you. I'd do it again, but…"

I *wouldn't* be kissing him again.

"Ayla, you were pregnant. Why didn't you tell us or me?"

Pregnant. Just like that, the aching in my chest was back. "I didn't know I was." I was having a baby—Griffin's baby. I should be crushed, but a wave of happiness washed over me just thinking about it. "A baby? How far along am I?"

"Fuck." Rubbing a hand over his face, he dropped his arm and took my fingers between his. "You lost the baby. You had a miscarriage earlier. The bleeding—"

A train slammed into my gut, and the ache was like a knife piercing my heart, over and over again.

"Stop. Where's my mum?" I did not want him to tell me more. I needed my mum.

With a nod, he stood and left the room. Only moments later, my mum was rushing in. She was crying as she hugged me tightly and kissed my forehead. "Oh, sweetheart, I'm so sorry."

I wish everyone would stop saying that.

"Tell me." I needed to know. I did not want to know any of it, but I needed to.

"It was an ectopic pregnancy. You had an internal bleeding, causing you to collapse when Dad was carrying you to the car. You had surgery to remove it. You were only eleven weeks..." she trailed off quietly. "It wouldn't have survived, honey."

Eleven weeks was still far enough to know. I did not even realise I had missed a period. Then again, I did not miss any. They were still normal. "I had no idea..." The bile burnt my throat as tears stung my eyes. "How could I not know?"

I had been pregnant, just like I wanted so desperately, with Griffin's child, and I had no damn clue.

For the rest of my life, I promise that I'll keep loving you.

Only, now, I was not pregnant, and I did not have Griffin. But I still wanted both so badly.

CHAPTER TWELVE

To say I had not been thinking about it was a complete lie. I had been thinking about it a lot.

Telling him that I was pregnant and then lost our baby could go two ways. One, he would be sympathetic and all sorry, but the response I was expecting would be a punch in the face. Kidding. He would not hit me, but his words would. He would accuse me of being just like her, trying to trap him into a relationship that he did not want, a child he definitely did not want.

Five days ago, my heart broke in a way I never knew possible. The loss of a child, an unborn, innocent child, gripped my heart and crushed it to pieces.

I lost a baby that he and I had made together, and it was all I could think about.

Eight days ago, I left him, and it still felt like the first day I walked out.

I would have probably gotten over him a little if I had not suffered the miscarriage. Harvey did not come back home with us. He left, and I was grateful he did. He was not helping by being here. It was only adding to the complex situation. I needed space and time and not someone trying to kiss me.

I could not believe he kissed me.

He knew that doing that would put me in a horrible situation. I felt as if I had cheated on Griffin, betraying him in a way he was expecting. He told me Harvey wanted me, and I had made it quite clear to Harvey that I could not have that kind of relationship with him.

Then what did he go and do?

Damn well kisses me and tells me that he loves me.

It was not fair. I was going to crush his heart. This could destroy our friendship all for nothing.

Griffin would assume that I left him for Harvey, and that was just a whole other something I did not have time to deal with. This was not about them; it was about me being hurt and neglected.

Griffin did not need me the way I had needed him.

His calls had stopped two days ago. I guess he had finally gotten over me. Of course, he would move on. He's fucking gorgeous.

Perfect even.

I was feeling bitter about everything. I did not want to feel this way, but I was. I told him to stop calling me, and he finally did. So, why did it hurt even more?

Because he gave up on you. Because you didn't want him to, my inner thoughts told me.

I wanted him to beg, fucking beg for me back, and he did not. We were done, and I was not going to go crawling back to him. It was time to grow up and move on. I could not go back, not when I walked out. Going back now, knowing that everything would remain the same, would only drive me miserable in the end.

I scoffed to myself. *Move on to what?* I worked in the same town he lived in. I needed a new job, and fast.

Gazing down to where my hand lay, my lips twitched into a sad smile. "I'm so sorry." I don't know why I felt the need to apologise, but I had been doing it constantly. I already placed myself in the category of bad mothers. I should have known.

I should not have been so worked up or emotional... should not have wrapped myself up in Karen and what she was doing. Maybe then I would have figured out, that yeah, my period was over a month late, and that would give me the initiative to take a pregnancy test.

My hand had been resting on my flat tummy like it had been most of the time since I came home, and my parents both put me on mandatory bedrest. Dad had taken a few days off work to be around in case I needed anything, telling me to just send him a text or to ring the bell he left on my bedside table.

They had been amazing and not mad at all about the pregnancy—mostly shocked. There were times where I would feel anger and hate, asking myself why. Why did I deserve this? Did I do something so terrible in the past that gave me this shitty situation to deal with? I had to put up with Karen. Surely, that was enough to pay for any sins I did.

Obviously not.

My friends, or should I say Griffin's friends, had not even tried to contact me. They just tolerated me because I was with him. They would all know we had broken up by now and were probably having a farewell-the-young-bitch party. Karen would be chanting, "I told you so. I told you so!" and then make her move on him.

My eyes narrowed to slits. I wanted to punch her so bad. I could just grab her by the hair and break her damn nose if I had the chance. That was how mad she made me.

The rumbling of my stomach brought me back to the reality of growing up. I should stop trying to hold on to the past. I was hungry, but I could not be bothered moving. I wanted to just lie there in the misery of all my *what if's* and dreams that would never happen.

Food was a thought I could go all day without remembering if it was not for my mother who kept me replenished and fuelled up. Just as she was doing now, walking into my bedroom with a bowl of soup and some heated up dinner rolls covered in butter.

It was my weakness. *Butter.* Yum.

"You didn't have to bring that up," I told her, sitting up from my lying position and muting the TV.

My dad brought it in, anything to keep his little princess happy.

Mum just smiled, setting the tray on my table and taking a seat on the bed like she had done in the hospital. "How's the bleeding today? Your incision?"

She had turned into my own personal nurse too. "It's okay. Sore, but guess that's to be expected."

The sore was rather mild for what I had experienced. The stitches would dissolve, and the bruising would fade. It would just take time, time to heal and time to recover.

"Are you going to tell him?"

"Cut right to the chase." I swallowed, reaching behind my back to fix the pillow that was making me uncomfortable. Sighing, I lay back down. "No. I don't know if I should."

"He has a right to know. It was his child too."

I gave her a look, biting my tongue from snapping back. "I know it was, but we broke up. What good is it telling him I was pregnant and lost it? It'll complicate everything even more." He would just assume I tried to trap him.

"Perhaps I should call—"

Babies need constant watch, and he did not want that. "No. Please. I'll tell him but in my own time. It's only been a few days."

I dropped my hands in my lap and chewed my lower lips as it began to tremble. "He'll think I had an abortion. That's what it was." Tears began to spill down my cheeks as I looked up.

"Ayla, sweetheart, you had an ectopic pregnancy. It will never be regarded as an abortion. You didn't choose this. You had a life-threatening condition. If it wasn't picked up, it could have ended your life. It was an out of place pregnancy. Your baby wasn't going to survive there, dear," she said quietly, taking my hand in hers and squeezing it with a gentle touch. "There'll be a time for you to start a family one day. It just wasn't meant to be right now."

"The doctor said…" my voice failed me again.

"That there's a good chance you'll fall pregnant again. The percentage increases. Just because you lost a fallopian tube, doesn't mean you'll struggle to fall pregnant, Ayla. It might just take a bit longer."

I did not want another baby.

"Now, eat up. You need your rest. I'll be in the kitchen if you need me."

"Okay, Mum." I smiled, and when she left, I picked up my roll and drowned it into the bowl of deliciousness. She could really cook.

I did not want another baby—I wanted *Griffin's* baby.

***

Two weeks later
Nothing had changed. I still missed him, and my heart ached more than ever.

Four weeks later
Who said time heals pain? What a load of shit. I was mad at the world for fucking me over and breaking my heart.

Six weeks later
For the first time since ending my relationship, I put on makeup, brushed my hair, and dressed in actual clothes—real clothes, not boxers or panties and an oversized shirt, but actual going outside clothing.

***

Ten minutes later
I was back in bed. It was a start, a very depressing start of becoming normal again.

It had been almost eight weeks, and my incisions had healed, leaving two little pinkish spots as a reminder of the loss I suffered through. The bleeding has stopped, and I was starting to feel almost normal.

I was even looking for a flat to rent, since well, I did not have a ton of money, and it was just me. I was thinking about getting a cat or a dog. They are meant to cheer people up. A dog would love me, protect me, and keep me warm at night.

God, I missed sex. No, I missed sex with Griffin.

His mouth… Those lips... That tongue… Cock… *Fuck.* I needed sex badly.

I went to call him, four times. I had even written out a long text message about the whole baby situation, but before I could send it, I erased every little letter on my iPhone. How pathetic. Texting him? *Cowardly.* I needed to do it face to face.

My phone buzzed on the glass wicker table beside me as I lay outside in the sun. Reaching over, I read the message. It was from Harvey, who had been texting me constantly.

His text blindsided me. I had not expected that. *Move in with me.*

I could not type back fast enough. *What?*

His reply was instant. *Just as friends, not lovers.*

Did he realise that I did not want to be his lover? *Let me think about it?*

No. Don't think. Just do.

I groaned. My heart was starting to beat faster, but my gut was telling me no. I had to slow down and not rush into anything. My vagina was saying he's hot, though. I bet he would not mind giving me what I need.

Damn it. I did not like being pressured into anything. *I'll let you know by my next shift.*

Three minutes later, he replied. *When do you come back to work?*

I needed to go back, back to my normal life. *In four days.*

I had taken enough time off to grieve. I had to accept that my life was changing for the better.

Lifting my leg up and placing them firmly to the cement, I stood and picked my phone up. No more texting for me. I had a cake to bake.

Mum was teaching me some new recipes, baking cakes and casseroles that were suitable for freezing. She and Dad both thought it would be good that I get into my own place and keep myself busy. They wanted me to move back here and run the new café. I knew she wanted to sell the other café but kept it open just in case I went back.

I guess if I really wanted, I could stay here with them. Mum would love it, and Dad could get used to it, and I would not have to fork out rent each week. Living alone is a whole new experience, though. Honestly, I was looking forward to making something mine. It would just be my things, and everything would be clean and tidy.

No crap left around or boys smelly socks thrown on the bedroom floor.

The thought struck me, and I wondered if Mack had confessed to Griffin. I hoped so.

Enough of them. Mum was already pulling out the flour as I walked in. "I'm ready."

She laughed. "Ayla, you don't have to help me cook."

"I have nothing else to do." I looked around. What a sad life I lead right now.

"Well, in that case, please go and get some eggs from the chickens. I forgot to buy some today." She reached behind her and handed me the small basket.

Taking it from her, I slipped my flats back on and made my way outside to the coup. Maybe staying out here was not such a bad thing after all. Bringing four eggs inside, I ran into Dad who was coming back from work.

He looked at me like I was broken and needed to be fixed and handed over a small bunch of flowers with a smile. "You look better today. Feeling well?"

"Well, I haven't cried."

"Good. I hate to see you cry."

That was what Griffin used to say, but he was the one who always put the tears in my eyes.

I inhaled the smell of wildflowers and smiled. "Thanks, Dad. Mum's inside."

"Give me a few minutes with her alone." He winked, and off he went inside the house.

Gross. The image of my dad feeling up Mum was disgusting and uncalled for. So, much to his annoyance, I walked in and cock-blocked him. He glared but said nothing as Mum laughed. She kissed him on the cheek and whispered something in his ear that made the glare disappear and a smile form.

As much as I hated seeing them flirting, I could not help but want that when I reach their age. It was something to look forward to, I guess.

The cake was amazing. I should know. I cooked and then ate it with Dad. It was just us with two forks and big appetites before we had dinner. I wanted an early night but ended up falling asleep playing *Candy Crush* on my phone. It was so addicting but also very annoying when I get down to the last life and have to wait a freaking hour to play again. So, like any normal human, I moved onto *Fruit Splash* and then *Farm Mania*. In the middle of a game, Harvey called with a cheery hello.

"What's got you so happy?" I asked, checking the time on my alarm. It was late.

I could hear his smile when he spoke. "I'm on your next shift. Plus, I wanted to hear your voice before I fell asleep."

Bloody hell. Why could I not love him? He was sweet, caring, and gorgeous to boot. "Guess who just came to the café?"

My heart almost stopped. "Umm, I don't know. Tell me."

"Karen." He snorted, and I began to breathe again. "She was pretty mad and asked for you."

Okay, now my heart was back at pounding against my chest. "What did she want?"

"Just wanted to know if you were on tonight. She left when she was told no."

"Oh."

I could hear him yawning as he started talking again. "Did you tell him about the baby yet?"

Jesus. I did not want to talk about that. "Nope. What are you doing?"

"Way to change the conversation." He chuckled. "I'm in bed. Why's that? You up for a bit of phone sex?"

I really wanted to hang up on him now. "Perve. No, just wondering. I'm passing out." I was not. I just wanted to end the call.

"Oh, sorry. Sweet dreams, princess. Goodnight."

"Night," I replied, short and not misleading at all. He was starting to smother me.

I went back to the games, but it was not long until I was passing out with my phone in my hand, more lives refuelling.

***

My phone was vibrating, and it was waking me up. *Ugh, go away. Leave me alone. I want to sleep.* Sleepily, I picked it up and pried my eyes open to see an unknown number flashing across the screen. I wanted to just silence the call, but curiosity got the better of me.

I answered. "Hello?"

"Don't hang up." Griffin's voice rushed out. "I'm only allowed one call."

"Oh, so after so many weeks, you think it's just okay to pick up and call me. No hello, how are you, but a don't hang—"

"Ayla... one call. I haven't got long."

Wait. *Just one call?* My brows dipped, and I took my finger off the red end button. "Griffin, what's wrong?" Something was wrong. I could tell.

"I need you to come get me."

I chewed on my lip. *Say no and hang up,* my mind told me. "I don't know if that's such a good idea." What was I whispering for? I did not even recognise my own voice.

"Please."

"I'm at my parent's house. Call Karen." Low blow, but he could call her like she would call him and he'd go running.

Scoffing, he cursed a muffled *fuck* and then spoke back into the phone. "I'd rather not. Please, I'll wait for you."

Now I was suspicious. "Where are you?"

The line was silent for a moment, and then I heard a quiet sigh. "I'm in jail."

Say no. Say no. Hang up. It's taken six weeks to start to move on. Just end the call.

There was no hesitation as I tossed the covers from my body. "I'm on my way."

CHAPTER THIRTEEN

What the hell was I doing?

I was getting up and dressed at two AM just because he called and asked me to pick him up from jail. How stupid. I was pathetic. I was not going to get there until at least four AM.

No, it was not pathetic, more like curious. He called and asked for help; it was the most I could do. I was not going to be doing anything else for him. There was nothing more to do. I would help him, bail him out, and be on my merry way.

Shoving a pair of leggings on, my heart was pounding, and my nerves were overreacting. I felt sick, nervous, and a little excited. I did not know why, but every crazy emotion was coursing through me right now.

As I opened my bedroom door, putting a jumper over my head, I bumped into something—someone. Untucking my hair with a flick, I immediately lowered my head and cowered like a little girl who could be easily intimidated.

"Where do you think you're off to, missy?" my father's deep voice asked.

I swallowed a gulp. *Not good.* "Oh, uh… Out?"

"Out? Where to? Look, if you're going out for some rebound thing, or whatever you kids call it these days, don't bother bringing any men back here." He warned.

"Eww. Dad, no. It's not like that. I'm just going for a drive." *Christ.* My dad and sex talk? No, thanks. "I'm not going out for a booty call."

"Booty call? I hope to god I never hear that term again." He seemed to relax, but he still looked confused. "Then where are you going?"

"Would you prefer the truth or a lie?" I asked, trying to end this conversation as quickly as possible. Why, though? It was not like Griffin was going anywhere.

Crossing both arms over his chest, he eyed me with caution. "Truth."

"I'm going to pick up Griffin from jail."

He did not look impressed. "I said, the truth."

"Then I'm going to have a threesome with two sexy men and get my rocks off."

"Ayla…" he grumbled, deep frown lines forming on his face. "That's a visual I don't need."

I rolled my eyes, trying to get past him, but he blocked my way. "Dad, I told you. Griffin called, and he needs my help."

I expected him to scold me or even send me marching back into my room, but he just sighed and rubbed his tired eyes. "Keys are in my briefcase. Drive carefully."

"You're not… I don't understand." Shouldn't he be telling me to let him rot in jail?

"Sweetheart, he called you for a reason. As much as he hurt you, I liked the man."

Maybe he would not if he knew how things ended.

"Just, drive safe, okay? Text me when you get there and when you're on your way back home."

Did that really just happen? He was okay with me going back to the man who knocked me up without even knowing it. I made a coffee to go. It would keep me awake as I would not get there for a good couple hours at least.

I was not speeding for him, and I did not like to drive in the night. I only did it often before when Griffin and I began dating, and our late-night sexting was not enough. We would drive and meet halfway to fuck somewhere in the car.

I arrived in town at about four am. I parked at the police station and nervously pulled my hair up into a messy bun and got out of the car. I walked towards the police station. I was nervous. I should not be, but I was. My body was shaking, both from the cold and from the nerves.

How could I look him in the eyes and not tell him about the baby? It was not right.

I was consumed by my thoughts as I took the steps to the main entrance. Would I crumble and become a weak woman and take the guy who hurt me back? Maybe he did not want me back. Or perhaps, maybe he did, and I would have to remain strong and tell him no.

"Miss, can I help you?"

I mean, I was finally in a good place and... What? I looked up, blushing as I finally noticed the woman watching me with great curiosity. Chick with tats and long, black hair... Yeah, I screamed bad girl, alright.

"I'm here for Griffin James."

"Name?" she asked, with a bored tone. She appeared to be around the same age as my mother.

"Ayla Matheson."

After looking over a logbook, she turned to a computer and clicked her tongue. "Okay. Well, it's four hundred fifty dollars upfront, and then I can release him. How do you want to pay?"

Well, just great! He could have mentioned that before I drove all this way.

"Do you take card?" I asked, hoping what little money I had on it would be enough.

Shaking her head, she pointed towards the main doors once again. "No, but there's an ATM around the corner. If you want to go draw the cash out, then we can process and release Mr. James."

I knew where the ATM was. I did live there for six months. "I'll be back then."

I walked in the morning frost, my teeth chattering. The air definitely kept me awake as I came back with the notes to pay for Griffin's bail or whatever it was. This guy owed me. I sat and waited for them to go and get him, thinking up all reasons he was in here in the first place.

Maybe he beat the shit out of Karen. *Ha, wishful thinking.*

A loud buzzer dinged, and a door unlocked. I looked up, and there he stood looking just like the way I left him.

He was still beautiful in his dark, tied back hair. His full beard was longer before, though, and he wore tired eyes. He really looked his age.

His eyes found mine, and a small smile broke out on his face. My heart fluttered with butterflies as he walked towards me, his large frame hovering above me, making me feel so small. "You came."

Not since you last fucked me. "Yeah, for a small price."

"Oh, shit. I didn't think you'd have to. I'll pay you back." For the first time, he looked embarrassed as he shifted on both feet. "Can I ask another favour?"

No, you may not. "Sure."

"Could you give me a lift? I kind of lost my licence." There was that look of embarrassment again.

"Griffin, I don't know if... Can you tell me why—"

A police officer walked over and cut me off sharply. He started talking while handing Griffin a thick manila envelope. "Mr. James, you have a court appearance in two weeks' time. Being convicted for an exhibition of speed crime can lead to some fairly significant consequences. You'll face reckless driving charges, as well as excessive speed, and have your licence suspended. If not, jail could be possible for up to ninety days. You're out on good behaviour until then, as this is a first crime charge for you."

Holy shit.

Griffin just nodded, taking the envelope and placing his hand against my lower back as we started to walk out. I pulled away almost instantly. "Sorry, habit."

I did not comment back until we were in the car. Secretly, I had missed his touches.

"You got drag racing?" This could get bad for him and his boys.

"Sure did." He laid his head back, closing his eyes. "I'm sorry you had to drive out. I didn't know who else to call."

"It's fine, Griffin." *Not really.* None of this was fucking fine. Everything was going ape shit. "How did they catch you? Why were you racing? What happened to poker?" I asked.

His jaw tightened, and she shook his head angrily. "No fucking idea. Call it being bored and needing a distraction." He knew. He just was not saying. "Got busted doing one eighty. Fucking cops, ay."

I took that for a change in subject. I needed to take him back home. "Where do you want me to take you?"

"Home. I need to get the money for you."

Home. Karen. Familiar. "Don't worry about it. It's okay."

"Ayla, I'll pay you back."

"You don't have to." I kept my eyes ahead as I started the car and turned the heat on.

"Why won't you look at me?"

Shoot. He noticed it. I did not want to look at him, not when we were so close together in the car. The feelings stirring in my lower belly... The head spreading to my loins... I began to crave his touch, his hands against my skin. I wanted his mouth against mine, exploring.

This was why I should not have come here. "Griffin..."

"Ayla, can we at least talk?"

"No." I had to stay strong. "I'm not going to that house again."

Blowing out a long breath, I finally turned and looked at him. His eyes met mine, and for a moment, I imagined us crashing our mouths against each other. "I didn't mean for us to go there. We can go somewhere else and grab a coffee and sit in the car. Wherever you want, Ayla, just please talk to me before you go back again."

We were heading for more heartache. Why would I want to go and put myself through this once again? Because I loved him and was not thinking straight. Because deep down, I had to tell him about the baby. Even if we were not together or even if he would hate me for it, he deserved to know the truth.

"One coffee. We can drive down to the lake and talk there for a bit."

Picking up a latte each from Banjos and a couple meat pies, sausage rolls, and raspberry white chocolate muffin, I drove us down to the lake and parked in front of the water, keeping the engine running so we did not freeze to death.

He rolled down the window and lit up a cigarette, inhaling with a long drag, then blowing it out slowly through his nostrils. "You remember when we'd drive down here?" This was our spot—in the summertime, anyway.

"You taught me how to skip pebbles along the water." How could I forget? "We almost got caught skinny dipping too."

He laughed, a loveable but sad laugh. "Yeah, I remember that. Funny how I never really thought about those times until you left. Now it's all I can think about—what we'd do, how we were." He licked his lips and glanced up. "I found the camping gear."

Oh. I wondered about that. "The milk…" I said, my eyes widening.

"I grabbed it after you'd left. Haven't driven that car since so probably a good thing you mentioned it. Wouldn't have been pretty otherwise." Maybe not for him. "Thanks for the rod and tools. You should take them back, get a refund."

"It was for your birthday," I reminded.

Shrugging, he muttered, "Pretty shit birthday when your girlfriend leaves you the night before." *Ouch.*

"I have something to tell you." I began, picking at the muffin in my shaking hands. *Christ, just tell him and get it over with it.*

"I know what you're going to say," he responded. I was barely audible, but I still heard and looked at him. He could not have known unless Harvey told him. "I'm not mad, Ayla."

I smiled a bit, slightly relieved. "You're not?"

He shook his head. "No. I understand and accept what happened. It was bound to happen, I guess."

"You don't know that." I mean, the baby could have been in the right place and survive.

Reaching over as he held his smoke out the window with one hand, he took my hand and squeezed firmly, but not too hard. "I do. You walking out like that, and I deserved it. I broke the one rule you gave me, and I haven't stopped regretting it since I walked through her door and you walked out of mine."

He was not talking about the baby. He did not have a clue about it.

I shook my head. This was getting too deep for me, but in a way, it was good because we were talking calmly and rationally about everything even if we were exes. "Everything went wrong, not just that. It was all leading up to that, Griffin."

"I know, baby. I know." He sighed and inhaled another drag. *Baby.*

"What did you tell the boys?" I asked. I wondered how my absence would affect them. "How are they?"

"Pissed at me. Mack refuses to talk, and Toby is a fucking pain, being a smart ass." He then smirked. "My sons have a case of broken heart syndrome just like their father."

"Sorry." I did not know what else to say.

He shook his head and rubbed his thumb over my skin, sending goose bumps up my arm. "Don't be sorry. I told them I hurt you."

Yes, he did.

I moved my hands away from his and looked out the side window before I began to feel all the emotions I had tried so hard to lose. My focus was on the rain droplets starting to hit against the window.

Resting my head against the cold glass, I closed my eyes. "Are you okay?"

"You broke my heart."

"Two hearts broke that night, Griffin. It broke my heart to leave."

I heard the window winding back up and his belt unclipping. His one hand slid around my waist, turning me to face him as his other hand travelled up towards my cheek. I tilted into him. Our eyes did not break contact as we looked at each other. For a slight moment, I wanted to kiss him. I wanted him to kiss me.

His face drew closer to mine, and I brought my hand up. I longed to touch his jaw, to feel his smooth skin, but I felt his beard of prickles instead.

"I'm so sorry for hurting you, pretty."

I lost our baby. The words were on the tip of my tongue, but I could not speak them. I did not know how to.

Closing my eyes, I slipped my arms around his neck and just hugged him. That was all I could do. He responded and clung to me just as tight, holding me the way I had been craving these past weeks. A hug from him was like heaven. It made me feel safe. It made me feel loved. But it also broke me, and I could not go back.

Pulling away, we broke contact completely, and I shook my head. This was wrong.

"I need to go now."

"I need you. Please, come back."

Fuck it. *Fuck him for doing this to me.*

I banged my head against the head rest and gripped the steering wheel tighter. "Damnit, Griffin," I growled, hitting it. "You can't say that to me."

"It'll be different."

"Has she been in the house?" I asked. Why did I care? Yes, I knew why I cared. Because I still loved him.

After a moment of silence, he spoke up and sighed. "It's not like that."

"So she has." I scoffed. I should have known. "Nothing would change, Griffin." Nothing ever did. "Not when nothing has changed with her and you."

"It would," he promised. "It will change."

I smirked, rolling my eyes at him. "I don't want to be with someone who is that close with their ex. It's like you are having an affair, not physically but emotionally."

"Bullshit. I have no feelings for her whatsoever."

"Prove it then," I threatened. "Prove to me that she's not going to be a problem."

Opening his mouth to speak, he closed it again, pinching the bridge of his nose. "I…"

He could not. I knew nothing would change. I knew deep down that if I went back, he would fuck me over worse than he already had done. "I love you, but you and I? We broke up for a reason. I think there's a reason why people don't work out, and that should stay in the past."

He nodded, not saying anything.

I drove him back to the house and did not bother to look out the window to see if she was there. She probably was, but I did not care. It was not my problem anymore.

Getting out, he bent down. "I'll go grab you the cash."

"No."

"You can't afford not to take it, Ayla." He was right.

"Just put it in my bank account or send it up to Mum's. Please, I need to go." I pleaded with my eyes, not wanting to stay there any longer. It was crushing me.

He nodded, and I noticed the sadness in his eyes as he straightened up. "Drive back carefully, okay?" He smiled, a sad one. "I still worry about you."

"Me too. No more racing, though. You've got two boys to stick around for. They need you more than you think." *Especially Mack.* He needed him and would need him more than ever when he finally told his dad the truth. "Stop the poker, too. Tonight should be a wake-up call about doing illegal things for a thrill."

Truth. Baby. He had a right to know, but I could not do it.

I drove away from him and all the drama that came with my love for him. I would probably regret it, but I would regret staying with someone who hurt me more, and it all came down to that.

Griffin would be the love of my life. Maybe we would be together another time, but right now, with Karen running his life the way she always has been, there was no chance for us… and for the first time, I was okay with it.

***

GRIFFIN

I reached for the base of my cock firmly as I spun her around to me. Her pretty little mouth hung open as I guided my cock in between her welcoming lips. Then I let go. Cum spilled out, and her tongue flicked the underside of my cock as my body twitched. A throaty groan escaped my lips with a hiss. Her mouth closed, taking me deeper, and my head dropped backwards.

She sucked and took it all from me—every last fucking drop.

My eyes lazily opened and saw my cum covered chest as my hand fell to the bed. My cock was flaccid, but my balls ached with a need for more. With my chest rising and falling, I caught my breath. *Ayla.* I could not get her off my mind.

She consumed me. All fucking day, she was all I had thought about.

I wanted her. Needed her. I would get her back.

Fuck it. Once again, I wrapped my hand around the base of my cock and slowly stroked at the image of her, trying to sate the cravings I had for her.

Instead of being able to taste… hold her… I had to jerk off instead.

I moaned her name over and over until I blew.

It was not enough. She owned me.

I would get her back and never let her fucking go.

CHAPTER FOURTEEN

Business was bustling. It would keep me busy, thank god. I needed and welcomed the distraction.

It took my mind off everything that I needed to forget. Being on my feet was a change from sulking for hours in bed—something I did for a whole week after my last visit with Griffin. True to myself, I stayed strong and did not go back.

He was not willing to change, and I was not willing to go back.

I knew what I wanted, and it was a man who worshipped the ground I walked on. I was a fucking queen.

Not quite, but I wanted a man to treat me like his queen.

I would be his lady on the streets and freak in between the sheets.

Ugh, I would need to find myself a man first, and I was not really looking.

My eyes were scanning the café as I grabbed a glass from underneath the counter and filled it with ice cubes. Harvey was flirting up a storm by the window, serving a group of women who flirted shamelessly back at him. For a man who confessed to being madly in love with me, he sure knew how to send mixed signals. I could not complain, though. It was not like I wanted to be with him. Men are so confusing.

My eyes were stopped by a flash of red. Her skinny frame waltzed right up the café, and I could not help but notice her pushed up breasts bursting out from the tight red halter top she paired with jeans and heels.

Beats me why Karen was here. I did not want to serve her, though, and I would not.

"Oh, she's been in every night looking for you. Literally every night."

Looking at Holly, I frowned. "Really?" That was a bit excessive even for her.

"Yep. I asked what she wanted, and she just said you are friends." She rolled her eyes. "That's the ex, isn't it?"

Unfortunately, small towns tend to know about breakups, and my co-workers knew all about it. Only Harvey and my parents knew about my miscarriage, though, and it was going to stay that way.

Nodding back, I turned away and stared at the coffee syrups. "Sure is. Can't we ban her?"

"Girl, he so traded up from that nasty ass bitch. He got himself some fine ass pussy. I just want to gag at what hers would look like. Fifty says she is all natural and smells like a—"

"Okay, enough about that." That was too much information, like way too much. "I'm okay with her being in here as long as she doesn't start anything. I'm taking the high road and being the bigger person, a better person."

Holly broke out laughing. "Better coz clearly, she's the bigger one."

Some lucky person got to mop up the spew all over the bathroom sink after a girl on her eighteenth decided to order and down six shots of tequila all on her own then come and eat the all-day breakfast special. Clearly, she could not handle them and puked her guts up as she ran into the bathroom.

That lucky person was me.

Washing my hands after I cleaned that god-awful mess up, the door opened and closed behind me. I did not take any notice until her reflection came up behind me. A smirk was across her puckered pout, and a tiny silver handbag was tucked underneath her armpit. Like, really? Why not do what a normal girl does and shoved everything in your bra?

"Been looking for you."

Walking to the dryer, I pushed the button and warmed my hands dry. "So I heard. What do you want, Karen?"

"What?" she shouted, over the noise.

Moving my hands away, the dryer stopped. "I said, what do you want? I have work to do, Karen."

"Fuck you, bitch." She spat, stepping in front of the doorway. "You think you're all high and mighty because you got in close with my kids. Well, I tell ya what, Ayla? They're not yours! They're mine."

That did not really make much sense. I looked around awkwardly. "Umm, okay? I know they're yours. I never said they weren't."

"I said I'd put you six feet under, remember?" she warned.

Christ. How could I forget? "Karen, you need to leave. I have work to do."

"I laughed so hard when he dumped your pathetic ass." She sneered. "He told me you walked out on him."

I ignored her. I was not doing this, not at work. It may be a café that opened late, but this is still my job, and it was important to me. I loved working here. I would not risk it for anything or anyone.

I was not going to react. Turning to grab hold of the mop and bucket, I went to leave.

I managed to keep my composure until she said something to me—something I was familiar with. "I'm not trying to replace you, but I'm not going away. So you should really figure out a way to get used to me being around because I'm here to stay."

Fucking bitch.

I turned around and narrowed my eyes. "What did you just say?" I asked. My hands were beginning to shake, and my palms were cloudy with sweat. My heart was pounding heavily.

Her smile pissed me off. She was smiling—not a fake one but a big, cheerful victory smile. "It's funny that you and Griffin broke up literally a week after you said that to me."

"What's your point, Karen?"

"My point—" she got in my face, her small frame appearing larger "—is that you are just a young thrill for him."

I was more than that. "You should leave." My voice was calmer than I had expected it to be.

In the past, I may have wanted to gauge her eyes out. Everything that had gone wrong between Griffin and me was mainly her fault. Things were not great, but they could have been better. She made them worse, and weeks ago when I found Griffin over at her house, I wanted to set her on fire. When I lost the baby, I wanted to beat the living shit out of her. But now? What's the point? Griffin and I were over, and I did not want to live in the past.

I was taking the high road.

"The night he came over, I took him into my bedroom and got on my knees to suck him off. He came for me, not you, that night." Her words hit straight through my heart like a dagger.

She was just trying to get a reaction from me. *Breathe and walk away. She's not worth it.*

"He's been coming over daily, and I'm always at his place just like old times. Little girl, I told you that he'd always come back to me, and he fucking comes for me."

Fuck the high road.

My hand drew backwards, and I slapped her hard across the cheek with a stinging slap. I grabbed her by her halter collar and with all my force, slammed her back into the wall behind her with a shove. Her hands wrapped around my throat, trying to cut off my oxygen as I pulled her hair hard.

Then she went fucking crazy.

She head-butted me in the face and almost broke my nose.

I was seeing stars as well as blood. "Motherfucker! Ouch!" I was literally swearing my lungs out.

Groaning, I poked her hard in the stomach, and she jolted down, trying to pry my hands away. On her second try, I drew my hand back and punched her in the face before pushing myself away.

I was not a fighter, but be damned if I would let her come in here and talk to me that way.

"What is your problem with me? You cheated on him, remember?" I yelled, bending forwards to catch my breath. Blood was still dripping from my nose. God, that hurts.

"He's the father of my boys."

"You sure about that?" I asked. Yeah, I really went there. "You fucked around a lot, from what I heard."

She went to lunge at me again with a deafening scream just as the door opened, and her friends came in. One of them was Helena. I could not believe it. Of course! Kill the girl who hurt their friend.

"Karen, you promised me," she said, mouthing sorry to me as she reached for her.

Grabbing her by the shoulders, she pried her out of the bathroom as she kicked and screamed profanities at me.

I burst into tears. He could not have done that. I needed to believe that he would not cheat.

Holly came running in with Cara, another worker. They were lovers. "Fuck. Your nose is like, broken."

"What?" I gasped, wanting to cry even more. More tears spilled out. I was becoming hysterical.

Cara flicked her in the arm. "No, it's not. Geez, don't scare her. It looks bad, but it's not broken."

Still crying, I looked in the mirror. There was blood everywhere, but my nose was not broken. Thank goodness. I probably would have been more upset about that. "She head-butted me." Then I began to giggle. "I poked her in the stomach. Oh my god, who even does that?"

The girls, looking at each other, both began to laugh until we were all cracking up in the bathroom. Holly had tears in her eyes, shaking her head and saying "No way, you didn't." I did. Grabbing some paper towel and running it under some cold water, I began to dab my nose and face clean from the mess. It hurt, and I knew I would be bruised in the morning. It was my first fight, and I came out worse than the other woman.

Cara whispered, "She is crazy, I swear."

"Tell me about it. She just attacked. Her words were so mean. I slapped her, but who the fuck head-butts someone?"

"Umm, you can't go out in that." Holly pointed out, nodding towards my white shirt. "It's got blood splatters."

Ah, just what I needed. "I didn't bring a change of clothes. Kind of didn't predict a bleeding nose tonight."

"Here. Cara, take your top off and give it to Ayla."

"No, it's okay." I quickly chimed in, holding my hands up as I glanced back in the mirror. The blood was not that noticeable anymore. "I'm good."

Two lesbians outvoted me, and I was eventually leaving the bathroom in skinny leg jeans and a white tank top. Cara had on two of them. The white one I wore went perfectly with my hot pink bra. That would teach me for not listening to my mum and her clothing advice.

The top earned me some extra tips tonight, as well as phone numbers and oddly, a piece of chewed gum. *Yuck.* But the numbers were from some pretty hot guys. I knew that moving on was inevitable. It had to be done—unless I wanted to stay single with a ton of cats that would only end up annoying me, and then I would have to give them away.

Why did this have to be so hard?

If I was going to move on, I had to do it like a guy. I had to rip that band-aid off, spread my tanned thighs, and fuck someone else.

Fuck someone else. My stomach knotted in guilt. I felt sick about the prospect of moving on without him.

I stopped thinking as I poured a double shot espresso, and the answer was right in front of me—smack bang in my face like Karen's revolting head.

We were already friends. It made sense. I could grow to love him. That's how it always starts. He was gorgeous, tall, and had a smile that melted hearts and also broke them the next morning after, but I could do this.

It was a great idea.

I was going to move in with Harvey, and that was it. I did not want to love him; I could not hurt my friend in such a way. If only it were as easy as getting under him... if only that were all it took to help me move on... If Griffin was having sex, then why should I stay celibate?

Making my way over to the booth he was sitting down in while on break, I flashed him a smile. "Hey, you." God, could not sound any more desperate.

His eyes were on my shirt and then looked back up. "You, uh... your bra is showing."

"Wow, give the kid a candy," I said, mocking him. "Yeah, got in a fight and had to change."

"Nice one." He laughed, not believing a word of what I just said. "So, what's up?"

"About your offer, and the other thing... You know, about us." I began, pulling him by the arm to talk to him without his fan club trying to listen in behind where we were. "I'm still at Mum and Dad's. I don't want to have to drive every night like I have been doing if I want to keep my job. I was thinking about moving to your place."

"Ayla... I—"

"I mean, I didn't want to at first. You know, with all that Griffin stuff." I was blabbering, talking through the crazy nerves. "I'm not promising anything."

"Ayla..."

"But I have to move on, right? We've always been great friends, and when you told me that you love me, it scared me. Like, *really* scared me. I didn't think I'd be ready for anything so—"

His hand covered my mouth, and my words became muffled.

"Shut up and listen to me." His voice was louder, angrier. His breath was against my face, and not in a good way. He was mad. My eyes widened. He sighed, running his free hand through his hair before dropping his palm from my mouth. "I met someone."

"Oh." Well, there goes that idea.

"I'm sorry. It just happened unexpectedly and hit me like a truck, ya know?" No. I did not know.

"Good." Wow, I had lowered myself to a new low tonight. "I have to get back to work." I had to take that job at Mum's new café then.

"I'm sorry."

I shrugged. I was not hurt, but I kind of was. "Maybe you shouldn't be going around confessing your love and kissing everyone then."

So he rejected me, not that it stung too much. I was just annoyed that I put myself out there like that and he turned me down. So much for always loving me. So much for the, "I'll wait for you, Ayla."

Bullshit. He could not be fucked waiting—just like Griffin could not be fucked treating me better than Karen.

Then again, I was only forcing myself to try things out with Harvey. He and I would probably have never worked, anyway.

This night was going from good to bad to worse. Everything was telling me to quit my job and move on... pack up the last of my dignity and just get away from this town.

I nudged some squealing girl in the side and glared at her. Yes, I actually glared at some blonde who was too happy for my current mood as she gossiped about her Tinder date going well.

Back at the bar, I was run off my feet. My nose was still throbbing, but the Nurofen helped ease that right up. Knock off was not too far away. For once, I was actually counting down the minutes. I wanted to leave, drive home, and cry my damn eyes out. After all that, I did not even want to come back to work again. I was the girl who got her ass kicked in a stall by an older woman, who was acting like an animal seeking revenge.

"Hey, guy down the end wants you to serve him." Holly came over, reaching in front of me to grab some more ice.

I glanced down, he had been sitting there most the night, at least four hours, anyway. He was talking to another guy and sipping on whatever he was drinking. His head was down at the moment, and a broodiness was about him.

Why did I always get these ones? "What does he want? A latte with soy milk?"

"Maybe he wants to get your number." Cara winked.

These two were funny. Not.

"Ooh, maybe he could be your rebound. You so need a rebound to get over your ex. Go and ride his dick or whatever it is you straight lovers get up to."

"Holly." Cara glared at her. "She isn't going to just throw herself at someone." Like I had almost done to Harvey. "Just get his number. Add it to the pile."

That pile was in the bottom of the trashcan.

"Maybe, I don't want to get a number from a guy in a café," I stated proudly and made my way over.

His dark hair was styled in a tousled bedhead—freshly fucked style, I would like to call it. He has a smooth, chiselled jaw and big, strong arms. Mmm. Nice, but I missed my long-haired man. A tattoo went up underneath his tight-fitted shirt, but I paid no intention to it. His hands were strong, holding the empty cup, as he drummed his fingertips against the glass.

"Another?" I asked. Two others turned around beside him, but I did not look. The guy did not answer and just slid his glass towards me. I would take that as a yes then. "Be right back."

It occurred to me that he had only been drinking water. I refilled it and brought it back to him. He did not say thanks and just kept his head down as I went about my night, serving and cleaning up another round of spew. When I came back, it was almost closing time, and his glass was empty.

This time, I just took it without asking and poured another refill.

"You do know I can shove some ice in a larger glass for you, right? Or maybe you want me to get you something else to drink?" Why did it bother me that he was just sitting here, drinking water? It was odd. Oh, unless he was waiting for someone, a date perhaps. For nearly five hours, though? That was a bit much for a date.

Ooh, or he could be my rebound. Could I really fuck a stranger, though? Griffin was a stranger, but that was different. I felt the connection between us immediately before we even kissed. One look in those eyes of his and my heart found its way home. I had found home, but now I was back to where I started and needed to figure out where my new home was.

Mr. Tall, Hot, and Handsome just shook his head. "I'm good."

That voice... That masculine, deep voice...

No. It could not be. He looked completely different. Griffin had long hair past his shoulders and a beard that almost reached his chest. He was scruffy and sexy. The man in front of me was clean shaven and handsome.

Then he looked up, and my heart stopped. *Home.* The drink in my hands slipped and fell to the ground with a smash. Water was pooling at my feet, and ice cubes were strewn on the wooden floor.

Still, I did not make a move.

My words finally found their way out. "You shaved."

"I did."

I suddenly felt like a girl standing in front of a cute little puppy and telling her parents how much she wanted him. I had that kind of emotion. I felt all that just by looking at him.

"You cut your hair."

My eyes were blurring. It was hard not to be breathless.

"I did."

"It's not long anymore." It was short and really dark. Gosh, he looked so different—good different. It suited him.

His hand raked through the top of his hair, scuffing it up even more. "It is."

"Are you going to say more than two words to me?" A smirk curved on my lips as I stared back, unable to move.

He cocked a grin back. Not taking his deep blue eyes away from me, he parted those soft, pink lips and spoke clearly. "I love you."

Don't say it. You broke up. Walk away. You ended it. It's over.

All those thoughts flew around my head. We broke up. I was the one who drove away, and I was finally at peace with my decision.

He began to stand, and I swooned inside. My eyes raked over his body, taking notice of his shirt clinging to his muscled torso and jeans hanging low on his hips. I looked up and drew in a slow breath as his eyes were hard on me. They were filled with primal need—lust and desire—but there was something else there, something new.

His tone now was a growl of possession as his eyes raked over my tits and then landed back on my face. "I love you, Ayla. I fucking love you. You want me to get on this bar and tell everyone in the café that I love you? I'll do it. I love you."

The other customers turned, noticing the interaction between us. I was blushing, terribly embarrassed.

I love you.

I should tell him to leave. I should have.

But he cut his hair and shaved his beard for me. He loved that beard. "I..."

CHAPTER FIFTEEN

He loves me.

I knew that, though. He was letting others know it and whilst he was completely sober.

I wanted him to get on that wooden bar and shout it to the damn world. I wanted to let everyone know and see this man declare his love for me. He deserves to humiliate himself that way. He could profess his love, and then I could reject him, crush him the worst way possible, publicly.

I could not do it, though.

Cara and Holly were both grinning from ear to ear as Griffin stood tall, awaiting my answer. "I…"

"If you don't tell him you love him, I sure as hell will. He's a fox." Some girl called out, and I blushed even more.

Instead of speaking, I untied my apron and tossed it on the counter, giving Holly and Cara a look, "I'm taking my break," I said before I start jumping up and down for joy, embarrassing myself further.

"How about you just knock off early? We've got this." Cara began to wiggle her brows, and Holly did the same.

I looked at the man declaring his feelings for me. "Give me five minutes?"

"You've got one."

Jesus. He was not messing around.

As I was slinging the strap of my bag over my shoulder, I felt a hand on my shoulder.

"What the fuck is this?" It was Harvey, and he was glaring at me, looking pissed. Oh no, he does not get to do this now.

"What's it look like? I'm leaving."

"With him?" He looked mortified.

"With him," I repeated and left it at that as I walked off quickly, ignoring his pleas to come back. What did he care? He had his new girlfriend, anyway.

Griffin was by the entrance door when I came out from the back. He got his hands shoved in his pockets as he looked at me, an unmistakable burning intensity in his blue orbs. *Fuck.* He had my insides going crazy. That smile, those eyes, his fucking hair, and clean-shaven face… My panties were almost soaked with lust for him.

"Where to?" he asked, sounding slightly eager that I had not rejected him—yet.

We began walking down the footpath, and I did not know where or what was going to happen. "I'm not sure. I was planning on driving back tonight after work."

"You're driving after a long shift?" he asked, bewildered. "I don't like that, Ayla. You could fall asleep at the wheel and crash or worse."

I groaned and gave him an eye roll. I was tempted to reply, "Yes, daddy." He sounded just like my father. "Yes, I know. Not my finest idea. The hotels were booked out." It was not like I could call him. Harvey was now busy. I needed a new plan. "Did you drive to the bar? You haven't lost your licence yet, have you?"

He laughed freely and beautifully. "No, I have my court appearance next week for that. I'm prepared to lose it for a couple years at least. I caught a cab."

"That's going to suck. You love to drive." He loved to just take long drives around the city, exploring new places. "You need your licence for work too."

"I was reckless. My own fault." He did not jump around taking the blame. "Let's just keep walking around. It's a nice night."

Nice night? Who was this man? He was being sweet and agreeable.

Grinning and letting out a soft laugh as I walked by his side. "So, have to admit I really wanted to see you on the stand on the bar."

"Thought for a moment. You would have wanted that," he murmured. "Still haven't answered me yet."

I knew that was coming. "I know, and I want to believe you, but—"

"I know what you're going to tell me, but I mean it when I tell you this: Everything will be different now." Stopping, he reached for my hand, leading us down the pathway towards a small park. "It won't be like it was before."

"You say that…" I began quietly, lifting my head and looking up at him.

Coming to a wooden picnic bench, he halted his steps. He then looked around and walked towards the grass, bending down. He patted it. "It's not wet. Let's sit on the hill."

I followed, and we walked a bit further in silence. We found a place to sit underneath a large tree that was facing a small duck pond where kids would come with their families and throw their day-old bread at them. It was nice to be here, away from the noisy traffic, and not feel the pressure of sitting in a close, confined space like a car.

"You were saying?" I pressed after we had both sat down. He was not getting off that easily.

He nodded, and I listened intently. It was just us, and no one else—no phones, no distractions. It was just him and me talking.

"My lawyer... I told him about the situation with Karen, and he's organising a hearing for custody arrangements. I'm not going to take them from her, but a line needs to be drawn. A split means one week with me, and the other with her, possibly on every second weekend with her. No coming over or helping when they're at my place. There will be no unnecessary speaking. All I want to talk to her about is the boys. We aren't friendly, but it'll be civil. Since the poker nights have ended, it'll be a set amount for her too. She was advised to find work, as freeloading off me for seventeen odd years isn't going to cut it anymore."

"You told her?" I asked, shocked and surprised as I sat up straight.

"My lawyer told her. I haven't been answering her calls or texts." *Oh, boy.* No wonder she was on a rampage. "I know I hurt you. I understand you are mad at me."

"I'm not mad anymore. I was but only because of how everything blew up." I sighed. It was the truth. There was no more anger towards him. It's just... "I'm sad."

He looked at me, elbows resting on his knees as he then dropped his head and looked down. "That's worse. I'd rather you hate me than be sad."

"Did she call you in about the racing?" I asked. I wanted to know.

"Yes. She knew I was going to apply for custody and went in and spilled her guts like a pig on the slaughter floor." *Yuck.* That was visual I did not want. He appeared vulnerable as his voice cracked from obvious nerves. "You said you could give me another shot if I quite being involved with Karen. Please, tell me you meant that."

I raised a brow. Did I say that? Lying back down, I rolled to my side and looked up to him. "I get that you and she can't cut all ties. It's impossible. You have kids together, and I understand that." That was not the part that bothered me. "You lost respect for me. You didn't respect me."

"I did."

He didn't.

"No, Griffin, you didn't. Texting her about broken DVD players or how to change a light bulb? That's not your problem. It wasn't just one text, it was the phone calls and constant talk about everything but the boys. The kids? Fine, talk away, but it was rarely about them. She came to our home and took food. She took my coffee, used my beauty products, and was always there. Her threats about putting me six feet under? Not on. You shouldn't let an ex talk to the woman you love that way." I sat up again, using my hand to keep my steady on the grass. "Could you even imagine how it feels having her in the home we shared? I felt like a third wheel sometimes."

"Ayla," he pleaded. "I'm trying here. I want to move forward with you, with us."

"I sacrificed everything I dreamed of for your happiness, and you just fucked me when I'd get mad or upset to distract me." I gave up the dream of being a wife and a mother for him. That was not just something; it meant everything to me.

Turning, we faced each other, and he ran a hand through my dark hair, sighing with a look of sorrow on his face. "I can't apologise enough. I just thought I was keeping the peace. I didn't want to be bitter and have the boys know that she and I were having it out. I couldn't do that to them."

I nodded. I realised that, but it did not change things. "She walked all over you—used you, and you let her."

"I know I did. You did deserve better. You still do."

"So do you. You don't deserve to be used." She took advantage of him so badly.

He rested his back against the tree, resting his legs effortlessly on the grass. The wind picked up, and my arms shivered. I wished I had brought my jacket. Without thinking, I moved and shifted my legs over, straddling his lap. His hands immediately wrapped around my waist and trailed his thumbs in circles against my hips. Just the heat of his body against mine warmed me. I just could not take my eyes off him. He was new to me again, like a new shiny object to play with. Only, I did not want to play. I just wanted him.

A tormenting battle was tearing me into two. I wanted him, but I did not want to go back to how everything was beforehand. Looking into his ocean-like deep blue eyes, I found myself melting against his chest.

"I'm cold." It was a lame excuse to get close to him, and I was sticking with it.

Griffin just smiled back. "I'm sure you are. You should have had a jacket. I'll keep you warm."

My hands lifted, and I began to caress his cheeks, softly holding him. "You shaved." He felt so good and smelt wonderful. My eyes were clouded in a haze of desire as our bodies lay close, our mouths touching almost.

His hands slipped around my lower waist and drew me in. "You wanted to see me," he murmured as his breath hit my face like a fresh breeze.

There was a lingering question on my mind that I just had to ask. "You didn't do it for your court appearance, did you? To make you look…" What was the word? I could not remember it.

"Ayla, I don't have to cut my hair to prove I'm a good father or a respectable person. I know I'm a good father, and I have people to back that up," he answered. Then his voice changing into a lower tone. "I cut my hair for you. I shaved my beloved beard for you, and I didn't even hesitate to do it."

"When did you do it?" I brushed my fingers against his smooth skin. "Did you cry?"

He laughed. His lips parted, and his tongue swept out, licking his lips. *Oh, god.* "No, I didn't cry. I did it once I got home after you bailed me out of jail. I needed you to see that I was willing to do what it took to get you back."

I nodded as my breathing began to quicken. "I can't believe you cut your hair and shaved your face." It was a grand gesture. My hands ran all over his soft skin, caressing and touching it. I could not get enough. "You look so different. It's almost like—"

"Like a rebound." He smirked and let out a pissed off growl, but his eyes danced with humour. "You have no idea how hard it was not to tell Holly to shut her fucking mouth."

I smiled, looking down then back up to him. "You hurt me. I'm afraid."

"I'll do my best to never intentionally hurt you again," he said with promise. "You're so beautiful. You consume me, Ayla. I can't live without you. I need you. I'll tell you how sorry I am, every single day."

Was that enough? I was still giving so much up for him. "We broke up. I wanted more."

"I know," he said quietly. He knows what I meant. I just didn't think he was able to give that to me. "I love you." Reaching up, he began to trace his fingers up my chin and cupped my face as I leant in against his hand. And then I remembered everything else that had happened tonight.

I hissed, pulling away from his hand and gently tracing my forefinger over my nose. "Sorry. It's just really sore."

"Are you alright?" he asked, his gaze growing concerned.

I had to tell him about this. He may not believe me, though. "Karen... She head-butted me." How humiliating speaking the words out loud! I wanted to shrivel up and hide.

"She what?" His voice boomed through the darkness and then lowered. "When?" He sounded pissed.

"Tonight. She turned up there at the bar. We had a scrap in the ladies, and she threw her heavy head straight into my face—hence the tank top. My other top got covered in blood." I could not look at him. I just felt so stupid for having to tell my ex-boyfriend that his ex-fiancé kicked my ass in a bathroom.

His fingers were once again underneath my chin, tilting my head back as he looked straight at me. "She's done that to me once or twice. You'll bruise, but I'll make sure it never happens again."

"How?" I did not believe him.

"Trust me, she won't step foot inside that café again."

I wanted to trust him, but he broke that trust once before, and he needed to earn it back. "Okay."

Both his hands held my face between his palms as he drew me back in. I was letting him. There was not a fight. I had missed him. I still miss him. "I love you."

"I love you, too." Oh, those powerful words felt good to say again.

He breathed what sounded like a sigh of relief. "I was afraid you stopped."

I shook my head slowly from side to side. "I could never stop."

His mouth closed in on mine, and our lips almost touched. My breathing was heavy but shallow. I waited for him to kiss me. I waited... and waited... and nothing.

He never kissed me. His head pulled away, dropping and resting in the crook of my neck as his arms wrapped around me tighter. He held onto me for dear life, leaving me no idea as to when he would let go.

Hours passed. It was only five minutes, but it felt like hours as I began to close my eyes from exhaustion. A yawn escaped, and that was when he finally pulled back. "You should be in bed sleeping."

"I should drive back home." Only I did not want to leave him.

"Stay."

I really should not. "Your…" His house. Karen. No, thanks.

His voice softly murmured, "Not there. I'll get us a hotel room."

"Griffin…" I became nervous, panicked even. "I can't… sex… we can't."

His eyes danced with desire. "Ayla, pretty, I wasn't even going to try and sleep with you. This isn't about sex for me. You're not just a pussy to fuck. That's just a bonus of being with you."

Oh, my. It was hard not to agree when he spoke to me like that. Plus, I really wanted a hot shower and bed to sleep in although it would be hard to fall asleep once we were in that bed together.

Funny how I could not get a hotel room earlier, but when Griffin called, they had one available. We walked back to the café to fetch the car, and he drove us down to a cheap motel that was not far out of the city. We did not really speak much, but I think words were not needed. The silence was comfortable. He went and grabbed the key as I waited in the car with the heaters on.

I stepped out to meet him, and he pointed to one of the rooms ahead. "Number eight."

His hand on the key, he pushed it into the metal hole. He turned it, and the door opened with a click. It was not anything spectacular. It was a cheap room, after all. It had a double bed, bathroom, and an inbuilt bench to make coffee—a seedy hotel room for a dirty night of fucking.

I yawned, stretching my arms out while kicking off my shoes. "There better be hot water."

"There will be. I asked about that. There are towels in there. Thought you might want to freshen up." He stepped closer, brushing my hair back from cascading the sides of my face and tucking behind my ears. "You're starting to bruise up. I'll go see if they have an ice pack or something. You're going to feel it in the morning."

"She said you… that you and her—" His finger pressed to my lips.

"No. I haven't and wouldn't."

I looked at him, like really looked at him, and cocked my head to the side, swallowing as I licked my lips and wondered if he was telling the truth although I knew he was. "You make all these promises now. What if the same shit starts to happen again, Griffin? I mean, what if we think that we're in love when really all that this is…" I waved a hand between him and me. "What if it's just lust?"

His brows dipped. "It's more than lust. You know that."

"Do I? You're my first boyfriend; I don't know how it's meant to go, but I do know how things were before. Me sacrificing my happiness for the sake of your relationship with her isn't what I want. I can't do that again." I refused to give in and be weak. I could not let him walk all over me again, same as with Karen.

"You won't have to. I told you, there's been no one since you walked out that night. I've been a miserable mess."

Chewing on my lower lip, I felt broken and bare to him. "You deserved to be miserable after how you treated me and what you've done."

"I know."

"That really broke me apart, Griffin. You in her house, lying to me." *And putting a strict no marriage and no baby ban on us.*

"I fucked up." His eyes were unsure. He could not tell what I was thinking. "Please, give me one more shot to prove that I won't hurt you again."

"But—"

"No buts, Ayla. There's been no one else since you—long before you, even," he spoke, stepping closer. "There's never going to be anyone but you," he yelled in an exasperated groan. "Don't you see? I don't want to be with anyone else. You own me, pretty. You have my heart. You own me. Don't you see that? If you're not with me, then I'm fucking nothing." He was baring himself to me, showing me the raw and hidden side that I never knew existed.

"Even if we've broken up?" I whispered, my eyes wide.

"Though we were broken up." He smirked as he grazed a finger gently over my nose, and I closed my eyes through the pain. When I opened them again, he was smiling still. "Go shower. You'll feel better afterwards."

Then his touch was gone, and I felt... empty. He had given me comfort, showed me the tender side I fell in love with again. My old feelings were beginning to resurface. I wanted him to hold me, but we could not. He was right; we had broken up.

So what the hell were we doing? We could not keep doing this secret meetings and moments together. It would only hurt us both, eventually.

Moving away, I turned and started to close the bathroom door shut when his voice brought me to a halt.

"When you said more, you were talking about what I couldn't give you, right?" If only he knew he had given me one of those things just fine. I, however, lost it and would not ever get that back.

I gave him a sad smile. I had my answer. "Yeah."

The hot water felt awesome against my naked skin. The water poured down, hitting my back as I stood facing the wall. I wanted to stay in here until the water ran cold. My exhausted body craved a massage, but a bed would do for now.

The shower curtain drawing back made me jump, turning to face a very naked Griffin as he stepped over the bathtub and in here with me. I went to cover myself, but like in the café, I was frozen to my spot.

"Griffin... What are you doing in here?" I blinked, making sure this was not a dream. My body wanted him. My heart needed him. Not once did I tell him to get back out again. It never even crossed my mind to kick him out.

He came towards me like a predator in the night. Hot water was falling over the both of us as he crashed his lips against mine possessively. A groan escaped his lips as he held me. His hands were dominating mine, pinning them up above my head as his hard body secured me to the tiled wall. I gasped against his mouth that tasted of mint mixed with a tinge of lime. *Oh, god.* I moaned. I moaned loudly and breathily. Another whimper came as he smoothly glided his tongue inside, over mine. Oh, to kiss a man without any facial hair. Passion took over, and his fingers clamped tightly before they loosened, letting them go. I was free, and I needed to touch him. My hands were grabbing his skin. Anywhere I could reach, I held. I needed him. I wanted him. I was *his*.

My back was against the wall as his erection pressed against my lower belly, stirring through to my core. The heat of needing him inside me was boiling up. I needed to feel his every ridge, the thickness taking me over and over. Our mouths finally parted, and I tangled my fingers in his short hair, tugging and enjoying its dampness. I kissed down his jaw, marveling at his soft skin. His hands cupped the curve of my ass, effortlessly lifting me up and slamming me back against the wall. I could feel the heat from his cock against my folds. I almost convulsed on the spot, but still, we did not go that far.

My arms wound around his neck as I kissed my way up his strong jaw, earning a throaty groan. I licked and sucked his lobe, and he found my mouth once again. We were kissing frantically, clawing at each other in primal need. This was enough—just kissing and holding onto one another. We pulled apart breathlessly after we had spent a great deal making out. My eyes slowly opened, and I could not help but smile. I realised his eyes were watering... and not from the shower. He had cried. I began to cry too, and his mouth gently placed another kiss to my lips.

With our foreheads resting together, our eyes connected. Our hearts were practically beating as one. He was home. I was home.

This was where we belonged, together.

"Marry me."

His words blew across my lips, a sweet whisper. It was not a question.

"Marry me," he repeated in a heavier, much more intense voice. Then he began to kneel in the bathroom tub on one knee.

Yes! I screamed in my head over and over—only that was not the word that came out.

"I lost our baby."

CHAPTER SIXTEEN

Kneeling at my feet, his expression changed and went straight from hopeful to confused.

"What?" he asked as he stood up, clearly not expecting that. His brows dipped low over his eyes that hid behind his furiously blinking lids. "Baby?" he whispered.

My heart was racing. How could a marriage proposal end up this badly? "I'm sorry."

"Ayla, what baby?" he asked again, repeating himself louder.

I finally found my voice, still feeling sick with nerves. "I was pregnant."

"And you didn't tell me that sooner?" he asked, incredulously. "Shit." He blew out a hard breath as his hands brushed through his hair. "When?"

Great, he was going to assume I was like here. "I didn't know until we were broken up."

"When, Ayla?" he asked more forcefully.

Okay, so no for small talking my way through this. "After we broke up. That first week."

"Did you take a test?"

"No."

"How did you find out?" He was shooting questions after questions, visibly frantic.

"I bled. Harvey was—"

"Harvey?" he glared. "You were with him."

Christ. I glared back. "Look, if you want me to answer you, then back up and let me finish speaking and stop interrupting me. Otherwise, this is only going to end with one of us storming out."

His jaw clenched, and his eyes darted away, but he nodded and took a step back away from me. "Go on." There was a hint of annoyance in that statement.

The truth, the whole truth… Just tell him.

"Like I said, I didn't find out until I was at my parents'. There was no test. I just started to feel sick. That same day, Harvey came up and visited me. He said you went and warned him to keep away."

"The fucker did the exact opposite," he muttered, unimpressed.

So much for no interruptions.

Ignoring him, I kept going. "I started to cramp, and then I had a massive bleed in the kitchen. I blacked out and woke in hospital. I didn't even know I was pregnant until I was told so. Mum told me it was an ectopic pregnancy and that nothing could have been done to prevent it. I was pregnant, and no, before you start accusing me, I hadn't stopped taking my pill or tried to get pregnant on purpose. I may have wanted a baby with you, but I wouldn't trap you or deceive you in such a way."

"You never told me," he spoke, sounding hurt.

"I was scared," I whispered. "You would have been so mad at me."

He took a step towards me again and looked down to my stomach. "You should have told me. I wouldn't have been mad at you. I know that you're nothing like her."

I eyed him. *Really? You really wouldn't have thought that, Mr. let-me-watch-you-take-your pills-every-morning.*

"I wanted to have your baby so bad." He knew this already. It was not a secret. "But I was eleven weeks along and had no clue."

"Make that two of us," he said with sarcasm, his brows still furrowed. "You should have called me at the fucking hospital, Ayla. That was almost what? Eight, nine weeks ago?"

I nodded. I knew this. "I'm sorry. I didn't know how to tell you."

"Harvey knew?" he asked, growing more uncomfortable. "I hate that he was the one who went through that with you. I would have dropped everything to be by your side and nurse you back to health, Ayla."

"I'm sorry," I repeated. I really meant that. "My body went into some kind of shock. I didn't know how to even wrap my head around it. Griffin, you scared the fuck out of me with your no babies speech. What do you want me to do? Call you up and say, 'Hey, I was pregnant but don't worry, I'm not anymore?' You think I would feel comfortable with that?" I shook my head, rolling my eyes. "I was afraid."

He glowered at me. *Sexy.* "I admit, my reaction to that wasn't well-handled. I didn't know what to do. I didn't want to hurt you, but I had to tell you how I felt. You were all gaga every time a baby was near. It was impossible not to see what you were craving."

And here I had thought I hid that well.

Bowing my head in shame, my eyes sprung with fresh tears. "I lost your baby. I just… How could I have not known?" It's something that I would always torture myself over. "I *should* have known."

"It wasn't your fault." He soothed my guilt away, lifting my chin, bringing me into his open arms, and holding me tight for a good few minutes. "Baby, I'm sorry you went through it alone."

Me, too. "How mad are you at me right now?" I asked, wondering if his taking his proposal off the table now that he knew I had hidden something this big from him. He had to be pretty mad. I had just sprung this on him at the most random time.

"Marry me, pretty."

I pulled away, opening my mouth with a soft answer. "Yes."

I don't think he heard me. He began to talk really rushed and nervously. "I've got a ring."

Whoa! Didn't see that coming.

"It's back home, but I brought you a ring. Weeks ago, the day after you left, actually. It's in the side draw, but I want this. I'm sure of it. I want you. This. Us. For the rest of my life. I need you, Ayla. You're the only pussy I want to fuck for the rest of my life."

Charming. Absolutely charming.

"Yes."

"Marry me."

Those words floored my heart to a halt again. "Yes." I smiled, and an excited laugh escaped my lips. "Yes! Yes! I will marry you!"

He beamed, and his eyes lighted up. That was the first time I have seen him smile heartily since we broke up. We kissed, and we kissed hard. The passion of fire was spreading through our loins, but then he pulled away all too soon, and I stood there slightly confused. "What are you doing?"

"Water is going cold," he chuckled, and sure enough, it was. I just did not feel the change.

The water stopped, and he drew back the old, ratty-looking shower curtain. "I'll get you a towel. Wait here."

I stood, dripping wet and shivering as he wrapped a yellow towel around his waist. He grabbed another, unfolded it, and opened it up for me. I stood as he began to dry me off, wiping the water away. Back on his knees, he patted me dry between my thighs and over my mound. When his face was at level with my flat stomach, he paused and grazed a finger over the two small round scars.

"You had surgery?"

I nodded, looking down. "They took out the tube."

"What does that mean?" he asked, standing once again. "You can't fall pregnant again?"

Was he worried about it? *Nah.*

"Yes, the tube was damaged. They had to remove it... but there's a good chance I can fall pregnant again." I hoped. Maybe, someday.

My hopes were dashed when he just nodded and continued drying me off. *Babies.* Not going to happen again, anyway.

I went to pull on my panties and was lifting my leg when he stopped me. Naked still, he stepped in closer. His erection thickened against my thigh as he looked at me. I tilted my head back, and he reached up, cupping the nape of my neck. His other hand drew in closer as his mouth neared mine.

I walked backwards towards the bed, and my calves hit the mattress.

"You said yes." His voice was a breathy murmur. "I have a ring."

My eyes hazed with lust. "You brought me a ring. I can't wait to wear it."

"I can't wait to fuck you while you're wearing it." *That.* "I really want to taste you." *Definitely that!*

Our mouths fit like the final piece of the puzzle. His hand slowly started to wander down my stomach, finding my fold to slide his finger up and down. His other hand cradled my head, running his fingers through my hair. A finger dipped inside me, and I moaned softly. I was so wet, soaked. His second finger entered, and I moaned against his mouth.

"Oh, god." That felt amazing.

His hand tightened in my hair, and he pulled on it. My neck was completely exposed. His mouth moved down to my neck, and I shuddered as I felt his hot breath against my skin. My hair prickled at the scalp. Oh, god. His teeth grazed on me, opening and closing against my flesh. His mouth sucked, tickling me with his tongue, and I felt my eyes rolling.

I missed this. *Hmm…*

His mouth went lower, down my chest to my breasts where his hot tongue trailed over. He flicked each erect nipple, teasing me as his fingers dip in and out in the same sensual pace. I clenched around him, roaming my hands through his hair.

His thumb twitches on my clit before his fingers slid back inside me and worked in and out, curling up towards my G-spot. "Don't sto—" Words failed me as my eyes rolled. I parted my lips as I sunk into the gratifying pleasure.

With a cry, my feet were out from under me, and my back fell flat on the mattress. His mouth moved lower, and his tongue traced down further to my stomach. Trailing around my belly button, he then kissed further down to the edge of my bare mound.

He kissed his way down. My breathing quickened when I felt his tongue against my swollen bud, already aroused from his thumb. He started to run circles around, knowing it would not take me long. His fingers worked faster as his tongue tasted me. I was soaking him. I could feel my juices soaking the sheets beneath me.

"I'm close." *Fuck.* I was going to come hard and everywhere.

"That's it, baby. Come for me." He growled against me, the vibrations from his voice breaking me apart.

Lifting my head, I glanced down through heavy lids to see him watching me hungrily. *Shit.* My orgasm tore through my lower belly. Curling my toes, I threw my head back, raking my hands through his hair and tugging them, arching up against him.

Grinding against his face, I blissfully came in ecstasy.

Moving up and over me, his hand wrapped around his thick erection, stroking up and down slowly. His eyes were already clouded with desire, and his voice was growing strained. "I'm not going to last long. It's been a while. Not even jerking off sated my need for your body."

"I… same." My naked body was underneath him, and I felt shy. "I'm scared."

Why was I scared? We were going to have sex, making love for the first time since we broke up. It was our first time as an engaged couple... oh, and since I lost our baby. *Shit.*

"We can't." My hands pushed against his chest. "I'm not... I'm not on anything."

"Nothing?" he asked. His eyes raked over my tits and further down to my spread thighs. "I'll pull out."

Pull out? He has done that plenty times before and came all over my chest. "Okay."

Steadily, he sunk into me in a sharp intake of breath. With his cock pulsing inside of me, my hands went around his neck, and I closed my thighs in on him.

Keeping each other close, we were home.

My chest was sticky with his semen, and he fell into the bed beside me. Quick was definitely right, but it did not matter. It was what we both needed—that first fuck of almost unbearable passion that bound us tightly.

And so our night went by with no sleep, just constant talk and laughter while I had an ice pack against my face to keep the swelling at bay. It was not going to help much, but the pain had died away at least.

Giggling, I lifted the pack and looked at him. "I can't tell my parents how you proposed to me."

"Why not?"

I raised a brow. *Really? Think about it, Griffin.* "We were naked in the shower. It'll be just like how they don't know the real way we met."

"Taking your virginity on table three at the café?"

I blushed, covering my face with my arm. "Don't bring that up."

Laughing freely, he took my hand from my face and kissed each knuckle. "Ayla, you could have told me you were a virgin instead of waiting until I was inside you to figure it out. I would have taken you somewhere else."

"I thought you'd change your mind. It could have been from your size. You just assumed I was a virgin." I was, but it was not something a girl on her twenty-first birthday would want to confess. "Plus, the motel was fun. That's where you fell in love with me."

"Sweetheart, I know I'm above average, but there's no way I wouldn't have guessed that."

I rolled my eyes and pulled my hand back, but he reached for it again.

"I like that I'm the only man to ever be inside you… to make you come."

"I like that too." I smiled, then a dreadful feeling went through me, kind of like guilt. "Harvey kissed me."

"What?"

Yeah, I should have mentioned that earlier.

"I didn't kiss him, just so you know. I made my feelings very clear that I wasn't into him." I sighed. "Actually, that's a lie. I thought that maybe you had moved on, and well, I went to take him up on his offer to move in and maybe start dating."

He did not say anything and just lay back and stared, watching the ceiling in the darkness. When he finally spoke, he was not yelling, but I knew he was fighting to stay calm. "When did he kiss you?"

"The night before I lost the baby."

"Four, five days after we'd taken a break?"

Baby, we'd broken up.

"How did he kiss you? What did you say? Where did he sleep?"

So many questions. I sat up and leant over him. "He slept in the spare room, and honestly, it wasn't a big deal. I didn't want it." That did not offer him any comfort. "Want me to show you?" I offered.

Raising a brow, he smirked. "Please do."

"You can't kiss me back. Keep your lips still." I leant further forwards, cupping his cheek and pressing my lips to his the same way Harvey had done. When I pulled away, he looked at me and burst out into laughter. "What?"

"Ayla, you're fucking kidding me. That was a peck, not even a kiss. I think I'll let that slide, but from now on, if he even looks at you the wrong way, and I'll lose my shit with him." He sat up, splaying his hand over my stomach. "Now, I'm going to show you how a real man kisses the girl he loves."

"You're up for that? Again?" I asked, with a wicked grin.

Oh, he was more than ready. He was close, and his balls were heavy as they slapped against my ass. My tits bounced with each thrust. I raised my hips up, creating a faster friction against him. He once again brought me to orgasm, and I came clutching his arms. Our eyes locked in on each other, and I knew he was seconds away from blowing.

"Pull out."

His voice strained. "I will," he promised. He would not forget not to.

His thrusts grew faster, and the head of the bed banged into the wall behind us. *Oh, shit.* He was fucking me, restraining me with his strong arms. He pinned my arms above my head and wrapped his other hand around my throat, squeezing gently. I could not move. I was crying out—sore, tender, and craving more. I did not need to guide him; my moans told him where to take me.

He took me to a blinding white place of pure heaven.

My eyes fluttered open, and I tried to talk. Instead, whimpers mixed with a jumble of words came out. I could not form a sentence.

"Griffin... pull out..." I grabbed his hip with my free hand, digging my fingers into it. I was trying to slow his thrusts down, but he kept pounding. We were pelvis to pelvis, animalistic—raw. His fingers gripped mine as he fucked me... until his cock twitched and pushed even deeper with three strong thrusts. His cock pulsed, spilling his fluid in satisfaction.

He came inside me unprotected with one hell of a guttural groan.

Oh, god. He was going to realise soon once the glory winds down and realise that he well and truly just fucked himself into the direction he did not want.

His ragged breathing calmed down after a few seconds. "I love you."

"You came inside me." I felt the need to state it very obvious.

"I love you," he repeated, ignoring me as he pushed himself up on both hands, hovering above me. He looked worried. "You didn't enjoy that? You look annoyed."

Of course, I enjoyed it, moron! "You know I did, but I told you I wasn't on any birth control, and you got carried away, then came."

"It was one hell of an orgasm."

I groaned with frustration. "Griffin."

"Ayla." He mocked back with a laugh. "Did you not come? Three times? You want a fourth? Shit. I'll fix that for you now."

He went to move, and I tightened my thighs around him to make him stop. "We just had unprotected sex."

His strong jaw tensed, and he leant down. Keeping his weight off my body, he spoke, "Our love is the type of love you don't just throw away. You fight for it, and I'm fighting, Ayla. I'm fucking fighting for it, for us. For everything you want, I want that too."

I had not expected it, but he was not mad at himself or me. He seemed normal, unfazed, and not bothered in the slightest.

He was gazing into my eyes. Each word that came out was a promise, a promise of a new path for us both, a different direction of a future, a future I had dreamed of with him: *marriage and babies.*

CHAPTER SEVENTEEN

"I have a question," I said to him as I lay naked in his arms, my fingers playing with his light spread of fine chest hair.

We have done nothing but lie there and talk after our love making. Both exhausted and slick with sweat, we tangled our legs and stole little kisses in between conversation. I could not stop touching his face. It was so soft and silky, smooth and clean. I could not believe he had a face underneath all that wire of hair before.

He had told me about the microwave dinners he had tried cooking for the boys, forgetting to peel off the foil wrapping, and then needing to buy a new microwave after it blew up.

I laughed. It felt so good.

It felt wonderful to lie in his arms and just feel happy again.

We talked more about Harvey and Karen, his plan to have the boys on a more permanent basis, and even of a weekend away to his parents. He was really trying. I could not wait to tell people we were engaged. However, I was not too sure if people would be impressed that Griffin had proposed on the bathtub floor in a seedy motel room, where we then proceeded to have some dirty, horny sex. *Oh, well.*

He stroked my hair softly. "What's that, pretty?" I *loved* when he called me that. It was more personal.

"If you were at the bar tonight, and Karen too… where are the boys?"

His answer was not immediate, but it was as if the wheels in his head began to turn, realising that they were both out without the kids. "That's a good question. She was meant to have them tonight."

"She's been at the bar every night this past week." My hand paused. "She wouldn't leave them alone, would she?"

"She's had the kids every night. I've been flat out at work. I kind of threw myself into it." He sat up, searching around for something and then sighed. "I left my phone at the house. I can't call them."

I looked at him cautiously, knowing that he was beginning to worry. I had to put aside my bitter feud with that woman and do this for him. "Do you want to go back there?" I asked.

He turned to me, raising a brow. "You hate that house if I remember correctly."

Point taken. "You know why." The ogre from across the road was the reason why. "But we're technically engaged." *Things will be different this time.*

"There's no technical about it, pretty. We are engaged." He lay back down, pulling the blanket over us both. "Let's get some sleep. There's nothing much we can do at four am, anyway."

"It's that early?" Time went by fast. I liked this bubble that we were in, just us.

His arm slid underneath the pillow my head laid on as he turned to his side, pulling me flush against his front. My back was to his front, and my ass was against his groin. Both of us were very naked. "I don't want to sleep."

"Me either," he whispered back, and I turned in his arms again.

"You're not going to regret it, will you?" I asked timidly.

"No." He knew what I was referring to.

I closed my heavy eyes as I lay against his chest, listening to the sound of his heartbeat underneath my ear. Today, last night... It was hitting me all of a sudden. I was utterly exhausted. "You didn't pull out."

"I was going to," he said, brushing his lips against my forehead. "But then I couldn't stop picturing you pregnant and how beautiful you'd look."

"Mmm." I smiled. I liked that. I really liked that a lot. "Promise you won't change your mind when I wake up?" I was afraid it was all just a big dream.

"Promise. Now go to sleep."

Peeking through one open eye up at him, I tilted my head back and held him tighter. "I love you."

"I love you, too."

I fell into a deep, completely sated sleep. Nothing felt so good to lie here, completely relaxed and at peace. It felt as though all my previous worries were vanishing away. We had grown so much in the time we spent apart, and I was not the only one who suffered. He suffered too in his own way. I can only hope that from here on out, we grow and take the steps forward to keep our relationship strong.

***

My body was not awake yet. It wanted to stay asleep, but someone had other ideas.

"Wake up. We've got to get up."

"No..." I moaned, not wanting to move. "Sleeping... Too tired." I was so not a morning person especially when I did not have coffee around.

"It's almost check out. Come, and you can sleep back at the house."

My eyes flung open but closed again. I was trying to force myself to wake up. This happened at least four times. Each time, Griffin was still in the same spot, watching me.

Trying to pull the cover up to just below my chin, I gave a little pout. "I don't want to get out. I'm nice and snuggly."

"And here I thought you were excited to see this ring I've brought you. Very well. I'll go pay for another night then."

"No." I was up. "I'm getting dressed." I was not moving, just grinning at him. "I want to see the ring."

We beat check out by three minutes. Griffin drove us back to his house—our old home together. I had spent the drive staring into the mirror, looking at the awful bruising forming around the top of my cheeks and underneath my eyes. Thank god, I was a girl who had concealer at home.

She was not out the front when he pulled up, and when we walked up to the front door, she still was not outside. That was new. Maybe she did not feel the need to pry on him because she assumed we were still broken up and over.

Oh, if only she knew.

Standing in the living room where we had had our last huge fight, a flood of memories surfaced again, and I swallowed, trying to pry them away. This was a clean start. We were starting over. We were both on the same page.

"You okay?" His arms slid around my waist, pulling me back against his chest.

Nodding, I rested my head underneath his chin. "I am. Tired, but I'm ok."

"Let's get you back to bed."

Without warning, he picked me up and carried me down to the bedroom. Everything was the same here. Nothing had changed except for me. I moved out and was gone for a while. Other than that, there was no sign of us ever living together or a girl being in the house.

Once I sat down on the edge of the bed, I smiled, watching as he walked towards his bedside table and pulled open his drawer. Searching around, I noticed a bottle of lube being taken out. He reached further in and pulled out something else.

A red velvet box.

Turning towards me, he paused, looking clueless. "Now? Or do you want me to propose again? Maybe over dinner? Romance... I should do it that way."

I stood, my smile not once faltering. "Griffin, put the ring on my finger before I go crazy waiting. You proposed perfectly." I did not want him to ask me any another way. The way he did it in the shower... it was perfect, full of emotion and so him.

The lid on the box opened, and I began to feel nervous. My eyes dropped down, and I felt every ounce of emotion I carried spring to life as he began to take out the ring with his large fingers.

"Hold out your hand," he whispered. His voice was showing his nerves. "If you don't like it, we can take it back. You don't wear rings, and we'd never really spoken about them. I didn't know what you would like, so I just went for pretty and expensive, and I remember you wanted sparkles." Sitting the box back on the dresser, he reached for my hand and slid the ring onto my finger.

Perfect fit.
Perfect ring.
Perfect man.

"I love it." It was stunning: rose gold, pear-shaped, and covered with little glistening diamonds. "You chose really well."

"Are you sure? Tell me if you don't like it, though. You said white gold, but I liked this one."

"Oh, I definitely love it."

A squeal escaped my throat as I held my hand up and wiggled my fingers, making it sparkle even more. My arms flew around him, and he picked me up and carried me back to the bed.

"I can't wait to marry you." I could not wait.

He grinned back. "Me either. Now, I want to fuck you wearing only that ring."

I laughed at that. With my back securely on the bed, he began tugging down my jeans and throwing them on the floor. "I want to see how good my ring looks as I'm holding your cock in my hand. Up here, baby!"

His cock looked amazing.

***

I called my parents, letting them know that I was alive and safe. I left out the staying with Griffin part, which was a conversation for when we are in person. I could not spring it on them over the phone. There was also our engagement, but I wanted to tell them that in person too.

Standing in the kitchen wearing a shirt of Griffin's and none underneath, he walked in as mum was talking about some cake she made that did not rise. Mid-conversation, my fiancé walked in wearing just a pair of tight boxers, and I looked up then back down. He was rock hard, again.

Arousal was taking over me as he came at me like a predator, pushing his body against my ass. His hands were starting to slide underneath his shirt. I had to end the call now. "Umm... Mum, I've got to go."

"Are you sure you're okay, honey?" she asked. *Jesus, yes. More than freaking okay.*

"Promise, I'll see you both later."

Ending the call and placing my phone back on the bench, I leant forwards as he ran his hard length up between my folds and slammed inside me. We both cried out in pleasure.

"Your mum... you told her?" he asked, easing back out again.

Don't stop. "No... I have to go back later today."

Only the head of him was inside me, so I tried to move backwards, wanting to engulf him completely, but he would not let me. "You're going back?"

"Mmm... Please, can we discuss this when I'm not twenty seconds away from coming?"

His hot breath blew against my ear. "Move back in. I can't stand being away from you any longer."

"Griffin..." *I don't want to live here.* "It's just..."

"Fuck me." A deep thrust, and his cock was buried to the hilt. "We'll move."

And that was how we decided to move and buy a house together.

I was sore and tired, and my thighs were killing me. We had fucked, fucked, and fucked some more. I was absolutely fucked and literally unable to move. I passed out once we had our second shower for the day and did not wake up again until his room was dark, and it was quiet.

Wandering into the living room, I saw him sitting on the couch with his legs propped up on the ottoman, cradling a laptop on his lap. Thank god. I could not do another round. My legs ached too much.

"Hey, you." I smiled, still half asleep. I took my spot beside him.

"Slept well?" he asked, turning to place a kiss on my forehead.

"Mm, I did. When did you get up?" I never heard or felt him move.

"Under an hour ago. I ordered some Chinese for us and then thought I would reply to emails before you wake up and drag me back to bed." He smiled.

Chinese. Yum. "I'm starving, and maybe we could look at houses?"

Eying me, he lifted his arm and wrapped it around my shoulder. "Ayla, you do know what I do for a living, right? Why don't we look at styles and build?"

"I work in a café; I can't afford to build a mansion." I pointed out. He knew this already.

"Stop worrying about the price and just look. You might see something you like. There is a lot of nice houses to design that doesn't cost a fortune."

Easy for him to say. "I'm only worrying because—"

Sighing, he went back to his laptop search. "You're not like her. So stop thinking you are and get the door. Dinner's here."

I laughed. "How do you know that?" I asked just as there was a knock on the door. Dragging myself back up, I called out and walked around the couch to the front door. "Fine. Make sure there's a walk-in pantry, and I want an en-suite for us with a huge bathtub!" If he wanted a list, I'd give him a list.

"Money's in my wallet," he added.

My head bowed, searching through his wallet for a fifty as I pulled open the door. I went to hand it over—until my eyes locked with the "delivery man." It wasn't a man nor was it our Chinese. She looked surprised to see me and shot me a glare. This would be interesting to see.

"Griffin," I called out. My nose could not handle another hit. "It's for you."

"What?" he asked and peered his head over the couch. "Shit. Karen, what are you doing here?" He was up and off the couch in seconds, heading to us at the door.

"I... I... Oh, I came to talk about the custody arrangements."

She was not here for that; I could tell.

"Now isn't a good time," he replied. "We're about to eat."

Speaking of food, the delivery guy turned up. About time. She moved aside as the young guy handed us two bags of food, and I eyed Griffin. *How much food do you think we're going to eat?* He shrugged and took the bags as I handed the money.

Should have realised that as I was reaching towards the guy with the money in my hand, someone was going to notice the huge diamond sparkling her way. Her mouth opened and snapped shut.

"Enjoy!" The young guy grinned after Griffin had told him to keep the change.

"You're... back together?" she asked, her words coming out like bile up her throat.

I nodded, and Griffin did the talking. "Yes. We're getting married."

Her eyes snapped to mine. *Oh, boy.* "You're marrying her? Are you fucking kidding me? How do you think the boys feel about that? You know you can't just decide all this on your own without consulting me. I am affected by this too. I don't feel comfortable with her around my children, Griffin."

"Excuse me?" he asked with a steady voice. "I don't have to ask shit from you. I'm a grown man. I make my own choices. Speaking of the boys, where were they last night?"

Oh, yes. She'd been out. Her eyes narrowed. "They're old enough to take care of themselves. I was out for an hour. After that, I came back home." I did not like that one bit. Those boys should still be watched. Maybe I was being over protective.

"After you decided to go to Ayla's work and attack her? You should have been with them, Karen. That's irresponsible."

She snorted. "Don't talk to me about being irresponsible, drag racing! You deserved getting busted." She smirked. She so told on him. Then her gaze came to me. "Oh, and if you mean after I kicked her ass, then yes, exactly." She was grinning. "How's the face?"

I was not going to give her the glory of knowing it hurt like hell. I just ignored her and turned to Griffin. "I'm going to take the food and keep looking at houses while you take out the trash." Yes, I called her trash. Petty, but Griffin chuckled.

He stepped outside, half-closing the door, and I could hear them well. She was never one for whispering as her voice screeched at him loudly.

"How could you go propose to her? She's a child."

He scoffed in disgust. "She's far from a child. It's none of your business, Karen. The boys love her, and so do I. You need to stop trying to assume there's something here between us." He went quiet. "I don't love you."

"You used to..." She pleaded, and my stomach knotted in jealousy that should not be there. "Don't you want your children to have a family? A proper family with both their parents together?"

I listened hard for his answer as I scrolled down on the laptop, pretending to be searching for houses.

He finally replied after a moment's silence. "I thought I loved you, Karen, but we were young, and I just thought with my dick. You tricked me by getting pregnant, and I stuck around for the sake of the kids. That's all. I'm sorry, but I can't give up my life just for the sake of our children. It wouldn't be fair, and they deserve to know what a family is really like, not one where their Mum and Dad are yelling and sleeping in separate rooms."

"You can't give them a proper family life with Ayla. She's not their mother."

He cut her off. "She's a mother to them. She may not be biologically related, but she loves them as her own, Karen. You just assume the worst in her. I wouldn't have asked her to marry me if I didn't think that part through."

"She's not their mother." She seethed in anger. "You hear me, bitch! You're not their fucking mother!"

I just sat there and did not bother to react. I knew I wasn't. If only she knew Mack called me mum, she would blow a fuse big time.

"Karen, enough. You need to go home to the children. If you have anything else to say to me, speak to my lawyer. I'm done. I gave you whatever you wanted, and you fucked me over with it."

"I want you," she whispered. "You'll pay for this if you marry her, I mean it."

"Goodbye, Karen."

I heard the door close shut and the lock flick over. It was time to change the subject for him. "So, I think I found one I really like. I'm just spending like you've got money to burn."

He smirked, coming back beside me. "Oh, yeah? Is that so?"

I turned and looked at him. His hand reached up and caressed my cheek. "I love you, Ayla."

"I love you."

"I'm sorry about Karen," he said apologetically. "She's delusional. I'm sorry I didn't see it before."

I nodded, thinking of all the drama it could have saved us if he did. "I think she's been hoping you'll go back to her. It's only hitting her now that it's not going to happen. Let's not talk about her. I just want to focus on us." I did not want her to put a damper on our evening together.

Not when I had my new shiny ring to stare at all day.

"Do you want to keep looking? Maybe we can go and do some more baby making?" he asked, wiggling his brows.

I laughed loudly. "Is that what we've been doing all day, huh?" I said, smiling as I nuzzled my nose against his. "How about we eat and keep looking at houses? Then maybe we can go give the ovaries a good shake up."

With a swift kiss, he smiled and pulled away. "Sounds like a plan to me, pretty. Now, let's see what I ordered. God, I'm hungry, and you need to eat."

He soon began digging through the delicious smelling bags of takeout. He had ordered all my favourites. Our night consisted of sitting on the couch, eating Chinese, and going through pages of homes to buy.

Turning to me, he moved the laptop from my lap. I eyed him cautiously. "Follow me." He stood, helping me up as well.

"What are we doing?" I asked as he led me down to the office.

"Do you remember the house I've been so busy building? The one out on a couple acres?"

"The really perfect one with everything in it?" I smiled, unable to forget that. "Have the owners moved in yet?"

He looked up, walking over with a black folder of paperwork. "How about next week?"

I did not understand. "Huh?"

"How about we move in next week?" He opened the folder, revealing drawings and interior designs. "It was for Christmas, but since it is finished now, why don't we move in next week?"

Then, it began to sink in.

"You built this house?" He nodded. "For us?" He nodded again. "So we were moving all along?"

"Yes. I was building us a home, a place away from here." He placed a hand over mine, squeezing gently. "I knew you weren't happy here, Ayla. I wanted to surprise you."

"Oh, Griffin!" I threw my arms around him, drawing him in. "I would love to move there, definitely."

It was a perfect night in, but even though we were in our own bubble of happiness, I had a feeling in the back of my mind that the perfect bubble was about to burst.

CHAPTER EIGHTEEN

"Hey, I told you not to pick that up," Griffin warned, taking the large box of bedding from my hands.

I stood in the driveway with a frown. "I'm able to carry things, Griffin. I'm not pregnant."

"You could be now. Just don't lift anything, Ayla. This was why I wanted to get removalists. They'd be able to do it all for us." My handsome, hairless-faced man wanted to hire people when we could easily do it all ourselves for free.

Just grinning, I shook my head. "Sorry, baby. I promise not to lift anything again, and why would I want to watch old men lift our things when I can perve on your sexy ass?"

"That's my girl." He leant in and kissed me before taking the box of bedding inside the house.

We were moving, if you could not tell.

We have done it. We went and moved into the house Griffin had built for me, together. It was exciting. We had brought new furniture and shopped together for everything. He had made a major effort, promising it would be different. Most of those purchases had been delivered yesterday, and today, we were getting the last of our things from the townhouse. And that was it. We were in our own house that we chose together. Well, we kind of did since he had been asking me questions about tiles and styles along the way, saying it was for the buyer.

All those visits were really him just making sure the builders were on track with the house.

He was putting up the townhouse for sale. It would be a clean, fresh start for us all.

It was a gorgeous and modern home on an equally stunning land. It was very farmhouse-like but modern with no dairy. The beach was so close that we could go down there for evening or early morning walks. It was different to his other house we were living in. This one was stunning on the inside with oak floorboards, white walls, and timber beams through the ceiling. It had a large kitchen without the dining room in it. I loved the kitchen, and its dark, handmade concrete bench island and black taps at the large sink. I would not even mention the pantry, which boasted another smaller kitchen. We now have six bedrooms which we could hopefully add to soon. When we walked inside, we instantly fell in love with it. I could see a little toddler running around, and Griffin could see all the places he was going to fuck me.

See? Perfect!

The dining room had sliding doors that opened up to a large deck. Now the view of the city was within our sights, and I knew that we would be spending many nights out there. We stood on the railing, watching the boys who were already off checking out the land, figuring out where they were going to make a BMX track for their bikes. Griffin wanted to get them motorbikes, but I was not convinced that they would be a good idea, as fun as they can be. We were getting those for Christmas.

My parents were not at all surprised that we were engaged. Griffin had called and asked for my dad's approval the day after he had been caught drag racing, and my father said yes. I could not believe it. Here I thought I was being sneaky when in fact, I had not been at all. They knew.

Griffin walked back down the front veranda steps, passing by Charlie and Paul who were carrying the LCD inside the house. "Don't drop that. Ayla will kill you both."

I laughed, shaking my head. "Yeah, he's right. I probably will." I turned to pick up a smaller box and heard a low cough behind me. "You're kidding, Griffin. What can I lift? I'm not going to hurt myself."

"Here, take these in."

I stared at him, unimpressed as he gave me his phone and wallet. "If I wanted, I could ignore you and carry something in."

"You could"—he said in a lower voice, coming in closer—"but you won't because, in the back of your mind, you're too afraid to."

He was right. My subconscious was afraid that I was pregnant with no idea again, and I did not want to risk anything this time. I only had one tube left, I needed that.

Snatching them up, I took his things and pretended to huff. "Fine. I'm going to start putting some things away. Can you ask the boys to come put their clothes away for me?"

"Yes, Mum." He smirked, patting my ass as I walked inside.

The boys both came running inside the house, and I raised a brow, peering around the kitchen island where I sat on my knees, putting away a box of baking trays. They both looked at me with wide eyes. They knew what they had done. "No running in the house, remember?"

"Sorry," they both grumbled together, going back to the back door and walking in again.

New house, new rules. No running, swearing, fighting, or slamming doors. Also, no Karen. The last one was the most important. *She comes in, and I'll be out for good*, I told Griffin that

He would make sure never to let that happen if he knew what was good for him.

When they walked into the kitchen again, Mack sat up on a yellow bar stool. "Dad said we had to do as you told us, and if we didn't, he'd get the belt."

I laughed. Yeah, empty threats worked well. "Did he really say that?" Suddenly, I was imagining my fiancé holding a belt in his strong hands and snapping it. *Oh, how I remember those days well.* Except the belt was hitting my arse as he pulled my hair from behind.

Toby nodded, sitting up beside Mack. "Yeah, but we know he's kidding. He said if we help really well, we might get a bike each."

"Oh, did he just say that?" I asked. Of course, he bribed them with a motorbike. "Well, all I would like you boys to do is unpack and hang up your clothes, then you can go play."

"Play? We're not five, Mum." Toby laughed and got up to go to his room. Mack followed, just grinning.

I would never get used to that. We had sat the boys down on the couch and announced our engagement to them. Mack asked if they had to call me mum, and I told them they didn't. There was no way I would put that kind of pressure on them.

Forcing them would only end in resentment, and that was something I did not want.

Toby then mumbled that if I would let them call me that, they would want to. I never expected that.

Of course, I said yes, but only if Griffin did not mind. It kind of turned him on, and he has been calling me that as well.

Karen had practically disappeared since we started moving out. She never once came to the house and have not even called. It was... dare I say, nice? *Touch wood.* I was not going to jinx this quietness from her.

Hours later, I closed the pantry door and bumped into Griffin's chest. His arms were instantly around my body. "Finished? I could think of a reason for us to go back in the pantry." His breath felt hot on the nape of my neck.

I nodded, trying to focus and turned in his arms, ignoring the innuendo to go for a midday quickie. "I'm finished. All that's left is to make our bed, and then the house is complete."

"Don't make it. We're only going to mess it up again."

"But..." *I have a new cover and everything.* "I went to Adairs. It's really pretty. I love our bedroom." It was a haven for just him and me.

"No buts especially tonight. You're going to need to hang on," he said.

Oh, I could not wait.

Charlie walked in, grabbing a bottle of beer from the fridge and cracking it with a sigh. "What a day. Definitely deserved this." I could not stop picturing him as a swinger. "Want one, bro?" he asked, grabbing another for Griffin.

My man took it with a nod. "Cheers. The women back yet?"

Maggy and Helena were at the store, grabbing some food for tonight. We were having a kind of housewarming party with friends and family, except for Griffin's parents who suddenly called this morning and told him they were unable to make it.

They would regret that. It was not just a dinner they were missing.

"Oh, hey. Guess what?" I said, slapping his chest as I forgot to tell him about my earlier call. "I got fired."

"What?" His frown was back on. "When?"

"Like three hours ago. Mum called and told me I was no longer needed. She has sold the café, and the new manager heard about my fight. So, I was pretty much fired." I was not happy about it. I loved that job. "You want to know the reason?" It was a great one. "Someone called and put in a complaint that I got violent in the bathrooms."

"Fuck off," Griffin said, almost growling. "You're kidding me?"

"She threatened to sue if they didn't fire me. Well, look who now is jobless." I hated that I was not working. It gave me something to do. God, I hated Karen with a passion. "She offered me a job at the new café in Mosman only forty minutes ago."

He pulled me to his side. "I'm sorry. Is the new café something you want to do?"

"No, it's okay."

"Probably for the best, anyway."

I eyed him, trying to take the drink from him, but he moved his hand higher in the air. "You're just saying that because you're happy I no longer have to work with Harvey."

"He kissed you."

"I thought it was a peck?" I teased.

"I should go break his jaw," he muttered and took a mouthful.

Laughing, I patted his chest and turned to Paul as he walked in to join us. "I'm going to make our bed. Enjoy your drinks, boys." They had earned them after all the hard work today.

"I told you not to make it," Griffin called out, and I just laughed, ignoring him.

Sitting on the edge of the bed, I got a fright when Mum walked in holding a metallic, silver spotted cushion. "I think these were just too lovely to pass up. They'll go well with the new couch."

"Thanks, Mum." She did not leave the room, and I raised my brows. "What's up?"

"Did I hear the boys calling you mum earlier?"

Oh, boy. "You did. They've done it since we told them we were engaged."

She nodded, gazing at me with that motherly look. "You're happy, yes?"

I groaned. *Please don't start this are-you-sure talk now.* "Yes, Mum. I'm very happy, and I love the boys. If I didn't, then we all wouldn't be here starting a life together."

"What about Karen?"

"I don't know. She's been quiet. I think maybe she's going to stop harassing us and be nice for once."

"Well, all I can say is it's a darn shame his parents didn't come by to help. I feel sorry for Griffin."

In a way, so did I. It must be tough to have parents who were judging you for everything you've done or thought you always needed to do better, be better. I got lucky with mine.

Even if I screwed up, they were always there for me to offer comfort and support.

When Mum left, I stood up and closed the bedroom door. I needed some privacy right now.

Dialling his number, I called Harvey for the fifth time this week. He was not answering me and barely spoke to me at work. It rang, and I sighed, tossing my phone aside after leaving another voice message. How could he just tune me out like this? He had been there for me constantly when Griffin and I were having troubles, and now that I was back with him, he was not to be heard of.

Men are so frustrating.

Fixing the bed, I made my way outside where the others were and took my spot on Griffin's lap. His arm wrapped around my waist, drawing me in closer… or maybe he did that, so my boobs were close to his face. You never knew with this guy.

"Are you nervous?" I asked, running my fingers through his hair.

"A little." He shrugged. "I guess. The judge didn't really say much to give any indication what the verdict would be."

"I don't see why you won't get half the custody. You're a good dad, and the boys want to be here." It was a fair proposal: one week here, one week there except Griffin did ask that he not pay Karen during the weeks he had the boys. His lawyer strongly agreed.

Placing a kiss to his temple, I just sat listening to them all talk. Then the conversation went to Griffin and his racing charges. He got off lucky with just six months' probation period and the loss of three points and a fifteen hundred dollar fine. He was not going to do anything wrong in the way of the law anytime soon.

Karen had been so sure he would suffer and do jail time, but as Griffin pointed out, she had no proof. Besides, it was a one-time event. There was no proof of anything—even of those poker nights he attended. There was no sign of him being involved. He pled guilty to speeding but fought the reckless and hoon charges.

With the fire pit burning a heated flame, we brought out some fruit and cheese platters, kind of a pre-welcome dinner fix. Mack was inside when I went to grab another box of crackers and some dips. He came up licking his lips hungrily.

"Yum, can I have some please?"

"Course." I glanced around, making sure we were not going to be overheard. "I want to talk to you for a moment."

He looked nervous, and his eyes lost contact. "Am I in trouble?"

"What? Course not, unless you've put a hole through your wall already?"

He and Toby got into a massive fight early morning last week. We had woken up to a startling bang, and Griffin found an Xbox controller hanging out of the wall. Apparently, Mack had a temper when pushed enough. He was grounded from reading Harry Potter for the remaining two days he was with his dad.

"No, I haven't."

"Good. Now, I want to know when you're going to talk to your dad about a certain something. You can't keep this from him forever." Griffin needed to know, and this secret made me feel guilty for hiding it from him.

His eyes grew wide. "You can't tell him. Please, you promised."

"I know I did, but you need to tell him. Soon, he would hate to find out through someone else." He would be more hurt by that. "Promise me that you'll tell him soon."

"Okay, I will."

I shook my head. "Not good enough. Promise me."

Looking up, he nodded. "I promise, Mum."

Ahh, melts my heart.

Good, about time. "Good boy." I reached over and handed him a bowl full of chips. "Take this out for me."

As I walked out, Griffin was on his way in with an empty bottle of beer. He winked and grabbed hold of my hand, pulling me back into the kitchen. He dragged me willingly down the hallway and towards our new bedroom.

Closing the door, I began undoing my jeans. "What do you think?"

"You're sexy as fuck."

Giving him an eye roll, I pulled down my panties. "Not me, the bedding. The room?"

He looked around as I lay naked in the middle of our bed, my thighs spread and inviting him into me. Then he began pulling his shirt off and working on his jeans. His eyes still on mine, he glanced to my pussy and then back up again. "Like I said, sexy as fuck."

His cock thrust in with such force that my eyes rolled to the back of my head. My back arched slightly to let him in me deeper as I slid up the bed, wrapping my legs around his hips and slamming my hips back down on his cock.

I was so close to coming when I heard a noise. "Someone's coming." *Oh, the irony.*

"No." Pausing, he glanced towards the door before looking back. The footsteps faded and went away. "It's okay. Keep going. No one will come in."

His rhythm continues, pulling in and out slowly as our bodies met thrust after thrust until his strokes turned violent, uncontrolled, and raw. Our mouths kissed deeply, and our hands grasped skin as we moved together. Tightening around him, I let go and lost myself in him. I grabbed his ass and pushed him in deeper as I grind up and down against him.

"I'm going to come." He grunted. "I'm coming."

My teeth bit into the flesh of his shoulder as I moaned loudly. "Oh yes… Come with me."

We cleaned ourselves up after that. I nervously giggled, hoping no one noticed we were gone for too long. As I changed into a new pair of panties, Griffin reached inside the closet and pulled out a pair of black dress slacks, a crisp white shirt, and a pair of suspenders. I turned, looking away from him as I continued to put on my panties and bra.

When I turned, he was already dressed and doing up his shoes as he sat on the edge of the bed. Tying his last lace, he sat watching me dress. God, this man in those clothing… damn.

Definitely husband goals.

"Can I help you?" I asked, walking over to the walk-in robe and pulling out a dress. It was a white backless dress with gold embellishments around the front that went around to the back and hang down along the free falling skirt like chains. It was simple but perfect for this occasion.

I slipped it on easily, and he kept watching me. "Just can't take my eyes off you right now. You're perfect."

"So are you."

Running my fingers through my hair, I came towards Griffin, unable to take my eyes from him. I scrunched my dress up around my thighs and straddled his lap.

"You're so beautiful, you know that?" He smiled, his hands holding onto my hips. "I wasn't too rough with you, was I?"

"Since when did you care how rough you are?" I asked, resting my arms on his shoulders. "You didn't hurt me. And no. I don't know, but I do enjoy hearing you telling me that."

He smiled, but it did not reach his eyes. "What if I lose the boys?"

"Baby, no," I reassured him, brushing a hand through his hair. "You're not going to lose them." I hated that he doubted himself so much as a father. "You need to think positive. It's all going to work out, and you need to believe that."

He nodded, resting his forehead on mine. "I know. I just worry. What if I can't get you pregnant?"

Oh, god. Way to change the conversation. "Griffin, we've been trying to get pregnant for like a week. The doctor said within two years is achievable. I'm not expecting anything to happen soon. I'd love it too, but I don't think it would be easy." I wished it was, though. "Let's not worry about that, or you'll drive yourself crazy."

"Hopefully," he mumbled and glanced over towards the clock. "Nervous?"

"Not a chance. It's almost six," I whispered in his ear. "We should go tell them what's going on. Yeah?"

His smile grew, and the sad man was gone. Griffin laughed as I moved from his lap to a standing position, turning and smiling at him as he smiled right back. "You sure about this? There's no going back."

I nodded. I was more than ready. "Yes. Come on."

I held out my hands, and he took them. We walked outside, and I noticed the car pulling up in the driveway. There was no turning back now. I grinned eagerly as Griffin went to answer the door and let the woman inside. After a briefing, she followed us outside. I stayed back for a moment while Griffin spoke to everyone.

"Ah, about time. Can I fire up the barbeque?" Charlie asked. "Where's the meat?"

"You're not getting anywhere near the meat, not after last time." Griffin laughed, looking back towards me. He looked incredibly handsome right now.

"What's going on? When are we eating?" Charlie's wife asked, frowning. "Why are you dressed up?"

"Soon." Griffin outstretched his hand to me, grinning widely. "Afterwards."

"After what?" Bryan asked. His voice came to a halt as his eyes landed on mine. "Oh, fuck you look—"

Griffin replied breathlessly. "Gorgeous."

My mum gasped, and her hands flew over her mouth as I walked towards Griffin, and his hand squeezed mine.

I smiled and finally found my voice. "So are you, handsome." His side-parted hair and the suspenders... Oh, my. He even added a bow tie. His white sleeves were rolled up to his elbows, revealing his sleeves of tats. Like I said, definitely husband goals.

I was so in love.

"Umm... What's going on?" Bryan and everyone seemed to have lost their words.

Looking back to Bryan, I answered him, "After we do something, we'll eat. But for now, you might want to go over to the garden." The garden had been lit up with a twinkle of fairy lights leading towards a tree where the woman now stood. I could not stop smiling.

Maggy sucked in a sharp breath as she took note of our formal attire. "Oh, my god! You're not... I can't breathe."

"Yes!" Helena clapped her hands together with excitement. "Please tell me you're doing what we think you're doing."

"Dad, Mum... what's going on?" Toby asked. His smile said it all, though. Mack just grinned.

A new home. A new start. A new life. Together, forever.

Griffin nodded, placing a tender kiss on my hand. "We're getting married."

CHAPTER NINETEEN

"I promise to always leave the lights on in the bathroom. I promise to mysteriously take three hours to make a simple breakfast as I have no idea how to cook. I promise to create a life for us of unexpected and strange adventures. I promise that I will love you."

Blink back the tears, damnit.

"I pledge to listen to your advice and occasionally take it. I pledge to never take score on *Super Mario*... even if I'm totally winning. I pledge to always admire your huge, strong, kind, and determined heart. I pledge that I will love you."

My heart is close to exploding.

"I vow to listen for as long as it takes for you to feel heard. I vow to watch in awe as you kick ass and take names. I vow to be your unrelenting cheer squad on the days it feels too much. I vow that I will love you."

I'm losing it.

"I believe that me-time is an actual concept that can be proven by science. I believe that carefully folded underwear makes you happy. I believe there is no time or place I'm more content than when you're close to me. Because of this and so, so much more... I believe that I will always love you, Ayla."

Tears were running down my cheeks as I became a blubbering mess.

His vows were everything, and so much more.

I could not believe he had come up with that on the spot. Seriously, who the hell knows how to speak romance like that? I could not even talk. I was too busy biting my trembling lip, afraid to open my mouth in case I burst into tears.

"It's okay," he whispered, reaching forward and using the pad of his thumb to wipe away the tears underneath my eyes. "Take your time. I'm not going anywhere."

Ahh… I could not take the feeling I was feeling right now. I wanted to throw my arms around him and kiss him like crazy—then drag him off to our bedroom and bang him like a hammer.

My vows were so going to suck compared to his.

"Griffin…" I began, taking in a steady breath to calm myself. "I love you."

He grinned, mouthing *"I love you, too"* back to me.

"You make loving easy. For starters, you're the best roomie I've ever had. Living in sin without our parents' blessings was totally worth it. I now know you are able to deal with my annoying habits, and I've discovered that you have very few. You pick up my half-empty coffee cups that I leave around the house, and you make me breakfast on the weekends even if it takes you hours. You stay up until I finish work even if you're asleep when I come home. I know you try to stay up.

"You always know where my phone and keys are when I go into full panic mode and scream that someone stole them."

Like my coffees. "With you, I have learned to take it slow—although I could have dealt with getting to this altar a little faster. When we met, all I knew was that you made me laugh and that you had a dorky look, which I thought was seriously hot. Only time would allow me to see your true colours. You're generous, loving, sensitive, kind, an insomniac, and a lover of man baths."

He burst out laughing, blushing slightly as his friends roared in laughter.

"I promise with all my heart to love you when times are good and bad. When you're sore on Monday from sitting the same position all day during Sunday football, when men hit on you, and when you need someone to lean on when work gets tough, I will always be your girl.

"When I'm scared, you make me feel safe. When I'm sad, you make me smile. We've had tough days, but there's never been a day where I have stopped loving you. I never want there to be one.

"I promise to continue loving your children as if they were my own as I officially become your partner in their lives. But most of all, I promise to love you under any circumstances; happy or sad, easy or difficult, through the sunshine and through the rain for the rest of my days. I am the luckiest girl alive, and I couldn't imagine growing old with anyone else."

I turned towards Mack and Toby who were standing near Griffin's side. I had something to say to them now.

"Thank you for sharing your daddy with me, loving me, and allowing me to love you with all of my heart. I was not there when you took your first steps, but I promise that I will love and support you in every step that you take in your life."

I was crying, and so was he. Mum was sobbing. Even Dad teared up. It was all happy tears around.

As soon as we were pronounced husband and wife, Griffin flushed me to his front and tongue down my throat, kissing me with the most passionate kiss I had ever felt before. His hands snaked around my waist and dipped me backwards.

I felt his smile against my lips. "Want to skip to the honeymoon?"

"Mmm... I do."

"Get off her," someone from the crowd said.

We finally pulled apart to see my mum dabbing her eyes as she came up towards us. "You're not skipping out on us yet. We're going to celebrate this wonderful surprise."

My hands grasped hold of his strong biceps as another camera flash went off. "I'm sorry I didn't tell you sooner."

Her brow raised, but I knew she wasn't being serious. "Yes, quite the shock to see your only daughter getting married."

We had not planned on it. It was just a spur of the moment thing. We had been discussing possible wedding dates and were leaning more towards in a year. Then we had shared a look between us and asked, why wait? We wanted this. We wanted to marry. We had that discussion, the baby talk, and then talked about a housewarming party. We decided to be different and combine the two without telling anyone.

My dress was bought last week, and Griffin picked up our rings yesterday morning.

"You look lovely." Helena gushed, coming over. "I can't believe you got married. I knew it'd happen soon."

I still did not know what to make of her and Karen. They were all close. It would only be a matter of time before she knew and rain hell on our lives.

Bring it on. We were ready for whatever was to come.

Griffin's hand slid down my ass and squeezed. "Who knew she'd look that good in a dress."

I laughed, lightly slapping his chest. "Excuse you. I like my jeans and shorts."

"Yeah. Well, I like you in that dress." His hand squeezed once more. "I also think someone should be helping out the big fella with that meat. I don't trust him to cook after last time." He turned to me and winked, both knowing it was not actually food poisoning I had, but a bun in the oven.

"Go help. I'll help inside," I offered, about to head on in.

"Oh no, you don't." Mum pointed towards the garden. "You two... over there and get some photos taken. Mack, Toby, you too, please."

After what I felt like a gazillion photographs, we were allowed to go back to everyone else. The food was amazing. Boy did I eat a ton of food. Griffin was pleased I did not want a drink. He was on baby patrol like you would not believe. It was insane. For a man who was happy to just give up marriage and babies, he had done one hell of a turnaround.

His hand grazed up and down my hip as I sat on his lap, feeling his warm breath hitting my neck. "What are you thinking about?"

"You," I replied.

"What about me?"

I nestled my nose against his cheek. "Just how I can't wait until you finger me with your ring finger."

Shifting in his seat, he gave a low cough. "Is that so? When can I do that?"

"Soon." I wanted to go to bed really soon. I went to move, but his arm tightened around me, keeping me in place. Someone had an erect cock poking against my ass. Drunk on happiness, I leant in with a giggle. "Naughty husband. You know I could just up and leave you here."

"You could, but then my father-in-law would also know that I was hard for his daughter, and I don't fancy being knocked out on my wedding night."

Yeah, my dad would definitely not appreciate that one bit.

I sat and waited until his raging hard on finally turned soft and got up to go grab something else to eat. I was quite impressed with myself that I had not spilt anything on my white dress. Griffin was still uber sexy with those suspenders and his bow tie now taken off. By now, the top three buttons of his shirt were already undone, showing off a hint of chest hair. My parents left with the offer of taking the kids to give us a wedding night, but we declined. We wanted to share the first night in our new home with the boys.

Plus, their rooms were way away from our bedroom. They would not hear anything, hopefully.

We laughed and talked about how Griffin proposed in the shower. Of course, I skipped the wanting my pussy for the rest of his life part. The night had been perfect—almost.

Karen's voice interrupted us. "The front door was locked. What's going on?"

Are you kidding me right now? Like, seriously? She was not meant to be here.

One day was all I asked for—one day to not have her in our faces. It was our wedding day, and I especially did not want to see her today. She was not even invited. This was Griffin's time with the boys, and Karen knew. She damn well knew that. My heart was not able to take any more. This woman could not take this day from us. It was our day. We were a family here, and

Karen could not ruin it. As much as she tried, she needed to get the hell out of our property before I lost it and smack the bitch out.

My eyes found Griffin. He was already standing, muttering fuck as he took off towards her, stalking and glowering directly at her. "You need to leave. Now." His voice was cold and harsh.

"I missed the boys. What are you—Why are you dressed up?" She went to touch his chest, and he flinched away.

"Karen."

Her eyes filled with tears. "Griffin... Please, let me spend five minutes with them. I miss them."

"Karen!"

"No. Please don't do this. You let me come over all the time before. Just five minutes."

Was she kidding me right now? What the heck?

"It's my damn wedding, for Christ sake. Do not come here and wreck this for us. You need to leave now."

Her eyes widened, looking around at everyone there and realising that her friends were celebrating with us. It must have finally hit her that it was done and over. She had no claim to him anymore. He was off limits—married and completely taken. I began to stand, and her eyes narrowed at me.

It was nothing compared to the slap across the face she got as the two boys came yelling excitedly towards me from the other side of the house where she could not see.

"Mum! We found a spot."

Toby cut Mack off. "We know where we want our bike track. Come and look, Mum!"

"Mum?" Her voice was a low, menacing hiss as her eyes glued to mine.

Every hair on my body stood on its end. *Oh, shit.* "Boys, go play," I said. They did not need to see any of this.

"Griffin, what the hell is this?" She went past him and came at me.

Maggy was running over to her along with Helena. "Karen, this isn't the time or place. You should go."

"Bullshit! You're all meant to be on my side. How could you? How long have they been calling her mum for? She isn't their mother, Griffin. I told you how much I didn't want that, and now you've gone and forced it on them!"

"I didn't," I said in a whisper. I did not force them to.

"I never asked them to. Neither did she. They asked her, and you know what? I don't care how you feel about it. You're completely irresponsible, leaving them alone for nights at a time. I found out about your weekend bender and leaving them to fend for themselves. Now get off my property before I have the police called and your chances for custody are done for." His hand thrust out, pointing back to where she came from.

Karen glared again, ignoring him and screaming at the top of her lungs. "Mack! Toby! Come here now! You're coming home with me!"

Both boys slowly walked over, but neither looked happy. Toby spoke up as Mack hid behind him. "We don't want to leave. We want to stay."

Her eyes narrowed. "Get in the fucking car now. You're coming with me. Do not make me walk over there and get you." She glowered at them, threatening the boys with an obvious punishment.

"Look, Karen, you need to leave. I'm calling the police." Bryan pulled out his phone and began to dial a number. He looked up at her with threatening eyes. "Last warning. You need to leave. Now."

Karen pointed and poked her finger into Griffin's chest, but he did not budge. "You fucked over the wrong woman. All of you can fucking rot in hell! I'm done!"

She left us all gobsmacked. We stood there, wondering what the hell had just happened. The boys were obviously shaken, and our night had come to an end. Nothing to ruin a party like an ex with a mission to destroy it.

I took them inside and led them to their new rooms. Not much was said as they climbed into their beds. I tucked them in, walking out once Griffin came down to say good night. She really knew how to put a damper on our evening.

Scooping my hair to the side, I went to undress when the bedroom door closed behind where I stood. "Here, let me help with that." His voice was soft, calmer. "I'm sorry for how everything turned out."

"Don't be. It's not your fault." The back of my dress unzipped and pooled at the bottom of my feet.

"I should have seen this coming. We can sell and buy somewhere else untainted by her if you want. I'll do anything to keep you happy."

I smiled. "I like this house, and she was just outside. Next time, I'll get the garden hose on her." *Or charge at her with a pair of hedge trimmers.* "She's becoming unpredictable. It's frightening." She was scary at the best of times. Now, she was just plain crazy.

"I'm going to call my lawyer in the morning. I think custody may have just gotten worse." He was right. Things were going to become harder for him now that she knew the boys both wanted to call me mum. "What you said tonight in your vows…

How you spoke to my sons, Ayla… I don't even know what to say to that. It meant more than you could know."

"I love you and understand you're a package deal. I love them like my own."

"I really don't deserve you… her coming here…"

Turning in his arms, I tilted my head back to look up at him and slide down one of his suspenders. "No more talk of her. It's our wedding night." A playful smile tugged at the corner of my lips. "Let me undress you and make love to your cock with my mouth, and then you can have your wild way with me."

"Jesus…" he groaned and fell into bliss as my warm mouth made him forget all the worries of tonight.

***

A ray of sunshine warmed up my naked back as I lay with my eyes half closed. The body pressing behind me gave me a smile as his arms drew me in closer. No words were said as my leg was lifted and he slid inside me. I moaned, wincing as we had only just fallen asleep not long so ago. He was still obviously, in the mood. Last night had been amazing, especially that part when he told me to hang on. Damn, he really meant it. He left no part untouched, kissing and sucking my breasts as he fucked me deliciously. His cock had me in every position possible, and we finished the night off with a tender lovemaking. I was utterly spent.

"Griffin…" I reached behind as I tangled my fingers in his hair, pulling him in for a kiss.

His tongue slid down my throat, and his body was heavy on top of mine as he begins to plow in deeper. Hard and fast, our breathing matched each other. My eyes closed, and I arched against him as we both come together.

No, less than two seconds after he rolled off me, our door opened, and two sleepy-looking boys stood at the door. "We're hungry."

"Give us two minutes. We'll be out there soon," Griffin answered, keeping the covers over us both—mainly me.

Toby rolled his eyes. Walking away, he called out. "You do know, that bed isn't as quiet as you think."

My face flushed with heat as I covered my eyes with my palms. "Oh, god." I wanted to hide. "Do you think they heard us all night?"

"No. Probably just then," Griffin grinned and planted another kiss. "I'll make a start on breakfast. You have a shower if you want."

"Nope. I'll cook and wait until you're ready to take one too." I smiled, reaching for a bra and something to throw on quickly before they come back in again.

Pancakes… waffles… bacon and egg…

The boys were still unsure of what they wanted to eat. Mack just wanted anything while Toby and Griffin were changing their mind. As they were having what sounded like an in-depth conversation about food, I made the whole lot.

"Someone's here, Mum." I looked up to see a shadow at the door when Mack walked over to take his plate of food from me.

Griffin and I shared a look. Mine said, *Please let me handle this without you going all caveman and beating the shit out of him.* He nodded and sat back down.

Harvey stood at the door with his hands shoved into the pockets of his jeans. "Hi."

"What are you doing here?" I asked, stepping outside with no intention of inviting him in.

"I got your messages."

"Nice to know. You could have replied back to one of them." I was not forgiving him easily. "Where have you been? You just dropped off the face of the planet."

He shrugged and blew out a long breath. "I heard you got married. When?"

So he knew that already.

"Last night. You were invited, but you know... never answered the calls at all." No, he was not invited due to Griffin's strict *No Harvey Policy*. "You should go."

"I'm sorry," he whispered. "I never meant to hurt you."

Ha, you never hurt me. Just embarrassed me, maybe.

Looking around uncomfortably, I said, "It's fine. I'm glad you found someone." Whoever she was, she must really be something for him to give up his playboy ways.

"She's pregnant... six months along."

Oh. My heart ached in jealousy. Well, then. I could not really say much to that. "Umm. I'm happy for you."

"I didn't think I wanted kids, but when she turned up and told me the baby was mine—"

I cut him off. I could not bear to hear any more. "Please. Just go. I'm happy for you, but you need to leave, Harvey."

"He won't let me in?" he asked, nodding as he spoke of Griffin.

"It's not just him. I think we need some time apart. I have to focus on my family, and you need to do the same. You're going to be a father."

"I wish we could have done this together." His confession made me feel guilty. I did not need to hear this. He should never have said that to me.

With a smile, I walked back to the door. "Take care, Harvey."

Griffin walked over to me as I closed the front door. "Are you alright?" He had obviously heard, and it was hard not to be jealous that Harvey was going to have a baby soon. It was something I wanted with all my heart.

Smiling, I slipped my arms up under his shirt and hugged him tightly. "I'm okay. Now, let's eat before we go search out this place where you're going to build a BMX track for our boys."

Griffin stopped me before I could walk away, his eyes searching mine for something. "Ayla, you'll be pregnant soon. I promise."

"I know."

I hoped so, but then again, when does anything ever go my way without me suffering some kind of consequence?

CHAPTER TWENTY

"What do you mean I can't pick them up?" I asked, frowning at the teacher from Mack's classroom.

The tall, slim woman held her nose high as she sighed heavily as if speaking to me was a problem for her. "I'm sorry, miss. You can't take them home."

"It's Mrs. James," I corrected, still trying to get used to that name myself.

"Miss Holloway, you can't stop her. She's our mum." Toby frowned, crossing his arms over his chest.

I smiled at him for defending me. He's such a sweet kid.

His teacher shook her head. "Karen Morgan is written down as your mother. I'm sorry, but you cannot leave with a stranger."

Toby's hands were in the air as he exclaimed, "But they're married! She's not a stranger. We live with her and Dad. Oh god, he's going to be so mad when he gets here. I can't wait. Where's the popcorn?"

She just ignored him. "I will wait for your father to arrive."

"I'm Mack and Toby's stepmother. Why can't I take them home?" It was our week, and Griffin had no problems with me picking the boys up. They were teens, for crying out loud. "You're making a big deal out of nothing."

"It's called protecting the children, Miss James."

"It's Mrs. James, and don't give me that."

Her brows raised. "You cannot take the children because there's been a formal letter, addressing us that you're not authorised to do so. Please, just wait until their father comes to collect them." Well then, that explained that. With a defeated nod, I took a seat beside Toby and rolled my eyes. He smirked, and Mack slumped forwards, burying his head on the desk.

"For fuck's sake." *God, my panties get wet every time he gets mad.* "This is pathetic."

Before long, my knight in shining armour was here—well, knight in a navy blue suit who rocked a week-old shadow around his chin. Standing up, he came over and kissed me on the cheek then looked at their teacher. "I thought this was cleared up. She's my wife."

I'm his wife! I loved saying that to anyone and everyone who would listen.

"Mr. James, there had been a formal complaint made about your... partner coming to collect your children."

"They walk home when they stay with Karen. What fucking difference does it make if my wife picks them up herself?" Griffin shot back, glaring.

"Maybe you could have a one-on-one session with Karen to dis—"

He cut her off once more. "Bullshit. This isn't even an issue. Mack and Toby are my sons. Ayla is my wife, and Karen is the only one with the issue. I'll be getting my lawyer involved." Turning from her, he motioned for the boys to grab their bags and leave. "We're going, and I authorise my wife, Ayla, to be allowed to pick up our kids from school. Write it down."

Did I say my panties were wet? No? Oh, ok. They are actually soaked.

Walking to my car, he sighed as he opened the driver's side door. "I'm sorry, baby. I thought this shit was over with."

I shrugged back as I slid into my seat. "It's okay. I mean, I don't know what the problem was. I dropped them off, and we were literally almost at the car when they were called back. I'm sure if the boys didn't want to come with me, then they'd have said so."

"I'll meet you home, alright?" he asked, leaning over me as I clipped up the belt. His mouth were mere centimetres from mine. "Drive safe. I'll follow behind."

"I like it when you're behind me."

"I like it when you're coming around my cock."

Laughing, I faked disgust. "You dirty man, get away from me. No sex for you tonight."

"Try to resist me, baby." His mouth finally closed the distance, and he kissed me longingly and tenderly before pulling away completely. "I love you."

With a smile, I replied, "Love you back."

There were a thousand things I wanted to say to Karen right now. She was doing my head in. Ever since Griffin had banned her from coming into our house or even getting out of her car, she had gone worse than before. He had a hearing coming up in four days, and I had a feeling things were not going to go so well.

Karen was due to take the boys back to her place tonight, and they did not want to go.

The boys wanted to live with us. They asked about that all the time, but Griffin, being the nice one, told them it was one week here, one week there. He was doing the right thing by Karen even though she wanted him to suffer.

Hell, she wanted him back.

***

Flicking the kettle on, I pouted as I faced the wall. "Why can't we go on our honeymoon? We've been married nearly two months."

"We could go to my parents. They still have no idea I'm married to the sexiest woman alive."

I laughed, facing him. "How come she did not tell them?" I really thought she would do so just to make drama for us.

"I think she wants me to start my own war with that one. Fuck, Mum's going to lose her shit."

That was an image I did not need in my mind. "You've got that right."

He just rolled his eyes. "We'll go on our honeymoon soon. I promise you."

"I need to find work soon. Maybe I could bag up groceries in the grocery store. Coles or Woollies?" It would not matter where, just as long as I brought something to the table, money-wise.

"Say you get a job, and then you end up pregnant, you won't be able to keep working." His voice turned serious. "I don't see why you have to work."

"Because I refuse to let you pay for anything. Besides, I enjoy working. It gave me something to do. You know, other than you." I grazed a finger over his hip bone. "Speaking of that, you want to go have a quickie?"

A low groan escaped his lips, and he sighed. "Wish I could, pretty, but I have to get back to work."

"Such a shame. I knew sex would stop after I married an older man." I loved to tease him.

Checking his watch, he stepped back out of the pantry and then came back in again, closing the door and smirking. "Very quick, and I'm not old. Just wise."

I came. He came, then he left back for work again.

Finally done making my hot chocolate in the new coconut flavour I got, I walked out with a smile on my lips. Griffin sure knew how to make a girl happy. Toby and Mack were in the media room watching TV, so I went to the back porch and sat on a lounge chair, curling my legs up as I watched the hail storm bucket down.

Life out here was so much different than in the suburbs. Well, being near Karen was more like it. I could come outside and not worry that she was snooping around. Our home was Karen-free, and it was an amazing feeling—like freedom. Griffin and I could breathe on our own without her interfering or always putting her two cents in.

Things had turned out so much differently since being here: me losing my job, and Harvey having a baby. I hated that I was so jealous about that. It was not fair. Then again, when was life ever fair? We had been trying to get pregnant for a couple months, almost three, and nothing was happening. I hated that I was getting my hopes up every month only to be let down. Sex was the best part, though. We were fucking like crazy animals most nights.

As I took another sip from my mug, the screen door flung open, and Toby stood there with a sad smile. "We have to go. She's here."

My mood suddenly dampened. I hated when they had to leave. With a nod, I stood up and walked over to him. "Go help your brother. Get his bag. I'll just go tell her you're on your way."

When the rain had eased enough for me to run over, I ran to her, and her window wound down. "Karen, can I have a word?"

"What? Where is Griffin?"

"He's at work."

"Work? You're here alone with them? Oh, I don't believe this."

"Just shut up for five damn seconds." I snapped at her, losing my cool. "You need to give it a rest. You and he were never married. Yes, you share children together, but that's it, Karen. You can't keep trying to push me out of their life." This was growing old. "Wouldn't it be easier if we could make an effort to get along? I don't want to always fight with you."

Her eyes darted away, and she pursed her lips. "I don't know what you're talking about."

"Really?" I scoffed. "Like the school letter? Saying I'm unable to pick them up? I'm his wife."

"Yes." She sneered, and the car window rolled up. The door flung open, and she stepped out. "I know that you're his wife. You married him. Big fucking deal! You're not their mum, and just because they call you that, doesn't mean it means anything. They're doing it to be nice."

"No, they're not." I shocked myself at how hard my tone was. "You don't deserve those boys. You deserve no one, you miserable, old woman. You can act all motherly, but I see right through you, and it's not a pretty sight."

She laughed, tucking a strand of her bob behind her ear. "You're just an easy fuck for him, and trust me, he'll be bored just like he was with me. You'll never really be family. You'll never have his mother's approval or his friends because they're all on my side. You need to realise that you're a dumb cow. You're no different from me, Ayla. I'll always be in his life. He and I are meant to be. He may not know it now, but he will soon, and then you'll be nothing but a regret in his life."

I rolled my eyes. "I'm nothing like you." I would never be.

"I heard you lost your job. Funny how you're living off him."

That was true. It was not my fault, though. "And unlike you, I did have a job. You've been freeloading off him for years. At least I have money saved from work. All you do is wait until the money hits your account, and then you're ready to party."

Her hand lifted, and I was ready for the slap across the cheek, but Mack ran down between us, facing me. "Mum, can you tell Dad that I left my book in his car?"

Karen looked at Mack and glared. "She's not your mother. You never call her that again or look out!"

Point proven. She's so mean to them.

I ignored her glares as I hugged them both, kissing them each on the cheek. I waved them off and finally walked back to the house, feeling sadder now that they were gone and the house was empty. This house was meant to be filled with noise and kids running around.

I wondered if I could talk Griffin into having two rather than one. *One thing at a time. I don't want to scare him off.*

Dinner was not anything exciting, just an easy lasagna. I sat alone, eating as I waited for Griffin to come home. The roles have been reversed. I wondered if he was this bored when he had to wait up for me. Probably.

So I headed to bed and pulled out my sexiest lingerie, taking about fifty photos just to get a decent one of me lying in the bed with a come fuck me now look. I took another shot of my legs spread with my finger deep inside my wet pussy and sent that to him, too.

The front door slammed with a thud, followed with his shoes being quickly thrown off and keys being tossed to the floor. His feet thumped down the hallway towards our room.

His eyes were filled with hunger as he began undressing. "Fuck, you're a naughty girl."

"Why?" I grinned, stretching out and pushing up my ass to reveal the black G-string. "You don't like?"

A groan escaped his throat as he came at me. His hands skimmed over my ass until I felt the sting of a firm slap. "You know just how much I like it. I was so instantly hard for you."

The material ripped and was thrown to the floor as he pushed apart my thighs even more, pressing his thick erection against my entrance.

"I was lonely," I muttered as I turned to look back at him. "I missed you."

"I missed you too. Now, I'm going to fuck you and then make love to you. I just need to blow really fucking bad first, then the night is all yours."

Biting down on my lower lip, I smirked. "Use my pussy, baby. Fuck it however you want."

His thrusts were to the hilt. My body bounced forwards as his hands wrapped around my waist and pulled me back with each forceful thrust. "I plan on it."

***

Placed at the dining table with a cup of tea, my laptop was on job search as I scanned for any kind of work available in the area. I was not going to be like her. I would not live off him. Griffin walked in, raising his brows as he glanced at the page then shook his head.

"I told you, you don't need to do that."

Picking up my hot tea, I paused as I brought it to my lips. "I want to work."

"Ayla, you don't have to work. I have a ton of money."

"I don't want to be like her." She was right. I was living off of him. I could not be like her anymore. "She told me… that you'll go back to her."

He frowned, sitting beside me and bringing my legs up onto his lap. "When did she tell you this? Because you know that's not true at all."

"We had a few words…" I paused, making sure his reaction allowed me to continue. "I called her a miserable old woman"—I felt horrible for it—"and told her she deserves no one."

His lips parted, but he did not speak. He just nodded then exhaled slowly. "She wouldn't have liked hearing the truth about herself."

I wanted to burst out laughing. He was right. "I don't think she did. She told me I was just a young pussy for you."

"You're an amazing pussy for me."

"Griffin, I'm being serious. She went off at Mack for calling me mum. I really didn't want to let her take them home for the week." I had the right mind to grab the boys and take them both back inside. Even if they were both teenagers, I felt the need to protect them.

He pulled me by the legs, drawing me closer. "I love you, you know that?"

"I had a feeling you might be, especially after earlier," I said, wiggling my brows as I relived the memory in my mind. "I love you, too."

The lid of the laptop closed, and he pushed it away. "Take a year off. If you're not pregnant within then, you can work. But I think you should take the year and have some time for yourself."

Umm… Who the hell is this man?

"Griffin, are you stoned?" He had to be.

He laughed. "I assure you, I haven't been high for a while. I'm just saying that you have been doing so much for the boys and me. You put up with so much between working and taking care of the house. You deserve a break, Ayla. Let me take care of you for once." His eyes were on mine as he reached up, caressing my cheek softly. "I want this. You've been through so much this past year: I treated you like shit, you've dealt with my psycho ex—and all you asked me for was a ring and a baby. I really want to give you that baby, so let's just take the year to fuck like crazy and try to knock you up without you stressing about work or anything else."

My jaw was slightly opened. I was shocked. "Umm…" What could I say to that?

"Say, 'Yes, Griffin, I'll take the year off.' "

Have you ever been drunk on words before? In a daze of lust mixed with arousal? That's what I was in right now. *Damn it.* He was turning me on with his words, and I was falling for it!

"Okay, fine. Yes, Griffin, I will take the year off." I sighed giving in. "No, wait. Just one question," I pointed out. "Say I get pregnant, what happens after that year is up?"

He laughed "Ah, baby! You already agreed." He grinned, closing in his mouth to mine. "And, baby, no way in hell will I let you go back to work after a year's up."

"But—" That was so not fair, but his mouth closed the distance, and I was too busy kissing him back to fight him off.

My hips ground against his, skin to skin, and my breasts bounced as I tightened my arms around his neck and kept rocking. His fingers dug into my ass cheeks, pulling me back and forth faster. I moaned loudly as a finger slipped inside my puckered hole. My every nerve was exploding with pleasure as I shook against him.

My voice breaking, I cried out with a whimper. "F-fuck me… harder."

He stood from his sitting position on the dining chair, and my legs tightly wrapped around his hips. He laid me flat on the kitchen table and slammed into me over and over as my orgasm shattered me completely, milking him empty inside of me.

Both of us was left breathless as his tired body lay over mine. Starting to kiss me from my neck to my collarbone, he reached for my hardened nipple and bit gently. "Let me pierce this."

"Mmm... Okay"

"Yeah?"

"Oh, you can do anything you want to me right now." I was that out of it. He could probably tattoo me, and I would not feel a thing. I was utterly exhausted.

His phone rang, and he went to pull out, but my legs tightened around him. He smirked and instead, picked me back up. Limp inside me, he walked us to the bench where his phone was vibrating. I giggled, slipping down a little.

"It's my lawyer," he said grimly. "I need to take this."

"Of course, you do." God, he definitely had to take this. Any news was worth hearing, and with his last hearing due in a couple days, we needed to be on the ball with what was happening. Even if it were close to midnight, he had to take the call.

We both stood naked in the kitchen as Griffin talked and paced around. He would give me a glance every now and then. I was not sure what to make of them. Was it good or bad? I could not tell. He gave nothing away. The boys expressed their wishes to live with us, and I hoped Karen was not going to do anything to screw this up.

When the call ended, he sat his phone back down and turned away from me. Both his hands gripped the bench top until his knuckles turned white.

I walked behind him and placed a palm over his hand. "Griffin..." I said in an unsure voice. I was suddenly afraid to hear what he had to say.

I did not miss the streaks of water running down his cheeks as he emptily whispered, "I just lost my rights of custody."

I frowned. This could not be right. Perhaps, I was not hearing clearly. "So what does that mean? When do you get the boys back?"

"I don't, Ayla."

I did not understand. "She can't take them from you." *From us.*

His spilling tears broke my heart. "Every second weekend. I get them pretty much four nights a fucking month."

CHAPTER TWENTY-ONE

"Do you want anything to eat?" I asked, climbing back into the bed where he slept, facing away from me. He stayed silent but shook his head. "What about something to drink?" I got the same response. "Okay, I'm just going to have a shower, and then I'll come back to bed."

The water hid my tears. I had been crying just as much as he had, only I did not do it in front of him.

Last night, he had lost part of himself to that evil woman. She had done the unimaginable and took Toby and Mack from their father. She outright lied, and he could not defend himself without admitting he broke the law and risking a jail sentence.

She really fucked him over. She well and truly had him by the balls and was killing him slowly while she sat back, laughed, and enjoyed every moment of it.

I paused, thinking I had heard him entering the bathroom, but when I opened my eyes and looked, he was not there. At first, I blamed myself, thinking maybe I had caused her to do this after our exchange yesterday. But that was not the case. She just wanted the kids and would do whatever she could to get them.

Wrapping the towel around my body, I walked into the bedroom. He was just lying there, still in the same position. His opened eyes had a look of utter heartbreak about him. I understood that it was painful, but he needed to get up and fight for them some more before it was too late.

"Griffin," I began, walking to the robe and pulling out some underwear. "Let's go have some breakfast."

"Ayla, I told you I'm not hungry."

"You need to eat," I urged, sitting on the edge of the bed as I pulled on a pair of ankle socks.

He groaned in annoyance. "I'll eat when I feel like it."

"Let's go for a drive, walk, or something?" He had to get out of there—anything to take his mind of what she had done.

"Christ, give it a rest. I told you I don't feel like anything to eat, and I don't want to go for a fucking drive. Just drop it!" His tone was loud and harsh as he snapped at me.

Don't take it personally. He's hurting, I told myself.

Standing, I pulled my jeans up and faced him. "Well, Griffin, you need to give that lawyer of yours a call and figure out what you're going to do."

"Oh, yeah? What can I fucking do?" He sat up, glaring directly at me with icy eyes. He was *really* mad.

Throwing my hands in the air, I pointed to the door. "Fight for them!"

"I have been fucking fighting!" He roared back, tossing the covers off his body. He took a step towards me. "She has me backed into a corner. Fuck me! You think I haven't been racking my brains trying to come up with a solution? She has me on video with the dates and knows if I come after her, she'll flaunt that fucking tape, and I'll have to submit a drug test which we both know will come back positive, and then what? They'll use that against me being an unfit parent. Jesus, Ayla. I'm fucked."

"Maybe you shouldn't have been smoking weed then," I muttered grimly. "You told me that you'd stopped, and that's probably why..." I stopped myself before I went too far. "Never mind, I'm going to make something for lunch."

As I began walking off, he followed. "That's probably why, what? Why you can't get pregnant? Because I was smoking now and then?"

I should have kept my mouth shut.

"Thanks a lot. Made me feel even shittier."

"I didn't say that."

"You were going to." Scoffing, he slammed his palm against the wall. "I want nothing more than to knock you up."

Oh, how things have changed from no babies to this.

I rolled my eyes. I was not having any of these. "Go back to bed. Sleep off your mood, and then we'll talk."

"Yeah, like I'm going to fall asleep now. Apparently, my wife thinks I'm a shit father who isn't fighting for his kids."

"I didn't say that," I said quieter. He was an amazing dad. "I just meant that there has to be a way around all of this. You're working, and she isn't. How can she get custody when they want to live here?" His jaw tightened, and he looked away. "Griffin, is there something you're not telling me?" He was hiding something. I could tell.

He glanced back, gave his balls a scratch, and shook his head. "Don't worry. You're right. I shouldn't have been smoking. It's my fault. I'm sorry."

"Griffin."

He shook his head again, pleading with his eyes for me to drop it. "Don't."

My concern grew as I stepped closer, reaching out to cup his cheek. "What aren't you telling me?" I asked, my voice fragile. Inside, I was afraid of his answer.

"Nothing."

"Don't lie to me."

He knew better than to lie. He lies to me, and he would know what would come out of it. Something was going on. He was not telling the whole truth about the situation. It did not add up. She was not working. How could someone just decide that the boys were better off living with her when they were clearly better taken care of with us.

"They wanted to live with her."

My whole body froze as a chill ran down my spine. "I'm sorry, what?"

No. That didn't even make sense.

His voice wavered. "They wanted to live with her. They didn't want to be here."

I was still confused. "What? Why?" His anger dissolved to sorrow, and mine began to simmer. "Me? They don't like me?"

"She's made them say something, forced them into it. I don't know. They were asked where they preferred to live, and they said with Karen. They didn't want to be here." He went to touch me, but I stepped back, needing space. "Pretty, you know they love you. It's not your fault."

"Like hell, it isn't! How can you even be near me? Jesus, you lost your boys because of me." It was like a slap across the face. "I feel sick." Literally, I wanted to throw up.

His eyes flickered to my stomach, and I shook my head. It definitely was not due to that. I just felt sick with hurt. This was all a mess.

His hands slipped to my shoulders, and his soft voice brought me back to reality. "Sweetheart, this isn't your fault. I don't blame you, nor do I believe that is what they really wanted. She's done some bribing, and as much as you want to help, you can't. We just need to take this with caution. The last thing I want is to hurt the boys any more than they have been."

"You couldn't go to jail for smoking, though?" That could not be true.

"Well, I don't know, but she threatened to bring up the racing again and even the poker. She's saying she has proof. It doesn't matter that the racing was a one-time event. She knows if she says we've taken the boys to them, then I'm screwed. It's all a headfuck."

I'll say. "So what do we do?" I asked, looking with hopeful eyes up at him. She was lying.

His response, as soft as his words were, did not offer me any comfort whatsoever. "I don't know."

We both went back to bed, and I never asked him to get back out again—not when I was feeling just as low as he had been. He deserved better, and only time would see that he truly was the better parent than that wicked, lying woman that's using her children as pawns in some sick, twisted game to hurt their father. She deserved no one, and I hoped she ended up getting what would eventually come to her.

***

A week went on, and we did not really do a whole lot. Griffin spoke with his lawyer at least once a day. The guy needed to pull his finger out and figure out something that would get our boys back.

It was just a waiting game. We had to wait and see it out. At least the boys were coming to stay with us this weekend. Only five more days.

I was hanging the washing out when Griffin walked outside, lighting up a cigarette as he made his way over. "How about we take that drive?"

"Today?" I asked, shocked. It was a Monday.

He nodded. "We never did get to tell my parents we're married. You can see my hometown, go out on Dad's boat, and fuck in the ocean."

I grinned. "I'm not having sex in the middle of an ocean. There are sharks about, you know."

"I'll keep you safe, baby." His arms slipped around my waist from behind as he pulled me back against his chest. "I just need to get out of the house and go for a drive somewhere. Being here, it's—"

"Too quiet?" I knew the feeling. It was weird that it was just us around here. The boys made noise and fought. I missed that. "Let's go then. You pack our bags, and I'll finish up here. Then we can head off."

Spur of the moment road trips bring back so many fun memories for us.

Three towns in, and I had swallowed his load. We had a thing where whenever we passed a new town, or somewhere we had not been, we fucked. If he was driving and could not stop, I sucked him off. Where was my orgasm in all of this? That would come in the next town over.

It was almost nightfall when he pulled into a long driveway. His parent's house was not the mansion I had expected, just a small house that looked on the older side—until we walked inside. That was where the money was. *Holy crap.* It was like walking into a museum. I was afraid to move in case I bumped and broke something.

"Well, this certainly is a surprising visit. To what do we owe the pleasure?" Paul, Griffin's dad asked, taking the bag from his son and setting it by the staircase.

Griffin just shrugged. "Thought I'd show Ayla around and take up your offer for that fishing trip."

Oh, yes. That was the reason we were visiting. I had my hand pulled up into my sleeve, nervous for when we had to announce that we had gotten married without them there. We technically did invite them, but they just chose not to turn up and visit our new home. Not our fault.

He smiled warmly. "Ah, yes. Tomorrow, we'll make a day of it. Ever been fishing before, Ayla?"

"Only with this guy," I grinned, nudging Griffin beside me. "I only hold the rod though."

"She does it well." He was being crude, and my cheeks flamed. I nudged him again, harder this time, with my elbow. Griffin just laughed as his father was unaware of our banter. "Where's Mum? She knocked herself out with one too many bottles of wine?"

I wanted to laugh but did not. On the inside, I was hysterically cracking up.

Paul laughed, shaking his head. "Oh no, she's in the kitchen. Talking with Jodie."

"Jodie?" I asked. I did not think he had ever mentioned a Jodie before.

"She cooks. Mum's probably going over the menu for tomorrow with her," Griffin answered as if having a personal cook was the most normal thing in the world. *Umm... No, moneybags, it isn't.*

I nodded. "Ahh, so you plan ahead. Good idea." Guess that was one way to be organised.

Griffin shrugged, pulling off his beanie and brushing a hand through his hair. His dad had not even noticed he had shaved the beard and cut the hair short. It was strange. They claimed to love him, but from what I had seen, they were absent parents. There was no real emotional connection between them; they were more like friends—acquaintances, even. I guess they thought money was enough to buy his love.

"Anyway—" Clearing his throat, Paul pointed up the staircase—"You two get settled in, and we'll have a bite to eat unless you've already eaten?"

"Nope. Starving." I grinned, following Griffin who already took our bags. "He wouldn't stop for food." He had no problem stopping for sex, though.

The bedroom looked like one of those posh hotel rooms, complete with a small mint on the pillow. I frowned, looking around more and noticing some old trophies and photos hanging on the wall. "Is this your old room?"

"Yep," was his sharp reply.

"But it looks..." How do I put this nicely? "It's really nice." Too nice for a kid's room.

"It's my mother." He grinned picking up the mint and began to tear open the gold foil wrapper as he flopped on the bed. "I think I was an only child for a reason. She didn't like mess and did nightly room checks. When I was around fifteen, I left some old, muddy soccer clothes out, and she went berserk."

"What did she do?"

"Hit me with some walking stick and then banned me from playing soccer again. Threw out all my stuff, and then made the room to her liking."

She sounded OCD and insane—extremely insane.

I sat by his feet, definitely too scared to make a mess of anything. "She loves the boys. Does she ever get mad when they make a mess?"

"Course, she does. Why do you think I never bring them here?" He grinned. "I grew up very well off, but I never wanted to be like them. Who the hell needs vases and statues in their house?"

I grinned. "Bugger, I was going to start buying them."

"I'll knock them over when I get drunk, baby. Waste of money."

"Luckily, you've got tons of it."

He laughed once more and then picked up the other mint from the other pillow. "*We*. Mine is yours, remember?"

How could I forget? He reminded me of that daily. "What does your dad do to have made so much money?" I did not know that much about his parents other than they were filthy rich and snobbish.

"Dad worked in a gold mine then started up his own trucking company. Mum used to work at a salon just before I was born." He placed the chocolate in his mouth and bit down with a wink. "Want some?"

Licking my lips, I gave him a slight brow wiggle. "You know I want some, Daddy."

His smile went wider to a shit-eating grin, laughing loudly. "You have to stop calling me that, pretty. I can't get a hard dick with you talking like that."

Laughing, I shook my head. "Nope. I love calling you that... only because you hate it so much."

With a soft sigh, he finished his chocolate and propped himself up with the navy blue pillows behind his back. "I feel empty without them around. I miss the sight of Mack reading his books or having Toby nagging about what he can eat. I guess when we have a little one, it won't be so quiet. Just wish things were different."

"So do I." I felt the same as he did. Without thinking, I asked. "Did Karen ever come here?" I looked down at the bed as I thought in my mind of her and him sharing this bed together.

"No. No woman has ever slept in this bed before. I'll finally get to fuck in it too." He winked, nudging me with his toes. "Maybe there's a hot chick who wants to get naked in bed with me?"

I pretended to be annoyed. "Hmm, looks like I'll be kicking some arse while we're up here."

"You don't want to share me?" He was teasing me back with a twinkle in his eye.

"I definitely won't be sharing you, never ever." I then gave a smirk of my own. "Unless you feel like sharing me?"

He snorted, turning serious. "Over my dead body would I share you. Even then, I'll make sure that never happens. You only get one cock for the rest of your life. Now come up and sit on it."

Laughing, I began to crawl up his legs and over his lap. "Mmm... is that so?" I definitely loved that thought. "Luckily for you, I only have eyes for one man, and he's got my heart."

"Same, baby." He smiled, reaching and running his fingers through my hair.

Completely straddling his lap, I leant in, placing my hands flat against his chest. "How about we get started? Or are you too sore after that last go?"

His hands were now on my ass, cupping as he gave them a firm squeeze. "Not sore." His eyes wandered down to my low-cut black top. "Those tits… I'm going to fuck them later too."

"What else?" I breathed out, feeling the heat pooling between my thighs. "Tell me what else."

My hand reached for his jeans, cupping his balls and giving them a squeeze as I rubbed my palm against him, stroking through his pants. He let out a low groan.

"I'll have you on all fours, slamming my cock into you from behind."

"Yes… What else?"

"I'm going to eat your pussy. I'll drown in it."

Oh, god. I almost came just imagining just how his tongue would lap me up, devouring me. I was stroking him faster as his cock strained against the fabric of his jeans. "I want that… so much."

His hands slid up my waist, working on my top. We broke away, sitting up as he lifted my top off and tossed it to the floor. I wasted no time in getting his off as well. His chest definitely did not need to be covered up right now.

"Is it wrong that I feel like I'm fucking a complete stranger with your haircut and all?" I asked. My fingers ran through his short locks, tugging on them.

A sexy hissing sound came from the back of his throat as he buried his face between my cleavage, kissing and nuzzling. "As long as you realise you're married to this stranger, then go for it."

Giggling, I grinded down against him, circling my hips to feel his thick erection against me. "I'll even moan your name when I come." His hips flexed up. "Oh, god. That feels so good."

His husky voice whispered in my ear, "I love hearing my name from you when you're getting off."

"Make me come. You owe me two." I was ready to collect them.

He was suddenly on my back. His hard body pressed against mine, grinding down against my hips as I wrapped my legs around his thighs. "Fuck... I could come like this." His mouth came crashing down, kissing me powerfully as our bodies rubbed against one another, hiding our moans through kissing. His hand was against my cheek as he kissed me deeply.

His tongue completely dominated my mouth, pulling away only to latch onto my neck. Cupping a breast, he pinched a nipple and created another surge in my lower belly. I could definitely come like this too.

"I love you." My fingers dragged down his back and over his ass, pulling him against me once more.

"You're the sexiest woman. Fuck, I love being married to you." He groaned and attacked my mouth once more with his.

"Married?"

The shocked whisper, so softly spoken, was like a bucket of ice and water being poured over us.

We tore apart, both looking in the direction of the voice.

Shoot. Not good. Very, very bad.

His mother stood there, eyes widened to the brim as she saw us half-naked and getting it on.

CHAPTER TWENTY-TWO

"Married?" she asked again, still staring at us.

Oh, my god. Get the hell out. My fingers tightened on Griffin's ass, warning him to get rid of her now.

"Get out, Mum, now!" Griffin's strained voice came from above me. His body had not moved from mine, and I think it was to keep my half-naked body out of sight from her. "We'll be down in a minute."

Her lips pursed, but she nodded. She backed out of the room before leaving, slamming the door behind her. Griffin fell beside me with a deep groan and adjusted his groin region, muttering about needing to blow before his balls fell off.

I just smiled, scrambling out of bed to find my shirt. "This isn't cool."

"Ayla, stop stressing."

My eyes widened at him. How could he be so calm? "Griffin, she walked in on us practically having sex."

"We weren't naked."

"I was about to have an orgasm. I think it's pretty close to sex."

"My dick wasn't in you."

Point taken. "Do you think we have time to—?" I desperately wanted to fuck. I was horny.

He smirked. "Baby, I know. Trust me, I want to as well. But we literally have—" he glanced at his watch—"forty seconds before she comes in here again."

He was not kidding. We were just on our way down the stairs when she flew back up them like a bat from hell. Spinning around when she saw us coming down, she stormed into a room off the hallway.

"Paul, get in here now!" she called out. "Griffin, you too!"

I cringed at her tone. "I should wait out here or drive back home."

Griffin took hold of my hand with a grin. "If I'm getting scolded, so are you, baby. You were fornicating her son."

"I'll tell her you forced me to call you daddy." I teased. "I'll say you're into that."

His eyes widened. "You wouldn't."

No, I would not, but seeing that reaction was totally worth it. "Come on." I sighed. "The sooner we do this, the sooner we can go have unprotected sex."

His hands slipped around my waist, pulling me flush to his chest with a grin. "I love it when you talk dirty to me."

The room we were in appeared to be a formal sitting area. His mother sat on the leather couch, holding a martini with two olives on a stick, while Paul stood by the fireplace, a cigar in his hand and a type of drink in the other. Scotch, maybe.

"When were you going to tell us? Did you elope?" she asked, finally looking our way. Her eyes glanced down to my ring, and I unintentionally covered it with my other hand.

Griffin rested his hand against my lower back and led me to the couch. "We had married a couple months ago. You were invited but chose not to come, remember?"

"I don't remember that." Paul looked absolutely baffled. "We haven't been invited. Were we Theresa?"

She shrugged. "There was a message left on the phone, but we don't attend anywhere without a formal invitation. There was nothing about an engagement, just about a moving-in dinner."

"It was a surprise. We chose to marry that night." I felt the need to say. Formal invitation my ass.

Sighing, she turned away. "Look, Griffin, I'm saddened you chose to marry without us. How do the boys feel about it? I can imagine they're quite upset."

The mention of the kids tugged at my heart. Griffin did not make it obvious to him. "They were extremely excited, and I'm sure you're well aware that Karen had full custody. It's going to take some time to adjust to that."

It would take *more* than time.

"Drink?" Theresa asked, changing the subject quickly.

I shook my head. Now was not the time for drinking. "No, thanks." See, I could be polite.

Griffin also said no. "No, thanks. Pretty tired."

"Didn't look that way moments ago," she muttered, bringing the glass to her lips. "You are in our home. I am appalled to have walked in on my child acting like a wild teenager."

I blushed. Griffin? Not so much as he responded back to her. "We're adults, you should have knocked."

She continued, ignoring him. "I don't know how I feel about you both sharing a room."

"We're married. We're not sleeping separately. Don't be ridiculous."

"Seems like you didn't believe in that before you married either," she said under her breath, not at all trying to hide it.

I was offended. I might look like the type to have had a few dicks inside me, but there was only one who has been there, and I married him. "That's none of your business." I could not stop myself. She was not going to walk all over me or insult us.

"In my house, young lady, it is my business."

"You should have knocked."

Her eyes narrowed, and her lips formed a thin line. "I wasn't expecting you to be half undressed, flaunting yourself."

I almost rolled my eyes, and Griffin sunk back more and stretched his legs out. "Mum, no disrespect, but you have to stop. Ayla isn't what you're implying, and I won't sit and listen to you insult her. She's my wife, and when the bedroom door is shut, you either knock or don't come in."

"I did knock!" She spat. "You two were… I can't even say it. I have heard and seen far too much."

Oh, god.

"We're adults."

"I felt like I had witnessed something pornographic. It was vile."

"It's called foreplay."

Her eyes bulged, and my cheeks flamed. He just blurted that right out without a care.

"Umm, well... not exactly," I corrected, not making our case any easier. Technically, there was no oral, and to me, that was definitely needed in foreplay.

Griffin stood up and cleared his throat. "Look, enough talk. I'm a grown man, and you need to accept that. As for Ayla, she's my wife which you also need to accept. If you have a problem with it, then we'll get a hotel for the night or go sleep on the boat."

That seemed to have scared her. Jumping up out of her seat, she shook her head. "No. You just got here, and it's been some time since we last seen you."

"Not my fault," Griffin said, once again taking his seat. "You don't bother to call me. I get an email now and then, asking how the boys are, and that's it."

She sighed, rubbing her temples as she picked her martini back up. "How's Karen?"

I blinked twice. Did she really just ask him that? *Umm, hello? Current wife in the house!*

"Probably getting off to finally screwing me—just not in the way she'd like."

I cringed at his reply. That was disgusting and so mentally disturbing on so many levels.

Paul coughed, almost choking on his drink as he set it down on the coaster. "We heard you lost custody of the boys. How could you let them slip away like that? You should have called us. We'd have written a cheque or helped you get a better lawyer."

"Because he was a fool in the first place. If they'd stayed together, then none of this would have happened. I tell you, throwing away your family and giving your children divorced parents is the worst mistake you could possibly make." Theresa rolled her disapproving eyes.

"Agree. If you don't love her, then you should have stuck around like a man."

I wondered if that was what his parents had done. Maybe that was why there were no other siblings.

"Oh, Griffin. Look at the mess your life has turned out to be: a failed relationship, two children out of wedlock, and well…" Her eyes flickered to mine, but she held her tongue. "We want what's best for you, that's all."

I smiled. My hand slid over his thigh and squeezed. "You do know your son is actually pretty amazing. He has a great job, lots of friends, and a wife who hasn't cheated or trapped him into anything. He's done wonders for himself and has not lived off mummy and daddy's money. You two can sit and go on about what he hasn't achieved, but you don't know him. If you did, then you'd see what a loving and caring man he is. You also would have come to the wedding… but you'll never get that chance, and you certainly won't be around for any future grandchildren we give you." Standing, I tugged on his hand. "If you'll excuse us. We're tired. I suggest you don't come in that room anytime soon; I won't be stopping." I informed them and walked off before they had a chance to speak back to me.

Screw them. They were horrible.

***

"You won't be stopping?" Griffin laughed, flopping down on the bed and wrapping his hand around his growing cock. A soft groan escaped his mouth. He was fully erect, stroking himself. *Oh, hot.*

Nodding, I unclipped my bra and made my way towards him. "Slow, not rough or hard. I'm going to make love to you with my mouth, and then I'll straddle your hips."

I was in the mood to make love, not fuck. I wanted him to feel just how much I loved and needed him… through my body. I wanted him to feel that he was the only man I adored.

His eyes were drowsy with lust. His head fell back, only giving me a nod.

It was a making love kind of night.

***

Who on earth wakes up at five am to go fishing?

Jesus, I was exhausted, and that was the last thing I wanted to go and do. The men had other ideas, though. It was actually odd. Last night's conversation had not been mentioned, and his mother was making breakfast. I thought they had a cook, but here she was, making waffles, eggs, and bacon.

Was this how the rich did things? Fought, forgot all about it, and then moved on to the next day as if nothing happened? At least they had not mentioned Karen's name. Any day that went without the mention of her was a brilliant day in my eyes.

"Bacon?"

I looked up from the paper to where Theresa stood, holding a plate with food on it.

"No, thanks." *I don't trust you one bit, and I'd rather stick to the fruit that I watched her cut up.* "Not really a big breakfast person."

"She usually just has coffee, and that's it." Griffin reached over and took the plate from his mother's hands. "But thanks. I'll eat this."

I gave him an odd look and just shrugged. How could he not see that this was all really weird and kind of creepy? His parents were acting like well-loving parents.

Surely, they could not keep this act up when we went out to sea.

But they did. They were polite, kind, and caring. Even Griffin had noticed it eventually after I pointed it out once or twice. Actually, he only noticed when his mother asked about my job and if I was searching for another. When I mentioned taking a year off, she did not even bat an eye. I did not tell her that her son practically forced me into it so we could spend the year trying to fall pregnant. She seemed a little okay with that. That was when Griffin had noticed something was up.

"Alright, what's going on?" he asked, throwing his line back out into the ocean.

"What do you mean?" Paul asked, baffled.

Griffin turned and looked from his father to his mother. "You're asking Ayla all these questions and being interested in her all of a sudden. Something's up."

"We can't be interested in our daughter-in-law?" Theresa asked with a small smile.

"Not without an agenda," he replied back. "What are you two doing?"

Paul sighed and shook his head. "Nothing. We're... we're trying."

"To do what?" Griffin asked back, running a hand through his hair as he picked up the can of beer and took a mouthful. His eyes widened mid-sip. Swallowing, he laughed. "You're trying to actually be parents?"

Oh, dear lord. They are bipolar.

"Umm, how about I take over for you?" I suggested, reaching for his rod.

Handing it over without hesitation, he went back to the conversation at hand. "You think one day is going to make up for all the shit you've said to me over the years? You implied Ayla was a…"

Yes, I could remember the hooker reference very well.

"I don't understand. Why now?" Griffin continued.

"You got married." His mother's sob changed everything. "We missed out on our son's wedding."

Griffin swallowed hard. "That's not my fault."

"But maybe you could…" She paused, flashing a hopeful smile at her son.

Shaking his head, he came back for the rod. "No. We were married the way we wanted to marry. I won't have another wedding just for the sake of you and Dad. You lost that moment. It's on video if you'd like to watch, but other than that, I won't have another wedding for your sake."

Ooh, harsh. But I guess they needed to hear that from him.

At that moment, I wanted to apologise, but I stopped myself. What did I need to say that for? I was not sorry; it was not our fault. They were to blame, and in this case, they lost out. Not us.

"You're going to have more children?" His mother just did not quit it. "I thought you'd had a vasectomy?"

I let out a soft giggle, unable to hold off laughing. "You wanted to get the snip?" I asked, and he shot me a glare.

"I didn't get that done, Mum," he said sighing heavily. "Ayla and I will have kids, eventually."

"There's going to be a huge age gap between a baby and the boys, how will you handle that?" she asked, holding her hands in defence. "I'm not judging, just asking."

"It won't be an issue. The baby will need a friend. Have to get working on another one afterwards," he answered, giving me a wink.

Oh, the stars. My heart was happy. He wanted more than one. Two, perhaps? Oh, this man was seriously making my ovaries swoon like nothing else. Two little babies with him? It would be perfect.

We had fish for dinner that evening. His mother even knocked on the bedroom door after we went upstairs for a nap that we did not take. Maybe they were having a midlife crisis. The next day, it was the same. We went for a look around his hometown: to a café where his parents wanted us to have lunch, then to a market. His parents were being loving and caring until we went home, and we were both left baffled, extremely puzzled by the events of what had happened.

"Did they just plan on stopping by? To visit sometime?" I asked, walking into our kitchen like a headless chook. I was really confused by their actions. "I mean, she yelled about us getting it on, and then she was nice."

He smiled, nodding. "Way too nice. Let's just not think about them. Want to watch a movie?"

"When have we ever just watched a movie?" I asked, raising a brow, then giggled as he could not tell me a time where we just laid and watched something without it leading to more. "Alright, let's watch a movie, and no fooling around."

That did not work. We fooled around and forgot all about the movie.

***

When Friday rolled around, we were both nervous for the boys to come stay. It did not feel like before. It felt like the calm before a huge, torturous storm. Karen pulled up in the drive, and I stayed inside as Griffin walked out onto the balcony and waited for them to come up to him. He was not going anywhere near her.

They looked dirty and unclean. Their hair needed a cut, and their clothes, draggy.

She just sat in her white 2000 Ford Falcon and eyeballed him—no kisses goodbye to the boys, no getting out to help them with their bags. They did it all on their own.

"Hey," he greeted Toby first with a hug and a kiss on the forehead. "How are you both?"

"Mum said she's getting us at lunchtime, Sunday."

Griffin frowned. "No. Seven pm is when you'll be dropped back home."

"Why?" Mack asked quite rudely. "She said she'll come here."

"You boys hungry?" I asked, trying to steer the conversation in another direction. "I made cake." No, I *brought* a cake.

Toby shrugged and dodged me when I went to hug him. "Ayla, can you bring it down to my room?" he asked, taking off down the hallway.

Ayla. I had gone back to being just Ayla to them. Not mum, just Ayla. "No," I told him. "We don't eat in the bedrooms."

"You suck!" he shouted, and then the door slammed.

My eyes met Griffins, and he took off down the hallway. "Hey, get back out here and apologise now. You don't speak to her like that, and you sure as hell don't come here and act that way."

The door flung back open, and Toby glared up at his father. "So?"

"So?" Griffin was just as taken by that as I was. "How about you go outside then come back in once you're in a better mood?"

"Fuck," he muttered underneath his breath, storming down the floorboards as he stomped past me, nudging me in the side as he did so.

Griffin went after him. "Watch your mouth, Toby."

This was not the Toby we had said goodbye to a couple weeks ago. He was moody, arrogant, and was just rude. Mack was still standing there, unmoving on his spot, until his gaze met mine, and he looked away immediately.

"Are you hungry?" I asked.

He shook his head. "No."

The front door opened and closed shut quieter. Toby reappeared and came towards me. "Sorry."

"That's okay," I said, unsure what the hell was going on. It was just as crazy as Griffin's parent's behaviour. "Do you have any homework that you need doing?"

"No."

"He does," Mack told on him. "He's just lying."

"Well, get it out, and you can do it," Griffin told them. "Would you boys like to get out and ride the bikes later?"

They shrugged and with a sad look about them, walked over to the kitchen and propped themselves up at the bench. Something was definitely wrong with them. They were not the kids I had known. Then again, they could be going through a tough time with the change of moving in permanently with Karen and only seeing their Dad twice a fortnight.

Griffins hand squeezed my shoulder. His voice was quiet, but I could tell he was just as confused as I was. "It'll be okay."

"How do you know?" I asked, looking up at him.

There was that look about him, determined and sure of himself. "I'm going to get to the bottom of this."

He walked over, and I followed cautiously. He stood on the opposite side of the bench to them, peering at each of them carefully. "What's going on?" he asked in a low voice. It was almost scary.

Mack looked up, shaking his head. "Homework."

"Not what I meant," Griffin warned. "What is going on? And do not lie to me."

Toby looked down at the kitchen counter and shrugged as well. "We're not allowed to tell you."

"Bullshit. Tell me now, or you'll be doing chores all weekend," he threatened. "There's a chook pen needing to be built. I'll have you both out there working your asses off, and then you can sweep up the leaves out of all the rocks from the storm the other night."

That was a job we were both putting off.

"Mack, you know you won't be in trouble if you just tell us the truth." I urged softly.

"Yes, we will." His eyes began to water. "She said she would throw all my books away."

Griffin and I both shared another look. She was using the kids in her own wicked game. It was sick.

Griffin's hand slammed on the counter with so much force, it made us all jump. "Tell me what is going on right fucking now, or you'll really be in for it," he said through gritted teeth, the threat cutting us like glass.

Mack burst into tears and shook his head as Toby finally spoke up and told the truth. "She told us to be naughty, so you would hit us and then we wouldn't have to come back here."

CHAPTER TWENTY-THREE

"What do you mean, hit you? I'd never lay a finger on you."

Talk about throwing a spanner in the works. Neither one of us saw that coming. Griffin looked as if someone had told him his parents had been killed. He was distraught, struggling to come up with words.

I had Mack in my arms as he sobbed. He could not stop crying. Something had happened, and my heart was telling me something was really wrong. He glanced up, rubbing his eyes as he spoke with a shaky voice. "I can't tell you. You'll get mad."

"Mad? Why would I be mad?" he asked, much calmer. His pacing stopped, and he joined us in the living room. "You boys need to start talking. You're confusing me."

Toby sat still, silent as Mack cried even harder. In the whole time Griffin and I had been living together, not once had I seen these boys cry. It was devastating, and my heart ached for him.

"Sweetheart, what's the matter?" I asked, softly.

"You know…" He sniffled back. "Can't you tell him? Please don't make me say it."

My heart was hammering like a drum. *Oh, shit.* She knew, and now his dad was about to know.

"Griffin, umm…" How the hell was I going to bring this up? I could not do it. I just could not tell him. It was not for me to reveal. "Mack, you have to tell your dad."

"Tell me what?" he asked. "Is something wrong?" His voice was frantic. Moving from around the coffee table, he came towards us with a worried look. "Mack, you can tell me anything."

Yeah, he might say that now, but who knows how he'll react. "Toby…"

"I'm not leaving him alone." Toby got up and came by his brother's side, playing the protective role. "Don't even think I'll leave."

I brushed my fingers through Mack's hair, hoping to calm his crying. "It's okay. I promise." I knew it would be. "You can tell your dad."

Pulling away, my stomach was in my mouth as Mack looked into his dad's eyes. Griffin was crouched in front of us both, and his hands wound into fists on my thighs. "Did you steal something or break in somewhere?"

"No."

His eyes flickered to mine then back to Mack's as his voice went to a low dull tone. "Did you get a girl pregnant?" *Oh, shit. History repeating itself.*

"No!" Mack loudly assured him.

"Oh. Okay, well nothing will be as bad as that." He breathed a sigh of relief.

"Like racing a car and getting caught?" I asked with a hint of a smile. "I could name a few others." Karen, Karen, and a big fat Karen.

He playfully glared at me. "Point taken." His focus went back to Mack. "Come on, son. You can tell me."

"I..." he stuttered. "I'm... I'm gay."

The whole room went eerily silent. You could hear the loud swallow that finally came from Griffin's throat as he took in his words, clearly never expecting to hear such a thing from his youngest son. It was not something anyone would be expecting, I guess. Then again, some parents would have an inkling of whether or not their child is gay. Mack showed no signs other than perhaps being quiet, timid, and shy. He loved reading and was a caring soul.

To me, it did not matter. Everyone deserved the right to love whoever they wished. Nothing should stop or try to change that.

I opened my mouth to say something, to break this uneasy silence, but no words came out. I did not have a clue what to say, and I did not want to force words from him right now. Mack was shaking in my arms as his face buried into the crook of my neck.

I could imagine how he was feeling; he was absolutely shitting himself in fear that he would be disowned or worse.

I gave Griffin's hand a small, reassuring squeeze, and he broke his trance, finally breathing a soft sigh.

Still, no words were spoken by him yet as his eyes went to mine, shooting me an accusing glare. It rocked me to the core. He was not pissed at Mack. He was pissed for being the last to know.

He knew that I knew and had not told him. Shaking his head, he simply stood up and turned around. Leaving the room, he went to the kitchen and opened up the fridge. Pulling out a six pack and tucking it underneath his arm, he then made his way outside. The backdoor closed with a quiet click.

I wanted to go after him, but I could not. He needed to do this on his own, however long it took. He had to be the one to break the ice and speak to Mack first on his own terms without me pushing him to do so.

Toby frowned, smirking. "I thought you were going to say you shagged a girl and got her pregnant."

"Please, don't say that." I sighed, rubbing my temples then giving Toby a raised brow. "If anything, I'd expect that from you, not him."

Toby snorted, sitting on the couch beside us. "I've never even kissed a girl, let alone boned one. I'm not that bad." *Boned, seriously?*

"Your father will be relieved to know about that." Hell, I was relieved to know he had not done any of that stuff yet. Mack's body began to shake again, and I pulled him close, kissing the side of his head and soothing him with words. "Shh, it's okay. Everything will be alright.

"He hates me."

"No, he doesn't hate you. He just needs a minute to think and calm down. I think he's upset that he didn't know sooner, but you told him. That's the main thing, and now you can keep talking. Can you tell me why you're supposed to be so naughty for us that it would cause your dad to hit you?" That did not make any sense. He would never lay a finger on them. Yeah, maybe a slap on the back of the head when they were being rude.

Otherwise, it would be in a playful manner, nothing like a punishment.

"I don't know." Toby shrugged. "I hate her. She wouldn't even let us call Dad and say hello."

"You have a phone." I reminded him. "Did you run out of credit?"

"She took them from us."

"How was the week with her? Did you do anything exciting?" Maybe they have had a good time with her.

Mack shrugged. "She's got a new boyfriend. They stay up drinking all the time. We had to walk to school on our own."

"That's a forty-minute walk. It rained during the week." I pointed out. Did this woman really not care about these boys at all? I wondered who this new boyfriend of hers was. "Does the man live at the house?"

Toby nodded. "We know. We got soaked and ended up late. He's there most the time. Doesn't talk much. They just tell us to shut the fuck up and stay in our room."

Bloody hell. "How about I get us some cake?" Cake makes everything better.

Mack nodded, slowly looking back up. "And ice cream?"

I smiled, relieved he had stopped crying. "Yes, sweetheart. We brought ice cream today for you both."

Toby stood with a grin. "What about sprinkles? Mum, you can't have ice cream without sprinkles."

Mum. I beamed. Fuck, I really did love hearing that.

"Yes, or toppings and whipped cream. Actually... we're out of that." I remembered and found myself blushing as I went to the fridge to start on their bowl of desserts. Griffin had eaten that last night with as much determination as he ate me.

Both boys jumped up, and I spotted Toby giving Mack a back rub. "Don't worry. I've got your back if anyone picks on you at school. I'll knock 'em dead."

"No fighting, Toby." I pointed out. "Well, make sure it's out of school grounds so you can't get expelled or suspended."

"I like the way you think." He winked and gave me a thumbs-up.

The three of us were in between mouthfuls of ice cream when Griffin walked back inside and strutted straight down to the bedroom. There was no pause or a look. He kept his head down and walked right by us. Mack made a sniffing sound, and I shook my head at him, telling him that everything would be alright.

He was on the edge of the bed, facing the wall when I walked into our room.

"How long have you known this for?" he asked, his voice barely audible.

"Since his birthday." His eyes lifted, and the hurt was in them. "He didn't tell me. I accidentally found out."

He stood up and ran both hands through his hair. "How did you accidentally find out?"

"I caught him and his friend…"

His pacing stopped. "Caught them doing what?" His words were rushed and frantic. "Jesus, what were they doing?"

"No. Not that." God, I would have died if I caught them doing that. "Just kissing, that's all."

"That's all? Fuck, Ayla. I feel like I've just been blown up by a grenade. You should have told me. That was months ago." Sitting back down again, he pinched the bridge of his nose. "You should have told me. After all the secrets between us and fights about trust, you kept this from me."

Yeah, I know I did, and I've felt like shit every day for keeping it from you.

How could I make him see that from my point without making matters worse? "It wasn't for me to tell you. I could have told you, but Mack begged me not to say anything. I promised him that. I couldn't lose his trust, Griffin. I love that kid, and if he hated me…" *It would hurt badly.*

"Ayla…" he sighed.

I dropped to my knees in front of him, looking up with sorrow in my eyes. "Please, don't be mad at him. He's so afraid, Griffin. He's terrified that you hate him."

His voice dropped. He looked worse than when Mack revealed he was attracted to boys. "I could never hate him for that. I just wish he told me sooner. I should have known that my son is gay."

"He hid it well." I did not think there was any telling if he was or not. It was just something for him to come and tell on his terms. "He's still the same boy."

"Just likes boys, not girls."

Yeah, that.

His sharp inhale caught me off guard, and I noticed he had tears in his eyes. "I can't protect him from those kids at school when they find out about this. He's going to get beaten up… teased." His eyes widened. "Fuck, Mum will just love this."

"Well, if she doesn't accept him, then she can go get stuffed." I was serious about that. "Don't worry about the school kids. Toby's got that covered."

"Need I ask?" he questioned.

I shook my head. No, he did not need to know that I have basically approved him to beat anyone up who teases Mack.

I rested my cheek on his thigh, and his hand automatically began stroking through my hair. "You need to go talk to him." I reached up, brushing my fingers over his. "I think Karen found out, and that is why they came in being that way. Toby said she took their phones from them and wouldn't let them call you when they wanted."

His jaw tightened. "Fucking bitch. God, if it were legal to kill someone, she'd be first on my list."

"Who'd be second?" I wondered.

"Harvey," he said without hesitation, and I smiled. I so knew he would say that. "I'd kill him with my bare hands if I had the chance."

I doubted that. "Should I be worried about your need to murder someone? Sleep with one eye open, maybe?"

Shaking his head, his smile softened. "I'd never kill the woman I love."

Standing up, I sighed, pulling him up with me. "Come on. There's cake and ice-cream."

"You're an amazing mother, Ayla. Really, you are." He smiled, bending his head down to give me a kiss. "The boys are lucky to have you in their life. I am too."

"I'm the lucky one. I get you and them."

Griffin took Mack down to his bedroom for a one-on-one chat while Toby and I stayed in the kitchen and ate our sweets. He showed me his homework, which he did have, and I sat with him, helping him work through fractions and other useless maths. Who the hell did fractions outside of school, anyway?

When the two emerged, Mack was smiling much brighter than before. Although, something was still wrong. If

Karen knew he was gay, then why would they need to be punished for it?

Griffin's hand slipped around my waist, and his kisses trailed down the bare skin of my neck. "Mm, you smell good."

"Hands off until later tonight." I smiled, trying to pry away from him. "How did it go?" I asked, looking up at the boys who were now in the living room, watching a movie.

"All good."

"Care to elaborate?" I asked, turning in his arms. He tried to come down for a kiss, but I leant back more. "What did you say to him?"

He smiled. "Nothing. It's fine, Ayla."

I laughed. "You're not going to tell me, are you?"

"Nope." His lips pecked my nose, and I gave his bum a squeeze. Pulling back, he just smiled again. "I just told him that it's going to be okay, and that I was proud of him for being able to tell you in the first place. For him to come to you with this even if he was caught, he obviously looks at you like a mother."

My gaze drifted back to those boys. They did not have a mother—at least not one who cared for them. "I want to be their mum."

"You are."

I shook my head. "Not what I meant." I wanted to adopt them as my own. "If only we could make that happen."

"Me too. She'd never go for that, unfortunately." He sighed and pulled away, leaning against the counter. He picked up the bowl of cake and began to dig in. "So, what's for dinner?"

"How about we be really lazy and order Chinese?"

"Done. So should I call the whale about what the boys have said?" he asked, "About their behaviour and being told to act that way?"

I laughed loudly with a snort. "Yeah, I think you should, but maybe call your lawyer and see what he thinks first. You don't want her coming after you for something else she's concocted up and try to use it against you." Who knew what else she could hit him with?

"You're right." Putting in another forkful, he paused and swallowed. Licking his lips, he frowned. "Why would I hit him over being gay? What would that prove?"

I thought about it for a moment, and he was right. It was still baffling. "Hey, boys. Come in here for a moment." I called out then looked at Griffin. "We'll find out in a minute."

Both of them came over and stood opposite us. "Yeah?" Toby asked while Mack shuffled nervously on his feet.

"You didn't answer before; Why does your dad need to hit you?" I asked. "Why do you have to be so naughty?"

"Does it matter?" Toby asked, sighing and looking ashamed.

"Yes," I responded. "You both matter."

Mack and Toby shared a secret glance that Griffin did not miss. "Come on. No secrets, boys. We can't help if you don't tell us the truth."

I thought Mack was going to run to his room, but when he slowly lifted his shirt up, it all made sense. My hands clasped over my mouth as I stared in horror at the sight of the bruises covering his ribcage and stomach. Turning slowly, I bit my trembling lip as more bruises appeared.

"She read my messages to Samuel and went ballistic."

It took us both a good few moments to gain some kind of control and unfreeze from the spot. The gay part? Yeah, I understand yelling, but to hit and belt him? No fucking way. There was no excuse for doing that to a child.

"Because she realised you and Samuel are more than friends?" I asked as Griffin visibly shook with raw anger.

He nodded, fresh tears springing to his eyes. "She was really mad. Called me a f—She said I was disgusting and abnormal."

"You're not abnormal. There's nothing wrong with you." I wanted him to know it was okay. I was beginning to cry. What has she done to those boys?

"You're dating Sam?" Toby asked through a mouthful of cake that he had grabbed. "You should have hit her back. She threw a glass sauce bottle at me once."

My head snapped to Toby. "She did what!" I practically yelled. Jesus, those Heinz glass bottles of tomato sauce were not at all light.

"Yep. I called her a mad cow, and she came at me like one. Bottles, hands and feet." He shrugged. "We're used to it. She told us if we told Dad, she'd kill herself."

No wonder they were terrified to do anything against her! I would probably do as my mother said if she threatened to do that too. It was sad that she had lied and hurt them. Who knew how long all of this had been going on for?

"You shouldn't have to get used to that," I said, giving his hand a firm squeeze. "Never."

"Ayla's right. I wish you boys would have told me. I could have helped you both. Don't worry. You boys aren't going back there." Griffin found his voice, but it was cold and shaking. In a millisecond, he was heading straight towards the phone and starting to dial a number. Covering his hand over the speaker, he spoke to me, firmly. "Ayla, take photos of this. I'm getting the police involved. Mack, strip to your boxers. You too, Toby."

I nodded as the boys began to undress in the kitchen, looking back to Griffin as I picked up the camera from the draw. I knew what was going to come. "You know she will use the tape." I was worried for him, for them all. "What if she comes at you with all she's got?"

His voice grew louder, bordering towards yelling. "I don't fucking care. She beat them, Ayla. She beat them, and if I have to go to jail over smoking pot or drag racing illegally, then she can be charged with child abuse." He put the phone to his ear and left the room as he began speaking down the line.

My heart broke for each of them—such angelic, sweet boys who now both wore panic across their faces and bruises all over their bodies.

One gay, the other straight. It did not matter. They were now the same. Abused.

CHAPTER TWENTY-FOUR

Photos were taken. Lawyers were called. Police arrived, and then we were all interviewed.

Mack was first, a shaking, crying, and afraid mess. They took him into a separate room. Although he still needed a parent, they thought he may speak more if Griffin or I weren't in the room with him. There was nothing for us to hide, and Griffin allowed it.

Mack copped the worst of the beatings we found out. His sexuality was just the tip of the ice. She had been flicking and pushing him around for years. He never actually fell down the back step and broke his arm. She pushed him, and he fell, landing the wrong way and breaking it.

I watched my husband fall apart over and over as he was reading back the statements. I, myself, began to cry, but I tried to remain strong. These three guys needed me. They needed a woman in their life to care for them. Karen and Griffin's mother weren't that type of woman. They were not caring or gentle.

They needed the loving, tender side of a mother—a woman who would comfort them when they needed it.

After Toby came out, he was quiet and scared. Karen was still their mother. She gave birth to them, and I could understand the need to protect her still, but they were doing the right thing. A mother should never bash their kids the way she had done. I just hoped they could forgive themselves for turning her in and speaking up.

They were brave boys and deserved more.

"How is your relationship with the mother?" The constable had asked me, her judging eyes awaiting an answer.

How was the relationship? I would have laughed if it was not such a serious question. "As you'd expect, tense."

Maybe not the right word. It was anything but.

"Do you and she get along?"

"No," I said, blunt and straight to the point. "She hates me."

Nodding, she began to write everything down. "And why do you assume she hates you? Do you and she ever exchange words? Have you ever done anything to upset her?"

"If you mean starting a relationship with her ex, then that would be it. I know she hates me as she's made it quite clear."

The writing stopped, and she looked up. Pausing, she asked me, "Has she ever made any threats towards you?"

I nodded, tucking a hair behind my ear. "She had me fired from my job. A few months back, she came in and started a fight in the women's bathroom while I was cleaning—"

"Did you ever strike her back?"

"I defended myself. She punched me first, and then I hit her back."

"I see. Was there a charge filed against this attack?" she asked, going back through her paperwork.

I shook my head. It was probably a bad move on my part. I should have done something about that right away. "There's no surveillance in the bathrooms, and it would have been my word against hers."

"Hmm..." She began to write again and sighed. "Anything else? Any threats made towards you or your husband?"

Plenty. I began to tell her about all the crazy things she had done to us and finished with threatening to bury me if her sons ever began to call me mum. "I have never pushed them to say that. They started it on their own, and she found out."

"Well, as you can see, if you're a mother, then hearing your children call another woman mum would be quite heartbreaking. Did you ever tell them to stop it?" I was really beginning to dislike this woman.

I just gave her an odd look. "Why would I tell them to stop it? Their own mother, if you want to call her that, has been beating them. They call me mum because I show them what a mother should be like. I treat them as my own children."

"Do you have any children, Mrs. James?"

Of course, that needed to be brought up. "No, I don't. Are we done now? I'd like to go and check on the boys. I didn't wait for her to answer me. I got up and left the room.

I gave Griffin an annoyed look and walked out. He came over, assuming I was mad at him. "Everything okay?"

"No. Just hate the police," I said with a grumble under my breath.

He chuckled, pulling me close and brushing a hand through my hair as his lips met my forehead. "I know how you feel, baby."

It had been a crazy evening; the police were thorough. They went back and forth with every little detail until the boys had talked themselves half-asleep. It was near midnight when they had all they needed and finally left. After tucking them into bed, Griffin and I had to sit down with his lawyer and go over what was to come next.

Even if we both knew, we still needed to hear those words.

We should not have smiled, but it was almost impossible once we were told that the boys were staying with us, that this was enough to keep them both and gain full custody. They just needed a Judge to sign off on everything tomorrow morning, and they would be ours.

Lifting his arm as he glanced down at his wrist, Griffin looked happy. "You think she's been arrested yet?"

I nodded, hoping so. "I reckon. They were going straight there to pick her up."

"Think she'll squeal like a pig on the slaughter floor?" he said, referring to his pot smoking and racing.

I nodded. "Yeah, but like your lawyer said, that's just a slap on the wrist compared to hitting the kids for so long as she had done."

"True."

She could blab her mouth all she wanted, but Griffin was not going anywhere. He had even told the detective about the racing one night, smoking as he gave a statement and offering himself up before she could try weasel some deal with a cop. The detective wrote it all down, but that was not their focus. He did not seem too interested in those as they were a thing of the past, and he was already paying for the driving.

Walking towards him with my arms outstretched and reaching around his waist, I clung to him. "We got our boys back, baby."

He offered me a smile, a gorgeous smile that reached his eyes. It was one I had not seen since he first heard they were not coming back here. "We got our boys back. We did indeed."

Sleep did not come as fast as I hoped it would. I was exhausted and lying in Griffin's arms as he slept soundly beside me. I felt drained, emotionally and physically. A headache was starting to come on. My nerves were tense.

Beginning to worry, I laid there and felt sick. *What if this does not go the way his lawyer promised?* My stomach churned at the thought of Karen indeed striking a deal and getting off. Griffin's parents could get involved. Maybe they would take her side.

Oh, god. My stomach rolled again, and I sat up with my hand clasping over my mouth. "Griffin."

"Mmm?" he mumbled, rolling over to his side. "I'm not snoring."

"No." I felt sick with worry. "What if this all goes wrong? What if the judge... What if you go to jail?" God, that was a real possibility. He could go to prison for his racing.

He turned the bedside lamp on, but I was already out of bed and rushing to the bathroom. I broke into cold sweat with tears in my eyes as I fell to my knees and threw up hard.

"Ayla."

I felt a hand slowly rubbing against my lower back, but I could not talk. I just threw up again. I was afraid of losing him. I could not lose this man.

I turned around as I wiped my chin and mouth with the back of my hand and shook my head. "I can't live without you."

Crouching down, he sighed and pulled me onto his lap. I was a sick mess, yet he was not bothered. *True love right here.* "Pretty, you're not going to lose me. We're going to be just fine. I promise."

"I'm scared."

"Me too. Me too, Ayla."

A hot shower and I felt somewhat better, but the queasiness did not ease up until the next morning when the phone call came in, and Griffin pulled me aside. We had gotten immediate full custody, and Karen was being charged with numerous child abuse offences. She had failed to provide a safe environment for them. After the police took her into custody, they searched her home and found traces of ice and other drugs throughout the house.

The next step was to tell the boys that they would not be going back home with her. They were with us indefinitely and completely with the custody finalised. We would tell them after Griffin comes to terms with everything that had happened this past evening.

"Do you want to go away?" I suggested. Maybe that camping trip could help.

"I feel like getting back into the tattoo chair."

"Let me tattoo something on you?" I suggested, really wanting to have a go at it.

He cocked his brow, smirking. "I don't want a flower or something girly."

I laughed, flicking him with the tea towel. "No, silly. I'll make it cool."

"Cool, huh?" He seemed to think about it. "Alright, then. I'll set the gun up later today, and you can give me some ink. Where do you want to work on me?"

A glanced at his groin, and he shook his head. I laughed. "Kidding. Maybe on your wrist? Under your watch band?"

"Ah, I know what you're going to put on there."

"My name." I nodded.

"I've already got that over my heart. Why do you want it there too?"

"Baby, if I could, I'd have my name all over your body for the world to see." I would, too.

***

After breakfast dishes, I took another shower as my headache had come back on. It was driving me mad. I felt like death and put it down to the night of stress we had endured. In other words, I was blaming Karen for the hell my head was in right now.

Drying off, I pulled open my draw to moisturise my face and glanced at the blue box. It was taunting me. *Pee on me, and you'll see you're not pregnant,* it seemed to say just like last month and the month before that. I don't know why I could not just wait until I was like a month late. Call it eagerness, but I pulled out the Clearblue pregnancy box and unwrapped the two sticks inside. I did not trust the normal tests. I needed to read the word pregnant or not pregnant. Otherwise, I would just be searching for two little lines that weren't there but my mind was imagining.

I waited and waited, and then the word flashed up on the screen.

My heart dropped as did the tests in my hand. Quickly tossing the box in the bottom of the small bin, I took the tests and shoved them in my underwear drawer, not wanting Griffin to see that I craved and took them.

All three of them were playing on the Xbox One when I found them in Toby's room. "Are you boys hungry for some lunch?"

"Dad said we can go out and get a huge burger."

I smiled, leaning against the door. "Oh, yum. Can I join or is this a boys-only lunch?"

"You can come. Mum's the exception." Mack smiled warmly.

"Hmm, I don't know. Maybe I want to spend the day at home playing the Xbox once you all leave. I could totally beat your high scores."

All three looked at me mortified. "No, please don't!" Toby begged.

"Yes, not again!" Mack groaned.

Griffin laughed. "Yeah, you erased like twenty gig of saved games. They've only just got back to where you erased it all."

I scoffed, rolling my eyes. "I didn't erase anything. It asked me if I wanted to format the device. How was I meant to know that it'd delete it all?"

"Formatting is erasing, Mum." Toby laughed, rolling onto his back and cracking up at me hysterically.

I pretended to be annoyed and scrunched my face up. "Fine. I won't touch anything. I'm coming with you now. Screw your boy's trip out. I'm tagging along, and you can watch me kiss your dad in public."

"Eww. Gross."

I just laughed. They made me smile so freaking hard at times.

***

Lunch was amazing and delicious. We had a great time. I did not know why, but when Griffin gave me that look, I had to wonder why on earth he was going to tell them about their mother here—in public and over lunch. Maybe because they looked so happy.

"I need to tell you boys something. Just don't go screaming at us or anything, okay?"

Then I realised he was doing it in public because he was nervous. He was worried that they would not be happy about this new move and that they would probably hate him. I reached over, squeezing his thigh to give him support.

They looked at us, and Toby frowned. "You're not breaking up, are you?"

"God, no. He can't get rid of me that easily." I snorted. "Like I'd ever leave your dad, anyway. He's got lots of money."

Griffin laughed, shaking his head. "Thanks, Ayla. Glad to know that's the big thing you like most about me."

"Not the only big thing I love," I whispered with my hand playfully moving closer to his groin region. He stopped me by taking my hand in his and lifting it, placing a kiss.

"Your mother has been arrested. There's a good chance she's going to jail," he told them in a shaky voice.

All humour was gone. Mack just looked at him. "How long for?"

"No less than five years. There were some other things that has become known, and she's in a lot of trouble." *Drugs.* "She didn't fight the charges and has admitted to everything."

Toby nodded, picking up his burger. "I don't want to see her ever again. I hate the bitch."

Griffin sighed. "You can't say that."

"Me, too!" Mack added. "I don't want to go anywhere near her again."

"Do we get to stay with you still?" Toby asked as if that part had not been made clear.

I reached over with my free hand and squeezed his forearm gently. "Of course, you are. We wouldn't have you live anywhere else."

"Ayla's right. It's just going to be the four of us from now on." Griffin assured them but then seemed to realise his choice of words. "No matter what, you boys will always have a home here with us. If you don't want to see her again, then I won't push you to do so. It's your choice, but at home, we have rules and expect you to follow them. Ayla's not going to be pushed around, and you have to treat her—"

"Dad, we know this already." Toby rolled his eyes. "She's our mum. We love her."

"Duh." Mack retorted.

I could not help but get in on it too. "Yeah, Griffin, duh."

"Cheeky," he leant in, ignoring the boy's groans of displeasure at the sight of us having a quick kiss. It was nothing over the top, but it definitely left me wanting more. That would come later once the boys are in bed and fast asleep… after I give him the best tattoo he would ever receive.

***

Griffin sat back down on the sofa in the shed after cleaning himself up as I straddled his lap again, taking hold of his hand tighter and getting a firmer grip on him. The gun was in my other hand, and I felt nervous but excited.

"You know, we could have done this when you were riding my cock."

"I wouldn't be able to focus." I smiled, trying to concentrate as his fingers slipped into the fabric of my panties. "Stop it."

"Like you told me to stop it half an hour ago? You begged for it." His voice was once again husky.

I pried his hand away from slipping into my underwear. "Stop it. You distracted me."

"I could distract you once again," he said, trying to pout. "Fine, I give up, but I want you afterwards. You're really sexy holding that in your hand."

I raised a brow. "Hmm, that's exactly what I thought when you first inked me. Maybe that's why I slept with you again."

He laughed as he leant forwards and kissed my nose. "Thanks pretty. I love you, too."

"Close your eyes." I urged him. "I need to focus, please."

He smiled an adorable grin but complied with my request. "Don't you dare draw a cock in there."

I laughed. "We'll, there goes my surprise." One eye opened, and he just shook his head. "Don't worry. I'm not. It's not going to say Ayla, though."

"No?" He seemed confused, and I just shrugged. I could not ruin the surprise.

The ink hit his skin, and of course, he faked a huge scream which scared me and almost had me falling off his lap. I could have injured us both with that. My heartbeat returned to normal once he promised to never do that again.

It took me a little longer. I was scared to go in too deep and hit some vein. He had told me about that once—blood everywhere and a man passed out on his floor. Not the image I would enjoy having in our shed.

"Okay. It's finished now." I set the gun back and admired my work of art on his left wrist.

Opening his eyes up, he lifted his wrist up and looked at it.

1+1=3

He stared at with a confused expression, scanning his eyes over the letters I had inked there. "I don't get it. Isn't it meant to be two? Not three?"

My smile did not falter. "Griffin, think about it. Really think about it. In this room, there's you, me and…" I lingered the huge hint in the air for him.

His eyes widened, and his mouth parted in a half-smile as he darted those blue orbs of his between us, directly on my stomach. "No…" I almost did not hear his gasp.

"Yes."

"Say it," he begged in a soft, pleading whisper.

"Best tattoo ever," I said through laughter.

Glaring at me, his hands slid to my hips and held me tight. "Yes, but not what I meant. Say it, Ayla."

"I'm pregnant."

CHAPTER TWENTY-FIVE

"It's so small."

"Tiny."

"Like, that is really, really small, Ayla."

Smiling hard, I fought to keep my mouth shut and inner thoughts clean right now. Just a subtle yep was all that was needed.

"That's your baby, growing healthy for eight weeks." The doctor pulled us out of our battle over how little the baby is. "How have you been feeling?" he asked.

Griffin did not let me have a word in. It was obvious how excited he really was about the pregnancy. "She's been sick, a lot. Like pulled-over-twice-on-the-drive-here sick."

"I'm fine." He was making me out worse than I really was. "It's just morning sickness."

"She's throwing up all day and night. Is that normal?" Griffin asked, ignoring me.

The doctor nodded, straightening his glasses back up. "Of course, some women experience morning sickness that lasts all day. It should start to fade towards the second trimester. Just make sure you keep your fluid intake up, and once again, if there's any sign of cramping of bleeding, please call my office immediately, just in case." *Just in case lose another baby.* "Other than that, you're good to leave."

As happy as I was, I was also terrified, constantly worrying that maybe I would lose this baby at any moment. It was a normal thought, so Griffin kept trying to tell me as he comforted me. It may be normal, but it still scared the shit out of me.

Paying the bill, we made our way back to the car hand in hand. Griffin silently beamed beside me as I looked up, and I wanted to shake my head and laugh. It was pretty cute. He was *really* happy. I had not seen him this happy since I married him.

After all the shit that has happened lately, he could be as happy as he wanted. Hell, I was on cloud nine and ready to shout it from the rooftops that I had his baby growing in my tummy.

A slight breeze picked up and blew my hair around. Letting his hand go, I tied it up. His hand did not move and only went to my ass as we kept walking to the car. He closed the car door, and I could have just burst into tears when he pulled out our ultrasound picture and stared in awe at it.

"I can't believe you're pregnant. We're going to have a baby."

"I know." I was pretty damn excited myself. "I can't believe I'm eight weeks. I thought probably four or five."

He looked up, giving me an adoring smile as he gazed at me. Reaching his hand up, he cupped my cheek. "Yeah, considering you only took a test a week ago, I have to agree."

One week ago, I had shocked the hell out of him with that tattoo. There was not just him and me in the shed; There was also a little baby inside me, making it the three of us. Too bad if it turned out to be nothing, and I had just inked that on Griffin's wrist for the hell of it.

Luckily, I was pregnant, and our baby was going strong.

"When do you want to tell the boys?"

We had not really talked about that much. I did not want to throw too much at them at once. I was not sure how they would take the news that they were going to be big brothers to a baby fifteen years younger than them. Oh, god, what an age difference.

"How about tonight once they get back from school? We can have a family dinner?" He suggested, dropping his hand and starting the car up.

"What if they get mad? Maybe they'll hate the idea." I asked, almost afraid of their reactions.

"I doubt that. Mack will probably be more excited than Toby. Toby will just be grossed out knowing we had sex." He went to pull out but hit the brakes and pointed. "Is that Harvey?"

My nausea picked up again as I looked to where he pointed. There he stood with a woman beside him—a heavily pregnant woman who, of course, was all sorts of beautiful. He looked happy, but in a way, he looked different. His hair was much longer, and the piercings were gone from his face. There was no facial hair or tats showing. He looked, well... not like the guy I knew.

A pang hit my chest. It was no jealousy that I felt. It was hurt for the friendship lost between us. I felt as if he only wanted me when Griffin was treating me badly. Then when Griffin came back, I was pretty much dropped for the new woman—the woman he was in love with.

"Are you okay?" Griffin asked, giving my thigh a rub.

I nodded. I really was okay. "Yeah, just wish he did not turn out to be such a dick." For making a move on me while I was suffering a broken heart.

"I ought to go over there and introduce him to my fist, fucking wanker." There was no love lost between those two.

I just laughed as he began to reverse once again and drove us home. There were no pit stops needed. I made it just in time to throw up in the kitchen sink.

"Are you okay?" Griffin came rushing over, his hand rubbing my lower back. Yeah, because that was going to help. "Fuck," he muttered as I threw up once again.

"Water," I mumbled, between hurls. This really was not fun, but in a way, it soothed me. As long as I was throwing up, I could be eased that my pregnancy was going well.

Cool liquid filled my mouth, and I swallowed, relishing the comfort it gave me. Griffin had not left my side and was all eyes on me. "Do you want to have a lay down?"

"Not really."

"What about on the couch? I could put a movie on for you?"

I did not feel like watching anything, really. "Maybe just turn the TV on."

"I'll get the hard drive and put on *Greys*?"

He knew me well. "Please."

"Anything for my pregnant wife."

Snuggled up on the couch, a water bottle plus a bucket was beside me with a towel in case I needed to throw up again. I swear, he was more concerned about my vomit hitting the new couch than anything else. His body was behind mine, holding me closely.

"Griffin... pause the TV." I told him, yawning and reaching for my phone.

"What's wrong?" he asked, doing so.

"Nothing. I just need to make a phone call." I could not hold off any longer.

Mum burst into tears when I had called her on the phone. I was going to wait, but in the end, I could not. We would tell others when I was further along, but for now, the kids and my parents were the only ones who would know.

Speaking of the boys, they still did not know. I could not wait to tell them either.

My bladder also could not wait, and I darted off to the bathroom.

I was standing in our bedroom, holding the photograph in my hands and smiling like a dork.

Griffin came up behind me. With a hand, he brushed all my hair from the side, leaving my neck exposed. "Am I allowed to be extremely turned on, knowing that you're pregnant with my child inside of you?"

I nodded, a soft moan escaping. "Mmm, course you are. Am I allowed to be lazy and not get on top this time?"

I shivered slightly, and my eyes closed on their own accord as I felt his lips against the nape of my neck, trailing soft kisses down that left a tingle of goosebumps right down my spine. "I'll be gentle."

"Oh, yeah? Like when you said you'd pull out, and you didn't?" I laughed, remembering that moment.

He laughed, turning to face me. "I didn't pull out because I wanted you pregnant, and mission is accomplished. I'm going to go slow because I don't want to hurt you or our baby."

Aww, so sweet. "Hate to break it to you, babe, but as big as you are... it kind of isn't that big, and it's definitely not going to touch the baby."

"I know that," he muttered, shaking his head at me. "I just... I want this baby, Ayla. I really want this."

As I went to undress, he stopped and reached for my hand. I was confused as he stood in front of me, halting my movements. "Did you not want to? We don't have to... I'm okay to just cuddle."

His eyes locked on mine. Taking a step closer, he shook his head. "Let me do this. I want you to feel it, Ayla... feel just how much I love you right now." Slowly, he began to continue undressing me.

As he promised, I felt it. I felt the love and need he had for me. His mouth took its sweet time bringing me to that glorious O, twice. It felt like forever when he hovered above me. His teasing thrusts filled me with satisfaction as I wrapped my legs around his thighs and locked him in close.

He really did want it gentle, slow, and tender.

Lifting my head up, his arm slipped underneath my neck, and I moved in against his chest. His arm curled around my face, and I traced a finger over his wrist. The tattoo has healed almost completely. "Are you sure you like it?"

"I do." Pausing, his voice changed, and he was leaning over me once more. "What's wrong?"

"Why would you think something is wrong?" He knew me well, that was why.

"You keep asking if I like it. Are you not happy with it?"

"I should have added the boys into my calculations. It's not just us. It's them, too." I had been kicking myself about that. "Maybe I could—" My words were cut off by a chaste kiss.

Pulling away, his hand grazed over my temple and down my cheek. "Yes, it would make things five, but pretty, this baby is ours first... just you and me."

"But it's not just us. It's them, too." I would hate for them to feel neglected and put out just because there was a baby coming along soon.

His chest rose and fell with a deep sigh. "When Karen told me that she was pregnant, I asked her to get rid of it. I'm not proud of that, Ayla." I did not think I would be either. His admission did not shock me as much as it should have. I understood, in some crazy way.

"You were young."

"I was too busy getting high and pissed to bother with the check-ups."

I nodded, not sure what else I could do. "That doesn't make you a bad father."

"I told her I didn't believe her, that I wanted to break up, then went on a boys' camping trip." A mocking laugh rumbled through his chest. "Came back, and she had the pregnancy test and ultrasound out on the table. Realised that, fuck yeah, she'd gotten pregnant, and my life was pretty much over."

"You're a wonderful dad to them, Griffin. It's okay that you were afraid at first. You've always put them first. Everything you do is in some way for them, to provide and protect them." He could not be judged on a thing that happened over a decade ago. He needed to let go and forgive himself.

"Wish I had met you back then."

"Creeper, I was like four back then. Are you trying to tell me that you want me to call you daddy and ask for a spanking?"

He laughed. I finally got a smile from him. "If I want to spank you, then I will."

"Shall I bend over?" I suggested, wiggling my brows. "Can I count, or would you like to gag me with my panties?"

"Pretty, I'd rather gag you with my cock, but you're off oral duties until you stop throwing up."

I pretended to pout in frustration. In actual fact, I could not be happier. That was the last thing I wanted in my mouth. I knew I would definitely throw up. I could barely stomach brushing my teeth without heaving over the sink and having my eyes water.

"So the tattoo is okay, then?" Time for a change of subject.

"The tattoo is more than okay. This is a baby between us. It's something you and I created."

"Oh, when you lasted like ten seconds?" I grinned, brushing my fingers through his hair.

He laughed softly. "I apologised for that. It had been awhile." His hand splayed out across my naked stomach, rubbing softly as he leaned over my body and smiled down. Looking into my eyes, he went to kiss me, skimming his lips across my jaw and whispering out those three words I adored. "I love you, crazy woman."

I would show him crazy when I was eight months pregnant and moody. "Crazy woman who's pregnant with your baby."

***

Dinner was in the oven, and my nerves were like a tornado inside my stomach. Toby and Mack were sitting at the table waiting to be fed while Griffin was opposite them, asking about their day at school.

"Why are we having dinner early?" Toby asked, drumming his fingers on the table with a yawn. "I have *Halo* that I wanted to play."

"You can play after we've eaten. We wanted to speak with you both. What's a better way than when there's food involved?" Griffin said, smirking as he stood up and made his way to the oven just before the timer went off.

Okay, since when did he ever help with cooking and dinner? He was really outdoing himself with all of this, letting me take it easy. I did not mind, but he better not get me used to it and then all of a sudden ditch the helpfulness.

"Griffin, I can do that."

"No lifting."

Oh, god. He could not be serious. "It's a casserole. Not ten kilos of spuds." I sighed, giving up and reaching for the ladle to dish the chicken curry over the rice.

"Why can't Mum lift?" Mack asked, taking his plate once it was ready.

"I can. Dad's just being ridiculous."

Sitting down, Griffin cleared his throat. "Ayla's pregnant. She can't lift, and I need you boys to make sure she doesn't pick anything heavy up."

Both boys, including myself, sat wide-eyed, shocked and staring open-mouthed at Griffin.

"Griffin!" I kicked him in the leg "What happened to easing into this lightly?"

"Ayla, we're having a baby. There's no going into this lightly. It's a good thing." He smiled, taking my hand and squeezing it gently.

"Gross. You two..." Toby pushed his plate aside, gagging. "That's just... I can't even eat knowing you and Dad took a trip to pound town."

"Pound town?" Griffin looked more impressed than disgusted. "Never heard of that one. May have to take another trip after dinner."

"Please stop," Mack begged. "I beg of you."

I laughed. "Yes, let's stop, but you still have to eat your food. So sit back down, Toby, and eat."

Mack cocked his head to the side. "When will the baby be here?"

"Just after Easter next year. Are you okay with that?" I began to feel nervous again. Maybe they were not happy about all of this.

Griffin and I shared a nervous glance. "You do know, that this doesn't change the way we feel about either of you."

"Chill, old man," Toby scoffed. "We get it. We kind of expected it. I mean, Ayla, doesn't have any kids of her own, and you're always banging."

"Do you have an ear at the door? We aren't always doing that," I defensibly said, my cheeks burning up.

"No." He shot back, looking equally embarrassed that I could suggest such a thing. "Just saying that you and Dad were going to have kids of your own. It's okay."

I wanted to believe him. I badly did. "Are you sure?"

Mack grinned. "Yeah, a baby! I bet it's a girl. I want a sister."

"Put some money on that, nerd, and you got yourself a bet," Toby said, smirking. In no time, he and Mack began to bet on whether our baby would be a boy or girl.

"Wait, it could be twins." I pointed out. "Maybe one's just hiding."

The cough of shock beside me was well worth it. Griffin cleared his throat with a glass of water. "Twins?"

I played along. "Sure, I mean, there's always that chance of one hiding. Two sets of twins could be fun."

If he weren't shaking his head so fast, I would probably be able to see beads of sweat forming on his forehead. "But we saw just one today. He said just one."

"Dad's about to have a heart attack." Toby snickered, and Mack grinned.

Putting him out of his misery, I rubbed his arm. "Don't look so ecstatic about it. There's only one. Relax." Although there were those cases, I thought it was best not to scare him anymore.

"Yeah, not funny," he muttered, shooting me a glare.

My smile did not falter even once. This was fun. "Aww, I think you're losing your sense of humour in your old age, baby."

Mack laughed. "Dad, can you imagine how cool that would be? Two babies."

"Be fucked if I'm buying a minivan," Griffin exclaimed. "I refuse to buy one of those, Ayla."

Oh, this was his concern. "Oh, truth comes out now. Don't worry. No minivan for us."

Blowing out a breath of relief, he winked. "Even if we did, you'd be the one driving it."

I laughed hard. "Afraid you'll lose your bad boy cred, huh?"

"You know it."

The boys finally passed out, and that meant we could go to sleep. I did not like going to bed before them. You never know what could happen. Pulling the covers up over our bodies, I yawned, rolling to my side as Griffin turned the lamp off.

"Sweet dreams, baby." I yawned, half-asleep already.

I felt his lips against the nape of my neck as his arms slid around to their usual place: one underneath my neck and the other around my waist. Only this time, his hand was holding protectively over my belly.

With a whisper, he softly spoke, "Told you they'd be happy."

Yes. He sure did.

CHAPTER TWENTY-SIX

Yawning as I rubbed my growing bump, I managed to open both my eyes and keep them open for a few seconds before they slowly began to close again. This was every morning for me: a struggle to get up and get out of bed to start the day.

Pregnancy had really kicked me in the ass and knocked all the energy out of me these last couple weeks. I blamed Griffin for the size of our daughter. I was going to be pushing out a good-sized baby and tearing my vagina to shreds in the process.

Walking out from his shower, naked and not a care in the world, Griffin shook his head, just laughing. "You know, you don't have to get up yet. Stay in a little longer."

"I need to clean, cook, and hide all those sex toys you brought."

"They're in the cupboard. No one needs to be in our room, so they're safely hidden from everyone except us," he said, pulling on a pair of boxer shorts. "I must say, I'm surprised you were up for that last night."

I would have rolled my eyes if I were not too tired. "What can I say. I was in a horny mood and just wanted to feel your cock fucking me." Pushing the covers off, I slowly started to get up, glaring at him. "Just be grateful that you got laid."

"True. Pussy has been on lockdown lately," he teased, walking towards me and helping me up out of bed.

I yawned again and flicked his arm in response. "My ass is on lockdown. Trust me, your cock in there is the last thing I feel like."

He roared in laughter. "I'm just kidding, pretty."

Doing his usual morning routine of dropping down to both knees and running his hands over my bulging bare stomach, he placed a string of kisses against my skin and talked to our child. It melted me every morning to see this, hearing him reading stories to the baby or just talking about his day and how much he could not wait to meet him or her. He had no idea that the baby was a girl.

I showered, and almost forty minutes later, I was joining the others in the kitchen. Seven months pregnant, I felt like it took me forever to do something as simple as walk from one room to another. I was expecting to see everyone, but it was only Mack inside eating a bowl of cereal.

"Where's your brother and Dad?" I asked, opening the fridge and pulling out the bacon. I could eat bacon all day long and be a very happy woman.

"Outside, they're cleaning up the barbie for lunch today."

That was another thing that had slipped my mind. His parents were joining us for lunch after a surprise trip announcement. They knew I was pregnant; They just did not really comment on it. It was the elephant in the room. It was there, but we didn't talk about it. It's sad, really. My parents, on the other hand, could not contain their excitement, and Mum often came to visit with little gifts for her grandchild.

The nursery was almost complete. Actually, it was complete, but I was buying little things online when I had insomnia. Our mailman must love me and my weekly packages.

"Why don't you see your friend anymore?" he asked, out of the blue as I sat down with my food. "You know, the one Dad hated."

That took me by surprise. It was hard to keep my shock hidden. I felt the need to point out an actual fact. "He still hates him."

Mack laughed, nodding. "Yeah, but only because he's jealous. Did you two have a fight?"

Harvey was not someone who I really felt like talking about. I have pushed it under the rug for so long, trying to forget about him and not care. It was hard, knowing he had become a father to a boy. He never reached out or tried to make contact, so I did not see the point in extending the same branch.

"Harvey moved on. Sometimes, people change and grow apart. It happens. Anyway, enough about that. Is Samuel coming over for lunch too?" I asked. It was normal for his boyfriend to join us. It was not a bother. They had been dating for quite some time, and he was always here.

His eyes widened. "But, Nan will be here."

Yes, she was not too thrilled knowing that her grandson was dating a dude. "So?"

His voice went quiet. "She won't be happy." Griffin's mother definitely did not like Samuel.

"I don't care. Invite him. He's part of the family."

Being heavily pregnant, my conversations were also limited. Before long, I began to feel puffed out and tired. I hated it. I needed a nap when I had not even started the day. Unfortunately, today was not a day that I could just lay down and rest. I needed to get stuff down and work like a boss around the house.

Pulling out the mop, I scowled as I filled the bucket with hot water and waited. A pair of arms sliding around my waist and a smile took away the annoyance I was feeling.

"You look tired, baby. Go lay down. I'll do all this."

Not a chance in hell. "As much as I would love that, I can't. You know I can't."

"Ayla, you're exhausted. Go rest. You need to rest, remember? The doctor told you to take it easy."

I hated that he brought that up. At four months, I woke up and went to the bathroom, only to find blood. I screamed murder. Not quite but almost, and Griffin rushed me to the hospital. I was having a threatened miscarriage. The baby was safe and sound, but there was a small bleed, and it could still lead to me losing it—my worst fear. From then on, Griffin had set me a rule to follow: When I was tired, I rest. Actually, I was to rest all the time and not do much.

It became boring after a while.

"I'm okay to mop." Turning around in his arms, I pushed my belly against his stomach and rested my head on his chest. "I don't want her to think I'm lazy."

"Pretty…" His finger brushed underneath my chin, tilting my head back as he placed his hand over my burgeoning stomach, spreading his fingers out. "You're close to giving birth. Rest now. It's an order."

This time, I rolled my eyes and cocked my head to the side. "I'm only thirty-two weeks or thirty-three, Griffin. I'm good for a couple more months."

Pulling away, he frowned and looked at me with an odd expression. "Ayla, you're thirty-eight weeks tomorrow."

I laughed. He was taking this too far by trying to trick me. I tilted my head back. "No. I'm not, I'm…" I started to work it out in my head, and panic seeped in. My breathing increased, and my lips formed an O. "But… No, no…"

"Yes. You're due at the end of the month. See? You're so tired, you're forgetting everything, Ayla." He was not scolding, just grinning because he was right. "Now, ass on that couch and relax."

This time, I did listen. I walked in a daze to the living room and sat down on the charcoal sofa. It was big enough to be used as a bed. We wanted a lazy couch, and this was definitely one. Yawning, I tried to get comfortable despite my restless legs. How could I have forgotten my own due date? Closing my eyes, I heard Griffin quietly giving out orders for the boys to clean their room and help tidy up as I slowly drifted to sleep.

***

I jerked awake when I felt a hand against my stomach. "What time is it? Your parents—"

"Are an hour away. Housework is all done, and you can rest up easy." He leant in, kissing me softly.

"You know." I smiled, making myself more comfortable. "How about we call the baby by her name?"

"You've picked out a unisex name?" he laughed, looking unconvinced. "No offence, but I'm not naming my baby a— Wait, you said 'her'?"

"I found out last week. I'm sorry, the doctor slipped up and said she was growing well." I grinned. He did not want to know, but I could not help myself.

"A girl," Griffin said to himself. His eyes were watching me closely in case I was going to tell him I was kidding. I did not, and he broke out into a huge smile. "Well, shit. I think I owe the older kids two fifty bucks each."

I exclaimed, "Griffin, not cool."

"I thought it was a boy. I was sure of it."

I started to stand up. "You are unreal." Betting on our child? How could he? Actually, it did not surprise me one bit, really. "I should have made a bet with you also then."

I felt his presence following behind me as I walked down to our bedroom. "Well, what's the name?"

"Hmm, how about you bet on that and lose some more money?" I grinned, flashing a smile over my shoulder at him. "Anyway, I think I like, Harper."

"Harper?" he repeated, sounding unsure. "Okay."

He did not like it. "We can think of some others later if you don't like it."

"No, I like it." He smiled warmly. "Harper James."

"Good, because I wasn't changing it." I winked as I pulled up my tank top and tossed it in the clothes basket, changing for a shower.

"Will your tits shrink again?" he asked, walking straight towards me, preying on my chest with open palms, and gently squeezing.

"What if my water breaks during sex?"

His face scrunched, then a smile crept over. His eyes danced with mischief. "Well, I guess it'll be no different to you squirting."

It was my turn to pull a face. "Gross." Pushing his hands away, I went into the wardrobe to grab another top. "And for your information, they will shrink, so enjoy. You won't get to see them this big again."

"Well, not until I knock you up again." He peeked in the walk-in and stood there, watching me change.

I shook my head but could not shake it fast enough. "No more."

"What? No, you don't mean that."

I laughed humourlessly. "Yes, I do. I am fat, tired, and aching all over. I'm not having any more."

His smile dropped, and his eyes shot me a glare. "Yes, you are. She needs someone to play with, so get used to the idea of another—"

I cut him off. "Griffin…"

"Ayla, it's going to happen. Deal with it."

As soon as he walked away, I let out a frustrated scream and finished pulling the top back on. He was not the one who had to give birth or grow a baby. No, he got to keep his body and shape. I was the one dealing with uncontrollable discharge and morning sickness all day.

I went to yell that out to him when I heard the doorbell ring and voices at the door.

Maybe I could just ignore them and go back to bed. *Yeah, tough luck on that.*

Samuel and Mack were on the couch watching a movie as Toby rode his BMX bike around outside. His parents were still here hours later with no intention of leaving. There was not one question about the baby, and whenever it was brought up by Griffin, they shot him down. Not so much his dad, but more his mother. She just glared at my belly.

Poor baby. She had done nothing to her. At least I was taking care of my baby way better than Karen had done.

"Oh, no. I'll do that," I told her, standing up as she went to clear the table. "I'm sure you want to catch up with Griffin." My back was aching even more, but I managed a smile and reached for the stack of plates to pick them up.

"Ayla, leave them." My overprotective husband warned me. "Sit and take it easy."

I halted, shooting him a glare. "I can manage."

"Leave them."

Why was I so annoyed at being told not to do anything? I should be loving it, but I was not. I felt agitated, annoyed, and really sad. Yes, my waterworks were coming on, all because he told me to not to do anything.

He noticed my eyes blurring and sighed softly. "Sweetheart…"

"I'm okay." I turned my eyes to his parents. "Hormones." I did not really know how else to explain it.

Paul smiled, looking slightly uncomfortable. It was annoying.

"Teresa," I began. "Look, I'm heavily pregnant. It'd be nice if you could acknowledge it."

"Dear… Oh, it's not that. We just feel… Well, we feel guilty." Her voice wavered. "We can't possibly be mad about the baby. It's wonderful, but we just."

Griffin stood up and glared. "What would you feel guilty for?"

Had I passed out? What the heck was happening? I felt in the dark with this conversation. What would he be so mad for? It did not make any sense.

"We didn't know she was hurting the boys. We would have never helped her otherwise."

My eyes widened, looking at Teresa as my mouth began to open.

Griffin's voice made us all jump. "You got her that lawyer, didn't you?"

Everything soon began to unravel. His parents tried explaining how she came to them in a state of panic, fearing that she would lose her children, and somehow convinced them that she could take better care of them than their own son. His parents saw how hurt and miserable their son had been when we came to visit, and all along, they knew everything.

They helped her take the kids from us, from him.

"Please, leave," I said softly, standing up. "It's time you both go." I could not hear anymore and did not want the boys to either. They would feel more than betrayed.

"Ayla, please..."

I rubbed my lower back. The aching intensified as I gritted my teeth and ignored it. "Please, you and Paul should go."

"Ayla..."

I could tell by his tone that Griffin was worried. "I'm okay. Just need a hot shower." For like, an hour.

"I can't believe you two watched how much she fucked up our lives, and you knew all along. You handed my kids to that bitch for them to get beaten!" He was seething with anger, pacing as he looked at his parents in horror.

"We know…" Teresa wailed, moving closer to him. "Do you think we don't regret it? Every day. Oh, Griffin, we regret it every day."

"You fucked up, Mum. Big fucking time."

I was frozen to the spot, unable to move as I felt a stabbing pain hit my lower back. "Griffin…" I breathed out, trying to hold my breath.

No one heard me.

"Griffin, we're sorry! Please, son. You have to see it from our side." Paul started, pleading.

"Griffin…" I tried again. My stomach was beginning to cramp up. "Baby…"

"No. I'll never understand. You paid her a good fucking lawyer and left your son to fend for himself."

I could not hold it in any longer. "I'm in labour! My water just broke."

Not the best way to go about things.

All eyes were on me. The three of them looked stunned as I stood there, tears streaming down my cheeks and water running down my thighs like I had just wet myself. This was it, what we had been waiting for, and now I was terrified.

"Are you sure?" he asked, looking completely freaked out.

"No, dickhead. I'm wetting myself for the fun of it." I could not believe he asked that. "I'm having contractions. Get the kids. We need to leave."

Our bags were already in the car. His parents offered to stay at the house with them, but he refused. So, they were in the waiting room with the boys and Sam while I was hauled off and hooked up to an IV drip, stripped naked in a gown, and laid on a bed, groaning in agony.

Griffin walked in looking like a ghost and stood by the door. "I'm terrified."

Now he decided to admit this. Mister, who was so excited for the baby to be here, now decided to tell me he was scared. "You have to be kidding me." I was the one who was terrified.

"No, Ayla. I am fucking scared right now."

I rolled my eyes. "Well, maybe just do whatever you did with the boys when they were being born?" He had to have some clue. "I'm new at this."

He shook his head. "Ayla..." His voice dropped as he made his way over, shame and regret filling his pained expression. "I didn't come in the room when she was in labour. I waited outside."

"And you tell me this now?" I snapped, reaching for his hand and squeezing hard. "How... I mean... Ahh, shit. This hurt so damn much."

"I never wanted them, so I didn't really come to any appointments or anything."

"Of all times. You could have told me this like, I don't know, yesterday maybe? Not while I'm almost a fist dilated."

A soft chuckle came from him, and his hand rubbed soothingly over my belly as I laid there trying to focus on my breathing. "I love you. Can I get you anything?"

Throwing my head back on the pillow, I began to cry. "I want the drugs. Get me the drugs!"

***

Thirty minutes later, I had pushed out an echidna. Kidding, but it felt like that.

I was completely in love as I held my crying baby daughter in my arms with my husband passed out on the bed beside us. Yes, he fainted when he took one look at the placenta and dropped down like a drunk man passing out.

I laughed quietly to myself. He can fuck me with a period, but as soon as he saw blood, he was out like a light. I was so glad the nurse was taking photos and videos for us.

"That's your daddy over there," I whispered as the doctors cleaned me up down there. "He's just having a nap."

I was too focused on her to notice the needle and stitch they were about to insert—her big eyes, dark hair, and perfect pout. I finally got that feeling, the feeling of having my own child and being so immensely in love that I would do anything for her. I loved the boys, but I did not ever get to experience this moment with them.

My whole world would revolve around her. Everything I would now do was for her. I was a mother, and it was the most incredible experience of my life.

"She's perfect." I heard a whisper from beside me. Griffin was on his feet as he slowly walked to the chair beside the bed. "She looks just like you."

I smiled, looking up towards him and meeting his gaze. "Thank you," I whispered.

He frowned, looking confused. Maybe he was still dizzy from the blackout. "For what? You did all the hard work."

Shaking my head, I melted against him as his arms wrapped around me. "For letting me have this, for being able to experience what it's like to have a child of my own."

He looked down, understanding fully what I meant. "I should never have made you promise something like that. I don't deserve you, Ayla, but I'll earn your love every day."

"I love you, and you deserve that." I smiled. "You and the boys deserve to be loved, and I will show you that every day."

"You're beautiful." Leaning in, he pressed his lips against mine. "I'm sorry for passing out."

I laughed against his lips, murmuring. "Don't worry. You can make it up to me with the next one."

His brows raised. "Another one?"

"Oh, yeah. I want more..."

"One, right? How many are we talking about here?" His tone was low. It almost made me laugh.

Shrugging, I looked back to our daughter. "I'm not sure yet. Harper needs some brothers and sisters."

"Ayla, how many? You can't just say that. Jesus."

I knew he was beginning to panic, and that made all the more fun taunting him. "I don't know. I'll let you know when I'm done."

"You said no more this morning. What changed?"

"Holding her in my arms, that feeling of explosive love I just experienced. I feel like I was born to be a mother, and it's crazy. I really can't wait to have another baby with you."

His smile grew, and he reached over and taking our daughter from my arms. "Yeah, I get that. I think we should introduce her to her two older brothers now, though. I'm sure our parents are hanging out to meet this beauty as well."

I agreed, then realised I was still all naked and gross with a doctor staring at my vagina. "Just wait until we're in the room, and then we can get them all in."

He nodded, sitting down and rocking Harper close against his chest. "I love you, my two girls."

EPILOGUE

I looked at the woman opposite me. Her hair was longer and untidy. I could not tell if she had lost weight, but she did look awfully thin with that face. Her eyes just shot daggers through my skull.

"You called me to come here. If you're going to sit and glare, then I might as well turn around and go home." I began to stand, but she shook her head, pleading with me to stay. Sitting back down, I sighed. "Karen, what do you want?"

Call me crazy for coming to visit this woman alone, but what else was I supposed to do when she called, begging me to see her. Ignore her and tell Griffin? No, I had not told him that I was here.

The good thing about having a baby? I could just tell him I had a doctor's appointment for the pill.

Karen slid over a piece of paper and shrugged. "I know it's late, but if you want them so badly, have them."

My eyes stayed glued to hers. "Why now?"

Shrugging once more, she licked her lips and dragged her fingers through her hair. "I'm not getting out of here anytime soon, and when I do... they won't want to see me."

True. "Are you okay in here?" I asked her softly. It was probably the most civil conversation she and I had ever had. "I mean, you aren't fighting anyone, are you?"

Smirking, she winked. "No one fucks with me. You should know that."

I bit my tongue and nodded. "Good. I guess that's a bonus."

"Look, Ayla, you can fuck off now. You got what you wanted, and I heard you had a baby a few weeks ago. Congrats, you got the family you always wanted from him."

"Not from him, Karen—" I took the piece of paper and stood, looking her dead in the eyes, "with him."

Turning away, I headed for the doors with happy tears filling my eyes and a huge smile plastered across my face. This was the last I would ever have to see her, and it made me so damn happy.

***

I did have to see the doctor for birth control—the mini pill—because I was still breastfeeding and planned on doing so for quite some time. After the doctors, I headed on home. I could not wait. I missed them terribly and wanted nothing more than to hug my babies and smother my man in kisses.

Pulling down the drive, Griffin was at the window, holding Harper and pointing out towards me. He was an amazing father.

I tucked the piece of paper in my back pocket and made my way up the deck to them. He opened the door and greeted me, "Hey, Mama. We missed you."

I smiled even more as Harper nodded, holding her arms out for me to take her. "Mama," she said and snuggled against my side, tucking her head underneath my chin.

"Did she have her sleep?" I asked, walking into the living room after I had kicked off my shoes.

"For a bit. She woke not long after you left." Griffin sat on the floor and began to pick up the toys scattered in front of him. "You'd think she'd have kept her good sleeping routine."

I laughed, lying back on the couch. "I know. At least we have another good little sleeper, though. I'm tempted to go in there and pick him up."

"Ayla, we both know better than to wake a sleeping baby. Leave him."

I grinned, poking him with my toes. "I missed him. He's so snuggly, though."

"Oh, dear. So when are we trying for number three?" He laughed, shaking his head.

Eyeing him, with a grin. "Maybe I'm happy with two. I could be done."

"Tough I think one more. When he's eight or nine months, prepare to be pounded into pregnancy."

"I love how you're so romantic with your words. One more, that's it, and you're getting the snip." I promised. "Now, what have you two been up to?" I asked, kissing Harper on the cheek. She was so beautiful and cuddly.

He went on, telling me about their game of chasings and then how she did a wee on her potty, which he gave her a bag of chips for. He was a really great and fun dad. He was so hands-on, and it made me fall in love with him all the more.

"How was the doctors? Are we right to, you know?" He smirked, watching his words around our daughter who already liked to copy us.

I nodded. "We're good to go, but I have to tell you something else first."

His eyes narrowed. "If you tell me you're pregnant from me blowing a load over your pussy the other night, then I'm sorry, but I won't believe you."

I burst out laughing, hard enough to scare Harper. "No, I'm not, and you can't say that around her."

"Sorry, what is it then?" he asked. Harper climbed up onto his lap and reached for the wooden tea set mug. She loved to play that with him.

Just as I went to open my mouth, a cry came through the baby monitor, and I jumped up. "I'll get him. You keep playing dolls with Harper."

"You can't keep that thing from me, Ayla. I'll find out soon enough," his voice called out. I just laughed.

In the bedroom, the cries grew louder as I leant over the crib and picked up Oscar, our sleepy six-week-old baby boy. Gah, I was still in newborn bliss from giving birth to him weeks ago. He took his sweet time arriving, not wanting to leave his safe, warm little home.

Perching myself up on the bed, I unclipped my bra to feed, and his cries instantly died down.

I stopped feeding Harper once she turned two, just before I fell pregnant with this little guy. We were definitely trying for him all day, night, and every chance we got.

Toby was at college. It was hard seeing him go. He was striving each day. Who knew underneath his bad attitude was a really smart boy who worked hard. Mack was the same, and as much as he wanted to go work at Hogwarts, he ended up asking Griffin if he could come work with him at his architect studio, a surprise we all were not expecting.

He and Samuel were still going strong.

Griffin walked in as I laid a passed-out Oscar back down in his Moses bassinette and came over to me. "Ayla," he began. "Harper's in bed. Now tell me."

"She asleep?" I asked, shocked.

He nodded, undoing the top button of the jeans he wore. "Oh, yes. Now tell me." Then he stopped and frowned. "Is this about Harvey?"

"No. I wouldn't see him. I told you I wouldn't. I promised you that, Griffin." After we had Harper, Harvey had shown up drunk out of his mind and begging for forgiveness. Like coming here at three am was going to win Griffin over. He then got mouthy when he was turned away and told Griffin he and I had screwed and that Harper may be his. *Jesus,* the shit that went down. Griffin lunged at him and did not let up easily.

That had been a tough time for us. It put doubts into Griffin's mind, and I think he wondered if maybe what he told him were true. I never spoke to Harvey again since that night. Last I knew, he and his girlfriend had broken up, and he had gotten someone else pregnant.

He smiled, relieved. "Good."

Giddy nerves filled me as he was not going to like this much either. "I went to see Karen."

He opened his mouth to say something, but then stopped and glared. "I'm sorry? You fucking did what?"

There was something about him cursing in a hushed whisper, carefully not trying to wake up the baby.

"She called me. I couldn't afford to not go."

"You should have told me."

I rolled my eyes. "You would have stopped me from going."

"Damn straight I would have. She's crazy and in the psych ward for a reason, Ayla. She killed her roommate in prison! You think I want you to see her? How the hell did she even get your number?"

I went quiet and reached in the back of my jeans, pulling out a piece of paper. "She signed, Griffin. She wanted to give me this."

His eyes scanned over the piece of paper, slowly reading everything written. "She signed just like that?"

I nodded. I did not want to get too happy, but this was a good thing for us. "I didn't think she ever would, but she did."

I was officially their mother. She had signed the adoption papers, and the boys were mine, *ours*. I wanted nothing more than for them to be legally mine, and now they were. Everything was beginning to fall into place for us. It had taken a while, but finally, we were going to be a complete family.

"We have to celebrate, get the kids together, and go out somewhere. Or we could do something here? What do you want?" he asked, glancing down at Oscar.

My eyes went to him and those half-unzipped jeans. My loins began to stir, and the blood heated through my veins. Arousal tingled through me. "You. I want you."

Slowly, he made his way closer and began to undress me. I let him, and then it was my turn to take everything of his off. The kids were asleep, and the boys were out. I was making the most of this alone time we had.

"I love you," I whispered, pushing him down on the edge of the bed.

"Ayla, you don't have to do that." He stopped and groaned as I ran my palm up and down his thick hard length.

"Yes... Actually, keep doing that."

On my knees, I leant in closer and started with one soft, slow, simple kiss. My eyes were still on his, letting him see the hunger gleaming through them. My warm wet, pink tongue peeked out to lick him from base to tip. Slowly, my eyes drifted shut, and a low hum of satisfaction vibrated down his cock.

"Ayla..." His soft moan heated the pool between my legs. "Come up here. Kiss me."

"This is my candy, my treat, my time to relish in you," I said, kissing slowly back up the way to his tip. "To show you just how much I appreciate, adore, and want you."

His cock twitched in my hand, and his palm smoothly glided against my cheek as he pulled me up towards him and flipped me onto my back.

Both his hands cupped my cheeks, and he kissed me hard and deeply. My legs wrapped around his as he entered me with a deep thrust, causing us both to gasp over each other's mouths.

"Oh, baby, want me... but I want you back just as much for the rest of my life. I want you, pretty."

The End

Can't get enough of Ayla and Griffin? Make sure you sign up for the author's blog to find out more about them!

Get these two bonus chapters and more freebies when you sign up at http://melissa-bender.awesomeauthors.org!

Here is a sample from another story you may enjoy:

Prologue

My cock throbbed.

The hot water spilled down my head, seeping into my shoulders and running down my back as I stood in the shower. I was unable to focus on anything but the familiar ache in my balls—the need for release.

It had been too long since I have had a good fuck, and just thinking about it could no longer cut it anymore. My dick needed some attention. I had tried putting it off, but as I closed my eyes and wrapped my hands around the base of my cock, it was too much to ignore.

I needed to come before I lose my fucking mind.

There she knelt before me. Her tongue slid across her upper lip, and her mouth opened just enough to take me. Her tongue flicked back and forth against the underside of my hard cock. It drove me wild.

The vibrations of my cock from her words drove me insane. She was making love to my dick, the same way I wanted to make love to her pussy. Slowly and lusciously, her mouth took me fully in. My head fell back instinctively, and my eyes closed.

"Fuck me," I moaned, my shaft growing stiffer.

The pace was too teasing. My balls twitched, and she stopped. My eyes opened, and I asked her to continue. I didn't beg, though. I never begged anyone for anything. Her green eyes widened, and they are teasing but still adoring as she pulled back and blew warm air on the tip of my cock.

I wasn't a patient man. I throbbed harder. Her thumb drew circles around my swollen head glistening in pre-cum. The teasing was almost too much. I needed to blow so hard. Her mouth fully engulfed my cock, sucking me in, licking and moaning against my cock. Her hand was stroking faster, up and down. Faster and faster.

All I wanted to do besides come was to taste her, to fuck her... to eat and fuck.

Reaching down, my hands combed through her red hair, taking a firm handful as I begin to fuck her mouth. My hips rocked back and forth as she sucked harder. Her eyes bore into mine. It was too much to handle, and I lost it.

Oh, fuck yes. I exploded with the build up from the week. Semen burst from my cock and coated the inside of her mouth. Her tongue stuck out, swirling around the head of my cock and taking every drop I had to give.

As I slumped against the cool shower tiles with my eyes half-opened, reality hit me. I was alone, with my cock in my hand and the load a fucking mess on the glass in front of me.

What the fuck.

I cupped a handful of water and splashed the screen until there was no trace of me jerking off like an adolescent teenager. Those years should have been long gone by now, especially if my girlfriend had something to say about it.

Both my hands ran through my dark, wet hair as I slumped with my back against the wall again, trying to control my breathing. What the fuck just happened?

More importantly, who the fuck was that girl I had just jerked off to?

If you enjoyed this sample then look for **His Rebound Love.**

Introducing the Characters Magazine App

Download the app to get the free issues of interviews from famous fiction characters and find your next favorite book!

iTunes: bit.ly/CharactersApple
Google Play: bit.ly/CharactersAndroid

Acknowledgements

To my friends, family, and readers.

Thank you, so much for your love and support with my 3rd published book. This year has been beyond a dream come true for me and it's only just began. Thank you for buying my book, for supporting my wildest dream. Not once did I ever expect to have an opportunity like this, and yet here I am. I am living my dream, my one true goal in life. Write, and publish a bestselling novel and I now have two of them.

Fingers cross this become a third.

I'd also like to thank coffee, for keeping me awake on my all-day writing sessions.

Author's Note

Hey there!

Thank you so much for reading Breaking Old Habits! I can't express how grateful I am for reading something that was once just a thought inside my head.

I'd love to hear from you! Please feel free to email me at melissa_bender@awesomeauthors.org and sign up at http://melissa-bender.awesomeauthors.org for freebies!

One last thing: I'd love to hear your thoughts on the book. Please leave a review on Amazon or Goodreads because I just love reading your comments and getting to know YOU!

Whether that review is good or bad, I'd still love to hear it!

Can't wait to hear from you!

Melissa Bender

About the Author

I'm wife to a FIFO miner. Mother of three. Passionate foodie and a vivid dreamer. Living in a small beach town in the lovely Tasmania. I spend my time between home and down at the beach, making memories and capturing the moments.

When I'm not glued to my laptop, I'm either in the kitchen creating recipes, cooking, or having a Netflix binge session. Often, I find myself drifting off into the world of make believe, getting lost inside the stories I write. I write because it's my passion. I want to create a world for my readers to get lost in. For them to swoon and fall in love the way I do with each character made. Oh, and I love starbursts!

Sweetly, Melissa xx

Printed in Great Britain
by Amazon